RU

by

Michaelbrent Collings

Written Insomnia Press

WrittenInsomnia.com

"Stories That Keep You Up All Night"

Sign up for Michaelbrent's Minions
<u>And get FREE books.</u>

Sign up for the no-spam newsletter
(affectionately known as Michaelbrent's Minions)
and **you'll get several books FREE**.
Details are at the end of this book.

DEDICATION

To...

Stephen King, for not leaving a human head on my doorstep,
but leaving me with many scary stories...

Dean Koontz, for showing me what craftsmanship is,
and always taking my calls...

and to Laura, FTAAE.

Contents

PROLOGUE

DOM#57-B
STONY CLIFF, OHIO TERRITORY
AD 1872
PROTECTOR FAIL FILE

Malachi waited in the saloon, his hand curled around a warm beer, and wondered how long it would be before he could just kill someone.

It was neither a beautiful day nor an ugly one. Neither was possible in this place, where nothing was real. Though of course it all seemed real. That was the trick. That was the joke.

That was the thing Malachi hated most of all.

He looked around the saloon, noting the planks that had been laid on the floor, the counter he leaned on, the rough framing of the windows. The windows were open, for which he was grateful. Whether this world was real or not, he certainly suffered in its stale heat, and any bit of ventilation was welcome. No breeze stirred the dust outside, though, not even when the passers-by kicked it up in dry puffs that settled leadenly back to the ground.

He peered out the window a long time, watching the people of this place walk by, carrying milk pails or books or nothing at all as they hurried to get to where they were going. He smiled tightly as the thought struck him that of all the people in the area, he was the only one who was really alive. They did not know it, but every single person in this tiny town was dead. Every person, that is, but one. And it was for that one that Malachi had come to this place.

It had taken him a long time to find the man. At first he suspected that his quarry would be located in the mountainous areas outside the town. A few settlements were sprinkled through the outlying regions of this place, and Malachi thought it likely that his prey would be hidden in one of them. As a result, he spent several days tramping through dirt and mud, fighting his way through the surrounding wilderness to find those isolated pockets where people could be found. Or, rather, where the things could be found. For though they masqueraded as living, breathing people, the man knew they were not. He knew their secret. He knew their death.

The one he sought was not among those groups. Malachi thought perhaps he had been fooled. Maybe this place had no life in it at all, but was merely a trap filled with trees and streams and fish and insects and people who were not really people at all, but something dark and terrifying. His fear that this place was such a trap led him to be more cautious and slower than usual, skulking around the outskirts of the town as he observed the goings and comings, the ins and outs, until he was certain he was not being monitored or surveyed. Once his fears were allayed, he came into the town, and made inquiries, and found his prey. He found where the man would be on this day that was not really a day at all, no matter how brightly the false sun seemed to gleam.

The bartender spoke, jolting Malachi suddenly out of his reverie. "New?" he asked.

Malachi shrugged. The bartender was a fat man, showing off a gut that bespoke prosperity in a place where existence had to be earned by sweat and hard work. His armpits were damp on this hot day, staining the otherwise white shirt he wore. A high collar pinched at his jowls, and Malachi wondered if the bartender had creases in his throat when he took the collar off at night.

The bartender watched him for a moment, seeming suspicious at Malachi's lack of responsiveness. The fat man's hand held a filthy towel that he used to wipe down the counter, sausage-like fingers digging into the stringy fibers of cloth that he pushed slowly across the wooden surface of the bar. Splinters chipped off as the rough-woven fabric caught at tiny fractures in the wood grain. They jammed themselves jaggedly into the cloth, adding their grit and texture to the fabric.

The bartender stared at Malachi, waiting perhaps for a clue about the stranger's business.

Malachi dropped his hand to his gun belt. The holster was completely enclosed, a solid pack of leather that gave no hint as to what manner of weapon hid inside it. Still, the fact that his hand now rested near the holster was enough to tell a smart man that he wanted no further questions.

The bartender was smart. He refilled Malachi's beer and moved away, picking up the spittoon that sat at the end of the bar. He handed it to a man who sat on the ground nearby, shining a pile of shoes and wiping used glasses.

Malachi watched the bartender do this and took special note of the shoe-shine man. He was fairly young, perhaps in his mid-thirties, and had black hair with a shock of pure gray running down the middle, like a skunk. Like a skunk, the man stank; Malachi could smell him even at a distance, his obviously unwashed skin and hair casting rank waves of odor all around him.

The man was obviously mentally impaired, his eyes dull and vacant, glassy. Malachi did not note any of the distinguishing physical characteristics of Down's Syndrome or Fragile-X in the man, so he thought it more likely that he suffered from Fetal Alcohol Syndrome or perhaps Lennox-Gastaut. Of course, the people here had no such medical term for this man. No, they would call him...what? Special. Touched by God.

As though God would actually touch such an abomination.

The skunk man looked at the spittoon dully, his lips dry and cracked and moving slowly as he tried to divine what was expected of him. The spittoon sloshed, a disgusting noise that spoke clearly of its contents.

"Throw it out, idiot," said the bartender.

Malachi watched it all. Took it all in. It was midday, so the bar was mostly empty. Three cowboys played cards at one end of the room, a haze of smoke hanging over them like they were devils freshly emerged from the brimstone of hell. They were grizzled men, unshaven and worn. Malachi could clearly see their histories from his spot at the bar, histories of toil and meaningless labor that were indelibly written in the slouch of their backs and the curls of fingers so tough and callused it was a wonder they could even feel the cards they clutched.

At the other end of the room a hooker slept against the piano, her legs wide apart in a gross parody of her profession. Rouge was smeared across her knees below the line of her bloomers, which could be seen under her red skirt. Her bosom heaved in and out as she struggled to breathe in the heavy heat of the day. A fly buzzed near her, then landed on her cheek and made its way across her lips and chin. She did not stir to wave it away, but slept on.

Four total.

And the bartender and the spittoon cleaner made six.

Malachi would kill the handicapped one first, if he could. They always seemed so harmless. It would be easy to forget that the shoe-shine man was every bit as dangerous as the others; that the retardation would suddenly disappear and be replaced by cold analysis. By a will to kill.

Malachi would not forget. It was his job not to forget, and he was very good at his job.

The saloon doors swung open then. Someone stood in the frame, the bright light outside hiding his features for a moment. In that instant he was just a shadow, hardly as real as the world outside or the light that glowed off his shoulders. In that instant he was a wraith, but then he stepped in and the sun fell away from him with a golden sigh and his face could be seen by any who cared to look.

Malachi saw who it was, but even if he had not, he would have known that this was his quarry by the subtle way the atmosphere changed in the saloon. With the newcomer's entrance, everyone seemed to shift toward him. They seemed, not more *aware* of him, but rather more *alive* around him...or as close to alive as such could be. Malachi had seen it a hundred times before, and it was always a tip-off.

Lucas – that was the name of his prey – tipped his hat as he entered. He kicked his boots against the floor boards, dislodging a few clots of dirt and horse manure picked up from the street outside. They fell in dry clods and broke apart on rough-hewn pine

5

floorboards that had been rubbed smooth by the years. The other men in the saloon nodded to Lucas as he stepped up to the bar. He put his boot on the rail affixed to the bar, standing relaxed next to Malachi, unaware and unsuspecting that death waited beside him.

"Whisky," said Lucas to the bartender. The bartender filled a shot glass, and Lucas lifted it to his lips. He noticed Malachi watching him, and nodded before throwing back the drink in one smooth motion.

Malachi nodded back. He finished his beer and threw a quarter on the bar.

"Keep the change," he said.

The bartender smiled at him, giving him a complete view of his three remaining teeth. They hung to his gums as tenaciously as the saloon clung to life in this dead town, but like the town were doomed to fail in their struggle.

"Would you like to see something?" asked Malachi, and the bartender nodded, eager to be friends with this big tipper.

Malachi drew his gun, lifting the holster flap and pulling out a shiny black Heckler & Koch with a sound suppressor threaded into its muzzle. It was a beautiful weapon.

It was also a gun that would not appear here for well over one hundred years, if time were allowed to continue unabated.

If time existed at all.

"What the hell?" whispered the barkeep. Malachi smiled again. Of course the bartender would not have seen anything like this before. The barkeep pointed at the suppressor's dark barrel.

"What's that?" he asked.

"So it doesn't make noise," answered Malachi. "Watch." He pulled the trigger, and the gun whiffed. The hollow point bullet took the barkeep in the throat, tearing his head off at the neck.

Malachi twisted, pointing at the back door where the skunk man was reentering the saloon with a now-empty spittoon. Another bullet flew from the gun, piercing the man's skin. Too fast to see, and the sound of its passage through the air almost unnoticeable as it traveled through the man's skull before exploding.

In the time it took to do that, he had already fired on the three card players. Three loud pops, and their bodies slid to the floor. Not drunk, this time, but decapitated and bleeding.

The whore was next. She never woke up.

It was just Lucas now. The man was shivering uncontrollably, his hands waving in front of him as he backed away from Malachi. Malachi smiled pleasantly, as though he were preparing to play a game of horseshoes rather than having just killed six people in the blink of an eye.

Urine dripped from Lucas's leather chaps.

"Please, no," he whimpered

Malachi's grin widened.

"It's my salvation," he said, and pulled the trigger.

Lucas fell to the floor like the others.

Malachi looked around. Seven bodies, only one of which really counted. He checked Lucas' pulse, and though he found no heartbeat, he emptied the rest of his magazine into the man. He smiled as he pulled the trigger, the fiery flashes of gunfire gleaming like the promises of angels in his sight.

He checked Lucas' pulse again, just to be sure, and nodded as he felt nothing. Life no longer stirred in Lucas, and so the man could be at peace. He was in Heaven now, Malachi supposed, and kissed Lucas' hand tenderly. He had to leave before anyone else came in the saloon, but he took a dangerous moment to glory in his actions.

It came to him then: the Dream of what would be.

He saw fire everywhere. Everywhen. Fire to consume the whole earth this time, and not just a small part of it. He saw babies writhing in pain as the flames licked at their tender bodies; lovers locked in intimate embraces, their cries of ecstasy becoming screams of agony as tongues of fire burned their horrible caresses to cinders; children playing and singing "Ashes, ashes" and then all falling down in a charred heap, their bodies disintegrating and never to be whole again.

The final baptism of flame would come, come soon, and it would end.

Everything would end.

Malachi smiled. He hated this place. But all of it, the endless searching for Lucas, the sleeping in the forest with snakes and ticks, the smell of horse feces and human excrement, it was all worth it in this moment of triumph and Dreaming.

Then he heard a noise. He turned around. The retarded man's corpse was twitching, his legs shuffling minutely, then seeming to gain strength.

Malachi cursed softly. He was not surprised, for he had seen this happen before. But it could create problems. He had to finish the job and leave before anyone else came into the saloon, or else the town might Activate. And while any such occurrence would come too late to save Lucas, a full-scale Activation would make Malachi's escape difficult.

Malachi pulled an implement from his pocket. It was shiny and metallic, the shape and size of a pencil. He pressed a button, and it snapped open like a spring-loaded telescope, ending in a wicked point.

He walked to the mentally crippled man. The headless body was moving fluidly now, sitting up and then flipping itself around so that it rested on its hands and knees. It had no sight – the eyes were gone – but the hands felt for Malachi's vibrations on the floor.

He knew what to expect, so when he approached the man, he was ready. The headless body lurched at him, and he sidestepped easily, kicking the corpse in the back.

The man fell, and Malachi jabbed his instrument into the back of what was left of his head. The point penetrated the meat easily, before grinding to a halt against bone. As soon as it stopped, he hit the button again. He had to be quick, for in that instant the man was already rising once more, turning toward him with hands that clicked together like pincers. Should they find him, Malachi knew he would be crushed in their vise-like grasp, his life torn from him by the fingers of a man who was not dead, because he had never been alive.

Malachi was quick, though. Quick enough to do what needed to be done, and survive. The instrument crackled with energy, and the smell of burning flesh wafted into his nostrils.

The idiot's body jerked like a fish on a line, and then fell to the ground. The tiny portion of his head that had remained was a charred nub now, burnt beyond recognition. It was dead. And, more importantly, it would not move again.

Malachi touched the button on the shaft of the metal implement a third time, and the probe withdrew to its original pencil-shape. He put it back in his pocket and headed to the door of the saloon.

He wanted out of this place. Out of this time.

And on to somewhen else, to kill again.

ONE – LOSTON

MEMO REPRO S-7/102467

Johnny was six years old when the man tried to kill him.

He was standing in front of the kitchen window that morning, pouring himself a bowl of Wheaties. The dry brown flakes rustled like leaves as they fell into his bowl, settling gradually into a small mountain that Johnny would soon destroy with a well-placed spout of milk, pretending he was a Rain God pouring out destruction on a mountain where his subjects cowered in fear.

Pouring that milk would represent the only concrete enjoyment to be derived from the cereal, as even with generous portions of sugar added to it, Johnny thought it tasted like nothing so much as dirt. And not just plain dirt, but dirt that had been left out in the sun too long and had somehow gone bad.

There were other brands of cereal, of course, but his mother didn't allow them. She believed cereal should have the consistency and taste of old particle board. If it didn't, it was at the very least bad for you, if not downright evil. So she fought the good fight against the sin of sugared cereal, waging battle against her enemy with Shredded Wheat and Puffed Rice and Wheat Chex, merciless in her attack and deaf to the cries of her son: the innocent casualty of a most cruel war.

Johnny begged and pleaded for a year before he got the Wheaties, which his mother saw as a borderline breakfast food: a shade of gray between the sides of good and evil. They were horrible, but still better than Shredded Wheat, so Johnny did the best he could with them: he shoveled tablespoons of sugar on the Wheaties and closed his eyes and pretended they were something...*fun*.

That's what he was doing that Saturday morning, when it all happened, when it all began: he was pouring cereal and minding his own business and wishing for some Froot Loops or even just some Frosted Flakes, but knowing with the grim certainty of a six-year-old of that neither was in his future. He would eat Wheaties until he died of fiber poisoning, and then his mother would be sorry. She would cry, and perhaps put a box of Froot Loops on his casket, but it would be too late. He would be dead, and the Froot Loops would go uneaten, and it was all Mother's fault.

He put cereal in the bowl. Milk on top. Sugar. Stir it up. Add a little more sugar. More milk so that it sticks. And some sugar. Taste. More sugar. It was a ritual that would end as it always did, with his eyes closed and his mouth working at a frantic pace as he choked down grainy masses of sugar and pulped Wheaties and then worked up the courage to ask Mother one more time for something tastier.

The ritual was interrupted mid-stream, however, as he noticed the man who was walking down the street in front of the house. He was clearly visible from Johnny's vantage point, perched as he was atop a chair in front of the kitchen sink. Johnny could see the man clearly by looking out the large window his father had installed only the year before, at Mother's urging. That window now provided Johnny with an easy view of the man, who stood a mere fifty feet away from the boy and his breakfast.

It wasn't anyone Johnny had ever seen before, and in a town the size of Loston, that was odd. Most of the town eked a subsistence living out of the almost-dry silver mine in the nearby mountains, and the rest raised several staple crops: corn, wheat, some potatoes. Almost everyone knew almost everyone else. In fact, the only people who didn't know everyone else were the members of the Town Council, who had the job because no one else wanted it and so they didn't have to worry about getting to know the folk they represented in order to keep their positions.

Johnny wasn't a Councilman, so even at his young age he already knew by sight most everyone in the town. But he didn't know this person. The thought struck him then, perhaps for the first time, that Loston wasn't the only place in the world.

The shot was less than a minute away.

Of course, Johnny didn't know that. He only knew that he was understanding the concept of a stranger for the first time.

Stranger.

Strange.

Different.

This was a different man, a man unknown. As such he was, in Loston, as starkly out of place in the bright sunny day as a vampire would have been.

The man was dark. He had black hair and a purposeful stride that reminded Johnny of the way his daddy walked when he was angry...usually at something Johnny had done. It was a long stride, with each footstep placed firmly and fixedly as though walking according to a very specific set of instructions, almost machine-like in its precision and placement.

The man noticed Johnny watching him and looked fixedly back. He stared at him from the street, gazing at him in a way the little boy didn't like, a pointed look that seemed to challenge Johnny's right to be alive.

Thirty seconds until the shot came.

Johnny was saved from being embarrassed at the man's scrutiny by the man's hair, which had one sharply-defined streak of gray in the front. Johnny nearly laughed when he realized the man looked like a skunk.

He's a skunk. Skunk Man.

The thought amused him almost enough to make him forget his discomfort at being stared at, and the only thing that kept him from giggling out loud was the fact that his parents were asleep in their room not ten feet away. So he clamped his teeth together, wheezing silent laughter in the back of his throat, knowing that if he woke up his parents he would be forced to trade watching Saturday morning cartoons for watching himself pull weeds out of the thick soil in his mother's garden.

The laughter threatened to overwhelm him, though, even as he tried to choke it down. In desperation, he clapped his tiny hands over his mouth and thought of his father being angry, and that seemed to help. It was enough to quiet him down again, at least for a moment. But it seemed his mind was feeling rebellious, for in the midst of his imagining a new picture burst full-force into his brain. He thought of his father, yelling, his hand touching his belt in an ominous way...and in the middle of the movie playing in his head, Johnny realized his father had a booger hanging out of his nose. Not a big one, just a teeny one. But the thought of *any* kind of booger was too much for the self-control of a six-year-old already wired from an earlier bowl of well-sugared cereal.

Skunk Man. Boogers. Daddy's got a booger and there's a skunk man walking down the street.

Johnny laughed a short, staccato laugh, like a high-pitched machine gun that fired a mere three times before silence fell again. It was enough, however: Johnny's father came out of his room, looking disheveled and a bit angry at being awakened too early on his one day off from the mine. Chore time.

Even confronted with the reality of an angry parent, Johnny's mind was determined to cause trouble. He kept seeing the image of his father in his head, red-faced, yelling, and now with boogers flying out of his nose like some kind of plague of Moses. The two images – his father as he stood in the kitchen and his father as he appeared in Johnny's mind – superimposed weirdly, creating a strange feeling of unreality in the little boy.

His father opened his mouth to speak. As he did Johnny glanced out the window again and saw the Skunk Man disappear around a corner.

And at the same instant another man – another *stranger* – stepped into the house.

He entered through the rear sliding glass door that Johnny's parents never locked. It was Loston, and no one came there to steal or even to visit, so what was the use of locking the door? Still, Johnny knew it was wrong to just walk into another person's house. But here was someone doing it. Just *doing* it like it was all right.

Like the Skunk Man, this newcomer was completely unknown to Johnny, who wondered at the sudden influx of strangers in the small town. Then all curiosity fled as the man pointed something at Johnny's father. A shotgun.

Johnny's father opened his mouth wide in an expression of surprise. Perhaps to ask what the stranger thought he was doing, just walking in like that. There was no fear in his eyes, possibly because the entry and threat had come too suddenly, too unexpectedly to be perceived as anything but one more annoyance on a very early Saturday morning.

Johnny's father never got the chance to speak. His final thoughts remained just that, and would never be heard beyond his mind, for the stranger's shotgun blasted out a gout of black smoke and a flash of bright flame and Johnny's father fell. Johnny fell, too, the shock and the sound driving him to the ground as powerfully and irresistibly as though he were a nail under a mallet. The blast had actual force, transcending sound and becoming a palpable feeling that slammed him downward to the cold tile of the kitchen floor.

As Johnny fell, he heard the stranger's shotgun roar a second time. He heard/felt/smelled something whiz by his face, hitting the window, which exploded in a shrieking screech of shattering glass and crushed wood, and realized that if he had not fallen he would be dead.

A piece of his mind screamed to him, You're hit! Buckshot had lodged in his shoulder, shattering his scapula and cracking his clavicle.

But Johnny did not feel the pain. Nor did he notice as the stranger cracked open the breach of the shotgun and shoved another pair of shells into the tube before closing the gun with a sharp crack. Johnny did not feel or hear anything at all at that moment, because at that moment all he was aware of was the strange sensation of looking at his father, lying on the floor beside him. At what was left of him.

The shot had exploded through his father's neck, tearing away flesh and bone and skin. The head was gone. Or nearly gone. Johnny found himself staring into the half of a head that remained: into the crater that had held his father's brains only a moment before. Into a sightless eye whose lid had ripped off but which somehow had escaped damage. The eye seemed to stare at him, but Johnny knew that was a lie, even before the eye turned red as burst capillaries inside the orb allowed blood to flow like cheap dye across a costly white cloth.

His father was dead, and the eye stared at nothing.

Then Johnny looked up, and forgot for a beautiful second that his father was dead and lying beside him in a pool of blood. He forgot because the man who had come in the house was now pointing the shotgun at Johnny, point blank and no chance of escape in sight.

The gunman himself commanded attention almost more than the smoking instrument of death he clutched in one white-knuckled hand. His clothing wrapped around him like a kind of glove, tight-fitting and sleek. It was made of a fabric Johnny had never seen before. Miniscule lights danced across the surface of the man's outfit, tripping back and forth like children playing hopscotch, a dizzying whirl of changing colors that would be beautiful in other circumstances, but now merely served to spotlight the horror of this moment.

The second stranger's hair was short and gray. Johnny could make out some kind of a symbol shaven into the side of the man's head. It was a cross, like the kind in the front of Aunt Wilma's church, only the vertical line of this man's cross ended in a lightning bolt. It had a jagged, ugly look to it, a dark totem to a twisted god.

The man's eyes were gray. The gray-white of new silver, still in the rock. The shining silver of a lake in summer, reflecting the sun off its surface. It was beautiful and terrible, a gray that would seduce and beguile even as death was in the air.

"For my God and my Redeemer," said the man.

His finger tightened on the trigger, and Johnny closed his eyes...

...and when he opened them again...

...he was seven.

Or rather, he was seven when he finally *remembered* opening them again. A year and more had passed since that day. He opened his eyes in his own room, in his own house, but it was a house strangely empty, for his father no longer lived there.

John's mother was at his bedside, and spoke to him quietly, of the six months he had been comatose, of the year he did not speak a word. She told him of the time and money spent on doctors who had come to help him, and above all of how grateful she was that he had come back to her.

He asked about his father, and she told him his father was dead. When he did not believe her, she showed him pictures of the funeral, and Johnny saw himself at the gravesite, slack-faced and tiny in a wheelchair beside the casket. He cried for his father, and then cried again because he had not cried at the grave.

His mother cried also, wept at his bedside, and thanked God and Jesus that her son had been restored to her. That was when Johnny knew that it was all true. He was the man of the house. He knew his father was dead, and that he himself was not, but the details of his survival were a blank, impenetrable wall.

Neither he nor his mother tried to break that wall, either. They simply went on with life as best they could, and lived as though Father were a memory, a pleasant dream that had faded with the summer's end. Johnny pressed his mother to tell him about the details of the day Father died but once, and she answered that it was best he didn't remember. Her eyes became dull and peered out at him from under thick lids that seemed suddenly both foreboding and sleepy. His mother would answer no questions, and so he asked no more.

He didn't even ask them of himself. Not even on the nights when he lay under his covers and the wind and snow blew angrily against the windows and terror held him in an icy grip. He did not ask himself why he was afraid, just closed his eyes tightly and tried to sleep.

Eventually he did sleep. But he woke often in the night, and cried out, reaching for something or someone beyond his grasp.

Mother would come, and hold and comfort him, and all would be well again.

At least, all would be well until the next time, when he would again wake, and cry out, and hear two words echoing in his thoughts. They were strange words, mysterious and nonsensical to him, but still they made him tremble with fear, and they haunted him.

Skunk Man.

MEMO REPRO S-7/102467

Two decades later John again met death, and again it somehow passed him by, if not actually missing him completely. John was twenty-eight. Full of life and apple pie, fresh out of Special Forces training. He still had no memory of his father's death, and still was not sure if the fact of his forgetting was a blessing or a curse. Two decades later, and John tracked across the pre-dawn fields of Iraq, between a dry canal and Highway Seven. His mind wandered, from past to future, and he wondered if he would ever go home, if he would do all the things he had heard about growing up. School, regular job.

Marriage.

That was the one thought of the future that preoccupied him more than any other. He felt a pulling inside him, a pulsing throb that seemed to hunger for family. That in itself seemed strange to him, for he had no experience with women.

He liked girls, it was true, but had never found one who excited him. Not that way. He dated in high school, having as exciting a social life as was possible in a graduating class of fourteen, but never went beyond kissing. His mother was proud of that fact, said he had Jesus in him and Jesus would protect him in his virtue and virginity. But the reason wasn't Jesus. John didn't know what it was, exactly, only that in the few times when more than kissing seemed possible or even likely, something held him back.

He was waiting for something. Waiting for someone, some siren in the distance. He didn't know who she was, only that he hadn't met her yet.

And he wasn't likely to do so now, either, hunched over with his pack heavy against his back. It weighed over a hundred pounds, and it was still one of the lightest in the unit. The packs strapped to the others' backs ranged from one hundred to one hundred seventy five pounds, containing between them everything the six man group would need to stay alive in Iraq for up to a week.

John's back burned, and courses of sweat cut trenches through the dirt and light camouflage paint that coated his face. A bead of perspiration dropped into his eye, stinging as the salt burned his cornea, but John did not move his hands from his weapon. He walked in dangerous territory, and did not savor the idea of dying because he was too busy wiping his eyes to return fire should he be fired upon.

His M-16 rested against his forearm, cocked and ready. He had never had to use a gun on live foe before but if it came to the choice of him or the enemy...well, John might be a virgin, but he had no pretensions to sainthood.

Like most of the others in his unit, he was a veteran in training terms, but this was his first time on an active mission. He was determined to do well; to justify his mother's faith in him and the tremendous amount of money that had gone into training him.

Vogel, the CO, stopped abruptly. He was short, with a brutish visage that concealed an alert mind and a whip-quick wit. He held a fist in the air, looking at the GPS unit he held in his hand. The tiny link was invaluable in this operation, giving them their position within yards and allowing them to coordinate their travel time to conform to the mission's needs. Without it, a man could easily become lost in the miles of endless desert where little distinguished one spot from another. People could die in this place.

Cowles uncurled his strong, short fingers. We're here, the gesture said.

Wordlessly, John and the others unlimbered their bags, and their backs cracked and popped in a mix of relief and umbrage at being so ill-used. The big green wart was what servicemen called the rucksacks, and the name was apt. Most Special Forces servicemen retired with bad knees from the heavy loads. That is, if they were lucky enough to retire, instead of being buried out in some dank jungle or godforsaken desert like this one.

The shoulder strap of John's bag caught on something underneath his shirt, hitching almost imperceptibly on the scar that lay beneath his clothing. It was a tightly knotted burl of tissue, the only tie he had to that day long ago when his father died and was forgotten as though he had never lived. He noticed the scar, as he always did, but as always thrust the thoughts it brought with it far away from himself. There was no time for memory today, even when memory was only a blank wall that stared at you from the past and revealed nothing.

John unpacked a collapsible aluminum shovel and began digging. The predawn light had brightened slightly, slight casts of pink now visible through the gray of dusk. He figured they had about two hours before the first people came down the road that writhed a serpentine path not one hundred yards from them.

The unit had to be gone by then, disappeared.

The squad was in Iraq as eyes on the ground, recon troops in charge of calling in information about who was traveling the roads. They had to be close enough to see everything clearly. Close enough to tell one tank from another if such moved down the road. CentCom wanted detail, and John's unit had to get it. But staying so close was dangerous, as it meant you could also be seen by anyone who passed by. So John and the rest of the unit were digging a hole in the dirt where they would remain, peeping out to gather intel, hoping that the hole they dug would not end as their grave.

Camp dug beside John. A rangy kid from Nebraska, Camp was the only one in the unit who looked more like a poster boy for The Great American Way than did John. The illusion shattered, however, every time Camp opened his mouth.

"I need some," said Camp.

John dug in silence, eyes darting back and forth along the side of the road. Intelligence reported the road was secure, but he knew that the only intelligence a good soldier relied on completely was what his eyes, ears, nose, and skin told him himself.

"Yeah. I need some," reiterated Camp.

John nodded in the hopes Camp would shut up. Sweat trickled over his eyes. He wanted to wipe his forehead but didn't. Part of the training. Keep your hands busy with the job and ready to grab a gun. Don't so much as think about anything else. You gotta pee, you get three guys to cover you before you put a hand on your zipper. Words to live by.

"If I don't get some soon, I'll die." Camp was becoming irritating as his half-veiled euphemisms continued to make their way to John's ears. A listening stranger would think that Camp was talking about the last time he'd been laid. Passing brass would nod to themselves and pretend they'd never been horny soldiers. They'd smile at the Good American Kid who believed in God and apple pie and bagging the occasional blonde.

John knew different. Camp wasn't horny, he was psychotic. Or at least he was pretending to be, constantly acting like he wanted to kill someone. The screening to get into SpecOps was rigorous, designed to keep out cowboys and wannabe superheroes, so John was pretty sure Camp was just putting on a show.

But not so sure he would turn his back on the guy.

"Yeah, gotta get me some. Feel the power."

"Shut up," hissed John. His eyes kept moving between Vogel, the other team members, and the roadside.

"If I don't get me some, I'm gonna –"

"If you don't shut up, I'm gonna kill you myself." The sentence burst out of John and he knew instantly that it was the wrong thing to say if he was trying to quiet Camp down.

"Yeah, that's it, you gonna give me some? You want to be my friend?" Camp had one hand on the knife he always wore: the one marked Mr. Happy in bold letters across the hilt. He unsnapped the sheath, caressing the finger-worn hilt with fondness. Camp slept with that knife. Even when he was picking up a hooker in the little bars the unit visited, even when the woman gazed at him with half-bored eyes, holding up her fingers to indicate how much, even when he chose one and took her, even then the knife stayed with him. That more than anything caused John to wonder if Camp wasn't faking it. If, somehow, he had managed to convince SpecOps that having a certified lunatic in the unit could be useful.

"Camp!" Vogel's voice was a tight whisper that nonetheless carried across the dry air like the sound of a cracking bone. Camp's hand dropped from the knife. He looked at Vogel.

"Camp, you talk another talk and I'm gonna eat your heart out through your ass. Hear?"

"Sorry, Cap. Just edgy."

That was the end of it.

The pit appeared quickly, deep enough for the men to hide in, and they each unlimbered the aluminum rods they would use to hold up the roof. The roof of the pit had to be undistinguishable from the surrounding earth, invisible. They had practiced the whole maneuver for weeks, getting non-SpecOps servicemen to look for their hideouts. The only way they were ever found was if one of the troops got lucky and walked across it.

Still, this wasn't base camp. This was behind enemy lines, and though CentCom Intelligence reported that it was winter and the road shouldn't be in use, none of the unit wanted to trust that information with their lives.

The roof went up, and the hole disappeared.

Vogel looked at it, carefully scrutinizing the area for any signs that the earth was anything other than hard-pack and sand. He glanced around the tight circle of men around him.

"What are the rules?" he whispered.

The five men whispered back, "Always know where you are. Always be cool."

"And if you don't know where you are?"

"At least try to look cool," said the men, grinning at each other. It was a ritual, Vogel's way of telling the rest of the Green Berets in his unit that the job was acceptable.

They all slipped through the small opening in the roof, closing it up soundlessly behind them, and it was as though the desert had swallowed them alive.

John took first watch, looking through a mini-periscope focused on the road. There was no traffic, so his mind wandered a bit, thinking how odd it was that a small group of men with enough schooling to run a country and enough armaments to blow one up were crouching in a hole near a deserted road.

What few people realized was that "special forces" wasn't just a euphemism for a bunch of killers. Special forces meant a highly trained *thinking* machine. Right now Vogel was getting out a small pad and paper, ready to jot down notes on anyone or anything that traveled the road: direction, appearance, any cargo, passengers. Any and all. The information would be sent back to Intelligence, where it would meet thousands of other bits of information, all waiting to be sorted and sensed.

They didn't have long to wait before the first travelers came along. It was a small band of Bedouins, their cloaks wrapped around them loosely, looking like dark phantoms moving heavily through the early morning light.

"Bedouins," murmured John.

"How many?" asked Vogel.

"Six."

"Armed?"

"Cloaked, so could be, but nothing apparent."

Vogel called the information in on the SATCOM radio they carried.

"They're nuts," said John to himself. It had to be over a hundred degrees out there, yet the heavily-wrapped men showed no sign of noticing the dry, dusty heat.

"All roads lead to madness," intoned Camp. It was a favorite saying of his, and Camp delivered the statement in the somber tone that told everyone he thought he was being deep and inscrutable. John thought about telling him it would have been better if he'd said "All roads lead to nutness," but thought better of it. For once.

John squinted into the periscope. "They're driving sheep," he said, and looked at Vogel in time to see the CO whiten slightly. Shepherds usually stuck to well-traveled roads. CentCom had said the road would be deserted, and the only traffic would be military companies.

CentCom was wrong. Within an hour, throngs of people coursed along the roadway, a living river of men, women, and children that showed no sign of drying up as the desert sun rose higher in the sky. John ceased describing each and every one – it would have been impossible – and just watched for military vehicles. There were none.

Still, the men in the hole twitched nervously. With that many people, some were bound to wander off the road. And if one came close enough, no amount of training in the world could guarantee their hiding spot or their survival.

Ten minutes later, it happened. Two little girls followed a small brown sheep that wandered off from their family's tiny herd. The animal bleated piteously, as though it worried that it might be dinner at the end of this particular trip, then bolted off the road, heading right at the squad's hiding place. The little girls did not wait to be told what to do, but ran after the sheep, calling after it as the rest of the group laughed and continued walking, trusting the children to bring the sheep back. John pulled back the periscope, waiting for the girls to corral the animal and go, praying that they wouldn't walk over the top of the dugout.

Tiny footsteps fell on the ground nearby, then one of the little girls' feet fell heavily against the roof. Thunk. It made a hollow sound, and the footsteps stopped.

Camp cursed under his breath.

The footsteps hurried away, and John waited for five minutes, then pushed up the periscope.

He stared straight into the face of one of the little girls, who was obviously staring at the tiny scope.

"Dammit," he whispered. "We're found."

"Who?" asked Vogel.

"Little girl."

As one, the other four men grabbed their weapons. Three of them had children, but they were willing to kill the little girl if necessary. John hoped it wouldn't be, and didn't know what he would do if so ordered. He knew that some in the unit were detached to the point of machines: the mission was all that mattered to them. John, however, was there because he believed that he was helping to save lives, in the long run. He believed in what he was doing, and that was what allowed him to sleep at night. But he did not know if he could face himself after killing a child, no matter how necessary the act might be to save the lives of his comrades in the unit.

Vogel shook his head, relieving John. He knew why the CO had made his decision for the unit to take no action against the girl. They could kill her, but her friend was gone. If one of the girls didn't come back, they would certainly be discovered. But if both were allowed to return...then the little girls would either tell or they wouldn't. All the men could do now was wait. Intel was sketchy about how the people in the area would react to the presence of Americans in their midst. They were just as likely to invite them to dinner as shoot them, so the unit had to be prepared for either.

John watched the child at last grow bored of holding her position and walk away. He exhaled as he saw her walk off, catch up to the group, and continue without comment until the group had gone beyond the range of John's scope. The rest of the unit could sense John's relief, and they too relaxed, settling into positions of less discomfort (actual comfort was impossible in this situation) and waiting for their turn to watch.

The relief was short-lived, however, as an hour later the little girl returned, leading a group of young men. They were not sheepherders, but were instead an armed group, clutching weaponry of various levels of sophistication and power. John spied them when they were still several hundred yards from the Green Berets' lair, but could tell in an instant that they were heading directly to the hide spot. The little girl halted and pointed at his scope, then stood her ground as the men continued without her.

He reported it to Vogel, who murmured, "We might be in trouble." Then the CO folded up the antenna and ordered everyone out.

The Green Berets exited the pit quickly, their pulses speeding up. Though they had popped the roof and exited in a matter of seconds, to John it seemed much longer, and he felt naked and exposed under the angry desert sun.

Vogel waited until the young men – they looked like Bedouins, but a bit harder and tougher than most – were about two hundred feet away, then shouted, "Salaam."

They kept moving forward as the little girl stepped back even farther away. That was a bad sign, as it demonstrated her expectation that this would not be a happy meeting. Then she turned and ran, and even at that distance John could clearly see the fear in her gaze. His heart sank.

Vogel – the only one who spoke Arabic – barked a few quick words. John knew he was ordering the men to stop, to stand down or risk being fired upon.

They didn't.

"Oh, hell," said Vogel. He moved his weapon into ready position, aimed at the young men. People on the road were starting to take note of what was going on.

"Pull the plug," said Vogel to John.

John nodded. He leapt into the pit and yanked a cord that was wired to a small explosive. It would burn all their supplies to slag, including classified maps and hardware they had brought. It would also leave them with only their hand weapons, some ammo, and the LST-5 radio they had brought for communications with base camp. Such a move was intended as a last-ditch effort to obscure their mission from prying eyes.

Camp was already on the LST-5, telling base they needed an emergency exfiltration.

Vogel started stepping backward, backed up by the other Berets, moving toward the canal. Calmly, though. The young men – about twenty in number – were unlimbering guns and looking less friendly by the moment.

A rumble caught everyone's attention as an Iraqi military transport pulled up, dumping Iraqi servicemen onto the road. They held outdated weaponry, some of them carrying breach-loaders that looked like WWII issue, but a gun was a gun and an antique bullet would kill a man just as dead as a new Teflon-coated one if it found its mark. Besides, their sheer numbers said they would beat the Americans in a fight.

Vogel reached the lip of the canal. John and the other Berets were already there, waiting for the next move to be decided.

One of the young men shot at them. As one, the Berets dropped into the dry canal, reacting with a fluidity that came from training, skill, and desperation. Sand and small rocks bit at their hands as they scrabbled over the lip of the canal, and all were bloodied when they reached the bottom of the short drop-off and began running east. Their response had been planned in advance, but though it was the result of previous deliberation, that did not change the fact that their flight was a run for their lives.

Camp was still on the LST-5, screaming for an exfil as they ran, snaking through the maze of waterways that led east. Bullets pinged off the canal's lip, then around them as the first enemy soldiers dropped into the ditch and began firing.

John spun around, dropping into firing position. He had an automatic weapon, and in the movies the soldiers always used such guns like huge scythes, fanning a spray of bullets across the area in front of them. This was real, though, and he knew that every shot had to count. One bullet, one fatality.

He focused on one man, and his vision seemed to telescope, bringing the man running at him into impossibly sharp focus. It was a Bedouin, pointing a revolver and screaming as he pulled the trigger jerkily. Bullet fire ricocheted around John, though he could not say whether it was that man's bullets or someone else's that were finding their way to him.

John pulled the trigger. His gun fired with a single short snap and the round took his attacker in the mouth. The man's eyes widened hideously and his head snapped back, bouncing off the rocky wall nearby and leaving a dark smear on the dirt.

John flinched. He didn't want to kill people, that wasn't what he was in this for. He wanted to keep people from getting killed.

Too late for that now.

He moved his muzzle a fraction of an inch and squeezed off two more rounds. Two more men dropped and did not rise again.

The other Berets were firing as well. Then the first wave of attackers ended, the enemy forces drawing back to recover from the Berets' sudden and effective counter-attack, and the unit turned and ran again.

The exfil spot was two miles away, which was not far when running around a base track, but could take an eternity when running through a slim canyon, pursued by an enemy hungry for your death.

It was a devastating run, broken every couple hundred yards as the unit turned to fire on the following soldiers. John was surprised that the enemy didn't run ahead and drop into the canal ahead of the unit. But the unit might have been moving too fast for that tactic, fear and adrenaline lending wings to their feet and allowing them to stay ahead of their shrieking pursuers.

When they reached the exfil spot, their ammunition was more than half gone. A helicopter would have to come get them, and do it soon, if it wanted to pick up something other than corpses.

"*What?*" screamed Camp. He was still on the LST-5. He looked at Vogel, eyes wide and empty as those of a dead man. His next words told John why. "They said they can't come in until nightfall. Too risky."

The other men's eyes instantly acquired that same dull look. Nightfall was ten hours away and none of them would ever see it.

Vogel's lower lip puckered, a queer look that made the CO seem less afraid than irritated. "Well, that stinks," said the look, "I was supposed to see a movie tonight." No fear, no desperation, just a severe professionalism that made even the impossible fight seem not only possible, but ridiculously easy.

"All right, kiddies," he barked. "Let's keep it pro. One bullet, one body. Just remember to keep one round in reserve."

None of them asked what for. Green Berets were worth more to enemy troops than their weight in plastique, carrying with them classified information about a plethora of different activities.

They wouldn't fall into enemy hands.

Not alive.

The next hour passed as a hell of death and fire. The Green Berets' exfil spot was a part of the canal that was a bit more rounded than the rest, providing a distinct landmark for the exfil chopper that would never come. John and his unit each took a position around the perimeter of the ring, pointing their weapons over the lip of the canal, picking off Iraqi soldiers and Bedouins one at a time.

None of the men in the unit fell, but John knew they would have to. Sooner or later, they were dead. The only questions were when and how.

He was down to twenty rounds in his gun. Two of the others had stopped firing, obeying Vogel's order to keep one bullet in reserve. They had already made peace and waited quietly for the silence of the end.

John fired again, and again, and soon had but four bullets left.

Three.

Another shot, and he was down to two, and the enemy kept coming, an unending torrent of men, willing to die for a chance to kill.

John drew a bead on what would be his last target before himself, but did not pull the trigger. A dull thudding noise rolled through the air in deep, thrumming waves. It was subliminal at first, felt more than heard: a presence that grew heavier in the hot, dry air until the sound could be made out and identified.

John knew they weren't out of it yet, but he joined the others in cheering as two choppers crested a low bank, heading toward them. The exfiltration unit had come.

The Pave Low, as intricate a piece of machinery as ever invented, hove into view first, its fiberglass rudders spinning almost silently. It was the eyes, the brain of their salvation, a great swollen giant packed full of computers and information systems. It paused in its forward movement, allowing the MH-60 Black Hawk that followed it to move forward. The Black Hawk was the gunship, the muscle behind the mind, and seemed to fly more heavily than the Pave Low, weighted down as it was with guns and weaponry, heavily laden with death.

The Iraqi soldiers who still surrounded the Berets' position screamed in anger and turned their guns on the two choppers. The Black Hawk's response came from its side-mounted Vulcan Cannon at the conversational speed of six thousand rounds a minute. The gun spat what appeared to be liquid flame, dropping twenty of the enemy in an instant. The rest dove for cover as the Black Hawk descended a few feet. It touched down with the Pave Low scant yards from the Berets, and they quickly scrambled toward the choppers, half of them heading for each.

John got in the Pave Low. There wasn't much room in the redesigned Jolly Green Giant 'copter, so he pressed himself against the computer banks that allowed the vessel to land within inches of a predetermined spot and within seconds of a target time. There was no room for weaponry, for the chopper's function was not to destroy, but to find and, in this case, to deliver.

Besides, it didn't need firepower with the Black Hawk escorting.

John looked out the side hatch as the Pave Low began to rise, seeing Vogel and Camp being helped into the already-ascending Black Hawk. The crewman who helped them in that other chopper glanced at John, and for a moment time froze.

The Bedouins, the Iraqis, the fight, all fled John's mind as he saw a shock of gray running through an otherwise dark head of hair.

Skunk Man, he thought.

The memories he had suppressed hit him with the force of an anvil dropped from the Empire State Building, cracking the sidewalks of his mind. He staggered, almost falling from the chopper before one of the other Berets caught him. John's mouth opened and shut, but no sound came out. Words floated back to him.

Daddy's got a booger.

Skunk Man.

John stared at the man, who stared back, and for a moment John remembered what had happened. He remembered his father being killed. He remembered why he himself hadn't died.

He remembered his father standing and walking after having his head blown off.

Then he blinked and the memories were gone again, fled behind whatever wall had protected his sanity for these years. John looked at the serviceman in the other chopper. At the stranger. At the Skunk Man. John did not remember anything after seeing the Skunk Man on his sidewalk on the morning his father died, but that memory was now as clear and clean as a pristine photograph in an album. John remembered the Skunk Man.

The man looked the same. Not close, but *exactly* the same. Twenty years hadn't aged the man, nor had his expression changed. He might have stepped right out of John's memory as a perfect reproduction of himself, and John wondered just what the hell was happening to him.

John would have dived right out of the chopper then, leaping for the other helicopter's strut – a suicidal move – had not one of the Pave Low navigators clacked a carabiner to his belt, securing him to the deck. The navigator reached out to slide shut the side door.

"No!" screamed John.

He pushed the man aside, his total attention still focused on the man. On Skunk Man, who had been on his street when his father died. Who had been there twenty years ago and looked exactly the same today.

Then the Black Hawk exploded.

John saw the white contrail of a hand-held rocket – probably black market Russian hardware – an instant before it hit. The small missile streaked through the open side hatch of the Black Hawk, and then there was a tiny snatch of fire, almost pitiful really, followed by a great gout of yellow and red flame. The incendiary tongue licked forth, singeing John's hair, as the Black Hawk exploded from the inside out, the machine dying along with its crew in an instant. Blackened machinery and the charcoal corpses of the vehicle's occupants fell the short distance to the ground, exploding outward in a wash of shrapnel that sent the Iraqis scurrying for cover.

"No!" John screamed again. He wasn't sure if he screamed for the loss of the chopper and its firepower, his friends who had been in it, the men piloting the saving machine....

Or for the loss of the man.

Skunk Man.

The Pave Low pilot pulled back on the yoke, and the chopper jerked high into the sky as though yanked by a great hand. Bullet fire continued to snap below them, the sounds growing thinner as the chopper ascended, until finally they were gone, lost in the endless desert where half of John's friends would remain forever, molded and joined to the helicopter that had come to save them.

The trip back to base camp was uneventful. The Pave Low kept below radar level, easily following the contours of the earth. The land rolled below them like a sandy sea dotted with bits of scrub that had somehow divined the secret of eking a life out of the death of the desert. John glanced at the pilot from time to time, noting how seamlessly the man moved with the machine, how melded they were, as if there was no chopper and no man, but only a weird hybrid of both. Then his eyes closed, and fear and terror fell away from him like a rush of water from a waterfall, leaving him dry and suddenly sleepy.

When the return trip ended, he asked the Pave Low pilot and a few others on base about the Black Hawk crew, trying to find out who the Skunk Man had been. But the two chopper crews didn't know each other: both teams had been recruited from different units.

He asked the base officers about the Black Hawk crew. Classified, they said. Per military protocol, they reminded him, Black Ops operatives were not known to anyone outside their unit. They smiled and shook his hand and told him to forget about them; they had never officially existed, anyway.

John received an award. A bronze star. Vogel got a silver one, posthumously, as did the other fallen men. John almost expected them to give one to the Black Hawk. But no, not to a machine. Only to the dead and those who had seen death.

John had seen death twice now.

And both times came with the strange man. The man who was now gone, a corpse that would smolder forever under the hot sun of Iraq.

The Skunk Man.

DOM#67B
LOSTON, COLORADO
AD 2013
3:30 AM FRIDAY MORNING

John woke up from the dream, and could not move.

In the movies, when people had nightmares, they always sat bolt upright, drenched in sweat and panting like a beaten dog. John never did that, though nightmares were his constant companion. When they came, the personal, unremembered demons of the night, he woke feeling heavy. His eyes would snap open, but he couldn't sit up if he wanted to. Two-ton weights seemed to press each limb to the rumpled sheets of his bed, and movement was impossible for a time after waking. All he could do was lay there, every muscle quivering from unremembered exertion, every joint sore from unknown strains, and feel the bed beneath him.

The bed was too large. It had been ever since Annie died.

He looked into the darkness, past the fuzzy outline of the pillow that half-poked him in the eye. A digital clock on his nightstand glowed like an iridescent monster of the night, laser-red eyes staring out with anger and bloodlust. Unblinking. Unmoving.

Gradually the monster's eyes resolved themselves into readable numbers as John's eyes cast off the lingering effects of sleep and his brain cast off the lingering effects of his past.

3:30 a.m.

He woke every night, and though the times varied, they were always at the half hour. Never 4:31 or 2:16. Always 2:30 or 4:30 or sometimes even 5:30 if he was lucky. Sometimes, when he cared to think about it, it frightened him that he woke with such precision; such exact timing. Biological clocks were generally well-tuned instruments, he knew...but that tuned?

The digital eye blinked. 3:31.

He still couldn't move.

35

Sleep had fled, and he knew that it would not return. He never slept again after waking in the night. When his eyes closed, the demons were real, and though he braved them every night, twice in one night would be too much to face.

Strength gradually returned as his heart ceased to pound against his ribcage. He sat up.

The covers fell away from his naked torso. Though nearing forty, John's body closely resembled that of an active twenty-five year old. His chest was still firm and muscular, athletic without being bulky. His stomach was flat, with traces of a washboard musculature showing through from time to time. Annie used to tease him about that, telling him he was vain for keeping up so. But he never worked out. He was just born with it.

Annie.

He felt the scar, as he did every night, and as he did every night he allowed himself to think about the dark flesh and the darker past it signified. The gnarled skin curled around his shoulder like a monkey tail wrapped around a tree. The scar tissue on his chest was smaller. The entry of the shot when he was young had left a mark, but it was barely the size of a silver dollar above his right pectoral.

On his back, though, the wound and scarring were greater. There the scar was a large fist of curled matter, darker than his olive skin. It seemed to swallow light, a malignant black hole above John's scapula.

He still didn't know where the scar had come from.

The whole shoulder had been shattered, he knew that much. He knew that his father had died, that he had somehow survived the aftermath of a bloody attack, and that he had taken a long time to recover from that day. But he had no *memories* of those facts. They were gone, not faded away but barricaded somewhere deep and secure, with thick walls that would serve equally well to keep intruders out...or to confine occupants within.

John took several deep breaths, and as always tried to remember what he had dreamed. What he had seen. What he had *been*.

That the dreams were important was a foregone conclusion. They started soon after Annie died. Every night he woke (always at the half hour!), feeling heavy, feeling the heart pound within his body, feeling...

(afraid.)

...alone.

That was how he knew the dreams had started after Annie was gone. He never felt alone when she was near. And she had always been near.

Now, as he struggled to remember his dream, the feeling struck him that tonight's sleeping journey was something of crucial import. It meant the end of something. Or the beginning.

Someone is coming.

He frowned as the thought echoed in his mind with a concrete firmness that was unusual. Where had *that* come from?

John stood, letting the covers fall to the floor. Annie wouldn't have scolded him for that. She would roll her eyes, and make some comment about living with a pig instead of a man, but she would smile lovingly as she spoke so that he would know she was joking and that she loved him.

He went into the bathroom, flipping on the light that hung over the sink. Seven bulbs were affixed, but only three glowed when the light was turned on. It was a vanity mirror, with enough light for Annie to apply her makeup or do her hair. But now that she was gone, there was no need for such illumination. John's lip curled in bitter almost-laughter as a thought struck him: "How long has my wife been dead?" And the answer: "About four light bulbs."

It was better with dim lights, anyway. Dim lights were less like hospital lights. And thinking that, he suddenly could smell antiseptic cleaning solutions, with the strong undercurrent of feces and death that always hung in the air of the terminal patients unit.

Annie weighed seventy-two pounds when she died. At least John was there when it happened. No surprise – he had been with her almost constantly. He remembered that he held her hand, and kissed it. She made no sound – she had been asleep for almost a week – but he fancied he could see her lips upturn ever so slightly. He imagined she was smiling as she died. And so he kissed her lips, and tried to smile, too, so that she would not feel bad for leaving him. She always got upset when he was feeling sad, and he didn't want to send her away thinking she had made him anything but happy. He kissed her, and left a trail of bright tears on her soft, sunken cheek.

John shivered, and tried to force his mind away from the image of his dead wife; tried to focus on his dream and attempted to recall that instead.

Nightmares were often safer and far less terrifying than reality.

The dream *had* frightened him, he knew. In fact, it still frightened him. His heart was racing, and sweat kept beading his hairline. But though the fear was real and palpable, he could not find *what* he was afraid of. As always, the dream was hiding in one of the many locked-away portions of his mind. John had no way to bring it back.

He turned on the faucet and wiped his face with cool water, letting it wash away the last vestiges of a dream that was already more ethereal than most. Down the drain, to mingle with all the other bad dreams that people washed away, a dense mass of nightmares that swirled and roiled and was finally swallowed up by the darkness below the town.

That image struck him, and for a moment he expected a hand to reach out of the drain and pull him in. A scaly hand, like a half-man, half-crocodile. It would pull him down, through the drain, into the sewers. And John would never actually *see* the thing's face. Fear had no face. That was why it was so frightening: because it could never be seen. But he would know that the thing was there. And that it was hungry for him.

He stared at the drain.

Nothing.

Words entered his mind, unbidden and unwelcome.

Someone is coming.

He shook his head, trying to cast the words away, trying to give himself peace from an unremembered past that he could neither escape nor embrace.

Nothing is so well-remembered as the aching emptiness of something forgotten.

He looked through the bathroom door, into the bedroom beyond. The bed lay there, rumpled and damp from sweat and fear.

Empty.

He shook his head once again, then moved to a chair and took up a book and read. The words passed obediently before him, straight as parade lines marching before the grandstand, but they left no mark in his mind. He could never remember what he had read during these nighttime sessions. He just read because it was better than laying awake in an empty bed and thinking of a time when it had been full.

At 8:20 that morning John drove his Suburban down the winding dirt road that led to the town's main street. The SUV thunked as it hove onto the concrete lip and then shuddered with relief at being on the only paved road that continued for more than two hundred feet in the entire town. John cracked the window to enjoy the early morning breeze that blew. It was cool and hinted of winter, though the real cold season was still months away. The air cut John's nasal passages pleasantly, leaving him physically invigorated, though it did little to brighten his mindset.

He looked over to the seat beside him. No one was there, and somehow that still surprised him. It had been long enough that the shock should have passed, but somehow it remained. The ache was always there, but in spite of that fact and the myriad reminders of Annie's departure, he always expected to see her beside him, smiling and laughing as she reached out to play with his hair.

He drove past the sign the town council had put up some five years before: Welcome to Loston, Pop. 1472 and counting.

The mountains loomed behind him. Colorado was nothing but one large mountain, it seemed, but parts of it stood higher than the rest. The mountains that guarded Loston were solid sentinels, vigilantly aware of all that transpired before them. The mountains had always made Annie feel safe.

John turned into the driveway of the high school, located right next to Town Hall. He parked the Suburban, got out without locking the door – no one had ever had a car broken into in Loston – and entered the office.

It was quiet inside, which was normal. The office was a well-oiled mechanism that functioned with the smoothness and efficiency of a luxury automobile. That was due in no small part to the woman whose flashing and – to the students – highly intimidating gaze now focused upon him.

Mertyl Breckman, the office secretary, noticed John immediately upon his arrival, as she noticed everyone who dared to brave her domain. Though she had lost the last of her teeth some four years previous, it seemed the two hundred students at Loston High still lived in mortal fear that she would bite them. Not even the principal commanded the respect that Mertyl did. When she was especially agitated her mouth firmed into a line that was colder than a Nordic glacier, and slower to warm. Rumors abounded that the reason LHS had such a small graduating class each year was that Mertyl ate anyone who was found wandering into the office without a pass.

John had no pass, but in spite of that Mertyl did something that would have shocked the collective student body.

She smiled at him.

He smiled back at her. When Annie died, Mertyl was one of the first people at his door, bringing a party platter of meats and breads. "You won't want to eat any of this, and you're a big boy, so I won't make you," she'd said, "but you remember that people will be calling on you and they'll want something to eat."

She had been right on both counts. Food had tasted like dry ash to him, burnt and soiled. But the party platter didn't last through the day, as well-wishers and mourners came to pay their respects and visit with one another and then eat a sandwich, as though Annie's death marked the grand opening of some strange new restaurant.

"How are you, John?" she asked.

"Same as yesterday, just a day older. You got anything for me?" He nodded to the orderly mail slots behind her. She kept them clean and tidy, just like the rest of the office, and, by extension, the school.

"Just a smile," she answered.

"You know what I like."

He continued his walk through the office, veering around the filing cabinets and out the back door, leaving Mertyl to her world of typing and clerical work.

It was less than twenty feet to his classroom and, as usual, the room was already full. John was a popular teacher – perhaps the only popular teacher at LHS – and his kids usually beat him in there each morning.

He stepped in just as the bell rang. Before Annie died, he tended to arrive an hour to an hour and a half early, turning on the computers and preparing for the day ahead. He would also be there so that any students who might be having problems with their schoolwork, home life, or anything else could come by and get his advice.

No longer. He just didn't have the strength. But he still loved the kids he taught, and they knew it and loved him back. The nightmares were what got him out of bed each day, but these children were the only thing that convinced him to leave his house.

"Good morning, ladies and gentlemen," he said, sitting down at his desk. The role sheet had already been filled out by one of his pupils, and he didn't bother double-checking it.

Their computers were already up and running. The kids waited for nothing but him. He looked at them for a moment, then a quick smile flitted across his lips.

"Let's lock and load."

Almost as one, the children slipped their disks into the computers. Hard drives whirred (a few of the older ones made a raspy noise, like the discs were being scoured by Brillo pads), and the new web pages they were designing appeared on their screens.

John walked between them for a few minutes, nodding, complimenting, pointing out ways that each could be improved. The children smiled at him as he passed between the aisles of the computer science classroom, and he smiled back. He would have thanked God for them every moment of every day, if he still believed in God.

One of the kids was particularly involved in his work, to the point that he didn't notice John quietly move behind him to observe. His name was Dallas Howard, and John watched him silently for a few moments. The young man worked quickly, fingers skipping quickly over the keyboard as he typed. John smiled as he watched the work progress.

Dallas had been a trouble student when he came to John's class. Failing most of his classes, in trouble with all the teachers – he brought a lifetime of attitude with him. The rest of the teachers at the school had given up on him, and he took their poor expectations of him and did his best to live down to them.

Not John, though. He firmly believed that no kid was a lost cause. He focused intensely on the boy from the first, pushing him to do better, to be more than he had been. Surly in the beginning, Dallas had gradually begun to respond to John's gentle prodding. Soon he was smiling when he sat down at his desk, waiting for the next assignment to be handed out, the next challenge to overcome.

John lay a hand on his student's shoulder.

"Good job, Dallas," he said, "pretty soon you'll be able to outdesign me."

Dallas didn't so much as pause in his work, but he did snort lightly, as if to say, "I already can."

"That good, are you?"

Dallas stopped typing for a moment, looking at John with playful teasing. "The worlds I create in here are already better than the piss-poor one God did for us."

He grinned widely, and John smiled back. A few of the nearby kids in the class heard the comment and snickered. One of them, a girl with a pair of rings in her nose, spoke up. "Want to be God, eh? You're the wrong sex, little man."

More laughter came with that comment, and John was pleased to see that Dallas could smile as well; that he was not taking himself so seriously anymore.

"You bring up a good point, Patricia," he said to the girl, then raised his voice to address the whole class. They grew silent instantly, all side-chatter ceasing as he spoke. John appreciated the fact that they liked to listen to him, but also felt the pressure each time as he strove to find something to say that would both interest and inform his students.

"Remember, ladies and gentlemen," he said, "the world is fast moving into an age where the computer-illiterate won't stand a chance. Tomorrow's world is going to be run by and through computers: a new age of machines merged with people, where they do the work we are either unwilling or unable to do for ourselves."

He paused for a moment, trying to figure out where he was going with this particular strand of thought. Very often when he taught, John found himself saying things that he had not thought about beforehand. It was as though the words came from someone else at times, emerging so quickly that they left him breathless and wondering just what part of his brain had come up with that idea.

Then he felt himself continue, saying, "So let's say Mr. Howard here is right, and he is becoming a god of computers." A few titters at that, and more than a few of the girls batted their eyes at Dallas, who was blushing a bit under the class's scrutiny. Blushing, but John noted with approval that he was not looking away from them. He was becoming a very strong and self-assured teen, so very different from the attitudinal, beaten-down youth of only a few months before.

John turned his attention from Dallas back to the class. "So what does it mean to be a god? How many of us have thought about the ethics of the computer age?"

John looked around the room. The kids all stared back at him, blank-faced.

"I see. Does anyone even know what I'm talking about?"

"Porn," said one of the kids. The rest of the class snickered. John laughed a bit, too, though for a different reason. It never ceased to amaze him that in all the changes in all the kids through all the years, one thing stayed constant: mention of anything sexual or any kind of bodily function was guaranteed to elicit a laugh.

"Yes, that's one thing we might have ethical concerns over, and certainly a subject we could spend a lot of time discussing. But I'm afraid that if we talked about that, then I'd just find out how hopelessly old fashioned I am and you would all have me blushing inside five minutes." More laughs. John drew a deep breath, still not sure where he was going with this but determined to find out.

"But there are a lot of other things to consider, too. Remember," he said, warming to his topic, "when you are given access to something powerful, you have a responsibility to use it well. The more power, the more responsibility. And I think we can all agree that one of the most powerful tools ever made is the computer and the other machines associated with it. We have to think about our responsibilities in using it well. And I'm not just talking about porn."

"What else?" asked Dallas, raptly attentive.

John paused. He liked to wait for several seconds after such shouted questions. Often the other students would rise to the challenge and begin an interesting discussion. No takers this time, though, so after a moment John continued speaking. "How about video games?" he asked. The class continued to stare at him in that semi-blank way that students did when they weren't thinking;

when they hadn't been kick-started *into* thinking. John was losing his audience. He had to get more participation.

"Does anyone know what the first video game was?" he asked.

One of the kids raised a hand. "Pac Man?" A few more shouted answers rang out as each student tried to guess the answer.

John let the guesses continue for a time, then shook his head. "Good guesses, but wrong. The first video game was called Pong. There were two lines and a ball that bounced back and forth between them. That's it. Nothing else."

"Booooring," drawled Dallas, his voice sounding like a foghorn as he drew out the vowel. The class laughed again, and Dallas clasped his hands over his head and shook them in victory.

Geez, thought John, he's coming along great!

Aloud, he said, "Thank you for that compelling gamer review, Mr. Dallas." Another round of laughs. "So who of you plays video games now?"

Three quarters of the hands in the class went up.

"What are some video games you like?"

The words came quickly, a shouted chorus of the newest titles. John waited until everyone had made a contribution, then held out his hands for silence. Immediately the students quieted, waiting for his point. "Good list there, ladies and gentlemen. Now, consider: in recent years, a major selling point for new systems is how life-like they can make their games. How real are they? How many pixels calculated per second? How fast?"

He stopped a moment, then turned to a young lady named Jerianne, a sallow-faced girl who wasn't interested in speaking much. John called on her a lot for that very reason, trying to include her and encourage her. Some students needed to be held back a bit, to be reigned in and corralled. Others needed someone to set them free.

"What do you think, Ms. Halley?

"Huh?"

"How fast are games now?"

"Dunno."

"They're making games that perform *billions* of pixel calculations per second. That's more than enough to make exceptionally realistic games. Cartoon-like, or even life-like."

A few of the students nodded, and John smiled inwardly. They were starting to focus on what he was saying.

"So here's a question, or maybe just a thought: when a five-year old played Pong, what was he doing?"

Silence. Then Jerianne answered.

"Playing a video game."

The class snickered again, but John silenced them quickly. "No, don't laugh. That's exactly right. He – or she – was playing a game. But now, when a five-year-old plays one of the modern breed of games, what is that child doing?"

"Playing a game," someone said. John shook his head slightly.

The class waited, then finally Dallas spoke. The kid was smart, and he gave the answer that was so simple it sounded stupid...which of course was why John wanted someone to say it.

"He's making decisions."

"What?" asked John.

"He's making life-and-death decisions."

Someone hummed Darth Vader music. More snickers. John chuckled, too, but his eyes were serious.

"Sounds funny, doesn't it? But maybe that's right. Isn't it just possible that a five-year old, someone whose own sense of reality isn't fully shaped yet, could confuse real life with a game? When you can't tell the difference between the people next door and the people on your video game, is there a difference? Are the people in the machines more real to some of us than the people in the supermarket?"

The class quieted. John smiled to himself again. He could see that some of them – most of them – didn't think his statement was correct. But that was all right. They were at least thinking about it, instead of just absorbing every single word he said without trying to make sense of it for themselves. "Kids today are all supermodels," he had told Mertyl once. "If they aren't physically bingeing and purging, they're doing it intellectually, swallowing everything that you give them and then puking it back at you at exams and hoping it doesn't leave a bad taste in their mouths. I want to be someone who teaches them how to eat a good, balanced meal that will actually help them."

Now, the class looked like it was preparing to tuck into a feast. The first words were confrontational. A small African-American boy named Jonas spoke up without raising his hand, his high-pitched voice lowered as he tried to speak forcefully. "You gonna spread that line about how TV and video games are the reason kids are shooting each other in L.A.?"

"Maybe." See what they did with that.

"That's crap, Mr. Task. You can't tell me that some kid plays a shooter and then goes out and pops his best buddy 'cause the game made him do it."

"You think it's crap?"

Jonas nodded. Standing up to the authority figure. That was all right with John. They were welcome to hold their own positions. He enjoyed it when they did, in fact, as long as they didn't stomp on anybody in order to stomp on that person's argument.

The class waited to see what John would reply. He didn't say anything, though, because at that moment the classroom door opened.

And she walked in.

John almost lost his breath. It caught in his throat, trapped there, and for a frightening moment John worried he'd forgotten *how* to breathe.

He didn't know why the girl affected him like that. His love for the children in his class was completely on the level of teacher to student, of an older brother who ached to show them the way through life. So why he should have this strong physical reaction to

47

the girl who stepped into the class was beyond him. It was strange; baffling.

More than that, it was...what?

It was recognition.

There was something familiar in her face, something about her bone structure. Something about her cast aside the gloom that shrouded John's past, and for a split second he thought he could remember. A bolt of lightning seemed to flash through him, burning out his insides and leaving behind cold ash that sent shivers up and down his skin. Then the moment passed and the gloom once again drew itself over his memory.

At last, his mouth remembered its job. "May I help you?" he asked.

The girl held out a yellow slip of paper. After a moment of serious deliberation he was able to move his feet and walk toward her. Further control returned as he approached her, and in the few feet between them he was able to convince himself that there was nothing special about the girl in the doorway. But only on the surface. Beneath his conscious thought he knew he was telling himself lies and knew that she was important.

The paper she held was a transfer permission slip. She was a new student. But usually new students came with a week or two's warning. John looked around, stalling while he simultaneously tried to figure out what to do with her and how to gather his shell-shocked wits.

The answer presented itself in the form of Dallas Howard's enraptured face. Obviously he had noticed the new student – Kaylie Devorough, the slip said – as well, and was equally struck by her, although for far more obvious and biological reasons than John.

A sly grin spread across John's face. "Well, class, it seems we have a new student. And you know what we do to new students around here."

A chorus of voices rang out. "We eat them!"

One of the kids cackled like a witch while two or three others dissolved into more genuine laughter. Kaylie stiffened for a moment, then relaxed as she realized that this class was likely to be less than torturous.

John turned to face the newest addition to his class. "Ms. Devorough, I'm Mr. Trent. Welcome to Computer Sciences. Today we're loading websites the students have designed."

Kaylie stuttered, "I don't...that is...."

"You don't know much about computers?"

She shook her head.

"That's okay, I'm not sure I do, either. So we'll sit you with someone who knows what he's doing." John pretended to scan the classroom, then: "Why don't you sit with Mr. Howard?"

John guided Kaylie to Dallas' desk, and the boy's face lit up. Was this Heaven? John didn't think so; indeed, he no longer believed there was such a place.

But, if this isn't Heaven, John thought, then at least it can be a good place. I can try to make it better.

Dallas' face was red, but glowing with excitement as Kaylie moved her slim frame near to him, sitting beside him and letting him explain what he was doing.

John pulled himself away from them with difficulty, trying to cast off the webs of strangeness that had spun themselves about him with the appearance of the new student. He moved into a different row, and work resumed as the class returned to their individual projects. John resumed roving again, wandering up and down rows in an apparently directionless pattern that somehow took him by each student who needed his help at just the right time.

He helped the students where he could, laughed with them where he could not, and above all tried to shake loose the thought that had come into his head. The thought from that night, and from so long ago. The thought that had returned to his mind with Kaylie's entry into the room.

Someone is coming.

FAN HQ, AD 4013/AE 2013

Malachi sat in his cell. Waiting. He lay on the cot that was the only piece of furniture in the spare chamber. Monks in the Dark Ages lived more ostentatiously than did he, and Malachi, though not proud of that fact, was happy to suffer for his cause.

He was nude. The darkness of the room caressed his body, touching it with the gentle feel of a lover. His eyes were rolled back in his head, as though he were trying to look at his own brain. To see why it made him think the way it did, as though visual perception of the gray mass would be able to further confirm what he already knew: genius resided in his mind. Genius and more.

Malachi was one of the elect. He had served well, and would continue to do so.

Fire flared in the darkness. The breath sighed gently from Malachi's lips as he watched the ghostly incandescence dance through the room. No heat came from it, only a dry coolness. That was what told him that the flame existed only to him.

A vision from God, it had to be.

The flame danced, and Malachi thought he could see the last bodies of the last men and women on earth as their lives extinguished.

The final face he saw dying in the fire was his own.

His hand clenched into a fist, as though tightly gripping the barrel of his gun. He remembered shooting Lucas, and replayed it in his mind: that wonderful moment when the man realized that his life would end. Lucas' eyes trying to look in every direction at once, as though the more he could see, the less he would lose.

The moment of clarity was something Malachi treasured. That moment when they all realized, yes, they were going to die. It came to everyone, though they all experienced it differently. Some refused to accept it until the last, others knew instantly.

Lucas had known from the moment Malachi shot the bartender. The urine that sprayed out of him testified to that, and he wished he could have taken a small trace of the fluid back with him. He supposed he could have, had he thought of it earlier. He could have emptied out a whisky bottle and stored some of Lucas' byproducts. Would the glass hold it? Or would it burst under the pressure of Lucas' holy secretions?

Malachi would never know. But next time, perhaps he would try. Perhaps he would make his next victim urinate into a cup. If it was a man, perhaps he would arrange his attack at a time when the man was aroused, to gather the man's seed, the fluid of life.

He would never take blood, though. Blood was holy. Sacred. It was the redeeming power that had brought him here, to this place, to this very room. It was blood that drove him to kill, to destroy, and thereby to create.

It was blood that Malachi had spilt, and would spill again. But he would not take it with him. The blood must soak into the earth, to become a testament to his greatness; to the Work he had done.

An intercom, small and all but hidden in the bare stone wall of his room, beeped.

Malachi ignored it for a moment. It beeped again, and he swung his legs over the side of his bed. A lighting-stemmed crucifix swung near his chest, its metal warm from laying against his neck. Malachi touched the intercom. At the other end of the line, he knew, another man would be reading a piece of paper. The paper would hold a name, a place, and a time.

"Yes?" said Malachi.

"We've found another one."

"Good."

"A woman."

Malachi's heart raced. The last one. The end was near.

"Even better," he said.

Malachi stood and began dressing. He pulled on the clothing quickly, because when he received new prey, he liked to move fast. But he still took the time to make sure the clothing was clean and comely.

He put on good clothing, because killing a woman was something that demanded respect.

FAILURE LOG
DOM#22A
LOS ANGELES, CALIFORNIA
AD 2013
10:00 AM FRIDAY

Fran heard the voice, just like everyone else. The difference was, she was actually *listening*. Because the words that the voice was saying meant something to her.

They meant her life could start again.

"This is your captain speaking. We'll be leaving in about two minutes, so you all just buckle up and sit tight while the flight attendants explain our safety procedures."

The voice was tinny: the same voice that Fran had heard countless times on countless TV shows and movies. Only this time it was real. This time she sat not on her couch with a lonely bowl of popcorn as her only company, but in the seat of the airliner. First class no less, with reclining leather seats that were far more comfortable than her sofa had ever been.

In the front of the section, the flight attendant began talking about emergency exits. Fran listened even more carefully now, as the pretty airline stewardess – no, *hostess*, they were called on this line – explained how the seat could be used as a flotation device in case of a water crash.

Fran's lips curled into a tight smile. Tight, because if she smiled fully, she'd start giggling. And if she started to laugh, she probably wouldn't stop.

We're flying over the Rockies. Where would we land in water?

And then, fast on the heels of that thought, came another: *I'm really doing it.*

She looked around, wanting to savor the moment. Leaving home for the first time. If she had had a camera, she would no doubt be busily annoying her fellow first class passengers by taking snapshots of everything from the elegant hostesses to the bald pate that was the only thing visible over the top of the high-backed seat in front of hers.

This was an adventure. She wanted to enjoy it, the only adventure she'd ever really had.

No, that isn't true.

For a moment the dull roar of the plane's jet engines became small explosions. Gunshots. The hostess continued pointing at the emergency exits with a too-wide smile, but Fran no longer saw her. For a moment, for one terrible moment, she only saw her husband's face. The shock as the strangers pushed into her house, screaming and raving.

The police said the men must have been high on something. PCP, speed.

But Fran had seen their eyes. There were no drugs coursing through the strangers' veins. Insanity, but no drugs.

Purpose, but no drugs.

Evil, but no drugs.

Fran did not sleep well for months after that night, terrified that the killers would return; that the dead would rise up and find her again. Because they had been looking for her, of that she was certain. The cops smiled and nodded and said they would look into it, but she knew that they wouldn't. To them, the case was an open-and-shut one that began and ended in five minutes in a small home in Los Angeles. They cared little that those five minutes had meant the end of everything to Fran.

That was why she was on this plane. After all this time, she had finally found the courage to admit what she had known since that night. Her life in Los Angeles was over. She was dead there, and her only chance at resurrection lay in leaving the place where her heart had stopped beating.

Fran had never left Los Angeles in her life. Had never had any aspirations other than happiness with her husband, working hard at his side to build a good life and, later, a good family.

She had the good life. Not for very long, but long enough. She was grateful. God gave, God took away. Fran had almost a full year with Nathan, and when he died, she went a little crazy for a time. But then she snapped back, as determined as ever to take life, wrestle it to the ground, and squeeze every last drop of happiness out of it.

But she couldn't do it in Los Angeles. She had to leave. She had to escape into real life again.

"Are you all right?"

Fran snapped out of her memories. The gunshots ringing in her brain turned back into jet engines, winding to a higher pitch as the pilot began to accelerate.

A flight attendant stood over Fran, a look of concern on her face. "Ma'am, are you all right?"

Fran looked down, and realized that the pressure of her memories had caused her to clutch the arm rests of the chair hard enough to crumple the leather.

Fran relaxed her grip on the seat.

"I'm fine, thanks."

The hostess, whose name badge read Ray-Lynn, peered into Fran's eyes for one last moment, then hurried to the fold-out seats where she would strap herself in during the rapidly approaching takeoff.

Fran closed her eyes, pushing the memories back. Enjoy now, she thought. Tomorrow's beyond your reach, and yesterday can't be helped, so just enjoy now.

The plane took off. Fran's stomach clenched as she suddenly became heavier. Her eardrums filled and then popped as her body tried to compensate with the pressure changes. The plane slowly rolled to its left side, a lazy turn that seemed to take hours before the plane righted itself and entered the flight path that would take the commuters to Denver, Colorado.

Last stop, Loston.

Loston, where Fran's cousin waited. Where a new *life* waited.

She smiled again, and looked around the cabin. Most of the other passengers took no note of her, but one of them, a little boy not more than ten years old, caught her eye. He looked frightened, gripping the seat with white hands that matched his white face, with little lips blue as the sky outside. Fran caught his gaze. She smiled. He tried to smile back, tried to be brave as his parents chatted nonchalantly in the seats behind him. But the smile nearly dissolved into tears as the plane bounced slightly. An air pocket, surely nothing more serious than that, but the child was rapidly approaching terror.

"What's your name?" she asked.

"George," he whispered, the word barely a breath across his lips.

"George. What a nice name. Like the curious monkey?"

George nodded. Still too scared to smile, but some of the fear had left his face.

"Are you curious, too, George?"

He nodded.

"About what?"

"Stuff."

"Really? How interesting. I had a friend once who was an expert."

"In what?"

"Stuff. He was an expert in stuff."

George's face loosened up a little more. He could feel he was being played with, and it didn't bother him at all. Fran had a knack for talking to children, and was using it now to calm this frightened boy.

"Yup," she continued, "he was a great expert in stuff. World-famous, in fact. He was curious, too, and decided to be a stuff expert. So he went out and examined stuff all year long, for ten years. Then he brought it all home."

"What did he bring home?"

"His stuff, of course. He kept the big stuff in the main room – the ballroom, he called it – and the smaller stuff in a dollhouse that he made special for small stuff. The medium-size stuff he just threw wherever."

George smiled. Fran decided he wasn't going to puke or cry. Good kid. She leaned across the aisle, as far as her belt would allow.

"But you know, the medium-size stuff didn't like that. Didn't like that small stuff got its own house, big stuff got its own room. So one day...."

"What? What happened?" George really *was* curious now. He had evidently forgotten about the air-pocket and about the plane itself as he leaned toward Fran, mouth agape and eyes agleam.

"Well, all the medium stuff rebelled. They called a secret stuff meeting, and decided they'd had enough. The next day my friend got back from a long trip, holding lots of new stuff. He went in his house, and BAM! The medium stuff grabbed him. Said they wanted better treatment. Said they wanted better food. Said they wanted their own *room*, by heck and by golly.

"But my friend had no more rooms. In fact, that's what he said, 'I have no more rooms.' So...."

Fran opened her mouth as though to finish her story. Then shut it and sat back. She was silent.

"So what happened?"

Fran looked at George again. He was straining across the aisle, now, as though he could influence her to finish the story by drawing close.

"What happened to your friend?" he urged, his little boy voice growing even higher in his excitement.

"I...I don't know, George." She shook her head as though debating. "What they did to him was pretty terrible. I don't know if you really want to hear it."

"I do. Tell me, please."

"Well...how old are you?"

"Nine."

"Nine. That's pretty old. But are you tough, George? Are you brave? Can you handle hearing about the awful thing the stuff did to my friend?"

George nodded, wide-eyed, not a bit afraid, having completely forgotten his fear of flying in the drama of Fran's small tale.

"Okay. But I warned you." She took a deep breath, trying to convey what a horrible, evil, slimy, bad thing she was about to relate, getting almost as caught up in the story as George was. "They took my friend into the basement. And tied him down. And then...," (one last pause for drama) "...they stuffed him."

"What?" George was incredulous.

"Oh, sure, they had all sorts of food waiting. Like Christmas feast and Thanksgiving and Halloween and Easter all wrapped up in one. Candy, bread, pies, meat, chicken, hamburgers from McDonald's, you name it. And they made him eat it until he was, you know, *stuffed*."

She smiled at George, who was frowning.

"That's it? The stuff just made him eat?"

"No, they *stuffed* him, George. That's what stuff does."

"That wasn't scary at all."

"Not scary? I had nightmares for months after my friend told me what had happened."

"He escaped?"

"Oh, they let him go. But they made him eat everything first. My friend weighed about six thousand pounds when the stuff was done with him. Sad sight, really. He couldn't get in cars anymore. Couldn't ride bikes, because they just broke under him. So did horses. Any time my friend wanted to go anywhere, he'd have to call the Coast Guard, and they'd fly in with a helicopter that had a special harness for moving whales, and they'd airlift him to the grocery store, or to my house for tea, or wherever."

George rolled his eyes. "Nobody's that fat."

Fran rolled her eyes back at him. "Says you. But as for me, I always make sure to treat stuff well. Especially the medium-sized stuff."

She grinned at George, and this time he grinned back, a jack-o-lantern smile that attested to the fact that he was still going through teeth. Probably had a pretty rich tooth fairy, too, judging by his clothes.

George had just been had, and Fran knew that he knew it, but neither one of them minded very much. The plane jostled again, another air pocket, and Fran saw the boy's face begin to bleach white once more. She thought quickly, trying to find something to say that would help him to conquer his fear, or at least to deal with it more easily.

"Say, George?" she said.

"What?"

"You are a pretty brave guy. And to tell you the truth, I've never been on a plane before and I'm a little scared. Would you hold my hand?"

She extended her hand. For a moment George was shy. Fran was a beautiful woman, and that fact was not lost on many males, not even those who were nine years old. But at last he reached out, interlocking his small fingers in her larger ones.

She squeezed his hand. "Thanks, George."

He smiled. Behind him, George's mom and dad were talking about their beachfront property in Malibu.

A moment later, the fasten seat belts sign blinked off, and the flight attendants began moving up and down the aisles, asking people what they'd like to drink.

Fran squeezed George's hand once more, then let go to unfasten her seat belt. George did the same, his fear forgotten. Fran watched his bright-eyed enchantment as the flight attendant told him he could have any drink he wanted. He wanted a root beer, and the hostess was happy to get one for him before inclining her head toward Fran.

"What would you like to drink, Ma'am?"

"Ginger ale would be fine."

The hostess leaned over the drink cart, selecting a ginger ale and a root beer. She handed George his first, and he attacked it like a camel just out of the Sahara. Then the flight attendant passed Fran her ginger ale and a napkin with the plane line's logo marching across the front. Fran put the napkin down and sipped the drink contentedly. Everything was as it should be.

And then the world turned upside down.

There was a clang, and the plane lurched violently, a shudder rippling through its frame. Fran thought for a moment it might be another air pocket, but since when did air *clang*?

The flight attendants all tumbled to the deck like so many straw dolls, and frightened cries echoed through the plane. They created a weirdly cacophonous chorus, a thin wailing as people shouted for parents and lovers and God to protect them.

Another clang, louder and more insistent than before, and this time the plane dropped into a sudden nose dive. Fran braced herself against the sides of her chair, struggling to stay in the seat that had repositioned itself above and behind her. People all around her fell forward, slapping hands and arms and sometimes faces into the seats in front of them as forward became down in a single shattering motion.

A flight attendant hurtled past Fran, following the drink cart that had already rolled to the front bulkhead and spilled its payload of soda all over the walls. The flight attendant shrieked as she landed on her arm. Even over the cries and the sounds of terror, Fran could clearly hear the woman's bone as it snapped against the metal bulkhead. But then the sounds in the cabin could scarcely be heard above the tumult of strained metal, firing jets, and panicking passengers.

Fran kept pushing against the seat in front of her, struggling to keep from following the flight attendant. There was no time for anything more than pure survival, but somehow she managed to turn her head…

…and it was then that she saw the second-most terrifying sight of her life. Not as bad as what happened to Nathan, but close.

George was struggling to stay in his seat. His thin child's arms quivered as he strained to remain in place, to resist the forces that pulled at him with a million strong hands. It was a miracle he had remained in the oversized chair as long as he had.

But miracles sometimes come with time limits, and George's time had run out.

The plane jolted yet again, and George lost his fight with gravity. He flipped head first over the seat in front of him, careening like a pinball into the aisle. His tiny body seemed to hang for an eternity, life and time slowing and the air thickening around him as though the very forces of nature were exerting themselves to keep the little boy out of harm's way.

Then even the forces of nature gave in, and George plummeted down to the front of the plane. Fran cried out, grabbing wildly out for him, knowing even as she did so that she'd never reach him in time.

George pinwheeled out of her range, smashed into a seat, careened back into the aisle, and then crashed headfirst into the drink cart. Time slowed again as Fran saw her young friend's head impact the metal cart, and almost gently fold under. His body drove down on his neck, pressing it to a twenty degree angle, then thirty, then forty, and somewhere along the way it snapped.

Fran screamed again, not with pain or fear, but with the searing vision of George's body in a heap against the cart full of his favorite root beer and lemon-lime and fruit drinks, his neck twisted at an impossible angle, his eyes sightlessly staring, and his little feet twitching a death-dance against the airplane floor.

Fran screamed until she couldn't scream any more, then she mouthed silent screams.

And still the plane fell.

A final metallic clang rose above the chaos, this time more of a crunch, and the plane abruptly righted. The movement seemed to come not under the plane's own power, but rather the jet was jerked into proper position by some outside force, as if God had a crane and had grabbed it out of free fall.

Fran glanced out the window, and saw something that sent shivers down her back, even though she could not say what it was she was looking at. Her experience gave her no words or concepts against which to place the huge metal shape that hovered above the plane and extended for hundreds of feet on either side.

She looked out the window opposite her, and saw the same thing. She also noticed that huge clawlike appendages had emerged from the side of the object and now grasped the plane, holding it steady below the behemoth that hung above them in the air, like an island in the sky.

People were still screaming, and all of a sudden the emergency exits burst open.

More shrieks. Fran looked at the exits, expecting anything and nothing all at the same time. She saw a man come through, bright blue eyes searing the compartment with a gaze like lasers. He wore a shiny, quasi-metallic suit, and a mask of some kind covered his nose and mouth.

For a moment, all Fran's overloaded brain could think about was the mask. Why a mask? He looked human (and in that split-second she had to admit to herself that an alien abduction was the thing she most expected to occur at this point), so why the mask?

Then she smelled something, something sweet and citrusy, but with a faintly bitter undercurrent. As she smelled it, her vision fogged. She tried to turn her head, but it seemed that someone was holding her muscles, keeping her brain from communicating its wishes to her body. Only her eyes moved, and they moved slowly, ponderously, and the last sight she saw before blackness utterly claimed her as its own was little George. He was crumpled on the deck, laying on his back with his head swiveled under him like a macabre pillow.

He was still. A moment later, so was Fran.

She closed her eyes and slept.

FAILURE LOG
LA/LOSTON TRANSPORT
SUBJECT A

Adam stepped into the plane, replaying what had happened and trying to see if it could have been done any differently. The mask he wore chafed at his mouth and nose, tiny fibers inside it filtering out the gas that still remained in the plane.

He looked at the wounded, the dying.

The dead.

He whipped around, fury rippling across his normally placid features.

"Get Dirk down here," he said to the woman who had followed him into the plane. Like him, she was dressed in a drab outfit, so gray it was almost colorless. It was the color of their home, and suited them. But it did nothing to hide the anger in Adam's eyes.

The woman turned and left. She did not salute, for that was a thing of the Past. Besides, this wasn't exactly a military unit.

Not exactly.

Adam turned his eyes back to the compartment, searching. Those eyes missed nothing. He noted every passenger's placement, divining from what he knew of the trajectory of their impact with his knowledge of their assigned seats to figure out where *she* would be.

Jason, Adam's second in command, stood beside him in the plane, his own gaze following Adam's. Jason was shorter than Adam, and was a quiet man, seeming to keep his own counsel more than most. That was all right with Adam. When he did speak, Jason always communicated something worthy of attention. That was why he was Adam's right hand, and why when Adam was eventually went insane or was killed Jason would take charge.

There was always the possibility Jason would die first. This was a dangerous business. But the odds were decent that Jason would hold to his sanity longer than Adam would, so it was right for him to be next in command. Jason had the best chance of carrying on Adam's mission when the inevitable finally occurred.

"She should be in 7-C, sir," said Jason.

Adam nodded and picked his way through the debris that littered the plane's interior. He tripped over a woman's handbag, the straps catching at his heel and sending him stumbling. He heard a dry crack as his foot landed hard on something.

He looked down and saw a young woman. She lay in the aisle, one hand thrown up over her face, no doubt to protect her beautiful features as she flew out of her chair. Her hair curled in a matted carpet over her face, knotted and gnarled from the cruel buffeting she had endured.

And now, on top of being tossed and thrown and most likely killed, Adam had stepped on her elbow, and he could see that it was broken.

This did nothing to improve his already bad mood. He muttered a curse, then stepped off the woman's arm. He gently brushed her hair away from her face, combing his fingers loosely through her hair. It was probably somewhat silly of him – uncharacteristically frivolous, even – to do so. But her broken elbow would not bother her, not in her present state, and her extreme dishevelment seemed to rebuke him. *You did this to me*, it seemed to say, and so Adam gently combed her hair away, softly put it as right as he could, then even more gently put her back in the nearest empty seat. It probably wasn't hers, but it didn't matter. Adam did it more out of respect than out of a desire to put things back the way they had been.

He respected all the people on board the plane. Some of his coworkers did not, seeing the plane's occupants as mere window dressing, but Adam certainly held them fond in his heart. They were, after all, the future. Or rather, they guarded its safekeeping.

He put the girl's broken arm on the armrest. She did not moan at all, though Adam could not tell whether that was because the synaptic inhibitors had done their jobs or because she was simply dead. Either way, she would not remember that any of this had ever happened.

Adam stood again.

7-C.

He found it easily. The woman had managed to stay in her seat.

"Thank God," he whispered.

He reached out to touch her forehead. It was smooth; cool. Unlined in spite of the horrible toll the past years must have taken on her. He traced the delicate curve of her chin, following her jaw to the point where it joined her throat. Skin so white, so pure. So real.

He took a deep breath, preparing himself for the worst, then touched her throat with two fingers. A pulse beat at his fingertips, strong and healthy. He let his breath out, his knees growing suddenly wobbly with relief.

She was alive. Today, at least, the world would not end.

I could love you, Fran, he said to himself. But that was a half-truth, at best. Because he already did. Not in the way some might think, but in the way of a father for his only child. In the way that only a man who has spent his whole life protecting a woman can feel towards her. "I do love you," he whispered.

She simply slept, like the beauty from the Old fairy tales. No kiss would wake her, though. Indeed, very few things could.

Someone coughed lightly.

Adam stood upright, spinning around so hard that he almost tripped again. Dirk, the man who had been in charge of the boarding process, stood behind him. He wore an ill-fitting mask that covered a mouth no doubt puckered downward in a pious frown.

"Idiot!" shouted Adam. The sleepers around them did not wake. "You could have killed her!"

"I'm sorry, there was a problem syncing our ship with the plane and –"

"I don't care what the problem was, Dirk. You could have *killed* her. Do you understand what that would mean?"

Dirk nodded. His eyes suddenly welled up and a tear streaked its way down his cheek, touching the edge of his mask and steering along the seal to his chin. Adam let up a bit. He didn't want to be too hard, but still....

"You are relieved of your duties as pilot. Have Abra take over," said Adam in a quiet voice. It was not meant to carry to the other men and women in the room. His decree was not meant to humiliate, but to teach. And above all, to ensure that the jobs that needed doing were done well. Dirk nodded and turned on his heel.

Adam followed him to the front of the plane, where the Cleanup Crew waited. They were Controllers, of course, as Adam was, but their function was more specific than most. They had to turn back the clocks perfectly; make sure that what they did left no trace, either in evidence or memory.

Adam looked at his feet. A little boy lay nearby, body smashed into a mangled ball by forces beyond his control. From the way his neck crooked, it was evident he was dead, and Adam resisted the urge to grow angry again. Anger would solve nothing and would not serve to teach any lessons, so he quelled it. He did this reflexively, subordinating the emotion almost as a matter of course. Emotions were a dangerous luxury, and one that Adam rarely indulged in.

"You'll have to fix that," he said to the Cleanup Crew, pointing to the child. They all nodded as one. Each had the exact layout of the plane in his or her head, where each item of luggage had to go, where each passenger sat.

They would make it right.

Adam sighed. I'm getting too old, he thought. But it was a lie. He was only fifty-two, and more than equal to the physical aspects of the challenges that lay before him. He would never see sixty, of course, as his death was sure to come before then, but until it did he would work and protect. He was a Controller, and that was what a Controller did: service and toil until death provided a release from both.

He looked at 7-C again, at the blonde-framed face that slept so peacefully in the midst of so many convergences of history.

"Fran," he whispered. He touched her lightly, a quick caress that was almost too fast to be seen. Then Adam stepped out of the plane. He would leave while the Cleanup Crew made all right again, and then would watch Fran as she reached her destination, the place she must go, if humanity was to have any chance at all.

Loston.

DOM#67B
LOSTON, COLORADO
AD 2013
9:30 AM, FRIDAY

The bell rang.

The kids stood immediately. They enjoyed John's class enough to be there on time and to actually pay attention. But not even special guest appearances by a Top 40 rock band could have kept them in their seats for one second – one *nano*second – beyond class time.

That was all right. John understood that, and was not offended. On the contrary, seeing their hurried walk as they crowded out of the classroom like a well-groomed and too-fashionable plague of locusts always brought John to memories of his own childhood.

And most of those were good.

The new girl, Kaylie, stood last in the line of kids pushing to get out the door. John watched her move inch by inch to the exit, walking to his desk without taking his eyes off her. He couldn't shake the feeling that he'd seen her before. And yet he knew he hadn't. Knew it with every atom of his being.

So why did he have some small, mostly-hidden part of him screaming that this girl was important? She was the most important person he'd ever met. She was....

The answer. To everything.

The thought jerked him to a realization of what he was thinking. It was crazy, he realized, and John had never had a crazy bone in his body. Not since he was a child, at any rate. And for a few months after Annie.

Still, no matter how hard he tried, he couldn't shake loose from feelings that had suddenly grown weird and conflicted. He wanted to call her; to talk to her. But to do that would be to admit that there was something not merely familiar, but *important* about her. To surrender his pretense of rationality and give in to...what?

I'll just call her over for a second to get to know her, he thought. I'd do that with any student. Not just her, so it's okay, right?

Right?

"Ms. Devorough?" he said.

Kaylie turned, and John was surprised to see fear skate across her pale face on like cool blades on a frozen lake. Fear of *him*.

No, it could be anything, he thought. She could come from an abusive home. She could come from a place where the teachers made fun of her.

All the more reason to talk to her.

The decision was made; had been from the moment she walked into the class.

"Could you come here for a moment, please?"

The girl nodded, but remained where she stood. The last of the students filed out of the room, leaving John alone with her. The empty space separating them seemed to scream at him: Run, get out, get out now while there's still time!

The silence between them stretched out, feeling more interminably desolate than the longest stretch of desert. The two stared at one another, and John felt himself becoming more and more nervous, almost to the point of nausea.

"Where are you from?" he asked.

Kaylie's mouth opened and shut in a semblance of speech, but nothing emerged. She was still as silent as she had been a moment before.

John stood and approached her, moving as slowly as he could, as though the girl were a frightened dog he had met in an alley. He resisted the urge to drop to his knees and offer her some food.

"I'm not going to bite you." He smiled broadly, hoping to jolly her loose from her nervousness. "Where are you from?"

She looked out the still-open door. Students passed it, shifting bags on their shoulders, talking to their friends as they hurried or dawdled to their next classes.

"I'm going to be late," she said.

"That's okay. It's your first day, and no one expects you to know where anything is. Where are you from?"

"I really don't want to get in trouble on my first day here."

"I'll write you a note. Is there a reason you don't want to tell me where you're from?"

She began edging to the door. "No, I just don't want to be late."

"Ms. Devorough, please just answer my question and you can go."

"Sorry, I don't want to be late," she said again, and almost ran out the door.

John watched her go, and wondered which was stranger: her actions or the icy fear that clutched him.

TRANSDOM#7
LA – LOSTON TRANSPORT LOG
SUBJECT A

Fran stretched her arms, feeling the bones in her forearms, shoulders, all the way down her back stretch and crackle. The flight attendant came by, smiling as before.

Fran could not remember the flight attendant's name, and looked to her name tag. Her name tag was gone. But it didn't matter. The hostess seemed just as happy without a name as she had with one. "Did you have a nice nap?"

Fran smiled languidly, like a Siamese cat well-sated. "Oh, I did indeed."

Other passengers were moving, too, each happy that they had arrived, each feeling particularly well-rested. Fran looked to her right.

"Did you fall asleep?" she asked. George nodded, tapping his feet impatiently, waiting for his parents to get his small carry-on. "Me too. Thanks for helping me stay brave. I don't think I could have fallen asleep without knowing you were around to watch out for me."

George blushed, crooking his neck to one side and avoiding her gaze. But he was smiling.

Fran winked at her little friend, and then he disappeared, whisked off the plane by yuppie parents who had never been aware of their son's fear or what might have been a moment of great personal victory for the young boy as he overcame it.

Baggage check was a flash; a breeze. She got out of the airport in under ten minutes, seated in a taxi bound for her new home.

She was ready for her new life. The old one had been wonderful. She hoped this one would be, too. Only this time, perhaps the good life would last. Perhaps it would last forever.

She smiled, already planning her happiness. That was what set her apart from so many others. She had seen life, and she had seen terror. But where many would see the cup half-empty, Fran saw the pitcher on the table beside it, just waiting for someone to start pouring. She would not hide in her fear, but would stand and smile in the sun as long as it lasted. And if night should come again...well, there was always another sunrise, just around the corner of the blackness.

***

Fran looked out the window for five minutes of the taxi ride to her new place. And then she fell asleep again.

A moment after Fran's head came to rest against the car window, the driver slumped as well. Neither saw the portal open directly in their path, the disembodied doorway that allowed the taxi to drive through a hole in what appeared to be the very air before them.

The gap sealed behind them, and it was as though they had never been.

DOM#67B LOSTON, COLORADO, AD 2013
3:30 PM FRIDAY

John put his key in the door of his Suburban. The day was over – the *week* was over – and the strange thoughts and concerns that gripped him during the first hour of classes abandoned him soon after, leaving him alone with his students and his normal thoughts. Or rather, what passed for normal thoughts in these days. Loneliness clutched him for a moment as he stood beside the door, a terrifying surge that passed through him and left him weak and nauseated. He gripped the door and realized that he had caught himself in the act of opening the passenger side.

For a moment, he almost believed all was right with the world. For a brief, beautiful second he thought that he could turn around and see Annie behind him, waiting as she always did for the door to be opened. He remembered that on their second date he had opened the door for her. "Why did you do that?" she had asked.

He sensed immediately that he was engaged in some sort of test. A thousand answers passed through his thoughts as he sorted, examined, discarded possible responses before finally settling on the truth as his best answer.

He looked Annie in the eye. "Because my mother told me that any girl I take out had better get royal treatment, or she'd come back from the grave and haunt me."

"Royal treatment, eh?" she asked, and he sensed the warmth that flashed in her eyes like a sunbeam through a winter sky. He had passed the test.

"Sure," he replied, heart skipping beats with every breath he took. He opened the door, bowed low, and said, "After you, my queen."

She curtsied and got in the car, passing him in a swift cloud of sweet-smelling air. He could still smell her on this hot day in the parking lot.

He could almost believe she was here.

But then the moment passed, and he knew she was not. She was not, and never would be again.

He moved swiftly to the driver's side, opening the door and throwing a handful of papers into the back seat. Class work that he would grade tonight.

He heard a car door open behind him, and at the same time a deep, rasping voice chipped out at him: "Casey's?"

John didn't even have to turn around to know who it was. Gabriel Harding – or Coach Gabe as he preferred to be called – was a thick, powerful man who looked as though God had taken a sequoia, shrunk it down to the more manageable height of six and a half feet, and put two eyes on the front.

John turned to his friend. As always, Gabe's whistle hung from his neck. The man wore it with more pride than a Congressional Medal of Honor, and when he wasn't talking, he held the silver instrument clenched between his lips. Gabe was an artist with a whistle, and there were some students on the campus who swore they had seen him use his instrument while cursing them and belittling their parentage at the same time. It was a feat a professional ventriloquist would find daunting, and not for a moment did John disbelieve the account.

"Casey's?" John repeated to himself, still shaking off the fog of his waking vision of Annie. He looked around. A long line of cars filled the parking lot as parents came for their children.

Annie was nowhere among them.

"Sure, that sounds good," he said.

"That's what I like to hear." Gabe got in his car and started the engine, backing his vehicle out behind John's car. He waited for John to pull out. He always waited, as though John were a prince and the high school coach his vassal, waiting deferentially a few steps behind.

John knew why the coach – normally not the most genteel of men – would do such a thing. Both men knew why Gabe held John in such high esteem, though neither would ever speak of the reason. To have one person owe another his life was a rare thing. And it created a deep, stable bond between them.

For a moment, standing there in the bright sunlight, caressed ever so softly by a thin mountain breeze, John saw his friend again, as he had seen him that day: bloody and broken, a dead man who hadn't the sense to lay down and expire. Then the vision passed, and John found himself in the parking lot again. His friend was not broken, but whole and unblemished. Still, the momentary tableau that had intruded upon John's mind left a mark. It felt like a premonition, as though something awful was going to happen to Gabe. He shuddered, and tried to expunge that thought from his mind. If anything happened to Gabe....

Then John would truly be alone.

Still trying to shake off the feelings of uneasiness that had suddenly gripped him, John turned to get back in his car. As he did, he saw Kaylie coming out of the school. Her head was bowed, her hair obscuring her features, but John recognized his new student instantly. She walked up to the curb where parents were picking up their kids and waited as a light blue Mustang convertible pulled up. John slammed his door shut without getting in and trotted to the sports car, hoping to see her parents, maybe schedule an appointment.

His sense of urgency from that morning returned with a vengeance, pricking at him like a spur. His trot turned into a run as he hurried to catch his student and meet her family, which he hoped would provide a key to revealing the enigma that the young girl presented.

He ran to the car and knocked on the glass. A man – John figured it was Kaylie's father – was sitting in the driver's seat, his face turned away from John as his daughter clambered in the car. The man did not turn, however, even as Kaylie closed the door and belted herself in.

John tapped again on the window. The sound was sharp, almost metallic, and seemed somehow out of place on this warm day. The man remained facing away from John, and now John noticed that Kaylie was staring at him in unabashed fear, the terror that he had sensed in her this morning no longer half-hidden, but easily visible in her eyes and the way her hands gripped the folds of her clothing.

John raised his hand a third time to tap on the glass, and a voice in his mind screamed at him, Don't do it!

But his hand and arm seemed under someone else's control, and so against his will he saw his knuckle rap two short taps on the safety glass of the car door. He almost expected the glass to craze beneath his fist, to hide whatever was in the car from John's prying gaze.

The glass did not shatter, however. Instead, the car's driver slowly turned toward him. John's mouth fell open as he came face to face with someone he'd never thought to see again.

Skunk Man.

It was him. The same face. Same hair. *And he hadn't aged a day.*

Forget *aging*, thought John. You saw him *die.*

On the other side of the glass, the man's eyes widened. Everything began to move slowly. John saw Kaylie pull at the man's arm. Saw the man's own hand drop to the gear selector.

You saw him die. Blown up in a chopper in Iraq.

Then time sped up again as the man threw his car into gear and pulled away from the sidewalk. The Mustang wasn't the newest model, but it still mustered sufficient power to leap away from the curb with a squeal of rubber.

John threw himself away from the car as it pulled away, narrowly missing being hit as the Mustang pulled out of line and began fighting its way past the one or two cars that blocked egress from the parking lot. Angry horns blared, and honked still more as the car rasped against a minivan that partially blocked its exit.

John jumped to his feet, subliminally noticing his stinging, abraded palms that had been rubbed a cherry red by their collision with the asphalt, and sprinted to his Suburban.

The door opened, and he jammed the key in the ignition, hardly waiting for the engine to turn over before throwing the car into gear and backing out of his parking space. He narrowly avoided a collision with Gabe's car, which still idled behind his, as he pulled out.

Gabe threw *his* car into reverse, pulling back a few crucial inches to avoid John's vehicle. John saw his friend's confused expression in the side view mirror as he popped his car into first gear and wound around a few cars. Then he was stopped by a pair of minivans several kids were jumping into. He couldn't thread his way around them: the school was on one side and a grassy hill on the other. Nor could he go between them. Even if there had been room, there were too many children milling between the two vehicles for John to pass without hitting someone.

John rolled down his window and leaned his head out to check where the Mustang was. He saw it pull past the last car, then onto the street.

John was about to lose them.

He thought for a second, then, ignoring his better sense, which was yelling at him not to be an idiot, he backed his SUV up a few feet. It tapped into the car behind him – Gabe's car, which added to the wide disbelief of his friend's expression – signaling the end of John's runway. It would have to do. He gunned the motor, then let out the clutch and his car surged over the curb, up the small grassy hill, and out onto the street.

The Mustang had a large head start, but was still on the main street.

And John was in pursuit.

CONTROL HQ – RUSHM
AD 4013/AE 2013

"We have a problem."

The words echoed in the silence of the observation pod, and then fell leadenly to the hard stone floor.

Adam halted the image on his own Control Time, ceasing his study of the bygone era, and immediately turned to face Jason. His second in command had spoken the words from his duty station, where the other man was watching one of the monitors on the wall.

Adam strode immediately to the younger man. "Enlarge it," he said.

Jason passed his fingers through the air in front of the monitor, piercing the invisible beams that formed a grid in front of the free-pixeled plasmatic display. The monitor threw out an image of itself, which seemed to hang in the air a moment, then floated down to floor level and expanded, becoming a three dimensional holographic image. The virtual world shown in the display swelled in size, swallowing up the front half of the observation pod. When it ceased its growth, a perfect cube six meters to a side stood solidly before them. It was a window into the world beyond, and Adam stepped into the cube, entering the scene.

He instantly recognized the area: Loston. He was standing on the main road, dust swirling along the highway. Two vehicles barreled past him, one in hot pursuit of the other. They passed near enough for him to touch, had they been more than holos.

"Give me a close up on the one in back. Center the holo on that SUV." he said, and though he couldn't see him, he knew Jason would be adjusting his controls to comply with Adam's command. The image moved to the car in back, an older vehicle that struggled to keep up with the more powerful sports car in the lead.

The holo kept the trailing SUV in its center, and as a result Adam himself appeared to be floating rapidly down the main street. Though he had done surveillance like this before, the effect always made him slightly queasy. He choked back his gorge, however, and peered into the driver's side window of the SUV that he had appeared to be floating beside. Now his nausea resurfaced, though for a different reason.

"John," he whispered. Then, in a louder voice, "Who's in front?"

The image recentered, moving Adam to the lead car, a Mustang. As it did, Jason's disembodied voice spoke. "It's a nobody. A bit."

Adam took note of the bit, observing the man's tousled, gray-streaked hair and fearful countenance. Then his eyes roved to the passenger, a young girl of perhaps fourteen.

"Who's the passenger?" he asked.

He could hear the sound of Jason typing hurriedly on one of the pod computers, a soft clicking that seemed to come from everywhere and nowhere at the same time. The clicking stopped for a long moment, then resumed again.

"That can't be right," came Jason's voice.

"What?" Each of the cars swerved to avoid a large pothole in the center of the street, and the holo bounced and jittered with them. The swaying movement of the image was not helping Adam's stomach.

"Records indicate...it's his daughter."

"His *daughter*? Bits can't have daughters!"

Jason's voice came back at him. "I don't know what happened, sir. The registry says it's his daughter."

Adam watched the Mustang turn off the dirt road. "Find out who made that entry and work back."

"The Fans?" asked Jason.

"Could be," answered Adam. "They might know about John and Fran, and if they do –"

"They couldn't. That would mean –"

"Exactly. Another traitor. So find out who made that registry entry and report to me." Adam watched the man driving the Mustang. "God in Heaven," he murmured, a swiftly-uttered prayer to stave off the fear that clutched his guts.

He touched a control on his wrist and the world around him dissolved, shattering into a trillion pixels that hung in the air for a moment before slowly fading.

Adam was already walking to Jason's station.

"We need to fix this," he said.

"What happened to John?" asked Jason. "It's just a *bit* up front."

"I would guess from his reaction that John has seen him before. So we need to get the bit out of there, now."

Adam turned back to the monitor, image now flush against the wall, but still showing the chase.

"This could destroy us all."

DOM#67B
LOSTON, COLORADO
AD 2013
3:40 PM FRIDAY

John dropped his Suburban into second gear, simultaneously breaking slightly. The shift in momentum made the SUV surge forward, dropping the front closer to the ground and making a more efficient turn.

John smiled grimly to himself. If the Mustang had stayed on the main strip, it would have outpaced his small car quickly, leaving him behind and helpless to pursue. But the driver of the car ahead was obviously a novice. He panicked, turning onto one of the dirt roads that led to the farms outside of town. He took the turn too fast and fishtailed, sending up a great plume of dust and losing precious seconds getting his car back onto the road.

In that time, John closed much of the gap between them. He took the corner perfectly, old reflexes and training surging to his consciousness for the first time in ten years. He upshifted, then braked and slammed his accelerator in a close series of movements that coaxed the maximum speed out of his tired old Suburban.

He was right on the Mustang's tail now, and damned if he was going to lose it.

***

Kaylie watched the road in front of them, clutching her backpack like a spiritual ward that would keep away demons. Her father sat beside her, his face haunted and waxy.

"What's going on?" she asked. She wanted to know the answer to that question, wanted to know so badly that she felt she could scream if it wasn't answered soon. Scream and never stop.

She could go mad.

She bit back the shriek in the back of her throat, though, and looked to her father.

"What's going on?" she repeated.

He didn't answer.

No answers for her. She did not understand what was going on, or why she had felt so much anxiety when meeting her new teacher that morning. She only knew that she must not – *could not* – answer his questions about her past.

Why not? she thought for the thousandth time. *Why couldn't I say anything? Why not just tell him where I'm from?*

And suddenly, agonizingly, Kaylie realized that she herself didn't know the answer to that question. She strained to think, to remember where she had been before that morning, but every time she did, her mind seemed to...*bounce*, somehow, and she found herself remembering only what she had had for breakfast that morning. All that lay before that meal was a fog.

She looked at her father again.

Who is that? If he's my father, why don't I remember him?

The man beside her cranked the wheel hard then, and the Mustang slewed to the left, losing traction in spite of the expensive racing tires that bit and tore at the road beneath them. The man looked afraid. He looked terrified, in fact, and Kaylie knew with dreadful certainty that her eyes appeared every bit as frightened as his.

***

John yanked his wheel to the left, surprised at the abrupt swerve the Mustang took in front of him. It had passed several small dirt roads, and when it took this one – chosen seemingly at random – it hadn't slowed enough to make a safe turn. If John had been watching the chase on TV – a police report or one of those tabloid "Real Police Chases, Real Police Blood" shows – he would have expected the Mustang to rise up on two wheels, doing a short moment of stunt driving before completely flipping over.

The car ahead of him didn't flip, though. John was fairly certain it had violated some serious laws of physics, but the muscle car kept its balance and sprinted ahead again.

John slowed for his turn. He didn't want to end up pinned in an inverted SUV.

The slower turn cost him time, and when he completed his change to the smaller street – a dirt road that was hardly more than a wide trail – he saw that the Mustang was hauling its way toward the mountains.

John jammed his foot down on the accelerator, managing to catch up to the gigantic plume of dust the Mustang threw behind it. Pebbles and twigs slapped his windshield with light snaps, as though someone with extremely hard nails was flicking his finger against the safety glass. The tapping unnerved John, and he let his speed drop a bit. He realized that pursuit at this point was beyond strange, it was foolish. Even if he could manage to keep up with the -

(*Skunk Man*)

- gray-haired man's car, he wouldn't be able to see through the dust cloud created by spinning wheels on a dry trail. John knew potholes – some small, some large enough to break an axle – littered this area. His foot eased off the accelerator a little more, and soon the car ahead of him pulled away.

The Mustang turned again, then disappeared behind a stand of trees. John watched the other side of the small copse, waiting for the car to emerge and continue its dogged climb up the mountainous trail.

It did not emerge, however, and John allowed himself another smile as he realized the car must have stopped, whether because of the driver's choice or because some accident had befallen the vehicle. He gunned his accelerator again, rapidly approaching the trees, then turning his wheel to slide sideways below a thick canopy of foliage. Then he jammed on the brakes as the sight that greeted him tore the breath from his lungs in one hoarse gasp.

The Mustang was nowhere to be seen.

Vanished.

DOM#67B
LOSTON, COLORADO
AD 2013
4:10 PM FRIDAY

Casey's was a place that reflected its owner: small, mostly quiet, and comfortable.

At the age of twelve, Casey ran away from home. He had lived in New York, in an apartment with his mother and two other women. All three were hookers, a fact that no one in Loston knew. The only things that they knew about Casey were the things that they had seen after his arrival in the small town at the age of eighteen.

In New York, Casey never had a father. Just a series of men who came into his life, usually with violence, always with pain. The violence might be directed at him, but more often it was aimed at his mother and her friends.

One night, after seeing his mother beaten mercilessly for the third time in as many weeks, Casey finally did something about it. The assailant was Tray, his mother's pimp...and a man who gave STD viruses something to feel superior to. A squat, fat man with a cartoonish overbite, Tray held sway over the three women in Casey's apartment, and, by default, over Casey himself.

Casey took the slaps, the taunts, the invitations to participate in "grownup games" that Tray extended on a regular basis. He took them for years, until that cold day in mid-December when Tray began beating Casey's mother again.

Nothing snapped in Casey, not exactly. He always thought of "snapping" as something that happened right before the people in the movies lost control and killed several of their friends in a frenetic rage.

Casey didn't erupt. He was calm. He was controlled. But he acted. Decisively.

Tray stood over Casey's mother, who was bleeding copiously from several wounds. He'd used his belt on her, the metal buckle slapping harshly against her body, actually ripping a chunk of skin the size of a golf ball off her back. And since his belt was off anyway, the pimp apparently decided that now was a good time to assert his authority in a few other areas as well.

He dropped his pants and pushed Casey's mother onto her back, ignoring her scream as the floor abraded her wounds. She kicked at him feebly, but Tray ignored the week blows. He lay on her with a grunt, forcing her legs apart.

That was when Casey buried the knife in Tray's back.

Casey was a small kid. A thin boy, often sick, unable to get heavy work at the docks or in a warehouse somewhere, too small to be intimidating.

Yet when he stabbed Tray, the knife went all the way in. Casey remembered being surprised at how easy it was, like the pimp was made of Spam or something. He missed the bones of Tray's back, his ribs and scapulae, sending the knife on a virtually unimpeded trip that ended in the middle of the pimp's heart.

The man died almost instantly.

Casey stuck around long enough to get his mother into bed, dress her wounds, and give her a kiss. Then he left, with nothing but his clothes, seventy-five dollars he found in Tray's pockets, and a heavy winter coat.

Seven years later he straggled into Loston. A bit of a frightening face, ringed by an ever-present halo of scruff, but his diminutive size mitigated the threatening aspect of his features. Somewhat. He got work as a night janitor at the small bar on Main Street – Mick's, it was called back then – and worked hard enough that no one asked him more than minimal questions about his past.

Just as well, because the past wasn't something Casey was prepared to discuss.

He worked at the bar for ten years, gradually assuming more and more responsibilities, and by the time Mick died at the tender age of sixty-two, Casey was more a son to the man than an employee.

No one was surprised that Mick willed Casey his bar, but what did surprise some was Casey's immediate remodeling. He got rid of the hunting trophies and stuffed heads that adorned the walls, replacing them with corn shucks and hay on the floor. He brought in a brand-new juke, and the kids started coming in.

He didn't mean disrespect to his unofficially adopted father. Quite the opposite. He wanted to remember Mick's bar with Mick in it, and each day without him there would be a tear in the fabric of that memory.

So Casey's bar was born, and though Casey got a little more of the profit, not much else changed. Not much ever changed in Loston, and he liked that. It was a nice place, and no one ever showed interest in his formative years. They minded their business, and the secrets stayed put.

Casey might have been surprised how many people in Loston felt the same way about their pasts and the secrets *they* didn't want to share.

But whether that would have surprised him or not, the sight of John Trent coming into the bar most definitely *was* a shock. Casey had known John for nearly twenty years, since the young man started frequenting the bar. John didn't drink much, but Casey's had a pool table, and John loved that game. "It's all about certainty, Case," John had told him during a moment when they were the only two in the place. "You hit the balls, and they *have* to go somewhere that makes sense. Maybe you miss, and maybe you miscalculate, but the game has to follow a logical course. It's kind of a nice feeling."

Never in all twenty years as acquaintances and friends had Casey seen John wild-eyed and dusty like he was now. His order, a shot of whisky, straight up, surprised Casey even more.

Casey poured the drink though. As he did he glanced at Coach Harding, who was playing pool in the back room, waiting for his friend. "Coach is here," he said to John as the younger man belted back the glass.

"What?" John's eyes seemed to take a long time to successfully focus on Casey. "Oh, yeah."

He put the glass down and headed to the bathroom, almost going into the ladies' room before entering the correct door.

Casey shook his head and went back to dusting the glasses, the chore he'd been doing when John came in. He wondered what it was that could have put his friend in such a state, but knew he wouldn't ask.

The past – even recent past – was usually best left alone.

***

John splashed water across his face. He noted his hands trembling, and concentrated on them for a moment, trying to stop the shivers that gripped his extremities. It didn't work, so he grabbed the sides of the sink. He took a deep breath, then let it out. Again. Another.

In a few seconds he was calm once more. He could even look at himself in the mirror and laugh about what had just happened. He decided not to tell Gabe about it, because the coach's only reaction would be to chortle and do some friendly mocking, most likely bringing up the story every time a friend or acquaintance of John was anywhere near.

"Stupid," said John. No way it could be the same man. No way.

Then why did he run from me?

The question stumped John for a moment, but he knew – *knew* – there must be some logical answer. So he pushed it back to the darker passages of his brain, surrendering it to his subconscious for further analysis.

He left the bathroom, going back to the bar. He ordered a beer this time. It was early in the day, but John relaxed his personal rules about multiple drinks for once. Besides, it was Friday. A hell of a Friday. Casey handed him the dew-dappled bottle and asked, "How ya doin'?"

"Fine, Casey," he answered. He didn't feel fine. In spite of the decision he'd just made not to say anything to Gabe, he knew he would. He had to talk to someone about what had just happened. It was his way. Annie used to call herself "John's Mind Massager" because of his need to talk about things. His mind worked better when he could bounce his thoughts off someone else.

John went through the small doorway behind the bar, entering the room that housed the pool table. Gabe was there already, shooting a solitary practice game. Two others sat in the room, old men watching Gabe play, quietly nursing drinks that would last them most of the evening. John had been introduced to both, but couldn't remember their names. He always got the impression they weren't happy with him, as though his relative youth was an automatic sin that could be neither denied nor absolved.

He nodded to them. They nodded back, reluctantly. John usually smiled when they did that, hearing a Pa Kettle chorus of voices hollering "Whippersnapper" at him in his mind, which usually made him smile. But this time he didn't smile, just went to the pool table.

As always, John's best friend didn't look up or make eye contact as he started conversation. He also had a habit of beginning his conversations with sentences that sounded as though he was already in the middle of the story, as though the listener hadn't paid attention and was guilty of missing the first half of the action.

Gabe held true to form today.

"So I'm wrestling this kid," he said, simultaneously smacking the cue ball into the two and sending it on a sharp bank that ended in dead center of the side pocket, "and I nailed him. Really got him locked up."

"Gabe," John said, "I –"

"And then you know what he did?"

"I want to ask you something, Gabe."

Gabe sent another ball to pool heaven, pausing not a moment in his speech or his playing.

"He called me a butthole. Now, that never bothered me before, but in a sudden flash of insight I realized that 'butthole' is probably the worst thing you can call someone."

Gabe sent another ball into the corner pocket and rounded the table to set up his next shot. John put a little more force in his voice as he said, "I need to ask you –"

Gabe held up a beefy hand, stifling John's reluctant query. "Think about it, John. 'Butthole.' You are a piece of void surrounded on all sides by stinking flesh. You are so low a piece of nothing that not even your butt wants to be a part of you."

Gabe grinned widely, proud of his personal epiphany. No doubt the movie rights were already sold: *I Was a Teenage Butthole.*

"Did you have a new kid in any of your classes today?"

Gabe appeared astonished by John's apparent lack of awe at the invaluable insight being lavished upon him. "Did you hear what I just said?" he asked, finally pausing his shots.

John surprised himself by slamming his beer down on the end of the pool table. Liquid splashed out of the open neck, sending a few drops onto the green velvet of the table.

"This is important, Gabe!"

Gabe jerked back, surprised at John's intensity. "Sorry. No, no new kids at all. Why?"

John released his death grip on the beer. He took a few more deep breaths, concentrating on all the reasons why he shouldn't be so upset, not doing a good job convincing himself.

"It's just that...forget it."

The two men locked eyes for a moment, and John expected Gabe to pry, to ask what happened? why did you go rocketing off like a QB whose girlfriend has said he'll get laid if he makes a touchdown? how come you almost creamed me in the parking lot? and a million other questions.

For a moment it looked like he would, too. Would ask all the questions that John couldn't answer.

Then John saw Gabe's eyes drop back to the table, as though dismissing the day from his thoughts. He put the last two balls away in a pair of straight shots, then began drawing the balls from the pockets and racking them for the next game. He handed John a cue stick, motioning for him to break. John did, after selecting a better stick. Gabe was probably his best friend in the whole world, but John knew that the coach would more than happily give his buddy a crappy stick for that little advantage in the game.

The cue ball shattered the tight triangle of resin spheres, sending them out in a nova of color. Two of the balls fell into pockets, a solid and a stripe. John surveyed the lay of the table and called stripes, then set for his next shot.

"So I have this second cousin once removed. From California," said Gabe.

John smiled, the familiar regularity of the game calming his nerves. "Congratulations. The government finally allowed your family to reproduce?"

He missed his next shot and Gabe lined up, chuckling. "Only the distant relatives. But seriously, this gal is hot. I mean, if I was from the South, I'd be all over her, and two-headed kids be damned."

"Thanks for the secret and disgusting insight into your life."

"But wait, there's more," said Gabe.

"Really?"

"Oh, yeah. See, her husband died a year ago, and she decided to move recently. Got a job teaching at a school. Guess where."

"Hmmm...."

"Here!" Gabriel was so excited at the prospect that he was no longer shooting. John didn't mind. The game was half for playing and half just an excuse to jaw for an hour. Besides, he always lost. The football coach was a surprisingly methodical and canny player.

"So she's coming on Sunday," Gabe continued, "and she doesn't know anyone but me, so I figured –"

"No. Forget it. Absolutely not."

"Come on, John. It's been two years."

"I know how long it's been."

"What, do you want to spend the rest of your weekends doing nothing but playing pool with a dried up coach whose teams are never big enough to even qualify for league play? Who hasn't ever seen one of his teams go on a road trip? Ever?"

"Sounds good to me."

"Well, I don't like it."

"This isn't about you."

"It sure as hell *is* about me. You know how long it's been since I've been able to go on a date? I'm always stuck playing with you. You're cute and all, but I'd like to go out with someone I could perhaps have sex with at the end of the date."

"You saying I'm not pretty enough to have sex with?"

Gabe stifled a grin. "Serious, John. You've gotta –"

"No. I mean it." John leaned across the table. "I will tell you when I'm ready."

"No you won't. You'll just sit there and mope and be a lonely piece of crap. And that's definitely not what Annie would have wanted for you."

John closed his eyes. He didn't want to talk about it, but he knew his friend wouldn't let up. Worse, he knew his friend was right. But over the last two years grief had become a comfort, a safe and secure place. He had lost himself in the fact that when you grieve over something, it's impossible to be hurt by anything new.

Gabriel's tone softened. He came around the table and spoke in a low tone, laying a comforting hand on John's shoulder. "Look, John, I love you, you know that? I don't want you to miss your whole life. It's too damn short." He took a deep breath. "She's a good girl, and she really does need to meet some people. And she lost her husband. You're kinda in the same boat, you know?"

John waited a moment, but the decision was already made. Gabe was right: this wasn't the way Annie would have wanted him to remember her.

"I'll show her around Sunday night. If she's interested."

Gabe let out a whoop, forgetting in his excitement that the two old-timers would frown on such an interruption of their treasured silence.

John looked at them as Gabe threw his hands in the air and did a mini war dance around the table. Sure enough, their eyebrows bunched so close around their eyes that it seemed their heads were imploding. Disdain practically oozed from them.

John seized the moment. He knew what he was about to do might get him killed, but it was worth the risk. Gabe passed by him, and as he did, John grabbed him in a massive hug. "It's all right," he yelled at the two old men, who almost fell off their chairs at what was to them no doubt verged on a sign of the Apocalypse: two men hugging. "It's all right," John reiterated. "The test turned out negative!"

He turned to Gabe then, who stared at him in complete mystification, and did the most daring and dangerous thing he'd ever done.

He kissed Coach Gabe Harding right square on the lips. Gabe stiffened, and John thought he saw one of the old-timers clutch his chest. He separated and looked at Gabe tenderly. "My friend is going to be all right. I love you, Gabe."

The old-timers hurried out, no doubt anxious to escape before they too were infected by contagious homosexuality. John didn't know what was funnier: their reaction or Gabe's. John didn't know how a man could be so completely homophobic, but Gabe had probably never even shaken his father's hand.

After a moment, Gabe came partway back from whatever place his psyche ran to during the brief contact. Looking like he was unsure whether to laugh, cry, or just go comatose, he said, "That was a crappy thing to do, John. I don't care if you *were* a Ranger way back when. Do that again and I'll kick your butt."

"Green Beret."

"Whatever."

Gabe went back to the game.

"Just one thing, Gabe. If things don't work out Sunday night...."

"Yeah?"

"What are *you* doing next weekend? You're a great kisser."

The coach framed his response with Shakespearean elocution and delivery: "Butthole."

John laughed. Gabe missed his shot, and John took a turn, somehow forgetting how odd it was that his best friend hadn't asked more questions about John's radically altered behavior earlier in the afternoon.

He didn't dwell on it, though. Not even for a moment. Not until much later, and by then, of course, it was too late, and his friend was already dead.

ATTN: DOM#67B
LOSTON, COLORADO
AD 2013
6:00 PM FRIDAY
STATUS CHANGE TO DOM#67A

Fran got in that evening. She was supposed to arrive Sunday – that was what she'd told Gabe she was doing – but she wanted to get there early, to get the feel of the area.

She looked at her new home as the cab pulled into her front yard. The house was small, but clean. A single-story place with two bedrooms, one-and-a-half baths, living room, dining room, den.

In Los Angeles it would have cost her an arm and a leg and everything in between. In Loston, she'd be able to afford it easily on her teacher's salary. Not for the first time, she wondered if the world hadn't gone a little crazy. Droves of people put themselves on two year waiting lists to pay five million dollars for a condo in California that they'd most likely lose to the bank anyway, while hardly anyone was moving to places like Loston. It just didn't make sense to her.

She shook her head as the cab pulled into her driveway. At least such cultural insanity would benefit her. The fact that no one wanted to live here made it easy and affordable for her to move into her new home.

She'd never seen the place – all her transactions had been negotiated online with a broker, with her cousin okaying the place as well – so she experienced the double thrill of seeing the house for the first time and knowing it was hers. When Nate died, he left her with a broken heart and a sizable life insurance policy that allowed her to pay for the house.

The cabby stifled a yawn. No such thing as a gregarious cabby in Colorado, she decided. She'd fallen asleep right outside the Denver airport and hadn't awakened until they passed a sign that said "Welcome to Loston" with an absurdly tiny population recorded below. And when she woke, there was no "Did you sleep all right?" or "Almost there," or even "This is cash, right?" to greet her return to wakefulness. Indeed, her cabby seemed quiet to the point of strangeness.

The cab stopped and she got out, bringing her overnight bag with her. The cabby went to the trunk and opened it, revealing a medium-sized suitcase. Fran had sent on the rest of her possessions earlier in the week, and the two bags were all that remained. The cabby bent to lift her luggage.

"I can get it," she said, yanking the case out of the trunk. She set it down and looked at the house again, enjoying the lawn, the whiteness of the walls, the small picket fence that pretended to mark the boundaries of her tiny domain. She inhaled, and smelled something...something wonderful....

"No smog," she said to herself, and giggled. You always heard about it in Los Angeles; when friends went to the mountains it was inevitably the first thing they said when they returned. But to actually *smell* it....

A sound cut her giggle off in mid-laugh. The dry crunch of tires on gravel sounded as the cab pulled out of her driveway. It was in the street in a flash, already pulling into gear and drawing away.

"Wait," she cried out, hurrying after the rapidly proceeding vehicle, "I didn't pay!"

The car continued driving. Fran ran after it for half a block, waving her arms back and forth, shouting at the top of her lungs (and marveling that in half a block there were only *two* houses!). The cab paid no heed, speeding off and rounding a corner.

Fran dropped her arms. Oh, well. She'd call the company when she got in the house. The phone should be connected.

She returned to the driveway, picked up her bags, and removed the key from her pocket. It turned smoothly in the lock, and she entered.

She didn't call the cab company, though. Instead she moved from room to room, enjoying the feel of a place that was truly hers.

She had owned her last home, too, but this was different. That had been a joint venture with Nate. This time she was on her own.

The thought made her sad for a moment, uncharacteristically so. She shook off her melancholy. "Chin up," she seemed to hear Nate say. "Keep your chin up."

So she did, raising her chin to an absurd height, stretching her neck out as she went from room to room, pretending she was a snobby Victorian heiress surveying her cottage in the country.

"It will do, Jeeves," she said to no one in particular, waving her hand in what she pretended would look like an aristocratic circle. Actually, she knew she likely looked like a nutcase with a sprained wrist, but she was having too much fun to care.

"Oh, the cab company," she said, remembering her mission. She had to call them and get the money over somehow. Credit card, most likely, as much as she hated the thought of performing such a transaction. She distrusted computers, though she knew how to use them, and the idea of someone keying in her financial numbers and billing her with no money actually changing real flesh and blood hands always bothered her.

She picked up the phone that sat in the front room, on an end table that her mother had given her when she got married to Nate.

There was no dial tone. She toggled the switch a few times, hoping to jolt the phone into responsiveness, but her effort came to naught. Gabe had promised he'd hook it up. She was early, but she thought for sure he would have done it by now. She supposed he'd forgotten.

She looked at her watch. It read four o'clock, which meant it was five p.m. here. Gabe would probably be home. She decided to walk to his house. It was only a mile or two, and she guessed there was still another good hour of sunlight. Monday she would look for a car.

She never made it to the front door.

Instead, she found herself laying in bed the next morning, feeling wonderfully well-rested. She couldn't remember getting into bed, but chalked it up to jet lag.

She had planned on spending the first few days getting to know her new town. Instead, she spent them inside her home, mostly asleep.

And as she slept, she had the strangest dream. She dreamt that the cabdriver she'd left Denver with was not the one who dropped her off in Loston. The one that had picked her up had brown hair.

And the one who took her to Loston and then left without taking her money had *black* hair. Black hair with a gray streak down the center.

Like a skunk, she thought, and then fell asleep again.

DOM#67A
LOSTON, COLORADO
AD 2013
10:00 AM SATURDAY

John walked down the aisles of the market. He stopped at a display advertising a buy one get one free special for pork and beans. He took six cans, tossing them in a cart already filled with canned food. When Annie had been alive, he'd eaten well. Not that she cooked all the time, not at all. They shared everything as equally as possible, and John cooked for her as often as she cooked for him.

But when she died, he became a bachelor in a way he'd never been the first time he bore that title: solitary, hanging out with one or two close male friends.

Eating a lot of chili.

The thought almost made him smile. Almost. But thoughts of cooking for Annie led inevitably to thoughts of feeding her in the hospital bed, spooning strained fruits and vegetables into her mouth, clearing off the dribbles, whispering to her that it was okay, and that she'd never been lovelier to him.

It wasn't even a lie. He saw her grow more beautiful every day he knew her, even at the end. Because when her physical body started to wane, her beauty changed into something that came from inside her. It shone from a pale, shrunken frame like a candle within a Chinese lamp, seeming to glow through her translucent skin. She was perfectly beautiful to him.

He walked the aisles for a few more minutes, even though he already had everything he needed in his cart. The store, like school and the time he spent at the bar, had become more than just a function or even a necessity. It was a proof he was alive. He lingered at those places, always half-dreading a return to his home because it was so full of Annie's presence, yet never able to stay away for that same reason.

As he turned the corner around the large advertising display at the end of the aisle (FRITO'S 99 CENTS!), he glanced behind him, to the front of the store.

And saw them. Kaylie and the Skunk Man. Already through the checkout process, they headed to the front door. John could see their blue Mustang parked in outside the huge windows that fronted the market.

"Hey!" he shouted, letting go of his cart and sprinting down the aisle. Kaylie looked back and spotted him. He saw her tug at the man's arm. He looked at her, then up at John, bearing down on them like a guided missile.

The man's face paled. He pushed Kaylie out the door in front of him, and John could see them run to the car. They hurled their groceries in the back – the convertible top was down – and didn't bother opening the doors to get in. They just hurled themselves over the tops of the still-shut doors.

John was at the door himself by then, running out the market and waving frantically. "Hey, I just want to talk to you!" he yelled. There was no answer beyond that of the car's speed increasing as it screeched out of the parking lot. A loaf of bread flew out of the car as it turned, a French roll that flew through the air like a soft mortar and landed in the gutter.

John hurried back inside the store. There was only one checkout lane open, and he knew the checker. He'd taught her son two years ago.

"Hey, Mary," he said. She smiled at him, continuing to help the next customer. She waved foodstuffs across the infrared scanner, a curious juxtaposition of machinery and organics.

"John, how are you? What was the yelling all about?"

"The little girl who just left –"

"With her father?"

"I guess so, I don't really know him." John moved aside for a moment to let her bag the groceries she had just scanned in. The woman buying the food – John had seen her around but didn't know her name – passed an electronic check card through the debit machine screwed in next to the cash register. "But the girl's in one of my classes at school."

"Lucky her. Chuck still talks about you all the time. Says his other teachers will suck forever in comparison. That's a direct quote."

"Thanks, Mary. He's a good kid. But about the little girl. Do you know her by any chance?"

"Nope. They're new, right?"

"Yeah. Have you heard where they might have moved in?"

"Sorry, John. No idea."

John cursed quietly. Mary handed the lady in line her receipt and the woman took her groceries. It gave John an idea. "Do you remember how they paid for their food?" He hoped it was credit card. If it was, he could take the number over to Tal Johnson, the sheriff of Loston and a good friend of his. Tal was hopelessly disconnected from social life in Loston and probably wouldn't have any idea where the new people in town were living, but he could use the credit card information to get their address, hopefully a current one in Loston.

John needed to talk to Kaylie's father. More than he'd ever needed anything before.

"How *did* they pay, paper or plastic?" said Mary to herself. She opened the top of the register, reeling through the yellow carbon copies of the receipts. "Paper. They paid cash." She eyed the long string of purchases. "Looks like they were going on a trip. Just moved in and already leaving."

DOM#67A
LOSTON, COLORADO
AD 2013
7:00 PM SATURDAY

Outside Loston, a door opened in midair near the foot of a mountain.

Malachi stepped through, entering from a place so shadowy it made the Loston evening seem noonday bright. He had changed his clothing, dressed in some Eddie Bauer jeans and jacket, Polo shirt, and Timberlands. The better to blend in with the locals.

A moment later, three others came through the door. Malachi watched them enter, surveying his small crew. Usually, when Malachi went on a mission, it was alone. However, this one was important. Crucial, in fact. If they were successful, it would mean the end. He would take no chances.

The three were garbed similarly to Malachi, with sturdy, warm clothing that was voluminous enough to hide an assortment of weaponry.

Todd was his second on this mission. His lean, muscled form stood at ease as he waited for direction. Malachi knew that the apparent relaxation was merely that: apparent. At the slightest hint of danger or necessity, Todd would spring into deadly action. He was a vicious predator, and absolutely faithful to the cause, so was an obvious choice for this important task.

Behind him stood Deirdre. Her dark skin blended with the inky blackness on the other side of the door, making her all but invisible until she stepped into Loston. She wore black leather pants and a dark brown leather jacket that made it even harder to see her in the night. It was nearing night in Loston, as well, so stepping through the door made her only marginally easier to see. Todd had argued against her wardrobe choice, telling her that it would make her stand out in a rural farm community.

Deirdre pointed out that Loston was predominantly white. A six foot tall black woman with a dangerous light in her eyes and a distinctly predatorial air would stand out no matter what she dressed in. Malachi had to admit she did look daunting.

Jenna was the last of the group. Like Todd and Malachi, she wore comfortable shoes, jeans, T-shirt, and a loose-fitting jacket that hid a number of machines that would make their quest easier. She was less experienced than the other members of the group, but what she lacked in experience she made up for in zeal. Besides, she was one of the members of the team that had discovered this place, so she deserved to be on the final mission.

Malachi looked at them one last time. They looked good. They were ready.

He nodded at Todd, who touched a button on what appeared to be his wristwatch. With a low whisper, the doorway to their time shut behind them, sealing up the naked air and leaving them alone in Loston.

"This is the most important mission we've ever been on," said Malachi. "We know she's coming sometime today or tomorrow. I want to find out where she'll stay, and make sure we're waiting for her."

"Where do we start?" asked Todd.

"Main Street."

"Anywhere in particular?" asked Jenna. Deirdre just watched, a trained black panther waiting for the kill command.

"Like always. We start at the bars."

The others nodded and Malachi turned to the glow that marked the nearby limits of Loston.

***

The game never changed. Neither did the outcome. Gabe would have felt bad for his friend, but figured that if someone *had* to lose, it might as well not be him.

He reracked the balls for the third time. Actually, John was playing pool well tonight, much better than he had yesterday after school, thought the coach. The first game had been close. The second game, John got his clock cleaned when Gabe put away five balls in one round. But John came back and won the third round, an unusual occurrence. It probably had something to do with his choice of conversation, which for some indefinable reason was making Gabe very nervous. Every time John mentioned this guy, this stranger with the gray-streaked hair, Gabe's skin started to crawl. He felt like someone was scratching his brain with long fingernails, raking furrows through his mind.

Gabe shook himself mentally, trying to shake loose of the rush of negative feelings this line of conversation was evoking in him. It was no use. The anxious – almost painful – feeling persisted, no matter what he did. Even picturing his daughter's face – serene, quiet and peaceful as she had been when he buried her – did no good. Nor did the fact that he owed John his life. For a moment, the past disappeared and all that was left in the coach was a searing, burning hatred.

He suddenly wanted to murder John.

"I swear, Gabe," the computer teacher was saying, "I've seen this guy –"

"Two other times in the past thirty years and he hasn't changed, yadda, yadda, yadda. I heard you. It's your turn to break."

John broke – badly, the ten and the fourteen hung right on the lips of the far corner pockets, but neither fell – then kept talking.

"The second time I saw him he got blown up, Gabe. Not shot, not hit on the head with a brick, not even get his head cut off. *Blown up.*"

Gabe had hoped that the game would distract John, but his friend was still doggedly pursuing the line of conversation he had begun some forty minutes before. Gabe had tried to turn him away from the topic several times, but to no avail. The coach lined up his next shot, but couldn't focus on the cue ball. His vision swam before him, momentarily clouding before returning to normal. He realized he was holding so tight to the cue stick that his fingers had gone numb.

He couldn't imagine why he was so nervous. So uncomfortable and angry.

So afraid.

"So how could I have seen that?" continued John.

"It's your imagination, bro. Listen, Franny's coming in tomorrow and I don't want her thinking you're a lunatic. Forget about this stuff."

Gabe lined up to put away the fourteen. It was an easy shot, one he should have been able to make blindfolded, shooting with his feet, and using a warped stick.

He missed.

John took the next shot, and Gabe thought perhaps his friend would let it go. He desperately wanted him to. Every time John mentioned this guy, this "Skunk Man" as he called him, Gabe wanted to go a little crazy. That scared him. In spite of his reputation as a loud, murderous coach, Gabe was about as pacifistic as anyone he knew. Sure, he spent some time hunting, but everyone in the town did. Other than that, the only time he had ever felt serious anger or rage was the morning Ruth died. And even that dwindled and disappeared when he buried her.

But the feelings that rose with every mention of the Skunk Man were anything but peace-loving. Gabe fought down urges of violence; of strange *other*ness that tried to persuade him to rip, to tear, to rend.

To kill John.

That was crazy.

Why would I want to kill John? he thought. I owe him everything.

Seven years before, a van had come into Loston. That in itself was almost enough to make front-page news on The Loston Rag, the two page newspaper that served basically as a place for people to sell used hunting gear and fishing tackle, with local interest stories squashed in the spaces between the ads. Anyone coming into the town got a nod of recognition, because visitors were scarce here.

The van quickly drew more attention than most passers-by, however. Bearing California plates, it later turned out that the men inside were on the run from the law. They were also on drugs, which explained their irrational actions to some extent, though no one would ever know exactly why they did what they did.

Whatever their reasons, they had come into town, stopped at the grocery store where Gabe had been doing his weekly shopping, and almost casually kidnapped his daughter, Ruth.

He remembered seeing the men walk in, spot her, and pick up the four-year-old girl from where she was standing in front of the gumball machines. She was trying to turn the dial on one of them, using a quarter Gabe had given her to get one of the large, bouncy balls she liked to play with. Gabe was not married, Ruth being a product of a fling he had had while in college in Denver, and he was glad of that fact. Because he knew that if he had been married, his wife would have been telling him not to spoil the little girl.

But he had to spoil her. Ruth was his light, the thing that brought meaning to his life and gave him joy. She was like a flask of living brightness, illuminating all around her with the heady luminescence of pure joy. How could Gabe hope to deny her what she wanted, when she gave so much in return?

Ruth turned the dial and opened the hatch, squealing in delight as the machinery clinked and a ball dropped into her tiny fingers.

That was when one of the men grabbed her. The ball fell from Ruth's little hand as she was roughly jerked away from her treasure, which bounced slowly away in ever-shrinking arcs. Gabe couldn't believe what he was seeing for a moment; was rooted to the market floor as firmly as though his shoes had been part of the linoleum. What could possibly be going on? he thought, the complete wrongness of the moment short-circuiting his ability to think coherently.

The three men rushed out of the store, passing Ruth back and forth between them like a screaming football. That was when Gabe finally moved, dropping his armful of groceries and hurrying out after them. They made it to the van, piled in, and screamed out of the market's small parking lot, fishtailing dangerously over the icy winter street.

Gabe was screaming insanely, but knew he couldn't help his daughter. They had walked to the market, and he had no way to follow after the van. Still screaming, he ran after them, fruitless though such a pursuit might be. It was his baby, his Ruth, and only death could keep him from following her.

That was when John appeared. He pulled his car up beside the coach, screamed "Get in!" and then stomped the accelerator before Gabe was completely inside the car.

Their pursuit took them high into the mountains. Neither man spoke, single-mindedly following the van through winding, frozen roads that quickly became little more than trails. At last, the inevitable occurred: the van hit a patch of ice and rocketed off the road, smashing sideways into a tree. The windows shattered with the impact, and Gabe feared the worst as he and John stopped and ran from the car.

The door to the van opened when they were only a few yards away, and out popped two of the three men that had been in the vehicle. One of them had a gun, which he fired, three sharp reports cleaving the mountain air as cleanly as a razor.

Gabe felt himself lifted off the ground, and knew he had been shot. He also heard a popping noise and knew that a round had punctured one of John's tires. He hit the icy ground hard, cold seeping instantly into his bones. He tried to stand, but found that the bullet had taken him in the thigh, breaking his leg and leaving him helpless to do more than watch and fight to keep from passing out.

John dove for cover as the gunfire opened up. He rolled, then came up suddenly in a bright flurry of snow that momentarily blinded the two druggies. Gabe couldn't even follow the other man's movements. John was like a man possessed, feinting and dodging with manic speed and precision as the two men – correctly seeing him as the only remaining threat – converged on him.

Gabe knew John only by reputation at the time. So he knew that he was generally regarded as a good guy, and knew that he had been a soldier. But that didn't prepare him for what he saw. John *destroyed* the two addicts with a skill and artistry that was frightening. He twisted as the one with a gun snapped off a pair of quick shots. One of them grazed his leg, but John didn't even slow down, gliding past the druggie's arm and breaking it, then whipping his arm up in the same movement, smashing the guy's nose through his skull and killing him instantly.

At the same time, John pulled the criminal's gun out of his now nerveless fingers. Turning fluidly to the other man, who was rushing at him with a snow-frosted tree branch, John calmly put the final bullet in the revolver's cylinder between the man's eyes.

Then Gabe saw a burst of movement as the final addict burst out of the van. He jumped out, then fled into the woods. Gabe saw him holding something: Ruth. She was a rag doll, loose as a half-filled sack of autumn leaves.

John turned to look at Gabe. Gabe knew he was bleeding badly; that he might very well be dead within minutes. Still, he didn't hesitate.

"Save her," he said. Or tried to. All that made it past his lips was a susurrant whisper. John dashed off into the trees, crashing through the snow banks and leaving a bloody trail behind him.

Gabe managed to pull off his belt and bind it around his leg as a makeshift tourniquet. Then he passed out, lying in the snow beside two dead men.

When he awoke, it was two days later. He was in a hospital bed. Friends and family were hesitant to speak of what had happened, so only gradually did he manage to wring the details out of them.

John had followed the man holding Ruth to the summit of one of the mountains, finally ending his flight at a sheer drop-off of two thousand feet. The druggie had dropped the girl in the snow a few feet away, trying to lighten his burden to more easily escape from John, who followed him like a coyote on the trail of a sickly gazelle.

It took more work and prying to get out what happened next. But Gabe was as single-minded as John had been, and soon was in possession of the remainder of the facts.

Ruth was dead, her neck apparently snapped when the van hit the tree. John saw this in an instant, and lay her tenderly on her back. He crossed her small hands over her breast.

And then he literally took the addict apart. The sheriff found the druggie's remains at the summit, where every one of his bones had been snapped, rent, or literally twisted to shreds. His jaw was the only thing unbroken, though it was racked open in a never-ending scream of pain.

John then returned to Gabe, holding Ruth's body in his arms. Neither the van nor the car would ever run again – one bullet had taken out the tire of John's car, another had sheared through the fuel lines and obliterated the engine block – so John *carried* both Gabe and Ruth down the mountain. He was met at the bottom by the sheriff and his deputies, who were only barely mobilizing to follow the criminals. After passing Gabe to them and seeing that someone would take care of both him and his daughter's body, John at last fainted, loss of blood from his leg wound finally claiming his consciousness.

The doctor who informed Gabe of this last bit spoke in a hushed voice that was part regret, part awe. John's lower leg had been broken by the bullet. Not shattered, but broken badly enough that he should not have been able to walk at all, let alone follow an able-bodied man up a steep mountain face, kill him, and then return down the mountain carrying not one but two other people.

Gabe took all this in quietly. His friends and family were clearly afraid he was going to react with hysterics, screaming at life's unfairness and shaking his fist at the sky. He did not, however. Ruth was gone, but he would not sully her beautiful memory by becoming hateful. All he felt was a deep, abiding sorrow. And an equally deep, abiding love for this comparative stranger who had risked his all to come to Ruth's aid.

Ruth was never very far from his thoughts. He cherished her memory, and every time he saw John it was all he could do not to embrace him and thank him for saving his life, and for trying to save his daughter's. He had known from the time he heard what happened that he would do anything for John. He would risk any loss, and would sacrifice anything and everything at John's merest request.

And that was why it was so unnerving that as John spoke, Gabe felt nothing but rage. Every clack of the balls on the pool table served only to heighten his anger, and every word John spoke was like a twisting knife, inflicting a psychic pain that Gabe found himself hard-pressed to hide.

The effort of quelling his feelings was making him shaky with tension and adrenaline. Had he not been so focused on controlling himself, Gabe would have wondered if he was going crazy. As it was, though, every tiny shard of energy he had was bent on maintaining control and an appearance of normality.

John seemed oblivious to his friend's internal struggle, which was good. Gabe didn't know *why* John shouldn't see him struggling, he only knew he shouldn't.

A thought came to his mind: *Keep it secret.*

And, on the heels of that, another thought: Keep *what* secret?

The question was too much for Gabe, and he forced it out of his mind. John took his shot, and for a moment it seemed as if everything would be all right. John put away the fourteen and then the ten, then missed an easy straight shot on the fifteen ball. Gabe dropped the four, then shanked his next, a two-ball combo off the cushion.

John lined up. "I can't forget about him, Gabe," he whispered.

And with those words, the rage that had hammered behind Gabe's eyes like a tsunami wave overpowered him. The anger flowed over his balustrade of mental defenses, blinding him and changing the face of his thoughts wherever it coursed. The wash of vicious spite cleaned his mental slate, stripping away the civilized habits and mores and exposing what lay below it. He felt himself – the person he thought of as himself – sinking away, disappearing as in a fog. Ruth's face swam momentarily before his eyes, then it too sank into the mist.

And then he was gone. Gabe was gone.

Replaced.

***

John missed the shot, and when he straightened he at last noticed the anguish on Gabe's face. It disappeared almost instantly, though, replaced by a strange blankness that was even more frightening. It was not the slack-jawed vacuousness of a mental patient. Rather, it was an utterly empty expression that reminded John of some kind of a machine, like a drill press or a heavy water sledge they used in the mines: quiet until it turned on, and then capable of incredible, frightening force.

Gabe spoke, and John recognized his friend's voice, but at the same time there was something different about it, as though someone had taken Gabe's timbre and tone and stripped it of all his vocal idiosyncrasies: a synthesized imitation of the real thing.

"Forget it, John," said Gabe. His eyes stared into John's, boring searing holes into John's brain. John stared back for a moment, then realized where he'd seen the look in his friend's eyes before. Gabe didn't look like a machine...he looked like a killer. It was the look of a sniper. Or one of the black ops assassins. Someone who was preparing to end another's existence. Someone who had relinquished his hold on humanity, if only for a few seconds.

John dropped his eyes to the pool table, thinking. It seemed to him best to pretend he hadn't seen the look on Gabe's face. That frightening look.

He took his shot, his mind moving quickly. Almost in spite of himself, his old training asserted itself and John's grip on the cue stick subtly changed. He was prepared to swing it like a club, or to use it to block an attack. He looked back at Gabe.

Gabe still looked the same: looked like Gabe, but *not*.

What's happening? thought John.

He didn't say that, though. What he said was, "You're probably right. It's my imagination." And he tried to put as much sincerity into those two sentences as he had put into any words he'd ever spoken.

It seemed to work. Gabe's face relaxed. For a moment his friend looked puzzled, as though stepping into a familiar room whose furniture has all been moved to new positions. Then he grinned, and John's heart slowed down a beat or two, coming somewhat closer to normal.

Gabe took his shot.

"When you going to see her?"

"Who?"

Gabe looked at him like he had just spoken utter nonsense. John relaxed slightly as he recognized his friend once more. Even so, he did not relinquish his grip on the stick.

"Franny, dim-bulb," said the coach.

"She gets in tomorrow?" John asked. Gabe nodded. "I'll swing by her place tomorrow night, then. Show her the sights of Loston."

Gabriel laughed, his voice normal, seeming his usual self once again, as though what had just happened were nothing more than a bad dream on John's part. A waking dream.

"Show her the sights of Loston, huh? That's the first fifteen minutes of the date," said the coach. "What'll you do after that?"

Gabe won the game during his next turn, and John left the bar. Gabe wanted to play a few more, but John begged off, saying he wanted to be rested for tomorrow evening. The reality was he wanted to get away from his friend who was suddenly acting so strange. He needed to think.

He put his pool cue up in the rack, standing it next to the others, all lined up like steadfast wooden and aluminum soldiers,

111

and stepped into the bar area. He waved goodnight to Casey, who nodded but didn't stop polishing his bar.

John went to the front door, waving to a few people he knew in the bar, and then opened it to leave.

He almost bumped into the people entering: two men, two women. One man and one woman were laughing, apparently having a good night. The other two – a black woman and a stern older man – didn't laugh. John had to suppress a shudder as he stepped past them. The older man's eyes quickly roved up and down, taking in John's appearance in an instant, before the party moved into the bar. The look unnerved him, and yet he seemed to have seen that look before.

He shrugged internally and stepped out of the bar. When he got in his Suburban, he realized what the look had meant.

He was casing me, thought John. He had seen that look, again in special forces training. How to rapidly assess a potential threat, noting bulges in clothing, physical prowess, and a host of other factors that could let a skilled observer know in a matter of seconds what dangers another person represented.

Why would he look like that?

Almost, he went back into the bar. To introduce himself, perhaps, and maybe get a bit of information from the man.

Almost. But instead he put his car into gear, and drove away.

DOM#67A
LOSTON, COLORADO
AD 2013
2:00 AM SUNDAY MORNING

Casey wanted to close up; wanted to go home and crawl into bed for five hours before coming back to get the bar ready for the Sunday lunch rush. The bar wasn't a restaurant or even a grill, but Casey noticed a lot of people that came in to ask if he had anything to eat stayed for a drink or two, so he had started cooking burgers and sandwiches for some of his customers. It made a bit more work, and a slightly higher amount of paperwork to be filled out each year for the state health commission, but it more than paid for itself in extra profits. So now he had to get the bar opened earlier than he used to, and Sunday was a good business day on top of that. He wanted to rest up for it.

Unfortunately, one small group of people remained. They had come in early, and stayed the entire evening, though they'd only purchased one round of drinks each, and as far as Casey could see, those drinks were still full. He had thought more than once over the evening that they might be waiting for him to be alone – as he was now – to rob him.

He dismissed the thought, though. He'd been robbed twice, and both times it had been people with a certain frightened, jittery look. These people didn't have that look. They sat utterly calm, like a deep pool of water on a still summer day.

At the same time, though, it occurred to Casey that even calm waters had been known to hide sharks.

Time to close up, he decided. He'd get rid of his guests – nicely, of course, but firmly – and go home for forty winks. Maybe for forty thousand. He told himself again that he wasn't worried, but he put his hand below the bar, where a shotgun – a sawed-off double barrelful of lead – hung on a spring-pivot. In a split-second he could aim and shoot it right through the bar, if necessary.

Anything he pointed at, he would hit. And anything he hit would go down and stay down.

Tal Johnson, Loston's sheriff, had given Casey the shotgun after the second robbery attempt. He'd handed it over, whispering, "I never saw this," when Casey got out of the hospital, where he had recuperated from a shot that glanced across his clavicle, missing his neck and head by inches.

Casey had laughed at the melodrama at the time, enjoying the sheriff's obvious pleasure at Loston's only chance to engage in vigilante cloak and dagger stuff. But now he was glad to have the gun.

"Folks," he said, making sure his voice was chipper, cheery, the last kind of voice in the world you'd want to hear angry. "We're closing up, I'm afraid."

Surprisingly, the answer to his statement came from the oldest of the group, a late middle-aged man who'd done nothing but case the bar out the whole time they'd been there. It seemed like he was looking for something. Or someone. Casey hoped it wasn't him, as the man wore a scowl more dark and impenetrable than the darkest night in the mountains.

That was why it was a bit of a shock when the man cracked a wide smile and said, "Oh, it's late. Terribly sorry, friend. We've been...traveling. It felt good just to sit down a while, and I guess we lost track of the time in your wonderful place here."

Casey smiled. His hand remained on the gun, but he was as susceptible to flattery as any proud parent. "Thanks for the compliment. She's a great place."

"Indeed," said the man. He stood, and the others followed suit. He walked to the bar and his hand went to an inner pocket.

Casey tensed, but the man withdrew a billfold, nothing more.

"How much do we owe you?"

"Four drinks, twelve dollars."

The man held out a twenty. "Here you go. If you can tell us of a good motel around here, you can keep the change."

Casey shook his head. "Sorry, I'll have to give you eight back. Loston doesn't get many tourists. Hardly any new move-ins, either. The nearest motel's about three hours west of here."

"Oh." The man's expression fell and Casey felt sorry for him. Driving in the middle of the night wasn't any fun after a long day of traveling.

"Sorry, friend," said Casey. He took the twenty and made change one-handed, a move he'd practiced many times. He knew it looked smooth and that the four watching would be unaware he kept his right hand below the bar. Unless they were up to no good, in which case the fear that he had something down there might keep them in line.

He handed the man his change. The man took it, laying the five down on the bar in front of Casey. "Well, thanks anyway." He pocketed the remaining three and then pulled out a gun.

Casey would have shot him, would have punched a hole the size of a serving tray right through the man, except the guy moved so smoothly. He didn't yank his gun out of a holster, trembling, as any other gunman might have done. He *drew* it out, not like a quick-draw, but like he was languidly drawing up water from a fresh artesian well. So Casey didn't react nervously, either, automatically pulling the trigger and blowing the guy straight to hell in two or more pieces. The guy *flowed*, and Casey was stuck somewhere between awe and surprise during the half-second he could have done something. Then the moment was gone and the man who stared at him from behind a gun was in charge, and Casey knew it.

"I know you have a gun under there," said the man. "If you so much as twitch I'll pull this trigger and your brain will be splattered into pieces too small for you to ever come back."

Casey knew then that the guy was insane. His three friends had pulled weapons during the short diatribe, too, all three taking them out with that same easy, almost casual style.

Casey was outgunned, outnumbered, out of luck. He was also supremely glad he had not tried to shoot earlier. From the look of these three, he had little doubt that such a move would have ended in his death. These people were dangerous, and his only hope lay in cooperating and praying that whatever they wanted took them away quickly.

"I'm taking my hand off the trigger," he said. His voice remained calm, well-modulated. Keep them happy, he thought. Pretend nothing is wrong, and live to see tomorrow.

"Slowly!" barked the other guy, a younger, good-looking fellow.

Casey moved slowly. "Thought you might be looking for something," he said as he withdrew his hand, centimeter by centimeter, from below the bar.

"Somebody," said the blonde girl.

"Looks like you found him," said Casey, trying to sound calm, as though this sort of thing happened every day. Stay cool, stay calm, and stay alive, he thought.

The older man laughed. The sound pierced Casey's ears like needles wrapped in barbed wire. "Not yet, my friend," said the man through his laughter. "We haven't found whom we seek." He leaned in, then, and Casey stared into twin pits of Hell masquerading as human eyes. "Not yet. But we will.

"With God's help and yours, we will."

DOM#67A
LOSTON, COLORADO
AD 2013
7:00 PM SUNDAY
** CONTACT – SERIES SEVEN/A-TYPE **

When the door opened, John's breath caught in his throat.

He remembered once at a Mexican restaurant he'd gotten a bit overzealous with the chips and salsa, swallowing a large piece of tortilla that went down sideways. It jammed in his throat, partially blocking his trachea and making it hard to breathe. Annie whacked him on the back a few times, then tried the Heimlich. Neither worked. He wasn't in any real danger of asphyxiation, because he could breathe around the chip, but the pain was excruciating, and breathing definitely *was* a chore. They'd gone to one of the two doctors who practiced in Loston, making an emergency house call, but the chip had popped back up as they pulled into his driveway.

John hadn't been eating chips – hadn't been *near* Mexican food since Annie died – but he had similar respiratory problems when he saw Fran as he had that night in Los Toros.

He dropped the bouquet he was holding, a small mass of tousled mountain flowers that seemed all the more beautiful for their chaotic arrangement. He knelt to gather them up again, and could not take his eyes off her, though it meant he had to crane his neck upward to see her.

She wore a white shirt and blue jeans, simple clothing that nonetheless draped her like it was tailored. She was slim, but not overly so. She had the look, not of a bulimic heroin addict, which John saw so many of the girls in his classes struggling to achieve, but rather the appearance of a truly healthy person. One who glows from without with physical well-being and from within with spiritual peace.

Annie had always looked like that.

The only ornamentation she had was a gold bracelet that hung loosely from her wrist. Completely unnecessary, in John's opinion, for no mere gold could match the glow of her eyes.

"Are you trying to hypnotize me?" she asked after a moment, and John's face went red as he realized how openly he had been staring.

"No," he said. "No, I...uh...." His brain completed the perfect moment by deciding now would be a good time to step out to lunch.

"It's John, right?"

Again, John's jaw pumped up and down for a moment before anything resembling speech emerged. "Yeah."

She smiled, a laughing, playful grin that invited instead of mocking. "Come on in."

She twisted sideways, but didn't move out of the doorframe, effectively forcing John to get close to her as he entered. He sensed that it wasn't a calculated move, designed to either seduce him or put him off, but was rather the action of a generous person whose personal space is completely inclusive of everyone around.

He noted an economy in her movements, too, a like a professional dancer, someone so in tune with her body that personal awareness became instinct. Her feet were placed just so, her body lithe and slightly leaning in the direction she would move, each placement perfect and yet totally unrehearsed.

Again, though she looked nothing like her, John was struck by Fran's resemblance to his Annie.

He moved past her, trying not to look too awkward as he passed close by her and then entered her house. Boxes sat everywhere in the small living room, most of them open but unpacked. The place was furnished, though, filled with comfortable chairs and soft lighting.

And books. *They* were unpacked, lining the walls, some on partially constructed shelves, some just lined up on the floor like silent guardians of literacy. John could not recall ever seeing so many volumes in one room before, unless it was in a library. He loved to read, himself, but his own accumulation of literature was dwarfed by Fran's collection.

Fran noticed his gaze. "Sorry about the mess. I actually got here two days ago, but I haven't done much. Just slept." She swept her hair back, a nervous move that conveyed her embarrassment at this fact. "Not really like me."

She seemed mortified by the apparent laziness such a fact conveyed, John noted. Good woman, he thought. She's a hard worker, and wants it to show.

Then he thought, That's the kind of woman I'd like to marry.

The thought bounced around in his cortex for a long second before he realized its significance. Whoa, cowboy, he thought. Let's get through the date before planning the wedding.

Fran changed the subject, saying, "If you can wait just a second, I've got to go change."

"You look fine to me." The words blurted out of him before he had time to think about their appropriateness. He blushed. This wasn't like him.

Fran smiled, looking sincerely grateful. "Thanks. But I would like to look a bit better for my favorite cousin's favorite friend who's taking time out of a busy schedule to be my new favorite tour guide."

John didn't know what to say to that, really, his brain having decided not only to go to lunch but also to stop for a movie and perhaps spend the night in a nice hotel somewhere. Fran saved him from revealing his sudden lack of brain function, though, by motioning to the flowers.

"Did you pick those yourself?"

"Yeah," said John. He was down to monosyllabic responses, he noted. Articulation and anything resembling a vocabulary were apparently at the movies with his brain. "They're for you."

"Thank you, Johnny." John jumped a bit at that. She noticed. "Are you all right?"

He refrained from saying the first word to pop into his head, which was "Yeah," nodding instead. "I just...someone else used to call me that."

"Sorry. I'll call you John."

"No, it's okay. You can call me Johnny."

He smiled at her. She smiled back, then took the flowers and put them in a vase that had been on the floor, stuffed with bunches of newspapers. Then she disappeared down the hall, stepping into one of the rooms.

John wondered if she was in her bedroom.

He wondered if he'd ever see it.

Hold on, tiger, he thought. Slow and easy.

Even as he gave himself that directive, however, he knew he was assigning himself an impossible task.

Fran stepped back out less than two minutes later. She had changed, keeping the jeans and the gold bracelet but adding a nicer pair of shoes and putting on a red blouse that heightened the natural blush of her cheeks. She was beautiful. John's breath caught in his throat again.

"Ready to go?" she asked.

He nodded, trying to remember how to make words come out of his mouth. "Nice bracelet," he said, which definitely ranked high among All-Time Dumbest Non-Sequiturs.

Her reaction was unexpected. For a moment, the glow in her eyes darkened as she fingered the gold links of the jewelry. "Thanks," she said. "It was a gift from my husband. I...I always wear it."

John was silent for a moment, unsure how to react. The specters of two dead lovers seemed to hang between them during a long period of silence. Then he pushed forward, clearing his throat and saying, "Anything you want to see first?"

Fran nodded and brightened almost immediately. "Take me to where you picked the flowers."

DOM#67A
LOSTON, COLORADO
AD 2013
7:10 PM SUNDAY

It was dark in Casey's basement.

He knew that, had always known that, but never had it so fully registered on him. The darkness hummed around him. It palpitated with its own deep, thrumming power, washing over him like dark waves that stood permanently at high tide. And yet the darkness that surrounded him was nothing compared to the darkness that he feared was coming.

He looked around. Could see nothing. His eyes were useless.

He could hear, though, and what he heard frightened him.

The man. The oldest of the four strangers who had taken him captive. In the few moments that they took binding his arms, Casey could tell that he was their leader. Malachi, one of the girls had called him. He was in charge. He was the most to be feared.

"The dark scares you, doesn't it?" said Malachi.

Casey wanted to answer, wanted to say, "Yes, sir, it does, please let me go, please," but the gag that stretched tightly across his cheeks and through his mouth prevented anything more than a low moan.

"Oh, I'm sorry." Casey felt the cool swish of air that accompanied Malachi's movements as he glided toward him. Or perhaps it was one of the other three, who were in the dark room as well. Though they hadn't moved since they'd brought him down here, below the bar, and tied him to a chair an instant before turning off the lights.

They sat there, silent, Casey gagged and bound tightly, slowly feeling his hands and feet go numb, remembering horror stories of POW's in World War I who lost their feet when their captors tied them too tightly and they rotted on their legs. He wondered how long that would take to happen, how long before his hands died and he lost his ability to serve at the bar. He wondered, and wondering turned to imagination, and imagination turned to fear.

Fear was what they wanted. He knew that; why else would they be acting like this? But knowing did not help him overcome the thick dread that froze his blood and made icy sweat ooze from his forehead.

A hand touched Casey's neck and he jumped, jerking violently away from the hand, almost knocking over the chair. Malachi caught it before it toppled, though, and whispered, "Shh, peace, my son. I'm just taking off the gag. You won't scream, now, will you?"

Casey shook his head back and forth. Screaming would be useless, anyway. They were in the bottom of a deep cellar, lined with stone and concrete and dirt to insulate the few expensive wines he kept for special occasions. Such a thick layer of dense matter would keep anyone outside the cellar from hearing him. He could drop a grenade on the floor and the only sound to penetrate above would be a slight tapping. No, he wouldn't scream.

"Good." The gag loosened, and Casey sucked in a great, gasping draught of air that tasted better to him than the finest Guinness.

"Now, my friend. Casey, is it?"

"Y-yes, sir."

"Sir. Good. Excellent respect, my friend. Keep that respect, and you will live through the night." Malachi paused a moment. "You are well connected, yes?"

"What?"

"You know the people in the town, correct?"

Casey was struck by the strange cadences of the man's tone and word choices. It sounded as though this Malachi was speaking English as one would a second language, translating rapidly from some unknown set of linguistics. Yet he spoke without accent, and obviously had no trouble following Casey's words earlier in the evening. Still, the wording of Malachi's question – "You know the people in the town, correct?" – struck fear into Casey.

"I suppose," he answered.

"Of course you do." Casey sensed rather than saw the man's predatorial smile growing larger, like the jaws of a Venus flytrap about to spring shut on a helpless fly. "Of course you do. I would like to know something, if I may."

Casey waited. He hadn't been asked a direct question, and he wasn't about to volunteer anything.

"Is anyone moving in to Loston?"

"What?" The question took him by surprise. It was the last thing he expected. Of course, he had no idea what these crazies wanted, so he guessed that *any* conversation he held with them would be one long succession of surprises. And none of them happy ones.

"Are the inhabitants here expecting any new people? Move-ins? Families?"

Casey sat silently for a moment, thinking. Fact was, he knew about as much about the town as anyone. A bar in a small country town was more than just a place to drink, it was a place to come together. It was a place where just about everyone in the town who was over twenty-one and still ambulatory would show up at least twice a month, and since Casey kept his ears open while he worked, he heard about most of what happened in the town.

So he knew for certain that there were two move-ins this week: a Devorough family that moved in Thursday night, and Coach Harding's cousin from Los Angeles, who was supposed to be arriving tonight. But he didn't answer right away, because he wanted to be absolutely sure he gave them a correct answer. He sensed that his life depended on it.

The pause, however, proved to be too much for one of the women. Casey had no doubt that the Malachi could wait until time ran out and God died of old age to get what he wanted, but one of the women – the blonde girl, he guessed – spat out the words, "Where's the girl?"

Casey heard Malachi grunt and turn. A light turned on, blinding him, but he made out enough through his tear-streaked vision to see Malachi slap the woman. It was a hard backhand that made almost no noise but would surely leave a sharp ridge of bruises along her jaw.

Casey only saw it peripherally, though, because as soon as the woman spoke those three words, something happened. It was like his tongue locked up inside his mouth. It wasn't that he resolved not to speak; rather, he suddenly felt he couldn't talk even if he wanted to. Nor was it merely imagination. He felt *something* change in him, and perceived an actual presence, a real though unseen power that froze his jaw and prevented him from uttering so much as a sound.

That was only part of him, however. Another part, a part that had somehow been subjugated in that moment, was screaming. "Yes, yes, I know, I know it all, and I'll tell you, too, if you'll just let me alone!" it yelled.

But the sound didn't come out.

Malachi turned back to Casey, the rage that had momentarily flashed across his face disappearing. The sharks were hiding under the calm surface again, but Casey knew they were still there, circling. Waiting.

"Now, who is new to your fair city?"

Casey opened his mouth, but no sound came out.

Malachi's jaw tightened. He turned back to the blonde woman and slapped her again. Harder, on the other side. She cried and fell, and he kicked her in the side. "You stupid *bit*," he said. "You shouldn't have mentioned the girl directly. Now he's locked and we have to break him."

Casey heard the word *break* and the silent screams that couldn't make it to his lips increased in volume, resounding in his head like thunder over a black sea.

The man turned back to Casey, and this time he held a small metallic box. He clipped it to Casey's wrist, then looked in Casey's eyes. Casey recoiled at the hatred and rage that glinted from the man's bright irises. "It's for my salvation," said the man, and pressed a switch.

Agony, liquid fire, ran up Casey's arm. It stabbed inward and upward, penetrating the bones of his arm, shearing inward to his trunk and legs, sparking through his spine. A million firecrackers ignited behind his eyes and burned his skull from the inside out. He felt his eyes melting in their sockets, and then drip in white-hot rivulets into his skull, searing his brain.

But while it happened, no sound emerged from his lips. He didn't scream. Couldn't, in fact. Whatever had kept him from talking apparently prevented *any* noise whatsoever.

Malachi pressed the switch again. The fire dissipated, leaving Casey gasping and sweating. He was surprised that he could see, that his eyes had not in fact melted. He also noticed that his body seemed to have suffered no external ill effects at all.

Which didn't make the agony he had just experienced any less real. It just made it more terrifying as Casey realized that whoever these people were, they had ways of causing pain that he had never heard of.

Malachi leaned close, then closer, eye to eye with Casey. "You can't talk at all now, though I'm sure you want to."

His hand dropped to the switch again, and Casey managed a whimper. His torturer smiled at the sound. "Good. As soon as you can scream, you'll be able to tell us what we need to know. And you will scream. Oh, yes, you will scream."

He hit the button again. Casey writhed in his chair, muscles cording up in arms made strong by years of pushing beer barrels under taps, of throwing out people who wanted to start fights. But his bonds held, and he still made no sound.

The man watched. And waited.

"You will tell us what we want to know," he said.

And Casey knew he would, eventually.

But first, he would scream.

DOM#67A
LOSTON, COLORADO
AD 2013
8:00 PM SUNDAY

Fran looked around and felt her jaw drop in amazement.

Though she was a self-admitted city girl, she thought she'd be prepared for the raw, uncut grace of the mountainous land Gabe had described to her over the last few months. But as John's Suburban wound up the side of the mountain just outside of Loston, her breath left her in gradual gasps of awe and delight. Part of her breathlessness was probably a product of Colorado's higher altitude, but much of it was simply the crisp beauty of the woodland terrain. Sheer rock cliffs jutted up from the ground like granite skyscrapers, more lovely than the clumsy steel and glass buildings that cluttered the Los Angeles skyline. Wild flowers and bushes were everywhere, even in the road, defying all odds to spring forth in the middle of a highway and standing defiantly forth to meet rushing cars that must repeatedly *just* miss them.

The land stole her gaze.

The air stole her breath.

And the man beside her had already stolen her heart.

When he first showed up at the door, she had been prepared for a "local yokel": some furry mountain man whose parents had most likely been close relatives. Her cousin was a wonderful guy, but she had vivid memories of him as a youngster. At the time, his greatest source of amusement when visiting her family in Los Angeles had been to pin her to the ground and perform what he grossly called the "spit suck": he would drool a long trail of saliva out of his mouth toward her face, waiting as long as possible before trying to suck it back in his mouth. And if it broke and sent a thick ooze of spittle raining down on her before he could suck it in, so much the better.

She had long since forgiven her cousin for such activities, but also knew that his level of maturity often hovered right around that of the adolescents he coached at the high school. It would be just like him, she thought, to set her up with someone who shared his sense of humor, in which case Fran had to be prepared to protect her bra from being snapped all night.

She knew who John was in general terms, of course; knew what he had done for her cousin in trying to save his daughter, Ruth. Still, just because he was a noble and courageous soul didn't necessarily preclude him from also being some kind of weird hillbilly whose idea of fun was getting drunk at the Piggly Wiggly before going out for a rousing night of cow-tipping.

But when John showed up, she had to admit she might have misjudged her cousin's taste.

No mountain man, he was a quiet, soft-spoken gentleman who had brought her flowers. *Flowers.* It had been years since a man had brought her flowers, and then it had been roses, expensive but easily purchased. These he had picked himself...and from the looks of it he'd driven quite a ways to do so.

His hair was brown, and looked as though it was perpetually tousled, always on the brink of being combed, but never quite there. The effect was not one of uncomeliness, however, but more of boyish play. His eyes, also brown, conveyed the opposite impression: a deep maturity tinged with knowing melancholy. They were deep limpid pools of experience that only those who have known passion – love, sorrow, hate, or something in between – can possess. She wanted to ask him from the first moment what had happened to him that he should have such profundity in his gaze.

He reminded her, somehow, of Nathan.

But, at the same time, John was nothing like her husband had been.

The sport utility vehicle jolted. She looked over at John, a bit alarmed at the sudden jump. He was already looking at her, a sheepish grin on his face. "Rock," he said. "Sorry."

"It's the mountains," she replied. "Don't apologize for rocks."

He shrugged, apparently embarrassed in spite of her words, then turned back (with difficulty? she wondered) to watching the road before them.

Ten minutes later they were at the end of the road. Literally. The dirt track turned around a sheer wall of rock and ended abruptly with only a sheer drop-off in front of them.

Fran looked out her window. It was dark outside, the deep dark of the country, but she could make out several hulking shapes, machinery of some kind. Beyond that, she could discern no details.

John got out, and Fran leaned over to open her door, but before she had a chance, it was already open. He held the door for her; held out a hand to help her exit the Suburban. And as before, when he had opened her door, she didn't get the sense he was doing it because he thought she was dainty and unable to open the door for herself, though. It was respect.

She looked around again. The nearby shapes were machinery, all right, though she had no idea what their use could be.

"What is this place?" she asked.

"Resurrection."

"What?"

"It's a mine."

John pointed over her shoulder. She turned and saw what must be the mine shaft entrance, locked up tight. A bright bird was painted across the wooden slats that shut off the mine from the outside world.

"It's a phoenix," said John. "Every 500 years it burns itself in a pyre, and a new one is born from the ashes. I guess the original owner of the mine hoped that would happen with the mine."

"It's a real mine?"

"Yeah. Silver. It's been operating since 1897. In fact, if it weren't real, Loston probably wouldn't even exist. Most of the people here are dependent on it for work, in one way or another."

"Have you ever been in it?"

John nodded. "Couple of times. They ask for volunteer help with the digging once in a while, so I go in and make like a jackass. There are a couple of miles of tunnels crisscrossing the mountain. I guess I've been in about half of them."

"Wow." Fran was giddy with excitement. She was standing outside a mine. Just like Tom Sawyer, who'd been lost in a similarly deep and dark cave shaft and forced to hide from Injun Joe, the crazy murderer. It was like a piece of literature coming to life and glaring at her, a bit of dream that was locked away behind a plywood door, but still closer than ever before. She pulled her attention from the closed shaft and looked around. "I don't see the flowers. Where'd you get my bouquet?"

"They're not here," said John, and pointed at a trail near the shaft that led even higher up the mountain. Fran followed it with her eyes until it disappeared in a thick copse of trees. When she looked back at John, he was grinning.

He had such a beautiful smile. Not movie star perfect, not a pinup smile. He had a couple of slightly crooked teeth, and a lopsided grin. It was a real smile, packed with life.

Fran wanted to kiss him.

"You up for a walk?" he asked.

In answer, she turned and began making her way up the trail. She heard the soft scuff of his hiking boots as he followed her up the trail. Other than that, he was silent behind her. Fran thought it was odd. *She* certainly made enough noise for both of them, huffing and puffing her way up the slope, her feet scrabbling for a hint of purchase on the loose silt of the path. It must be the altitude, she thought. Not used to it yet.

Suddenly she slipped, her foot coming down on a pile of apparently solid rock that disintegrated suddenly, leaving her feet scrabbling wildly for purchase before she fell backward. John caught her, one arm around her waist, one hand locked onto her wrist. His grip was tight; secure. It was like being held by something more than a man, something with the solidity of iron, something safe.

He pulled her easily back to her feet, and then she felt his arms leave her waist. Before he could completely disengage from her, though, she swiveled her hand around and took his. He seemed surprised, and perhaps she saw a glint of something like dismay. But he did not try to take his hand from hers, and he smiled again.

The smile propelled Fran the rest of the way up the trail, where she spotted the flowers he'd picked, tight blue petals clustered around a dark core of pistils. She clapped in delight, dropping his hand in a moment of girlish exuberance, then bent over and began picking bunches of them. She stopped after a moment, though, laughing at herself.

"I already have a quite a few of these at home, don't I?" she said.

John, still smiling, said, "There's more here than just flowers, you know."

"Really?" she asked. "What else?"

Again, rather than answer with words, John pointed. Up. Straight up. Fran's gaze followed the line of his arm and she gasped.

"Oh, wow. You don't see that in California."

"You don't see it anywhere with an altitude of less than ten thousand feet."

The stars hung in the heavens, but they were no stars that Fran had ever seen. Stars to her were the pale pinlight flickers that occasionally broke through the clouds of methane and smog that shrouded Los Angeles. They blinked and twinkled as their rays fought through some of the highest pollution levels in the world, most failing to penetrate or simply being overwhelmed by the competing glare of the city below.

Here, the stars were enormous: luminous patches that didn't flash or twinkle, but blared forth in a symphony of pitch and wave, of beam and ray. Each one seemed to be separated from the next by a thick blanket of deepest velvet that circled and curved around the bright radiances to form a celestial orchestra of brilliance.

John pointed at different groups of stars. "That's Orion, and Cassiopeia, and the Bear...."

Fran followed his gestures, closing her eyes at times to imagine the mythical battles that were still being fought above them, the hunters seeking prey, the lovers who would always yearn, but never know the touch of those they wooed, separated by eons of time and distance.

She shivered. It was a pleasant trembling that reflected her sense of wonderment and pleasure at being in this place. But John immediately took off his coat and wrapped it over her light jacket. "Sorry," he said, "I didn't even think to warn you that it'd be cold."

"That's okay," she answered. "Won't you catch a chill?"

"No. I'm used to it. It's practically summer here."

They stood a moment in silence, looking at the grand dome above.

"What's winter like?" asked Fran. To her surprise, John laughed, a coughing chuckle that came from somewhere deep within. "Did I say something funny?" said Fran.

"No," he said, shaking his head. "I just remembered something funny. Something that happened to...someone I know."

"What?"

She watched as his laughter died. She saw a struggle play itself out within him, visible as a mouth that suddenly straightened and a shimmer in his eyes. He wanted to answer her, she was sure. But he was also keeping something hidden.

"Come on, Johnny," she said, "let's not start keeping secrets already."

And just like that, he won the struggle. Or perhaps lost it, she didn't know for sure. All she knew was that he took a deep breath and began to speak.

"A friend of mine got set up on a blind date about six years ago. So he shows up at the girl's house, not very excited because he's just a shy guy, and lo and behold, this goddess opens the door. Most beautiful woman my friend had ever seen."

"What happened?" asked Fran.

John looked away from her as he spoke, retreating into a world that was his, apparently unable to maintain contact with her while he was there. "It was winter – that's why I remembered this story just now – and so my friend decided to take her up to the mountains and go sledding. Nice date, no pressure, just a little safe, harmless fun."

"Sounds nice."

"That was the plan. But he forgot chains, and the sled broke, and it started to blizzard and they didn't get along at all and it was probably the most miserable day of his life. So he's taking her home and she says she has to get out of the car."

Fran giggled. "In a blizzard?"

"That's just what he said, too. So she said she...well, she had to...."

John made a helpless little movement with his hand. One that Fran had seen from hundreds of students requesting a hall pass in the middle of class time.

"She had to pee?" asked Fran.

"Yeah. She'd been holding it all day and she was about to have an accident. So he pulled over and let her out."

"What happened?"

"Well, my friend waited. And waited. And waited. And then he heard a noise. The girl was shouting for him. So he got out of the car, went around back, and there she was. Sitting on the bumper."

"What was she doing?"

John almost laughed then, but bit it back. "You know what happens when you lick a light pole in winter?" Fran nodded. "Well, it turns out that if you have to pee and you decide to sit on the metal bumper of a 1989 Chevy, the same thing happens."

Fran erupted in laughter. "Oh, no!" she barely managed to form the words. "She was...."

John nodded, laughing now as well. "Stuck tight. She would've ripped off half her behind if she'd tried to move."

They both doubled over then, howling and clutching at their stomachs like a couple of happy lunatics dancing below the full moon.

"What did they do?" said Fran when she managed to stop laughing long enough that articulation was possible.

"Well, he had to unstick her somehow, but there wasn't a whole lot of warm water around. He opened the radiator, but there was no way to get the water inside it out to her. So he went back and tried spitting melted snow on her butt."

That line was enough to send them both into another torrential fit of hysterics.

"It didn't work," continued John. "So finally...." He laughed more. "He unzipped his pants and peed on her until she defrosted!"

Fran laughed so hard that this time she *did* fall, losing her balance completely. Her arms pinwheeled and she grabbed John's shirt. John, laughing in no small way himself, followed her right down. He kept laughing until Fran rolled over on top of him, arm half wrapped around his broad chest. His laughter caught and died instantly, and she worried she might have gone too far. She wondered if she should move her arm and pull away from him.

Why? she thought, and stayed put. "I guess they never went out after that," she said.

John's eyes got that faded look again, and Fran knew he was remembering something beyond special. It was the look Nathan used to get when he was walking through his memories, a quiet, almost pained expression that bespoke love and tragedy together. "They got married about three months later."

"What?" She was surprised at that answer.

John nodded. "I guess their thinking was that the worst was behind them."

"And were they right?" Fran drew in close to John, almost laying on top of him, nose to nose, mouth to mouth. "Did they live happily ever after?"

133

John's face became even more serious, if possible. Solemn. Sad. "They lived very happily. Maybe the happiest ever. Until she got cancer and died."

Fran almost started to cry for the pain she saw in his eyes. She moved forward quickly, because she knew he'd pull away if she did it slowly, and kissed him on the cheek. Then she rolled over, laying beside him now. A moment later she pulled his arm under her neck, using it like a pillow.

"Which one is Cassiopeia?" she asked.

John pointed. "And the Bear?" she said. Another gesture. Fran asked him about all the stars, it seemed, through the hours until the sky began to brighten in the east. It was the sun, and John took her home in the burgeoning light of a new day's dawning. And for the first time in a long time, Fran could look at the day and know that Nathan was still gone, but perhaps she would no longer have to be alone.

DOM#67A
LOSTON, COLORADO
AD 2013
3:30 PM MONDAY

Over one full day.

The sign that hung on the door upstairs had one word scrawled across it: "CLOSED."

No one had come. Casey was a man who liked his privacy, and no one would think to intrude with inquiries about why he had closed his doors for the first time in well over a decade.

No one would come.

And no one would hear him scream.

Malachi leaned in close to Casey. The blood that streamed from Casey's nose and ears oozed in sticky rivulets down his neck, joining the darkening patches of brown and crimson that already stained his shirt. Tears dripped their own salty paths down his face, mixing with the blood into a thin streamlets of sickly pink: small tributaries of the larger rivers of pain that tracked their paths over his body.

Casey had been crying for hours, and bleeding for more, under Malachi's terrible ministrations. But still hardly a sound had escaped his lips, though he'd prayed to God and Jesus and the Holy Virgin and all the Saints and every other person he could think of, asking them all to let him die or at least let him tell the crazy man what he wanted to know.

Malachi pulled out a small box, and Casey wanted to shriek but of course could not. Malachi had withdrawn several implements and instruments in the past hours. Each had been unfamiliar to Casey, but each had brought new and unimaginable pain.

Malachi touched a button, and out of the box popped a thin spear about ten inches in length. It looked like a surgical tool. Malachi touched the button again, and a low hum began. It originated at the box and traveled in tight reverberations up the length of the metal spire, seeming to hover in a dark mass around the deadly point.

Malachi smiled, and Casey knew this was it. This was the end, and he was grateful because if it was the end he could stop hurting. He had heard of men in so much pain that they were afraid death was coming, but Casey was well beyond that stage. *His* only fear was that death would not come soon enough.

The crazy man pushed the point slowly *into* Casey's eye. One half of Casey's world disappeared, and the pain that traveled through his body was so intense, so frightening. He felt with peculiar distance the sensation of his bowels and bladder letting go.

"Tell me," Malachi whispered.

Please, Mary, Mother of God, he thought. Please, Mary Mother of God, he prayed as he had been praying for hours. Please hear my prayer and let me speak.

And at last his prayer was answered. Casey opened his mouth wide and *screamed*. He screamed until his lungs gave out, high-pitched yowls of animal agony and rage that slowly petered into whimpers and wheezes.

The madman before him smiled. He lay a hand on Casey's head, like a patriarch of old giving a farewell blessing to a journey-bound son.

When Casey was finished screaming, Malachi leaned in again. The needle was still in Casey's eye.

"Where are the new move-ins? A girl?"

"Sherman Street," panted Casey. It was hard to speak: Malachi had pulled out all of his teeth some hours before, so his voice sounded mushy and soft. "Gray house. North side of town. Corn fields around it."

"What is her name?" asked Malachi. "What name is she going by here?"

"Kaylie Devorough," answered Casey. He wanted to pass out and not wake up, but his body somehow held itself together.

"I knew it," said the blonde girl. "I knew they'd change her name."

"I wonder what reason she's been given for changing it," said the other man – not Malachi, the younger one. The one with beautiful eyes and a smile that was brightest when Casey started screaming. The black woman remained silent, as she had during the entire time in the basement.

Malachi cut off their conversation with a curt gesture. "Anyone else coming into town?" he asked. Casey just stared at him a moment, not comprehending the query, his mind stretched to breaking.

Then the question percolated through to the small fraction of his mind that was still capable of responding.

"FRAN!" he screamed. "NOW LET ME DIE!"

The force of the shout shook him to the core, but his four assailants didn't react, and Casey's pain- and fatigue-sodden mind slowly realized *he hadn't said anything*. Nothing at all. He could not say what he wanted to say.

"No," he gurgled, and saw Malachi smile again.

"Is he lying?" asked the black woman, her first words in Casey's hearing. Her voice was soft, he noted, but it had a slight rasp to it, like her throat was coated with chalk dust.

Malachi looked at Casey, still holding the needle that had punctured the bartender's eye and still remained planted in the orb. "I don't think so," he said. "He's broken."

He laid his other hand, the one not holding the box, on Casey's head again. Casey didn't know what he was going to do.

"Goodbye," said Malachi.

***

When the bartender was dead, Malachi stood a moment with his hand on the man's cool head. Part of that was just to make sure the man didn't reanimate, though Malachi was fairly sure he'd fried out the man completely.

Part of it was just to feel the moment. Even with a soulless one, the moment of passing was a moment of virtue. Of love. Not for the bartender, of course, but for the fact that each of these moments was a moment closer to the realization of Malachi's task.

He smoothed down Casey's hair, through which wisps of smoke slowly curled.

"What now?" asked Todd.

"We find her house. She'll probably have a Protector with her," answered Malachi.

"Do we hunt them down?" asked Jenna.

"No, we'll just wait for them to come to us." He nodded at Casey's body. "It looks like everyone in Loston has been put on Alert, so if we attacked her in public, it would never work. We'll wait inside her house. When she comes in, we kill her privately."

"What if someone else comes in first?" asked Jenna.

"Then they got in the way." He went to the stairs that led back to the bar. Then stopped and turned back to Jenna. "You spoke too soon, asking about Fran the way you did. And if you ever do something like that again, you won't be helping us anymore. I'll kill you and leave your body for the worms and your soul for Satan."

He ascended the stairs without waiting for her reaction.

DOM#67A
LOSTON, COLORADO
AD 2013
3:40 PM MONDAY

John weaved through the students milling in the halls of the school, and found himself smiling again.

It was unusual for him to be here at this hour. Normally he took off instantly, beating the students out of the school and hurrying home to be alone with his thoughts. But he'd awoken that morning with a sense of...something new. Something that he hadn't felt in a long time.

Happiness.

"So it went good last night?" asked Gabe. He walked beside John in the halls, having a harder time weaving his way through the crush of students trying to get to their lockers as quickly as possible so that they could vacate the premises.

"Yeah."

"Mertyl said you didn't get back before she went to bed. Must've been a doozy of a night."

John chuckled. "The best thing about small towns is the seventy-year-old woman that lives next to every house and works for the FBI." They reached the door to the office.

"Don't change the subject," said Gabe, frowning, though his eyes danced and John could tell he was already planning the reception and compiling a list of people he'd send announcements to in his head. "Have you seen her today?"

"Nope."

"But you waited for her in the break room didn't you?"

John grinned – felt good to smile like that – and opened the door to the office. "Sorry, Chief. No time to chat; gotta pick up my mail." He swept into the office, leaving Gabe behind.

Mertyl sat, as ever, in her customary spot guarding the front of the office. She smiled at John, and seeing her reminded him of why he was really there. His good mood evaporated like a drop of water in a bonfire.

Kaylie hadn't been in his class that morning. Her desk stood empty.

"Hello, John," said Mertyl. "How was school today?"

"Great, Mertyl. How was your day?"

"Usual. Wally had a hangover when he came in, but that's getting to be a pretty normal thing, I suppose."

Wally was the principal, the most tightly-buttoned person John had ever met. He and Mertyl liked to joke that at night he went home to a secret crackhouse where he spent the night boozing and doing all sorts of inventive drugs. John smiled at the quip, but the smile was a tight one. Nervousness fluttered in his stomach, though he had no idea why. He was just asking about a student, and that was well within his rights.

So why was he so edgy?

"Mert, I wonder if you could help me out."

"Sure. What can I do you for?"

"One of my students didn't come in today. Could you find out why?"

"Sure, John." Mertyl rifled through a pile on her desk. "Who was it?"

"Kaylie Devorough." Mertyl's hands slipped on the papers for a moment. She recovered quickly, but John noted a fleeting expression dance across her features. Too fast to be made out, but something strange. Then Mertyl's smile returned.

"That's easy, John. Her father called in sick for her."

"What's she sick with?"

"He didn't say."

"Where do they live? I'd like to see her about some things."

Mertyl stilled, leaving John with the momentary impression that his friend had been stolen away and replaced in the blink of an eye with some sort of wax replica, or a marionette that perfectly resembled Mertyl in every way, lacking only a soul. Again that

140

strange look surfaced. This time it stayed, remaining on her features as she said, "We have no record of that yet."

John was a bit daunted by the forbiddingly emotionless look on the old woman's face, but he pressed on. "Come on, Mertyl, how could that be? We don't let them into school unless their records are here."

Her face grew cold and hard. "We have no record. Leave it alone."

John frowned. Her speech disquieted him. Just as Gabriel's tone had altered in the bar the other day, Mertyl's voice now seemed as though it was hers, and yet at the same time somehow *wasn't*.

"Hey, stranger."

John turned gratefully away from Mertyl, smiling as he came face to face with Fran. She smiled back at him. Out of the corner of his eye, he saw Mertyl abandon her post, going into the ladies' room in the short hall off the side of the office. That was strange, too: in all the years he'd worked at the high school, John had never seen Mertyl go to the bathroom and leave her station during work hours.

"Hello?" said Fran, and John realized he had not responded to her salutation.

"Sorry, Fran. Thinking." He shrugged his shoulders in the universal code for "I'm an idiot sometimes."

"Thinking, eh? Don't hurt yourself."

"How was your first day? How's English 11A?"

"Well, they're monsters, but at least there aren't any drug runners here."

"No, not many of those in Loston. Not unless you count the kids who steal chemistry equipment every year to build stills in their parents' barns."

"They do that?" She laughed, a mellifluous sound that tinkled through the air and seemed to brighten it. He smiled a bit wider, his momentary disquiet dissipating in her presence.

"I...that is...." Once more, his tongue seemed to thicken in his mouth as he struggled to find words to say to the lovely woman who stood before him. "Uh...thanks for last night. I had a good time."

"Me, too," said Fran. She gazed directly at him, no shy girl. He was again struck by her confidence and frank nature.

"Sorry I didn't actually get to show you much of the town."

He was about to add "Maybe some other time" but before he could, Fran said, "That's okay. You can do it tonight. I'll be ready at seven." She touched his arm briefly, and then was gone in a cloud of vanilla.

John stood quietly for a time, still trying to come to grips with the conflicting emotions he felt. He wanted to be with Fran. But at the same time he wondered if being with her was somehow a betrayal of Annie's memory. Intellectually, he knew that was ridiculous. Indeed, he suspected that if Annie could somehow speak to him now she would probably chide him for withdrawing from life so completely. But he couldn't completely shake the feeling in spite of that fact.

In the midst of his musings, John realized he was alone in the office. He could see the file cabinet that held names and information of all the students at Loston High. Kaylie's address would be in there. He took a step towards it.

Mertyl came out of the bathroom. "What are you doing?" she said, almost barking the words.

"Waiting to say goodbye to you, Mertyl," he answered. And then turned around and left the building.

CONTROL HQ – RUSHM
AD 4013/AE 2013

Adam slapped his hand down on the console, a nearly silent display of his anger and despair.

"Sorry, sir," said Jason.

Adam ignored him. Continued studying the wall monitors, looking for any sign of the missing man. Each inhabitant of Loston was there, represented by a prismatic holo that could be instantly enlarged to show where each person was and what he or she was doing. But Adam was not interested in the population as a whole. He only wanted to know about one of them. Casey had disappeared from the screens a few hours before. There were several things that could mean, none of them good. Adam feared the worst.

"No reading at all on him?" he asked.

"None," answered Jason grimly.

"So he's gone. "

Jason shook his head. "He could be just out hiking or something. We have trouble picking up signals in the mountains."

"For two days?" Adam shook his head, as well, somehow making the movement bleaker than when Jason did it. "No, Casey's dead. And that means *they're* inside Loston. Somewhere." He paused, thinking. "What about Devorough?"

Jason hesitated. Then said, "He still hasn't turned up, sir. Neither has his...daughter."

Adam glanced at Jason, and saw that his right-hand man must be thinking the same thing he was: Devorough couldn't *have* a daughter. It was impossible.

Wasn't it?

Adam felt things surging out of his control. He had to put things right again. Soon.

"God," Adam whispered. He finished the prayer in his head. *Please, God, don't let the world end here.* Out loud, he said, "We have to find them."

"Should we go in?"

"Not yet," he answered. "But get a squad ready."

DOM#67A
LOSTON, COLORADO
AD 2013
5:45 PM MONDAY

The office was deserted; had been empty for the last hour and a half. The light was dim, the setting sun casting its last rays of orange through the frosted glass windows.

John stepped out of the bathroom, where he'd hidden while waiting for everyone to leave. He had a bad moment when he heard Janice, the woman who served as part-time janitor, come in the room. Luckily, Janice was a bit lazy as a custodian. John heard her check the soap dispensers, load paper towels by the sink, and then leave without checking the stalls.

An hour later he came out of the stall, waiting that long to make sure he didn't bump into the principal or anyone else trying to put in a bit of extra work. He didn't know why, exactly, but something told him that what he wanted to do would not be well-received by the staff of Loston High.

Once in the office, he went directly to the filing cabinet. It wasn't locked, but then there was no real need for it *to* be locked.

Was there?

He opened up the second shelf from the top, fingering through Mertyl's neatly-arranged files until he came to the right one: Devorough, Kaylie D.

He pulled the file. Grades, transcripts from several other schools, and a photo all spilled out. John pushed them aside, looking for his new student's address. He found it on a mailing slip: 1089 Sherman Street. He knew the area, had probably actually passed by the house numerous times, but couldn't remember exactly what it looked like.

He replaced the information, then put the file back in its designated spot. Mertyl, as careful with her system as she was with everything else, might notice tomorrow that it had been pawed through, but John hoped that by then it wouldn't matter; that he'd have resolved the questions that held sway over him. He hoped that would cure the strangeness that had infected him and seemed to be quickly spreading to his closest friends in Loston.

He glanced at the wall clock: 5:45 p.m. Sherman Street wasn't too far.

If he hurried, he could get this taken care of and be at Fran's on time. Assuming nothing went wrong.

DOM#67A
LOSTON, COLORADO
AD 2013
5:55 PM MONDAY

When they had first entered the house on Sherman Street, Todd and Jenna had raged. It was empty. Nothing, not a scrap. They saw a child's doll in one of the two bedrooms, but it was the only article in an otherwise empty house. It sat against the wall with its arms folded, like a little girl sitting reverently in the front pew at a funeral.

"What are we going to do now?" asked Todd. "She's gone."

"Maybe she hasn't arrived yet," said Deirdre. Once more, Malachi appreciated her quiet, self-contained confidence. She was far more disciplined than Todd and Jenna.

"Then what's that?" asked Jenna, pointing to the doll. She had a point. Malachi believed that Fran would not visit this house again, if she had even been permitted to get here. Still, perhaps something could be learned.

"We wait," said Malachi. He stepped into the other bedroom and closed the door, leaving it open a crack so they could see into the hall. "If she hasn't arrived, we'll kill her as soon as she steps in the door. And if she left, we wait for whoever comes her next – and someone will, I promise you, they always come in to make a last sweep – and make him tell us where they've taken her."

He smiled, a tight-lipped grimace that transformed his thin features into a death's head.

***

John stepped up to the house, checking the address to make sure he was at the right place. 1089 Sherman. This was it.

It was a small enough house, not large like some of the big family homes that squatted outside Loston.

No lights were on inside, but he knocked anyway. No answer.

***

"Wait," said Malachi when they heard the knock. "Wait until whoever it is come in. We want this to be private."

***

John put out a hand, touching the door handle. It didn't turn. Locked.

He stood for a moment, asking himself if he really wanted to do what was coming next. But he had already decided. He walked around the side of the house, stopping in front of a window. It was closed, a screen over the glass, and curtains drawn within. He figured it belonged to one of the bedrooms.

He withdrew a small penknife and popped out the screen, then pressed his fingers against the window, pulling at the glass. A lot of the houses in Loston didn't even have latches on the windows. And often the ones that did weren't engaged, their owners assured that no one would dream of breaking into a house in a place like Loston. With luck, John could open the window, hop in and look around, and no one would be any the wiser.

He pulled, and the window slid open without a sound.

His lucky day.

***

Malachi and the others tensed as they heard a rasping noise. Someone was entering the house.

***

John slid through the window, dipping his head below the curtain and seeming to glide to the floor like a legless phantasm in a haunted house.

He closed the window behind him, then looked around the room. It was empty, save a tiny doll sitting against one wall.

John walked noiselessly into the hallway. He looked across the corridor, where a closed door waited. The other bedroom door was ajar. He headed to it.

Then he veered down the hall, deciding to check the front rooms first and finish with the bedroom. Though he had come in through a window – and such an action was so completely unlike him that he couldn't really understand where it had originated – he didn't like the idea of violating the sanctity of someone's bedroom if he could help it. Perhaps the front rooms would turn up the answers to questions he didn't even have formed in his own mind.

***

They saw the flash as someone walked by their room. It startled them; they had heard sounds, but had not heard anyone actually come in the house.

Todd looked at Malachi, mouthing the words, "What now?"

Malachi was about to answer when they heard the front door open. Distracted by the presence of a stranger in the hall, they hadn't heard the latch disengage.

Now there were two people in the house.

Malachi decided to wait and see what happened next.

***

John stepped into the living room at the same exact time someone else entered through the front door. It registered on him that this room was as bare as the other had been, but that was before he locked eyes with the man who had stepped in.

"Skunk Man," whispered John.

Devorough stared blankly at John, his jaw slack, as though he were some patient in a mental hospital, too doped up to recognize anything around him.

John and the man both waited, a frozen tableau, before John broke the silence. "Mr. Devorough?" he started.

Devorough seemed to animate a bit. His mouth closed for a moment, then in a dreamy voice he said, "She forgot her doll. I came back for it. The place has to be clean."

John didn't know what was going on; was too confused and frightened by half to make any sense out of Devorough's strange words. He pressed on, though, wanting more than ever to pierce the shroud of mystery that had suddenly wrapped around his life.

***

Malachi held up a hand. They could hear the conversation in the next room. They might find something out. One of the men had mentioned a girl, and he wanted to hear what he could before going in and blowing both of them back to Hell.

The first voice came through the door. "Mr. Devorough, I'm Kaylie's teacher, and...."

Teacher? Malachi frowned. No matter what false name the Controllers had given her, why would Fran have a teacher? This wasn't sounding right.

"...well, this is gonna sound crazy," the first voice continued, "but were you ever in the military? Do I know you?"

There was a long pause. And then a sudden, violent crash.

***

John expected several things. A laugh, perhaps, with an accompanying "What are you talking about?" If not that, then a mere "I'm calling the police" was also something he would have been ready for. He even felt prepared for Devorough to rip off his face and reveal an insect-like alien beneath the skin that would grab him and take him aboard some mothership hovering a few miles above the earth, undetected by NASA's best scientists, there to be anally probed and made to mate with the bug women.

But he did not expect Devorough to attack him.

The man screamed, a crazy, ravaged cry that seemed to tear out of him, and John instinctively threw up his hands as Devorough rushed him.

Devorough's hands were like flesh-sheathed pincers that felt more as though they were powered by pistons and steam than by muscle and tendon. John pushed the man away, kicking him in the groin and forking at his eyes automatically, old training surging up to take control of his reactions.

Devorough defended against the eye-gouge. John's foot, however, connected. It was a solid hit, slamming Devorough's genitals straight on. It should have dropped him, but the guy kept coming. He didn't even slow down, in fact. He pushed into John, punching him back into the wall hard enough that he felt his ribs bend and the air whoosh out of him.

In the movies, such a hit was always a chance to hear the good guy scream in rage and then come on with renewed vigor. Reality was different. John couldn't breathe; for an agonizing moment he couldn't even *think* about breathing. Then his body recovered enough to suck in a huge gasp of air.

Too late for further action, though. Devorough had the upper hand and he kept it, pressing John into and up the wall, keeping John's feet off the floor, keeping him from regaining his balance. Both Devorough's hands were occupied, though, so this time when John's two fingers stabbed out, it was a success.

One jammed into Devorough's cheek, bruising John's knuckle. The other slammed home, plunging into the gooey mass of Devorough's eye, ruining it forever. John felt no qualms about the action: he knew instinctively this was a fight to the death, with no second place award. But still, in a place in the back of his mind, he knew that he would later agonize about the move; would replay it over and over in his mind to see if there might have been some other way of dealing with the situation.

If he survived, that was. If he was dead he wouldn't have the luxury of feeling guilty.

Devorough stepped back – without a sound, though he should have been *screaming!* – and John found his footing again. He grabbed hold of Devorough's neck and pulled, throwing his hip under Devorough's and swiveling his feet as he simultaneously yanked on Devorough's head and neck. It was a hip-toss, and John planned to throw the other man down as hard as he could, adding his own body weight to gravity's taut pull and hopefully crushing Devorough's ribs into pudding.

It didn't work. Devorough pulled himself high, defying physics and leverage to yank John into the air again. It wasn't form or technique, it was sheer brute strength.

John had never felt such power. It was as though a monster, a juggernaut, a *leviathan* was attacking him. He had fought large men before, and his training allowed him to win. Technique provided him with enough advantage to come out as victor. But here, it seemed that training was nothing. And technique was just a silly fairy tale that evaporated in the face of rough, brute strength.

Devorough slammed John into the ground, a throw that seemed almost clumsy in execution. For all its lack of smoothness, though, the move was effective. John landed on his tailbone, bruising and perhaps fracturing it as he landed. He cried out, a staccato yip that was broken off as Devorough's hand wrapped itself tightly around his throat.

For a moment, John thought he was going to be slowly strangled, the oxygen and life crushed out of him. Devorough's grip changed, though, and John gasped quickly as the other man's hands left his trachea, inhaling with relief. The relief quickly fled, however, as Devorough switched his hands to a firm hold on his chin and the back of John's head, and began twisting.

He's going to snap my neck, thought John.

And there was nothing he could do about it. The pressure was slow, even, unrelenting. And inescapable. John could actually hear the vertebrae in his neck popping and crackling as they struggled to maintain themselves under stress which nature never intended them to feel.

He heard a bang, a loud clattering sound that he knew must be his neck breaking. John thought the pain would cease with the noise, but miraculously it didn't. It got worse, a sheer agony that ripped through his muscles and set them afire.

Then he felt Devorough's hands loosen and the man's body fell next to John. A hole the size of a cat was punched through the Skunk Man's torso. John could actually see through the gaping wound to the wall behind as Devorough fell.

John looked behind him, and recognized the four strangers he had bumped into at Casey's coming in the bedroom door. They held guns.

The one in front, the oldest one, smiled. He looked at Devorough's body and whispered, "Thou shalt fear no evil." He aimed his gun at Devorough's body, which was still twitching.

Do bodies twitch *that* much? he thought. John had seen bodies before, and they'd never convulsed like this one was doing,

The older man pulled the trigger of his weapon.

John threw himself to the side as the shotgun blasted. He felt the heated shot whiz past him as he hit the wall under a large window, but wasn't harmed.

He looked at Devorough, whose head was now splashed all over the room, body ending in a mutilated, ragged stump of a neck that dripped blood everywhere.

Devorough was no longer twitching. Once again, the Skunk Man was dead.

CONTROL HQ – RUSHM
AD 4013/AE 2013

Adam was poring through the unsealed portions records databases, trying to figure out exactly what was going on in Loston, and as always, he scanned the electronic files with trepidation. To look too far into the matters they contained could mean death, and worse, so it he felt a mixed sense of frustration and relief when his studies were ended by the sound of trouble.

"Sir!" Jason yelled. "One of the bits just went offline!"

"Was his cam recording?" asked Adam as he made his way to his right-hand man's console. Jason nodded. "Then let's find out what happened."

Jason keyed in a command on his console, and they turned to the screens that hovered over the walls. One expanded, and began to play out a scene. It was confused and jerky, but Adam could see John's face for a moment, and then another face. Light hair, dark clothing. Adam's breath caught in his throat as he realized who it was.

"Malachi," he gasped. Then he turned to Jason. Gesturing at the monitor, he snapped, "Who was this? Who did we just lose?"

Jason checked his record bank. "Devorough 42261-6. That's who just went down."

"The *bit*?"

Jason nodded, his face ashen. So he recognized Malachi, too, thought Adam.

"The records maintain that Devorough is offline and in storage," said Jason, "but the console also shows him as the one we just lost."

Confused and worried by this new bit of information, Adam turned back to watch the scene. It ended when Malachi pointed his gun at the cam and pulled the trigger.

"Locate them," he said to Jason.

Jason began working, and Adam began to pray.

Just one break, God. Just one little break, please.

DOM#67A
LOSTON, COLORADO
AD 2013
6:30 PM MONDAY

The man who had pulled the trigger turned his attention to John. John cringed. He had never in his life confronted a gaze more filled with malevolent insanity. It seared through him like a red-hot poker, burning out courage and security and leaving behind it an ashy trail of fear. John shuddered. He knew instantly that Devorough, for all his chaotic action and superhuman strength, was far preferable to this man, this devil in human guise.

"Have to make sure they stay dead," said the man, and John was struck by the incongruously happy voice that came out of the man's mouth. "It's how we bring about the end of days."

John tensed, preparing to jump to his feet. Instantly all four strangers pointed their guns at him, aiming with military precision. John remained down, kneeling with his hands up.

"Not so fast," the man said. "You don't do anything until you tell us where she is." And then, insanely, he said something which made no sense whatsoever: "I'm human, by the way."

John looked at the people threatening him. There was the older man who had spoken, who was so obviously in charge there was no need to ask to whom John must direct his attention. Behind and to his right stood a younger man, pale blue eyes crackling with an only slightly less intense version of the same insane energy that riddled the older man's irises. To their left stood a petite blonde girl. She held her gun in rock-steady hands, but John noticed her feet shuffling back and forth.

Nervous, he thought. She's the weak link.

He filed away the information for later use.

The last person in the group was a black woman, dark and dusky as a sunless night over a tropical forest, her clothing seeming both a part of her and of the dark quarters in which they now stood.

John remained silent. He knew from experience what to do and what not to do in a prisoner situation. Rule number one was only speak when asked a direct question.

Apparently these people hadn't studied their hostage etiquette. The younger man stepped forward, forcing the other three to shuffle sideways and draw a bit closer to keep their guns on John.

The man kicked John, then hit him with his gun. "Tell us!" he screamed.

John went down again as his already-abused body suffered further damage. He felt another rib bruise. The pain was bad, inconvenient, but not unbearable. He stayed down, though, arms crossed in front of his stomach, and began crying hysterically.

He could hardly breathe between the tears and the sobs that shook his entire frame like a wind-tossed leaf, and each shudder took its toll on John's bruised neck and chest. But it was worth it. The young blonde girl stepped forward, prodding his shoulder with her gun.

"Shut up," said the woman. Her voice was like steel, but John could detect a tiny quaver around the edges. "Tell us where she is."

She prodded him again.

Mistake.

John exploded upward, twisting to the side and pushing her gun to the floor as he jumped. The gun boomed as it went off, and at the same moment John stood, using his powerful momentum to hurl her into the younger man. They both tripped, arms pinwheeling to maintain balance, then fell backward into the other two.

In the same motion, John heaved himself up and back, through the window behind him. He fell through in a tinkle of glass and felt a shard pierce his lower back, hopefully nothing serious, and then the breath whooshed out of him yet again as he hit the ground outside. He sprang to his feet and was running even as he heard his attackers struggling to their feet inside the house.

John ran to the corn field that butted up against the Devoroughs' yard, plunging head first into the stalks.

He could hear muffled grunts at the house as his four assailants came through the window in pursuit of him. They plunged into the rows of shucks as well, hurrying to catch him as he fled.

But John was no longer fleeing. He ran about six feet into the thick patch, just far enough to be out of sight from the house, and then dropped to his belly, laying flat in the dirt.

It was a gamble, but his car was in front of the Devorough place. Escaping on foot was something he didn't want to try, especially if it meant running into the nearby mountains. He wanted someplace populated, so he had to make it to his car. Once there, he could get into Loston and go see Tal, the sheriff.

Four sets of feet crunched by him, one set – belonging to the young man – coming close enough that he could have seen John had he merely looked down for a moment. Luckily, for all their apparent facility with guns, John could tell they had no idea how to conduct a thorough sweep of a cornfield.

John waited until he heard them plow deep into the rows, then stood and ran with all his might. His legs pumped like the pistons of an angry locomotive as he fairly flew to his car, expecting at every moment to hear the explosion of a shotgun and feel the tearing pain of shot ripping into him.

With that thought, the scar on his shoulder twinged, as though it was remembering its birth. John had no time to think of that long-forgotten day, however, and dismissed the thought. But he did not send it far. He sensed that what had happened that day would prove important; that it might even be crucial to staying alive.

He made it to his car, yanking the door open and throwing himself onto the seat. A small cry escaped his lips as he sat. The shard of the window glass that had imbedded itself in his back was still there, and as he sat down it was pushed further inside. John hoped it wasn't severing any nerves or causing serious damage, but he didn't have time to stop and try to get it out.

He turned his key in the ignition and rolled out, casting one last look at the house.

He had escaped death tonight. Not once but several times. But he felt no relief, merely a burgeoning sense of despair.

As though what had happened was only a small taste of things to come.

"The end of days," was what the older man had said.

John hoped they weren't his.

CONTROL HQ – RUSHM
AD 4013/AE 2013

"How did this happen?" barked Adam.

"I don't know, sir," said Jason. "As soon as we were aware that John had recognized Devorough we tried to call him in."

"And?"

"He didn't come. Kaylie showed up – she's in the Clinic – but Devorough never did."

"Wonderful. Didn't you ask her where Devorough was, and how she came to be his daughter?"

"Yes, sir, but...." Jason's voice trailed off.

"But what?"

"She'd been wiped. Nothing left. She couldn't even talk."

"Damn. That's the work of someone inside." Adam turned to the wall, a single enlarged screen there the focus of his attention. It showed the last thing Devorough had seen: a freeze frame view of the bullet that ended his life. And behind it, that face that Adam had hoped never to see again. "Malachi," he whispered. The name pulled at him. Weighed at him. Dragged him down to despair.

"Sir," said Jason. "What do you want us to do?"

Adam turned to the Controllers and tried desperately to think of an answer to that question.

DOM#67A
LOSTON, COLORADO
AD 2013
6:50 PM MONDAY

Sheriff Tal White cultivated despondency like others raised roses.

Functional depression wasn't merely his hobby, it was his way of life. People laughed at him behind his back. He knew that, and it served only to sadden him. A vicious cycle.

Single, he graduated Loston High, took a correspondence course in forensics and criminology (amazing what you could get for yourself over the computers these days!), and then lobbied – successfully – for the job of Loston's sole Sheriff. He told himself he got the job because people secretly admired his fortitude in the face of despair.

In reality, no one else wanted a job that paid slightly over thirty thousand dollars a year and tended to result in lowered sperm counts through exposure to extremely high levels of boredom. Nothing ever happened in Loston.

At the swearing in, no one came but his parents and his little brother. "Just a perfect way to start the job," he said directly after the ceremony, and not even his family could tell if he was being sarcastic, self-pitying, or sincere. "Figures."

Tal had no real friends, and he preferred it that way. He knew very few people in the town, aside from immediate family, and didn't particularly *want* to know many folks.

But he *did* know Loston's most popular high school teacher. So when John Trent slumped through the front door of Loston's sheriff's office/prison, Tal jumped to his feet. John was a mess. Great purple bruises ringed his neck, and his pants looked wet with blood.

"What happened?" asked Tal incredulously.

The computer science teacher looked at him, grinned in a bemused "hellifiknow" way, and then passed out.

***

They walked out of the corn field, shaking loose twigs and angel hairs – the wispy golden threads that hung from the ripe ears of corn – from their clothing.

Without a word, they all agreed that they had been given the slip. Without a word, they went back to the house. Without a word they knew what they would do next.

They would search Devorough's body for the key to his car, a Ford that was sitting in the driveway. Then they would get in and go to the town Sheriff. The man they had pursued would go there. He would *have* to. He would literally have no choice, as that decision would have been inculcated into him through countless years of subtle indoctrination. So they would go to the Sheriff, as well. They would find that man. They would torture him until he told them where Fran was.

And then they would kill him.

***

John wasn't unconscious for very long. Maybe a minute and a half. When he woke, Tal had already laid him down on his stomach on a cot. Loston was small enough that the entire Sheriff's station consisted of one front office with a door in back that led to a small, three-cell prison. The cot was in the front room, next to the door to the jail area, wedged between a desk and a folding table that held a percolator. John moaned.

"Jesus, John," said Tal, interest warming his characteristically phlegmatic voice ever so slightly. "What happened to you?"

"Glass," answered John.

"I know." Tal held out a shard. Blood caked the clear surface like some evil stained glass window at a satanic church. "I got it out and bandaged you up. Not cut too bad, but it'll bleed more if we don't get you some stitches. I'm gonna call a doctor over here." He paused, then repeated his earlier question. "What happened?"

"I don't know." John sat up. The wound at his back was a dull throb under a tight bandage. Of more concern were the jolts he felt at his ribs. Not broken, but severely bruised for sure. "I went to a student's house and when I got there her father went berserk and tried to kill me."

"*What*? So he's the one who put a piece of glass in you?"

"No. But when we were fighting these four lunatics showed up...." John's body shook as a violent spasm wracked him, a convulsed shudder that sprang from a newly opened well of fear and disorientation. Chills racked him for a moment before he was able to get himself under control again.

"It's okay, John." Tal gripped his shoulder. "What happened next?"

"They killed him." John took a deep breath and continued slowly, pressing out each word as though it cost him. "Devorough – that's the guy I went to see – he went insane, attacked me, then when he was about to kill me four people showed up and killed him. Then they tried to kill me, too."

Tal stood. He went to the percolator and poured a cup of coffee, bringing it back and handing it to John. John sipped it gratefully. It was hot – too hot to drink, really – but the heat was welcome, scalding his throat and serving as a proof that he was still alive.

"So these four fellas –"

"Two men and two women. I can describe them to you."

"In a sec. They say why they tried to kill you?"

"No. They asked where she was, and then I got away."

"She?"

John shrugged and took another sip of his coffee. "Damned if I know."

Tal eyed him for a moment. "We really ought to get you to the doc."

"I'll be okay. I'm more interested in finding out what just happened."

"Why were you at this fella's house, anyway?"

John stopped drinking. He looked at Tal, trying to decide what he would tell the droopy-eyed officer. In the end, respect and faith in the law won out over his desire to avoid sounding crazy, so he told the truth. "I...I thought I'd seen him before. Hell, Tal, I *know* I'd seen him before. Once when I was a kid, once when I was in Iraq. And he hadn't changed a bit, not in almost twenty years."

Tal's expression showed that he didn't think much of that fact. "Some people don't change that much."

"But this guy didn't change *at all*. And when I saw him a few days ago, he was still the same. It's been over thirty years, Tal."

Tal's face grew hard. John could see the Sheriff didn't believe him.

"It sounds nuts, I know. But get this: when I saw him in Iraq, I saw him die. He got blown to pieces." John looked down at his coffee, studying it as though its murky liquid might hold answers to the insane night's unasked questions. One accusatory thought kept surfacing in his mind, though he did not voice it aloud: "Maybe I'm crazy."

As if in answer to his silent self-doubt, John heard the distinctive click of a gun hammer being pulled back. He looked up and saw Tal aiming his police special at him.

The look on his face hadn't been disbelief, John realized in the milliseconds before acting. It had been that same hard look that shone in Devorough's eyes.

Right before he tried to kill John.

Again, instinct took over. As Tal's finger whitened on the trigger of his gun, John hurled his coffee at the man. The burning liquid hit Tal in the eyes, scalding them, perhaps permanently damaging them. John hoped not, Tal was – well, not exactly a friend, but a good acquaintance. John taught Tal's brother Joey some years back, and liked the whole family. But there was no time now for friendly remonstrances. Tal was trying to kill him.

The sheriff shrieked as the brown spray hit him in the eyes and the gun went off. John heard the frightening zing of a bullet going by and the wall behind him thudded.

John took advantage of the other man's momentary incapacity and jumped at Tal, who was still clawing at his eyes. He took the sheriff by surprise, boxing both the officer's ears and then punching him in the crook of his arm. His aim was true: John hit the nerve ganglion near Tal's elbow, and the man's gun hand opened automatically as the blow paralyzed his nerves. John caught the gun before it even hit the ground. In one smooth action it was up and pointed at Tal's face.

The sheriff's visage was frightful. Bright red tissue surrounded his eyes where the coffee had splashed. But worse than that was his expression, which looked as though he were fighting some horrible internal war with himself. He kept mumbling something to himself, and John couldn't quite make out what he was saying.

"Tal," he said. "It's me. I taught your little brother, for Heaven's sake."

Abruptly, Tal stopped mumbling and bent over to pull up his pants leg. An ankle holster hung below his calf.

"Tal. Tal, don't touch that gun."

Tal popped the latch on the holster. John's finger tightened on the trigger of the police special, but he couldn't do it. This wasn't a war, at least not like any he'd been in. Nor was it a sudden attack. He had a moment to think, and discovered that he couldn't just shoot Tal cold-bloodedly, however necessary it might be for John's own well-being.

Tal, on the other hand, apparently *could* shoot John. As the ankle pistol came out, John threw himself through the door to the prison. It wasn't locked, or his trip might have ended then and there in a flurry of point-blank shots.

John landed on the hard concrete floor of the prison, a small cry escaping his lips as he landed on his tailbone, still bruised from his encounter at the Devorough place. He covered his head with his hands as gunfire ricocheted off the door and its frame.

Then the fusillade halted for a moment, and John looked around, taking stock of his surroundings. Three cells, no hiding places. One back door, but John knew that it was locked, double locked, and made of stainless steel. There were keys, of course...on Tal's belt. But somehow John didn't think the Sheriff would just relinquish them.

Click.

Click.

Click.

John heard the Sheriff reloading. He cocked his own gun, chambering the next bullet. "Tal, you're my friend, but you come around this corner and I'll kill you."

He didn't know if he actually would or not. He doubted it.

He looked around again.

Click.

Click.

Nothing. He ran down the short hall to the back door, but as he expected, it was locked.

A heavy bootfall sounded behind him, and John faced the open door, gun aimed at it.

At the same moment a tinkle sounded, the bell above the front door ringing brightly as someone entered the Sheriff's office.

DOM#67A
LOSTON, COLORADO
AD 2013
7:25 PM MONDAY

Tal's thoughts were fuzzy. Confused.

Can't think. Can't concentrate. Can't think.

He knew he held a gun. He knew he had fired it. But he couldn't remember why.

Go into the prison. Use the gun again. Shoot something. What? Don't know.

When the door tinkled, he turned.

"May I help you?" he said to the four people who entered. His voice sounded strange, even to him: emotionless; dead and dry as a petrified stick. He held the gun in front of him, regardless of what the visitors' reaction might be.

The one in front – an older man – brought up a gun of his own. The man smiled. He fired. Something hit Tal in the chest and he heard the new arrival say, "We'd like to report shots fired."

Tal slammed into the wall next to the prison door. He slid to the floor, leaving a wide swath of blood smeared down the wall behind him. His eyes rolled back, and when everything went dark he wasn't sure if it was because his eyes were closed or if he had just forgotten how to see.

Just the perfect way to end my day, he thought. Figures.

And he died.

***

John heard the report, heard the terrifying explosion, and heard something hit the wall. He hurried to the door that led to the office, knowing that what he'd heard was Tal hitting the wall, probably dead now. One more corpse in a night already packed with death and fear. John hoped that Tal was close enough to the door that he'd be able to grab the Sheriff's key ring and escape out the back, because he was sure that the crazies he had encountered at Devorough's house were responsible for the gunfire he'd just heard.

Who are they? he thought. But he had no time to find out now. The question would have to be answered later. If he survived.

He risked a glance into the office, darting his head through the doorway. Tal's body lay within inches of him, but before he could grab the keys he saw them – the four crazies. They saw him as well, and opened fire. John ducked back into the prison as the shots hit the wall, gunfire deafening him in the confined space. The wall buckled but didn't disintegrate, its steel core holding up against the flurry of gunfire.

"Where is she?" The older man's voice ricocheted into the prison like one more bullet, pinging against John's ears harshly before imbedding itself in his mind.

"What the hell are you people talking about?" John yelled back. "Why are you doing this?"

He checked the gun he still held to make sure it was fully loaded. One shot already gone, only five remaining in the cylinder.

Another round of gunfire sounded, and bullets hit the door. One rammed its way through the frame, missing John by inches and leaving the doorway permanently open.

John could see Tal's foot through the doorway.

The exit lay beyond the open door, on the other side of the hall. He'd have to cross their line of fire to get there. Assuming he could even get the keys without dying.

"Don't play stupid, bit!" It was the blonde girl's voice. "Where's Fran?"

John paled. Thoughts of Fran and his date had flown from his mind in the course of the last half-hour. But now they rushed back, her name triggering intense fear – not for himself this time, but for her.

How was *she* involved in this?

***

In the office, Todd waited impatiently for an answer. Where's Fran? The question hung over them like a guillotine, sharp and potentially deadly to their cause.

No answer came, and Malachi nodded. The four spread out, heading for the door, weapons ready. Todd noticed Tal's feet begin to twitch, and was about to signal to Malachi that they had to take care of that problem.

Before he could, though, he saw their quarry's hand poke around the doorframe. The hand ended in a pistol, and before any of them could move it had pumped every round into the air around them.

One of the bullets caught Todd in the neck. It exploded through his windpipe, and for a sharp moment he felt the strange sensation of his own blood filling his lungs, then he knew no more.

***

Click.

The gun was empty. John had heard a thump through the gunfire, the characteristic noise of a body hitting the floor. It was a noise John had heard before, but not one he had ever hoped to hear again. This night was refamiliarizing him with all sorts of things he had thought were behind him.

He hoped he'd dropped the crazy bastard who'd killed Devorough. John would equate that with personally killing the devil.

He dropped the gun and grabbed Tal's foot, pulling the Sheriff's body into the cell with him.

Tal's foot was twitching. The reflex action gave John the willies, but he pried Tal's ankle gun from the sheriff's dead hand. It was a six-shooter, small but effective at close range.

John hoped it wouldn't come to that.

He focused on Tal's belt then, searching for the keyring. He found it and yanked it off. A belt loop on the Sheriff's pants snapped.

"Come out, bit!" The voice startled John. It was the older man. Not dead, then. John focused on the open doorway, wondering if he should risk running across now, or if he should pump another bullet or two into the room.

"Come out or it'll go harder on you!" screamed the voice.

"You need to go home and tell them to increase the dosage!" John hollered in return. It was stupid, a stupid thing to do, giving away his position in the hall, but John had to give voice, to speak, to tell the lunatic in the office that he was still alive and planned to remain so.

A shot zinged in through the open door. John dropped and rolled away as the bullet's impact showered bits of plaster into his hair.

He sat up.

And found himself inches away from Tal.

Who was sitting up as well.

Alive.

"Oh my God," said John. He watched in shocked horror as Tal reached for his gun. He was breathing, even though he had a hole punched straight through his chest. John could see blood pumping out of the meaty crater, as though circulating through arteries, then veins, returning to the place where the heart should be. There was no heart, though. It had to be gone, splashed against the wall of the office.

Tal, his eyes staring blankly into John, seemed to realize his gun was gone. He flung himself at John, going for him with his bare hands.

The movement snapped John into movement, and nearly snapped his sanity. "Ohmygodohmygodohmygod," he said as he threw himself backward, crabwalking convulsively away from the dead man. Tal's hands snapped like lobster claws only millimeters away from John's foot.

John threw himself across the open doorway, expecting to be taken in mid-flight by a hail of bullets. He made it unscathed, running to the door.

He turned, and saw that Tal had made it across the doorway, too, on his feet, hands reaching out for John. Blood – his own – dripped from his hands in cascades, a macabre vision from the most dire chapters of the Bible seeming to come to life before John's eyes.

John screamed, holding onto sanity's last thread with a grasp that grew ever more tenuous. He brought up the gun and emptied it into Tal, blowing great bloody holes through the sheriff, who stepped back with each shot but *didn't fall*. John almost wept with fear as he saw blood pour from each new wound, yet each new wound failed to topple the man who had converted to an undead monster from beyond nightmare.

The last bullet hit Tal solidly in the temple, snapping back his head and forcing the sheriff to take a single step back.

The other man, the *dead* man, now stood framed in the open doorway to the office.

***

Jenna fingered her weapon silently.

What do I do now? she thought. Todd is dead.

The words ran bitterly through her head, almost a chant of confusion and despair. She had loved Todd for years, ever since she had met him, in fact. He was in love with her, too, and had told her so. They could not marry, they would never bear children. Attempting to bring more children into the world would be a fool's game, not to mention acting against their beliefs.

After all, if God had decreed that all must perish, then to bring a child to light would be sheerest blasphemy.

So no children. Only work, and toil, and the cause. And love. She cried, looking at his body, lying still and damp on the floor of the office of this hateful place. The weeping was silent, though, turned inward so only she could hear the wailing sounds of mourning.

I loved you, she thought. Go in peace, my darling.

Then Jenna raised her eyes from the body of her love and saw the man – the *thing* – in the doorway. She screamed and opened fire. It was the sheriff, not the one who had killed Todd, but the gunfire drowned out the pounding ache that erupted in her heart when she saw her love die. Todd was gone, but fire remained.

She screamed, and the scream came from the base of her soul, a primal cry to expunge the pain of her loss. Todd was gone, but the cause lived, and to serve it the things of this place must perish.

Malachi and Deirdre also opened fire beside her, their combined gunfire deafening in this confined space. But the noise was welcome music to Jenna, for as long as she heard the song of the weapons, she could not perceive the cries of her heart.

***

John watched what looked like a hundred holes blast through Tal's already wrecked body. The sheriff's face smacked wetly as low-caliber shots punched through it, his cheekbones slowly dissolving under the torrent of lead. A shotgun blasted, and his right arm came off at the elbow. Another, and his kneecap shattered.

And still he lurched toward John, using his one wrecked leg like a broken crutch, wobbly and inefficient...but still moving slowly towards him.

John turned to the door. It was locked, and he had no idea which was the right key. Tal's ring looked to hold about thirty thousand bits of jangling metal. He tried the first. Nothing.

Behind him, he heard Tal's body hit the ground. He dared a look back, and saw that he –

(*it, it had to be an it, no man, just a thing*)

– was still crawling toward him, inch by inch, foot by foot.

John tried more keys. None of them worked.

Tal's face, no longer recognizable as belonging to his friend, leered up at him, a bloody pulp. Two or three remaining teeth seemed to grin a mad, ghastly jack-o-lantern smile at him, loosely hanging from exposed jawbones and pulped flesh.

And John still hadn't found the right key.

Bloody fingers – two left on one hand and four remaining on the other – reached out towards John, pinching open and shut convulsively. John knew that if he fell next to Tal –

(*no, it isn't Tal, it can't be, this has to be something else*)

– he wouldn't get up again.

The broken fingers brushed against his leg, and John screamed. A strange mewling sound, like that of a kitten being slowly tortured to death, came from Tal's wrecked mouth: the Devil calling for John's surrender.

John kicked convulsively, knocking the fingers away. Disgust skittered through his body and he had to fight for control of his bowels. Tal almost grabbed his kicking foot.

Then one of the keys turned.

John pushed the door open and ran.

***

Deirdre heard an alarm sound.

He must be going out through the emergency exit, she thought.

Silent and dark, she hurtled through the door to the prison, Malachi and Jenna only seconds behind her. She turned the corner, and saw the sheriff, recognizable now only by his tattered remnants of uniform and the pieces of a badge that still clung tenaciously to his ruined torso.

He lay on the ground, scrabbling against the doorframe as the emergency exit swung slowly closed. He left bloody smears wherever he touched, painting crimson swaths like impressionistic sunsets across the sidewalk with his body.

The door shut, clicking against its metal frame.

The beast turned to them.

Deirdre looked calmly at it. She felt no horror at this moment, nor fear. The sheriff was just a thing, just one more obstacle standing between her and Heaven. So she calmly reloaded her gun and did her best to destroy the thing and send it back to the devilish place where it was born.

Malachi and Jenna joined her attack, their own weapons blasting at the beast's body.

Slowly, shredded muscle pulling and pushing against shattered bits of bone and cartilage, the sheriff yanked itself around. It began making its way toward them, its extremities ever-shrinking under their withering assault. Yet still it pushed to them, scraping against the ground with ruined legs.

Deirdre knew it would never stop until it was dead. When its arms and legs were gone, it would stay twitching, its trunk orienting on them. That was why they had to be so careful: death was not the end. It was just a horrifying change into something else.

The thing scraped toward them.

Malachi held up a fist, signaling them to stop. Deirdre ceased fire instantly, immediately reloading her weapons in preparation for the next conflict. Conflict was inevitable now, and would come more and more often as this longest of all nights – perhaps the beginning of an endless night for the human race – wore on.

Jenna kept firing, screaming at the tops of her lungs, yelling Todd's name over and over. Malachi pushed the barrel of her gun down, slapping her at the same time. Jenna's cries broke up jaggedly, hoarse, whispering gasps replacing them.

Malachi walked to the sheriff's still-animated corpse. He pulled out his needler, the implement he had used on Casey, and thumbed the button, triggering the spire's extension from its small housing. He jammed the spike into the base of the sheriff's neck, hitting the button again.

The sheriff's body went rigid, wisps of smoke curling from it as what was left of its brainstem fried in a curdling pool of cerebrospinal fluid and blood.

He had looked human.

But then, they all did.

Deirdre holstered her weapons and followed as Malachi reentered the front office. They pulled the door shut behind them, secreting themselves from prying eyes. She glanced out the glass window inset in the door and saw no one on the street.

"Will anyone come about the noise?" she asked.

He shook his head. "The whole town is probably closeted up in their houses. If the *Controllers*," he spit out the word like a venomous mass, "stay true to form, the whole town is going into lock-down."

"So people won't come out, but we'll have to be careful," she said, more for Jenna's benefit than for anything. The young woman looked as though she was hanging over an edge, the thin twine of her sanity acting as her only slight support.

Malachi nodded and looked like he was going to say something more, when a scream jerked his gaze to the prison door. Deirdre looked there, too, and saw Jenna, her finger pointing into the office, terror leaving ghost trails across her face.

"He's moving!" she shrieked.

Deirdre looked over and saw that Todd was indeed twitching. The twitches, she knew, would rapidly become spasms as the brain rerouted its impulses through different parts of the body. Within seconds, nerves would be regenerated, control reestablished, and life would begin. But not life as they knew it. It would be a different, frightening life with a malevolent will.

Malachi quickly walked to Todd, jammed his still-extended needler through the dead man's eye, and triggered the switch.

Todd's eye seemed to deflate. Deirdre was startled for a moment until she realized that the needle wasn't sucking up the viscous fluids of Todd's eye. Rather, the intense electrical charge that the needler funneled through the spire was cooking the eye matter, burning it to a small lump of ash that sat at the hollow of Todd's eye socket.

As always, Deirdre couldn't pull her gaze away from the grisly demise of one of the creatures. It was a child of Satan, most assuredly. Soulless, inhuman, yet so hard to kill. Only a direct hit on its brain stem or using the needler to fry its entire brain could stop it.

Sometimes not even that.

She shook her head. Humanity was at the brink.

At last Todd's body went limp, rigid muscles relaxing, this time forever.

"He wasn't – I mean, he didn't –" Jenna was babbling in the doorway, her body shaking almost as convulsively as Todd's had just a moment before.

Malachi pocketed his needler. He smiled grimly.

"No, he wasn't," he said. "He wasn't human."

Then he began slapping Jenna.

***

Malachi's hand stung. But he didn't stop with simply slapping his underling. He grabbed the girl, curling his strong hands tightly around her upper arms. He shook her, banging her against either side of the doorframe.

Jenna cried out, the pain he inflicted apparently piercing the haze of fear and hurt that she felt.

"He wasn't human," Malachi said again, and those words seemed to hurt her worse than the slap or the pummeling. He moved in closer to her, pulling her to him, switching his grip, cradling her head now with his hands, pulling her face to his. "He wasn't human," he whispered.

"But I loved him," whispered Jenna. "I thought he was real."

"Believe not all signs, my child. For Satan shall have power. Yea, even enough to deceive the very elect."

Jenna sobbed and fell against Malachi, weeping out her pain against him, as was her privilege. He was the Father, the Brother, the High Priest, the Comforter.

She pressed into him, and Malachi pressed himself into her, molding his body to hers as he whispered words of comfort. She was pleasant to look upon, unscarred and unscathed by the deadly landscape of their true home, but he was starting to think he shouldn't have let her come along. She was too flighty, too hysterical. He much preferred the quiet, deadly competence of Deirdre.

Malachi pulled Jenna even closer. His lips found her ear, and he said, "If you don't shape up I'll kill you without honor."

He felt her body stiffen in his arms as fear ran through her. It excited him, and a dull heat spread from his loins through his chest and burned dully in his heart. If he did have to kill her, he knew he would use her first, making her pleasure him in every way possible before sending her on to the next life of reward...or of pain and damnation. The choice of which realm she would inhabit in that next existence would be solely his, and that knowledge aroused him even further.

He felt *alive*.

He pulled away, looking into her eyes. The fear was still there, but she was getting it under control.

Good.

DOM#67A
LOSTON, COLORADO
AD 2013
8:10 PM MONDAY

Fran went to the door, smoothing her hair self-consciously. The bracelet Nathan had given her got caught in her hair, though, and she only ended up messing it badly.

Great.

John was late, more than an hour late, and she wasn't very pleased with that, but even so, she couldn't help but be happy that he'd arrived. She wanted to look her best.

She planned to tease him a bit, of course, couldn't let him off the hook *too* easy, but then she would quickly move to the more important business of having a good time with him.

She opened the door, and the teases died on her lips as she saw the barrel of a gun, inches away from her face.

"May I come in?" asked John.

She nodded, stunned, stepping back to allow him entry. He walked through the door, keeping the gun trained on her, dead center. He carried it like he knew what he was doing, and she had no doubt that he'd put a bullet in her head if she so much as sneezed.

"John," she managed. "What's going on?"

"I was kind of hoping you'd be able to tell *me.*"

"I don't...." The presence of the gun unnerved her. It seemed to grow larger before her eyes, the bore enveloping more and more space, quickly becoming a black hole that sucked everything into it.

She flicked her eyes to John's face, and thought she saw a trace of sympathy flash across his visage. Then it disappeared, replaced by a cold, methodical calculation.

"Sorry about the gun. I hope it's not necessary."

"Necessary? John, for God's sake, what's going on?"

"I saw this guy when I was a kid. And then almost twenty years later, in Iraq. And he hadn't changed a bit. Not one hair any grayer. I was going to talk to him, but before I got the chance, he was killed. Blown up in a helicopter."

"What does this –"

"And then I saw him again a few days ago. Very alive and still the same. After thirty years, still the same."

John stopped and waited, peering intently into Fran's eyes. She looked back at him, not exactly sure what was going on, and noticed for the first time how disheveled he looked. His clothes hung loosely on him, and his shirt was torn, a great rent that began somewhere on his lower back and continued around to his belly.

Blood stained his hands. Lots of blood. More was scattered across his shirt and some had dried on his knees, as though he had knelt in a pool of it.

She didn't know what to say so she waited. A moment later John lowered his gun. She exhaled, suddenly aware that she had been holding her breath since he entered.

"Sorry," he said. He stuck the gun in the waist of his pants. "Every other person I've told that to has gone nuts and tried to kill me."

The words, "Are you insane?" almost popped out of Fran's mouth. But then she looked at John, looked at his face and his eyes that held no madness. Fear, yes. Confusion, definitely. But they were clear of the clouds of darkness that she had seen before.

She had seen madness before, the night that Nathan died. In the eyes of the two men who had come for her, she had seen evil and madness. John's eyes held neither. So she bit back her question and exchanged it with another:

"Would you mind telling me what exactly is going on?"

***

Malachi watched as Deirdre looked through the papers that now littered the police station. They had spent the first five minutes after John escaped looking for clues of his whereabouts or anything else they might find useful. The search proved to be fairly easy; the sheriff's papers were all filed methodically and each paper was triple-indexed as though it were the most important document ever produced.

"I found his address," she said.

"No good," he responded. "He'd stay away from there. He's gone to the girl."

He glanced over at Jenna, who sat next to Todd's body, holding his hand.

"I can't find her name in the town register," said Deirdre.

"Of course not. They wouldn't be that stupid."

Next to Todd, Jenna pulled out a small book. She opened it and began reading. "Yea, though I walk through the valley of the shadow –"

Malachi's short laugh cut her off. "You can't pray over a thing like that. Not over such a monster."

Jenna's face bleached. She looked at Malachi, shock dulling her gaze. She was silent a moment, then gulped and her eyes cleared a bit as she asked, "What about me?"

"What *about* you?"

"Am I...," she nodded at Todd's body, unable to say the words.

Malachi laughed again. It was a cold sound, as devoid of warmth as a glacial cave. He brought out his gun, pointing it at Jenna. "Do you want to find out?" She waited a moment, then shook her head. "Good. Because we need you. Now get over here and help us find that devilspawn of a girl. Help us find Fran."

DOM#67A
LOSTON, COLORADO
AD 2013
8:15 PM MONDAY

In the small town of Loston, things were usually quiet. That was part of the appeal. Part of what kept people there: it was quiet. People could keep to themselves, if they liked.

Secrets could be kept.

Everyone in Loston had secrets. *Some* knew what *some* of theirs were. But nobody knew them *all*.

Tonight, though, the characteristic quiet of the town was broken by several unusual noises. Not everyone heard them, and those that did just nodded to themselves and called the noises a backfiring engine. They all knew that guns had been fired, and not for hunting, because the shots came from the middle of town. But for some reason, not a single person who heard the noises felt any inclination to investigate or even to call someone about them.

Instead, all the folks of Loston did one thing: they sat. They sat on their chairs in darkened living rooms, darkened bedrooms, darkened kitchens. All the lights in Loston were out, and the people sat in darkness.

And watched.

They looked out their windows, waiting.

***

What am I waiting for? thought Mertyl Breckman. She didn't know. She only knew somehow that she needed to sit quietly, sit tight, and watch hard. Harder than she watched over tardy students asking for a hall pass. Harder than she had ever watched anything before.

She wondered if she was watching for whoever it was she had been warned of. Several times in the last days and hours, she had heard the words flit through her mind: "Someone is coming." She did not know where the words came from, but every particle of

180

her being told her that the words were real. A warning. Had the person – the someone – at last come?

She did not know. But she would watch from her spot in front of the large window that faced onto the street. She would find out what was coming.

She had forgotten to turn on the heater before taking her place in the chair, but she didn't feel the room grow cold around her. Nor did she feel the arthritis depart her joints for the first time in fifteen years, as though her body was getting ready for something.

Changing.

She felt nothing, in fact, and in a few moments thought no more of what she was doing. She would know what to do when the moment came. Until then, she would sit, and wait, and watch.

Someone is coming.

***

The sentiment echoed in the mind of Dallas Howard, who had been glad when Kaylie didn't show up to school. That rather surprised him; when Mr. Trent had the cute new girl sit next to him on her first day at Loston High, Dallas thought he had died and gone straight to heaven. But still, when she failed to show up after that, he felt a strange relief in the pit of his stomach. It was as though her very existence was somehow wrong, and a deep-seated part of him knew it.

At the moment, though, Dallas felt neither relief nor adolescent sexual tension. He felt surprisingly little, in fact. He sat before his second floor window, looking onto the deserted street in front of their house.

He knew without being sure how that his parents were in the living room, sitting in front of the bay window, surveying the same street as he.

What am I looking for? he thought.

Someone, came the answer.

Someone is coming. Someone is here.

***

All of Loston was quiet.
They had all changed.

TWO – RESURRECTION

DOM#67A
LOSTON, COLORADO
AD 2013
8:20 PM MONDAY

John winced as Fran pulled the bandage tighter. The wound on his back had opened at some point, and blood had stained the bottom of his shirt and soaked his underpants. Fran got gauze out of a first aid kit, put anti-bacterial cream on it and rewrapped the wound as he recounted the events of the strange evening. Her movements were sure and precise, and once again John thought what an amazing woman she was. He had seen grown men swoon while preparing a field bandage for wounds less bloody than his. Not Fran. Mere blood seemed neither to deter nor to frighten her in the least.

As he told her what had happened, he felt rather than saw her shock and disbelief. And he felt something else, too, below the surface of her apparent incredulity. It was as though she didn't want to believe, but a part of her that she had locked far away couldn't help but trust his bizarre tale.

When he got to the part where the crazies mentioned her name, she jerked slightly. She put a final piece of tape on the wrap and John replaced what was left of his shirt.

"What would anyone want from me?" she asked.

"I don't know. I really hoped you would," John answered. He swiveled. He was sitting on the couch, and had turned to allow her to fix up his back. Now they sat side by side. He looked at her. Her brow furrowed in thought and concern, normally not the face a woman would make if she was trying to look her best. Even so, John felt something in the pit of his stomach, a fierce attraction to her that seemed to belie the doings of this strange and frightening night.

"No," she said at last, "I can't believe all this." But something in her eyes spoke different words. John thought what she really wanted to say was, "Please don't let this be true. I can't handle it."   And, perhaps, even lower and more well-hidden, "Again?"

He chose not to speak of what he felt, however, and instead just said, "Fran, you saw my back.   Do you think I just tripped through a window on my way to bed or something?"

"I know you were hurt, John.   But all this about people attacking you for no reason, dead people standing up and walking around...it just doesn't fly."

"Fran, I'm telling you –"

She stood and backed away from him.   "John, we had a really nice date the other night.   But that doesn't mean –"

"Yeah, we did," he said, cutting off the stream of denial he sensed was about to come from her.   He had to convince her. Beyond the matter of survival, which he felt sure would rest on both of them knowing as much as possible of what was going on around them, he couldn't bear the thought of her being afraid of him or believing he was insane.   "We had a great time.   And did I do anything crazy?"

She shook her head, slowly.   She bit her lower lip, as though she were about to cry, but John knew she wouldn't.   He sensed a strength in her that was beyond anything even the men in his unit had had.   She was a survivor.

"No," he continued.   "I didn't do anything strange at all. Fran, I'm scared.   Not just for me, but for you.   Whatever is going on, it involves you somehow, and when I heard your name, and that those bastards wanted you, the only thing I could think about was getting over here to protect you."

He stood, slowly, stepping toward her, expecting her to dart away from him like a frightened deer faced by a howling pack of starving timber wolves.

She didn't.   She stayed.

He swallowed and continued inching closer to her.   "I've never told anyone the things I told you the other night.   Not since my wife died.   Do you understand what I'm saying?"   He wanted to say more.   Crazily, he wanted to tell her he loved her.   That surprised him, and so he left the question as it was, cutting himself off before he went too far and perhaps caused her to be even more frightened than she already was.

He could see her struggling with all that he had said. "John, I don't know."

"Please, Fran." He was right in front of her now, standing close enough to touch her, and still he inched forward. "I'm frightened for you." Their breath mingled as he leaned down, eye to eye, nose to nose.

Lips to lips.

"I need more than anything for you to trust me right now," he said.

He kissed her.

For a moment she held still, as though afraid to move. Then she responded, and he felt her lips, soft and cool against his mouth. They kissed, and it lasted an eternity and at the same time was over far too quickly. The feelings John was keeping half-hidden within himself exploded through him like a life-giving spring, cooling him and buoying him up. He was happy, as he had not been for the first time since his Annie died. In spite of the blood and fear, his heart was light, and he suddenly realized how much he wanted to kiss Fran again, and to hold her forever. He suddenly felt hope.

Perhaps the night had been worth it after all.

CONTROL HQ – RUSHM
AD 4013/AE 2013

Adam's guts constricted inside him, a coiled mass of tension tied in a Gordian knot.

What do you do when the fate of the world sits on your shoulders? he thought, and not for the first time in his tenure as a Controller. As always, the only answer that presented itself was that he should keep doing his best. Press forward, he thought. Press forward and do the best you can, Adam. Hopefully God will pick up the slack.

He watched the screens on the wall, each showing a different view of the strangely deserted streets of Loston. Two of the screens held no picture. Only a word: OFFLINE.

Jason watched the screens with him. Slightly behind him and to the right stood Sheila, Jason's wife. Not many Controllers married, because of the emotional threat involved. But Jason had elected to marry Sheila, and though Adam disapproved of the decision itself, he certainly approved of Jason's choice in mates.

Light brown hair that held itself in tight curls against her pixie's face served to emphasize her slight frame, but Sheila was a strong-willed woman. And not just strong, but happy, a characteristic in short supply among the Controllers. Sheila often had the power to light up an entire room with the brightness she exuded, but was still a damn fine Controller when the time came, methodical and efficient.

Tonight she didn't light up the room. Her expression was dark as a deep midnight sea.

"What are we going to do?" she asked.

That was the very question that had been troubling Adam, and still no answer had emerged from his self-doubt. "If I send in a recovery squad, the entire town will have to be shut down," he mused aloud. "But if not, the Fans might get her before she's safe."

"We can afford to shut down the town," said Jason. "If it's a question of her or them, I think you should terminate all of them, go in and wipe out the Fans, then –"

"At least one of the Fans is human, too," said Adam. "Confirmed."

Both Jason and Sheila paled.

"Goddammit," whispered Sheila. Usually the blasphemy would have brought a swift scolding from Adam. Not tonight. "Who?"

"Malachi."

"And he'll know what we're going to do, too," said Jason.

"If we stick to procedure," said Adam. He watched the screens intently, along with several dozen other Controllers, awakened in the middle of their sleep-cycles just for this. No one spied any movement. All of Loston was waiting, and that should make it easier to find anything that was out and about in the suddenly silent town. But still there was nothing.

"What else can we do?" asked Jason.

Adam sighed. "We wait. As soon as we can pick her up without anyone in the dome detecting it, we'll go in. Otherwise we run the risk of a full Activation and a bloodbath. Not to mention the fact that if Malachi somehow sees us go in, that increases the chances of his tracking us here on the return trip." Adam did not have to remind his people what such a discovery would mean. That was one of the ever-present threats that every Controller was aware of.

"I'll get a crew and a jet ready," said Sheila. She kissed Jason's cheek and disappeared from the control room.

"Jason, I want a story put out on John."

"Where?"

"All media. Tell them he's a dangerous criminal. That'll keep him running with Fran. And maybe we can protect the minds of any bits he contacts. If they're afraid of him maybe they won't give him a chance to talk." Adam did not know how much of the truth that John may have figured out in the last few days. Probably not much, but even his suspicions might prove deadly to the people of Loston, if he was allowed to share them. So Adam needed a way to keep John isolated; to keep him from talking. The general media alert, sent through the town, seemed the best way to accomplish this, though it was not without its risks.

Jason concurred, nodding his head and gesturing to several other Controllers to begin that process. But he also said, "They might try to kill him, though, if they think he's crazy."

Adam sighed. Too many things could go wrong. "Hopefully they won't succeed."

DOM#67A
LOSTON, COLORADO
AD 2013
8:30 PM MONDAY

Malachi threw the papers down on the sheriff's desk. Several of them fluttered down to the floor, where the remains of Tal Johnson and of Todd lay. "You two are useless!" he screamed. Spittle flecked his lips, and he felt himself losing control.

This would never have happened when I was a Controller, he thought. Such emotional outbursts were coming more frequently though, and he wondered if he was going mad, even as he struggled to get himself back under control; to rein in his murderous rage. Madness was inevitable, he knew. The barren wastelands of his home were so irradiated that eventually everyone went insane. But that could not happen to him now.

Not now, not with the end so close.

Jenna cowered visibly at his outburst, and even Deirdre, stolid and immovable as flint, seemed to shrink in upon herself. Malachi smiled a bit at the sight. The fear of others had always had a calming effect on him.

"What do you want us to do?" asked Jenna.

Malachi opened his mouth to answer, but suddenly the TV came on. So did the radio. He heard another radio playing in the prison.

"This just in," began the TV reporter.

Malachi watched the newscast and smiled. He knew what the newscasts meant; knew that it would be dangerous to go out now, looking for John and Fran. But he wouldn't have to go looking. Someone would bring them to him. He knew that Adam and the other Controllers had co-opted the town media to send out a primitive alert, telling everyone in the town that there was a dangerous criminal in their midst. Sooner or later Adam's plan was sure to bear fruit. Someone would spot John or Fran.

And what would such a concerned citizen do? Call the sheriff, of course.

Malachi smiled, then sat down next to the phone and waited for the call.

***

Gabe lived just down the street, but Fran automatically went to her car. She was from Los Angeles, and no one went *anywhere* on foot in that city. Whether the travel was six feet or six miles, the car was the preferred – and sometimes it seemed like the only – method of transportation in the city of angels. Like most inhabitants of the metropolitan, Fran despised the congested traffic of the city. But like most of her fellow Angelinos, she rarely thought to walk, as though acceptance by the city came only after a promise to travel exclusively by car.

John stopped her, though.

"No," he said. "Let's walk."

She looked at him quizzically, then shrugged and nodded. It had been hard enough just getting John to agree to go to her cousin, though she knew he and Gabe were best friends.

When she had broached the subject of going to the coach for help, John shook his head. "I don't want to," he said.

"We have to let him know what's going on. Maybe he's noticed something, too."

"Besides, that way I'll have another person vouching for your sanity" were the words she *didn't* say, but both of them heard them, nonetheless.

Still, John wasn't going easily. "What if he turns on me, too?"

"He's my cousin, John. And I didn't do anything to you. Mental health is a genetic ailment that runs in my family."

So he agreed. But Fran didn't want to push her luck by insisting on driving, so now they were walking behind the four or five houses – spread out liberally across an area that in LA would have held several dozen – that separated her home from Gabe's.

Even in the midst of the dark night, even avoiding lights and sticking to the shadows that draped thickly over the Colorado landscape, Fran still had to marvel at the beauty of this place. Thick foliage sprouted from every available surface, evergreens predominating, sending their needled fingers high into the thin mountain air. They seemed to guard the landscape, subtly imposing yet also somehow comforting, conjuring up childhood images of Yuletide and fireplaces in the snow.

Below the trees, the ground was thick with grass and shrubs. It crackled softly underfoot as Fran moved forward, creating a pleasantly whispering noise that would have soothed her in other circumstances. Unfortunately, however, she was not on a nature hike. She was following a man who clearly feared for his life, though whether he was right to do so she could not yet say. She knew that she had strong feelings for John. They were surprisingly strong, in fact, considering the short amount of time they had spent together. But she had not felt such an instant kinship with anyone before. Perhaps not even Nathan, though she had loved him almost from the first moment they met. Did she love John? That was a question that she dared not answer. Not until she knew what was going on tonight. Not until she understood for herself what was making him so afraid; so furtive as he hugged the shadows and almost disappeared into the night.

That in itself was a skill that surprised her. John seemed to become little more than a shadow himself at times. He moved with a silence and ease that was almost spooky. Where Fran's footfalls crackled and whispered as she stepped through grass and mulch, John's movements could be followed only by sight. If she had closed her eyes, she could not have pinpointed his location. Even with her eyes open, she was hard-pressed at times to keep up with him. He was little more than a specter in the night, and as elusive and ethereal as any ghost. Though a city girl, Fran was aware that not everyone from the country could walk so silently through the night. John's movements spoke of skill and training. She wondered where he had learned to walk like that, and what other secrets this man might hold.

About three-quarters of the way to Gabe's house, John dropped suddenly to the ground, yanking Fran down with him.

"John, what's –"

He cut her off with a finger to his lips. His eyes momentarily studied the house nearest them. Then he peered behind him, glancing at the other homes they had passed and the two or three still between them and Gabe's place.

"See that?" he asked, pointing at the house next to them.

"I don't see anything. It's dark."

"Exactly. They're *all* dark."

She looked around. He was right. "So, maybe they're all gone. Or asleep." She knew it sounded weak, and didn't believe it herself. Everyone on the same street gone? Where? There was no place to go *to* in Loston. Not at this time of night. Yet it was still too early for bed. Lights should have been on, sounds coming from the homes, perhaps even kids playing in lit yards. Instead, there was nothing. "Maybe just gone," she repeated quietly.

"No," whispered John. "They're in there."

"Why would they be sitting in dark houses?"

"Because if it's light inside you can't see out the windows."

Fran looked at him in disbelief.

John nodded. "They're looking for us."

He began edging farther away from the houses, staying low, heading for a small line of trees that ran most of the rest of the way to Gabe's house.

Fran wanted to laugh. She wanted to laugh and stand up and tell John he was being ridiculous. But she didn't. Because she knew he was right. Something inside her knew that the silent houses were not empty, but filled with vigilantly attentive people. Watchers. How she knew this she could not say, but she knew. Undeniably and indisputably, she knew. She *was* being watched.

Hunted.

The night, comforting and lovely just a moment ago, turned suddenly dreadful and weird, a lovecraftian landscape of hidden monstrosities. The trees were no longer guardians, but sentries, striving to divine her location and give her away to those who hunted her. The mulch that had whispered below her feet now seemed to shriek in pain, much too loud to be missed. Surely someone must have heard that, she thought with every step. Surely someone will come. Someone will find us.

They stayed in the trees the rest of the way, moving to Gabe's house furtively, and the urge to laugh suddenly seized Fran, in spite of – or perhaps because of – the fear that still touched her neck with its icy talons. It was all so like a movie, the hero and heroine making their way slowly to the safe house, staying in the trees, hunched over to provide small targets.

The trees, gnarled and bent with the passing centuries, crowded around them. She remembered a movie, a scene from the Disney version of *Alice in Wonderland* where Alice got lost in a forest and saw strange creatures. To most, she supposed, the movie was meant to be amusing, a playful romp through a child's imagination. To Fran, however, the whole movie had been an exercise in quiet insanity. And when Alice got lost in that strange, pastel-colored forest, Fran cried until her parents took her from the theater.

The thought was juvenile, and again Fran wanted to laugh, but a part of her also wanted to scream. To shriek until the fear she suddenly felt went away, driven out by sound.

She bit her tongue, and also bit down the hysteria that threatened to overtake her. It was all so like a movie. But she knew that this wasn't mere cinema. John's story was too much like hers. Too much like what had happened to Nathan, on that frightening evening years ago.

What was happening was real, and to take the night lightly would mean death.

So she played her part, and lamented that in this instance, the hero and the heroine had no guarantee of living through to the final credits. Indeed, if what John said were true, the chances of survival were slim.

And *was* what he had said true? she thought. How could it be? What was going on?

Fran felt John's hand on hers, and he tugged her in a different direction.

"Come on," he whispered.

She realized that, submersed as she was in her thoughts, she hadn't realized their approach had ended: Gabe's backyard lay before them.

They went to the house. Like the others on the street, it was black within: a looming beast with darkened eyes. The family homestead, so convivial and inviting when she had seen it before, now loomed before them and evoked fear and dread.

John went to the side door. He hesitated a moment, then knocked on a nearby window. Even to Fran, the sound seemed strangely hollow, as though the sound waves vibrated not against air, but against some thinner version: something that carried nearly all the characteristics of the real thing, but wasn't *quite* exact. But even though the noise was hollow, it seemed far too loud.

Again she thought, Surely someone heard that. They're going to find us.

Don't do it! she wanted to scream. *Don't let him know we're out here!* If she could have turned back the clock in that instant, she would have. She would have changed her mind and urged that John *not* go to her cousin. She didn't know where she would have gone instead, but she felt a presentiment of doom that could not be dispelled by her cousin's familiar abode. She looked at John, and the starlight glinting from above shadowed his face strangely. He looked like a hollow-eyed cadaver, she realized, and again felt that sense of fearful destiny.

She was gripped by the belief – no, by the utter assurance – that John was going to die.

Then the doorknob twisted, and a dark form lurched out from the blackness within the house.

DOM#67A
LOSTON, COLORADO
AD 2013
8:45 PM MONDAY

Fran's cry of fear startled John. But it was no monster who lurched at them. Fran's cousin stood in the doorway. The room behind him was dark and forbidding, a deep pool of black where nothing could be seen. The darkness shadowed Gabe's face, making it hard to see his features. Still, John thought Fran should have known it would be Gabe standing in the doorway; should have realized that there was nothing to fear.

Unless she was starting to believe that John was right, and there really *was* something to be truly, deeply afraid of.

Gabe looked at them, his eyes catching bits of moonlight and reflecting them, miniature stars in the deep night of his eye sockets. For a moment John thought that Gabe didn't recognize them: he looked slightly dazed and disoriented. He blinked rapidly, as though casting off the lingering cobwebs of sleep, and seemed somehow unsure.

Different.

Then the look changed and Gabe's characteristic smile spread across his wide face. "John. Franny. What are you doing here?" John shrugged. Gabe's smile disappeared. He looked more closely at them, at John's bloodstained clothing and Fran's worried eyes. "What's up, folks? You okay?"

"We've had better days, Gabe," said John.

Gabe stepped into the house, motioning them to follow him in. After a moment's hesitation, John did so, still holding Fran's hand. It felt good that she was there with him. It felt *right*.

Or as right as anything could feel on this night where nothing was as it should be.

The room they entered was the laundry room. It wasn't odd for houses in Loston to have such rooms, nor was it odd for them to be dark when no one was in them. John did find it odd, though, that Gabe had answered the door without switching on a single light.

When they stepped from the laundry room to the hall, there was still no light. The entire house was dark, as had been all the other homes they had passed. The darkness pressed on John, weighing him down like one of his frequent nightmares. Only he knew he was not dreaming; whatever this night held, it was all too real. He could see shadowy forms through doorways and halls, dark outlines that he knew were just bookshelves and appliances, but that still filled him with dread and foreboding.

John forced a smile. "Why the gloom and doom, Gabe?" he said, trying to keep his voice casual.

"Just watching TV in the living room," Gabe answered. "Helluva news story on tonight." He laughed, but the sound was devoid of warmth. His voice was strained, as though he was trying desperately to seem normal through forced jocularity.

As Gabe had indicated, when John and Fran entered the living room, the TV was playing soundlessly. TV reporters gesticulated wildly as they spoke, and several police liaisons came onscreen as well. Whatever was going on, it seemed it was, as Gabe had said, a "helluva story." But no matter how strange, tragic, and frightening that story was, John knew it would not even come close to the events in *his* life that evening.

Helluva story.

Gabe shut off the TV, and for a moment they were all pitched into darkness. John tensed, and he felt Fran's hand tighten on his own. Then the lights came up as the coach found a light switch and flicked it on.

"Cop a squat," said Gabe, gesturing at the couch.

Though he had spent several years with a daughter in the house, before her life was claimed by those crazies from California, Gabe's home had been and continued to be the epitome of bachelorhood in the mountains. The furnishings consisted of a couch, a loveseat, and a La-Z-Boy recliner, all done in the same deep shade of red. Sports calendars rested on every vertical surface, placed between rifles and hunting trophies that hung from the walls. The entire space was festooned with signature proofs of virility and manhood, almost to the point of overkill.

Still, John usually felt at home in the place. It was the house of his best friend, and countless hours had been spent shooting darts at the board or playing pool in the basement. Tonight, however, nothing made John feel at home. He felt disoriented and dazed.

Fran, seeming to sense his discomfiture, squeezed his hand encouragingly. Bless her, he thought. She might not believe him entirely, but that didn't mean she wasn't going to encourage him and try to keep him from being on edge.

Gabe waited until John and Fran settled, then said, "I've got some food in the oven I've gotta take out. You want anything?"

John and Fran shook their heads, and the big, solidly-built man ambled through the kitchen door, which swung open on well-oiled hinges, then fell shut behind him. The whisper of the door was loud in the quiet room. The noise gave John the chills, and he shuddered.

"See?" said Fran. "I told you normalcy runs in my family."

John nodded, but wasn't convinced. He had glimpsed the kitchen as the door swung open, and the sight did little to encourage him. It wasn't unlike his friend to be cooking – Gabe was a fine cook, able to wield a spatula with the same finesse he exhibited with his treasured whistle.

But still, John understood that when people were cooking, most of them turned on the lights.

***

The phone rang. Malachi picked up the receiver.

"Hullo?" he said, and sniffled. Deirdre knew immediately what he was doing. To a friend of the people who worked in the sheriff's station, Malachi's voice might be unfamiliar, and therefore suspicious. But if he had a cold, the caller would expect his voice to be different than usual. "No, Tal's home heavin' his guts out," Malachi said thickly. Deirdre admired his performance. He sounded as though he really *were* sick. "Well, who de hell do you think it is?" he asked. A pause, then, "Yub, id's Bill. Hode on." He blew his nose loudly next to the receiver. "Oh, I got a cold. What can I do you for?" Malachi listened a moment. "Really? Well, you just keep on doin' what you're doin', and I'll be there in a few.... Right.... Just stay calm.... We'll take care of everything."

He hung up and smiled at the two women.

"What?" asked Jenna.

"Once again, the Controllers have completely stuck to their program."

He picked up his gun and headed to the door, grabbing the keys to one of the police cruisers off a board on the wall.

***

John and Fran were still alone. Even Fran, obviously determined to believe that everything was all right here, that her cousin was going to help them, had a frown tugging at the corners of her mouth.

"Hey, Gabe?" John called out.

"Yeah?" came the coach's voice from the kitchen.

"What are you cooking?"

"Just some bread."

"Come to think of it, I am a bit hungry. Can I have some?"

A long silence greeted his question. Fran looked at him. Her eyebrow cocked, and John could see she was surprised at his hunger. But he wasn't hungry in the least. Just trying to find out if Gabe was actually cooking anything at all. Somehow, he doubted that there was any kind of culinary activity going on in the coach's dark kitchen.

The kitchen door swung open again and Gabe reentered the living room, still wearing a jovial smile.

The smile seemed forced.

"Sorry, John. Looks like I burned it. You know how I am with food." He laughed, and John managed a chuckle. Fran smiled a wan smile that grew tighter with every second. John didn't know why, but he was convinced that Gabe was playing a part of some kind. He felt like he was a lackadaisical understudy in a play, only half-sure what was going on around him and completely in the dark about what his next line was supposed to be.

"So how was your night on the town tonight?" Gabe asked, sinking stiffly into the La-Z-Boy.

John tried to appear relaxed, to put Gabe at ease. Whatever was going on here, the coach seemed to have some part in it, and John didn't want to spook his friend. Keep calm, keep cool, and find out what was going on. That was all he wanted right now.

"Well, Gabriel," said Fran, "that's what we came to ask about –"

"You know Gabe," John cut in. "I don't think I'd mind burnt bread. I'm pretty hungry."

Gabe straightened up again. "Oh, you'd mind this stuff. I turned it to charcoal." Gabe turned back to the kitchen. "But I've got some Wonder bread in the fridge. You want me to make you a sandwich?"

John's voice halted Gabe at the door.

"How come it doesn't smell like burnt bread in here?" he asked quietly.

Gabe stood still a moment, then spun suddenly. He grabbed a rifle off the wall and aimed it in a sinuous motion that John knew came from long hours hunting in the woods. While waiting in a deer blind or hunched in some brush, a good hunter had to be able to go from complete silence with his gun at rest to full aim and fire in only a fraction of a second. Gabe was an excellent hunter.

He was also a crack shot. Whatever he aimed at, he hit.

"Gabe!" screamed Fran. "What are you –"

"You just ease away from him, Franny," said Gabe. John saw that the rifle was aimed at his head. Not a shotgun, so Gabe wouldn't worry about hitting Fran if he had to shoot it, but the bullet would still blow John's whole head off at this range. "Come over here where it's safe."

"Don't do it, Fran," said John. He put his arm around her.

Gabe cocked the rifle. "Don't touch her, John. I mean it."

John slowly pulled his arm back.

"What are you doing, Gabriel?" asked Fran. She looked back and forth between the two men. John sympathized with her confusion. Another layer of madness had been added to the already insane night. He himself would have been hard-pressed to maintain his calm in such a situation, and again he admired her apparent fortitude.

When it became obvious that Fran wasn't going to move, Gabe seemed to weigh his options, trying to divine some way of getting his cousin away from John. At last, he slowly moved to the TV set in the corner of the room. He kept the rifle aimed at John, but he reached behind him with one hand and flicked on the television, then had the hand back on the rifle barrel in a flash, so that John had no chance to move without being killed.

The TV came on, a white pinlight appearing in the center of the screen that rapidly expanded and took shape. Whatever news report had been playing before was still going strong, and a lanky journalist was now onscreen. "...Once again, reports are flooding in from three different counties. No one knows what caused the murder spree, we only know that its effects have been terrible and widely felt."

The news anchor spoke with professional detachment, but John felt a very real nervousness under the man's cool exterior, as though something extremely horrifying had happened. The dread that had been with him since he first saw Devorough now rose again, rearing up and pawing at John's throat with icy claws.

"The death toll has reached seventeen," the reporter continued, "in the wake of two shocking attacks over the last day and a half. Reports are still unclear, but several eyewitnesses have identified John Trent –" John jumped. Fran glanced at him, then turned back to the set. "– a teacher at Loston High School, as the man responsible for the shootings."

Behind the newsman, a pair of coroners pushed a body by on a stretcher. The man on it had a blank gaze and gaping mouth that John had seen too often: the stare of the dead.

"The cabbie," Fran breathed.

"What?" asked John.

She turned to look at him, and John saw that she was afraid. Not just of what might be going on, she was afraid of him, and that knowledge worried him more than all the events of the night.

"The man who picked me up at the airport. "

On the TV, a picture of John with his squad filled the frame. "Trent, an ex-Green Beret, is considered highly dangerous. Police are urging anyone who comes in contact with him to avoid confronting or even so much as speaking to him."

A new face now appeared on the screen, a strong-jawed man in an army uniform. "Men like Trent are trained not only to use their weapons, but their words. Even talking to such a man could prove fatal."

Gabriel shut off the television. Once again, he motioned with the gun. "Now why don't you just move away, Franny."

John was aghast. He had no idea what was happening. Of course, the whole night had gone on without him understanding one whit of it, but this new development shocked him in a way he couldn't fully comprehend. To be implicated in what were apparently a set of violent murders....

He looked at Fran, who still gazed at him with fearful eyes. She was tough, he knew, but he didn't know how much more of this she would be able to deal with. "Fran," he said. "I didn't –"

Gabe interrupted. "You say one more word and I'll kill you right now."

John looked at him. He saw his friend meant it. He knew that Gabe was rattled; shaken. But he also saw determination there and he realized that he faced death now at the hands of his best friend.

He stared into his lap, trying frantically to figure out some way to talk to his friend. He desperately needed to explain things to Gabe.

He did not know what was happening, but he knew that he had just seen a classic example of government propaganda on the television. To put out a false news story, with that many people involved, spoke of a high level of government involvement. Probably federal. John had seen that kind of thing before, during counterintelligence training. If you had a cooperative media, putting out a false story could get quick results when you wanted to apprehend someone. John had no idea what was going on or what he might know, but to tell Gabe might only implicate the man.

Flashing lights illuminated the windows behind Gabe then, whirling pinwheels of red and blue that signaled the arrival of the police.

A car door opened and shut outside. Another. And then a third.

John tensed. He knew who was outside, and it wasn't the police. Gabe must have phoned the sheriff's office when he went into the kitchen. And of course he would not have reached Tal, who had been splashed all over the interior of the prison block. No, it would have been the others.

It would have been *them*.

Gabe moved to the door, keeping his rifle trained on John. Fran continued looking back and forth between the two men, torn between whom to believe but obviously leaning toward Gabe's story.

"I called the police from the kitchen," said Gabe as he moved to the door.

"Gabe," said John, reaching out for him, "don't –"

"Shut up! I want to believe you, John, but right is right and I had to call 'em."

"Don't go to the door, Gabe."

"If you're innocent, we'll clear this all up in a jif."

He reached behind him.

Touched the doorknob.

"Gabe, *don't touch the –*"

Gabe turned the knob.

Shots punched through the door, knocking fist-sized holes in the thick wood of the door and its frame. The shots took Gabe in the chest and head, pulping him. He sunk to his knees, then went facedown on the floor.

Before Gabe had time to fall, John had already grabbed Fran and pushed her over the back of the couch, hunching over her cowering form as the shots continued, this time peppering the front window.

Fran screamed as two shots slammed through the couch, narrowly missing her and John. Stuffing floated down around them like feathers before settling to the floor. The red couch fabric mixed with the stuffing, and John thought it looked like bloody popcorn.

A pause came in the firing. Fran started to move, but John pressed her back down. "No," he said. "They're reloading."

Sure enough, a moment later more shots blitzed the front room. John listened to the shots, concentrating, trying to pinpoint the number of shooters and their locations. It was hard in this confined space, the thunderous sound of the gunfire bouncing off the walls and fixtures, creating twisted echoes that inhibited any sense of direction.

Another pause came in the firing. John looked at Fran. She was biting her lip, trying not to scream.

"Only two people are shooting," he told her. "The third is probably circling around back. Next pause, you run up the stairs as fast as you can. Understand?"

She said something, but her answer was drowned out by a storm of bullets shattering the rest of the room. She nodded through the melee, and John kissed her on the forehead.

The gunfire ceased, and Fran sprang for the stairs. At the same moment, John screamed. "Oh, God," he cried. "My arms, *my arms*! Please, God!" His terror and agony sheared through the momentary still.

DOM#67A
LOSTON, COLORADO
AD 2013
8:49 PM MONDAY

Fran stopped in the dark stairwell as John continued screaming. She was terrified for him, as he had evidently been shot. But she was also confused: in spite of the fearsome sounds of agony he was making, she could not see any wounds on him. He didn't *look* as though he'd been hit.

He kept screaming, but waved her up the stairs.

Then she understood.

He was faking it, luring them into complacency with his apparent injury. And doing a good job of it, too. She could hardly believe he hadn't had his arms blown off at the shoulders, the way he was shrieking.

He waved at her again, and she turned back to the stairwell. Before she completed her rotation, though, she spotted Gabriel.

Her cousin lay face down in a pool of what looked like gallons of his own blood. She saw the mangled meat of the entry wounds in his back and neck and head, and almost lost control of herself.

"Gabe," she whispered. The sound was drowned out by John's agonized screeching and the pounding swell of blood that crashed and coursed through her ears. She could hear her heartbeat, like rhythmic mortar fire, and that was what convinced her, more than anything, that this was real. She had toyed with the idea that perhaps this was all a dream. That maybe she was just asleep on the plane to Loston. That she had never met anyone named John, and all this would turn out to be just a nightmare.

But in nightmares, you couldn't hear the sound of your own blood, moving with adrenalized speed through your body. No, this was all real. It was terribly real, and her cousin was dead.

Gabe moved.

Fran gasped, then stepped toward him. He was moving, crawling inch by painful inch toward her.

John saw her move and, still howling, sprang to his feet. He grabbed by the arms and ran her to the stairs, practically hurling her up the first three. She hit her knee hard on one of the steps, bruising it badly. She did not cry out, though, too frightened even to scream.

"Go or die!" whispered John in between his shouts of panicked agony, and then turned away without waiting for her reply.

Fran looked up the stairs. It was dark above and she was afraid. Afraid again. Like that night so many years ago. Nathan had died, and she had almost died as well. But she had survived, and more than anything had been comforted by the fact that such terror could never visit her again. But it *had* come again. The terror was back.

And once more, as she had the night Nathan was killed, Fran found herself running for her life.

***

John resumed his position, hunched behind the couch. He screamed a moment longer, then let the cries peter out into a sustained whimper. It would sound as though he was losing strength, further adding to their attackers' confidence. Besides, a whimper would be harder to pinpoint.

He crouched, ready to move in a nanosecond, splitting his attention between the front door, the kitchen door that opened nearby, and the hall entry through which he and Fran had entered.

The kitchen was where the woman came in, and John almost didn't see it, because the second before the door swung open a noise distracted him, a rasping sound that John had heard before. The noise sent a chill through his body, and he almost convulsed with the force of his sudden terror. The noise that frightened him so was the same he had heard at the sheriff's station. It was the noise he had heard when Tal began crawling toward him. It was the noise of a dead man moving.

Gabe. John could hear his dead friend was crawling toward him, pulling his way over the hardwood floors, clawlike fingers scrabbling for purchase on the slick surface. The rasping noise distracted him, and for a moment he forgot his training, forgot everything but that noise. He was, for a moment, transported back to the day his father died. He heard that noise, then, as well. The noise of a dead man moving.

Then the kitchen door swung quietly inward, pushed open by the long barrel of a shotgun. The momentary glimpse into his past was forgotten as he hurled himself at the door, smashing it into the gun and his attacker's fingers. He heard the woman cry as two of her fingers snapped between the door and the warm metal of the shotgun. The door swung open wider as John grabbed the barrel of the weapon. It was the blonde girl, still howling but holding onto the gun with a death grip.

John yanked the gun, pulling her into the room with him, and at that moment heard the door kick in behind him.

He was a Green Beret, had been very good at his job, and had little doubt that he could take the girl in a one-on-one confrontation. But this wasn't a movie. One more person at his back would quickly finish him off.

***

Malachi leveled his weapon at John, waiting for a cleaner angle. He didn't give a damn if he hit Jenna or not, but he wanted to be sure to finish the man off in one shot. He wanted to be sure he blew John's head off.

Malachi waited a fraction of a second longer...there!

He pulled the trigger.

But at that precise moment, he felt a hand – strong, painfully strong – grip his leg and then yank it out from under him.

The shot went wide, plowing into and through the wall about a foot from John's head. Plaster and wood erupted from the target, raining splinters down on everyone nearby. A shard hit Malachi in the cheek, bloodying it slightly, but he had no time to notice the pain or wipe his face. Still being yanked about by the strong hand that had caused him to miss his shot, Malachi teetered for an instant. He saw John continue fighting with Jenna for the shotgun, then he lost his balance and fell on his back.

The man they'd shot – undoubtedly Gabriel, the man who had called the sheriff's office – leered down at Malachi, his face three-quarters destroyed, a tangled mass of flesh held together by gristle and bone and partially-torn cartilage.

The monster's undead hands encircled Malachi's throat and began to twist and pull. Malachi felt the blood flow cut off and almost immediately grew woozy.

Then the beast stopped.

It pulled its hands away as though recognizing its master, for so it did. Malachi smiled at what remained of Gabriel Harding's face.

Malachi could not be harmed by the monsters. Could not be killed by those undead. He was elect, and he was protected by a divine right locked into his genetic makeup.

His smile widened when Deirdre entered the room.

She quickly sized up the situation and strode to where the creature still knelt over Malachi, its ruined mouth opened in a forever scream of sudden understanding as to what it truly was. Deirdre did not wait for Malachi's orders. She put her shotgun against the creature's temple and blew its head off.

***

John saw Malachi pulled down and felt the shot pass wide over his shoulder and slam into the wall. But he had no time to marvel at his good fortune or to cheer the evil man's fall. The woman he faced demanded all his attention, fighting with venomous zeal and horrendous ferocity. What she apparently lacked in formal combat training she made up for in energy, and John had to put his all into the pressing task of staying alive.

The woman rocketed her knee into John's crotch, trying to cripple him. John sensed the attack before it came and pitched his pelvis forward. The move shifted his anatomy slightly, moving his testes out of harm's way so when her knee hit him it missed his genitalia. The attack bruised him, smashing painfully against the back of his crotch and jarring his already tender tailbone, but wasn't the crippling hit it would have been had she caught him square on.

He wilted, though, as if she had connected perfectly, then in the next moment straightened again, driving her shotgun into her chin. Her head snapped back, knocking into the wall behind her, and her fingers loosened on the gun.

John yanked the weapon away from her and planted the stock firmly in her gut. He heard the air whoosh out of her lungs as her diaphragm was crushed backward with the force of his blow. She fell, the wind knocked out of her and perhaps sporting a few broken ribs, and then John turned to the scene behind him.

Gabe – moving again, moving like Tal, moving though clearly dead – lay across Malachi's chest, staring into the madman's eyes. For a moment it looked like Gabe – or the thing Gabe had become – was going to kill Malachi. Then he stopped moving, suddenly frozen in place and apparently unable to continue his attack.

Malachi smiled.

John didn't know what was going on, but he wasn't about to stay and find out. He turned to the inky stairwell and ran up, hoping to find Fran and a way to escape from this deathtrap. Before he could move, though, he felt the shotgun pulled from his grasp. The woman, crumpled below him, had torn it away from him. She aimed it at him, but he kicked the shotgun hard, knocking it from her grasp. She cried out as the gun flew out of her hand, and John hoped he had broken her fingers.

He snatched another rifle off the wall next to him, knowing that Gabe kept the weapons loaded in case of intrusion, then hurried up the stairs without looking behind him.

He heard a shot. The noise made him jump and look at himself, half expecting to see blood pouring from a massive exit wound in his chest or stomach.

Nothing. The shot either went wide or was meant for a different target. And he had to get to Fran. She stood at the top of the stairs, peering down at him from the darkness. If he'd been one of their attackers, she would be dead right now, he thought. But what did he expect? She had no special training, no preparation for this kind of action. When he thought of it, he was amazed at her ability to get through this as well as she had.

He pulled her away from the steps, moving down the dark hall to Gabe's bedroom, passing several doors on either side.

"What happened?" asked Fran. She was trying to be tough, but John saw tears glisten behind her eyes. "What happened down there?"

John didn't answer.

"Where's Gabriel?"

Her voice was small, so pitiful that John went against his instincts and took the time to answer: "He's dead.

Now Fran started crying. John shook her. Gently, he didn't want to hurt her, but hard enough that she looked at him. He spoke quickly, intensely, still edging them toward the master bedroom.

"I'm sorry," he said, "but we don't have time for that right now."

"This is just like before," she said, and for a moment John worried that she was going to go catatonic on him, forcing him either to leave her, which would be unthinkable, or to carry her, which would be undoable while fighting his way through crazies and people who turned into zombies.

She quickly shook herself out of it, though, walking with him to the master bedroom. As soon as she was through the door, he swung it closed behind them. It shut silently, but with a grim and disturbing finality, like the door of a tomb sliding shut with not even a last whisper of comfort for the dead.

***

Malachi looked up the stairwell, searching for movement. Deirdre stood directly behind him, her pant legs stained from the knees down with Gabriel's blood and brains.

Behind her stood Jenna, checking to see if her secondary gun – a powerful Magnum – was loaded. Blood dripped steadily from her mouth, down her chin, and onto the floor. The bright red of the blood contrasted starkly with her pale complexion and blonde hair. She looked like a vampire, a devil that had just fed and yet still hungered. A strange kind of toothless vampire, though. Malachi could tell from the way her lip hung that most of her teeth had been smashed out of her mouth.

"Jenna, cover the front. Deirdre, go around back. I'm going to go up and either kill them or flush them out to you."

The women nodded, quietly exiting the house.

Malachi started up the stairs.

***

John looked around the room, trying to spot anything that might help them. He left the lights off, though, so as not to give away their position in an otherwise darkened house. That made seeing a bit difficult, but he could make out enough to start thinking of a way to escape this waking nightmare.

The room was decorated the same as the living room: trophies, calendars, and a preponderance of red. No guns, though. In their place, Gabe had chosen to hang a pair of old-fashioned railroad conductors' lamps on two of the walls. Before flashlights, the conductors had used the red kerosene lanterns to warn oncoming engines to reduce their speed or that a track change was coming up. Two of those antique warning lights now hung from the walls of the dead man's home, ancient but still useable. Unfortunately, John didn't see any immediate need for a warning signal. He was already all too aware that he and Fran were in grave danger, and did not think lighting a lamp to commemorate that fact would do much in the way of getting them out of peril.

John didn't see anything that looked immediately useful. He knew that an eave extended about three feet around the outside of the house between the first and second floor. If they could get to it, they would be able to jump safely to the ground and run away. He moved to the bedroom window, hoping that their attackers were all inside looking for them. But as soon as he approached the window a shot blasted the windowpane to splinters. He quickly ducked and moved to the back of the room, near Fran. He assumed that there were still just the three remaining people after him, Malachi and his insane harem, but he didn't know for sure. It was entirely possible that they could have sent for reinforcements who were waiting outside for them. Either way, he and Fran couldn't get out the window without being killed.

Who are these people? John pondered as he looked around the room. The planted story in the news indicated some level of government involvement. So maybe the attackers were black ops agents. John didn't think so, however. They were too uncoordinated. And Malachi didn't look like someone that the military would use for anything but target practice. Unstable, clearly insane.

Still, John knew the government must be involved in some way. They had to be; that was the only explanation for the bogus news story and the APB that was certainly circulating among nearby law enforcement officials. But he had no idea what it was he could have done that would warrant Uncle Sam's sudden interest. Maybe it had something to do with Fran.

That would make sense. There was no denying that Malachi's group was after her for some reason, and it would be too much of a stretch to think that the government's involvement was with regard to an unrelated matter. However, when he had pressed her for answers she hadn't been able to give him any. He had sensed at several times in the evening that she was hiding something, though whether she hid it from him alone or from herself as well he could not be certain. Still, he was sure that whatever it was, her knowledge did not extend to an understanding of why they were being pursued.

He glanced at Fran to see how she was holding up. Her complexion was still pasty, but she gave him a thumbs-up.

He smiled back, and wished he felt half as confident as he was trying to look. He still had not managed to find anything that might help them escape. No hope filled him, only despair and discouragement.

He had the very real feeling they were both going to die.

DOM#67A
LOSTON, COLORADO
AD 2013
8:53 PM MONDAY

Malachi stood at the top of the stairs. The hallway extended in only one direction, with four doors lining it.

Each would have to be opened. He knew that as he opened each door and peered into the rooms beyond, he would be highly vulnerable. But he had to send the women outside to cover the house, so that could not be helped. He would simply have to be careful, and trust in God to protect him.

He was sure God would do so. After all, Malachi had known from a very young age that he had a special part to play in the final battles. Surely God would not let him come so close to fulfilling his ordained mission, only to snatch victory from his grasp. He felt all fear leave him at that thought, and believed for an instant he could see fires licking all around the doors in the hallway. It was a holy vision, it was the Dream, now so close to becoming a reality that he was starting to see it in vision even while in the midst of his holy combat.

Surely, he could not fail.

Thus bolstered he moved to the first door, swinging it open and extending his gun with the same motion. The door opened to some kind of crafts room. It looked like it had once been a guest bedroom, now converted to a small taxidermist's studio. Apparently the heads he had seen on the walls below were prepared and mounted here.

Malachi glanced around the room, but saw immediately that there was nowhere to hide. The desks were small, mostly of the type that a person could buy at a corner store: cheap, collapsible tables that provided no cover whatever. The closet had had its doors removed and stood empty. Nor could he see any attic door in the room. The space was empty of prey.

Malachi moved back out into the hall, stepping softly, ever-alert to any noises that might tip him off as to where his quarry was hiding.

A shot rang out from the far room.

He immediately started toward it. Then stopped.

What if they had separated? What if Fran was in the last room, while John waited in a side room?

Malachi cursed inwardly. He was used to dealing with single victims. The addition of another person meant new strategies he was unversed in practicing. Still, God would provide.

After a moment, he opened the next door in the hall.

He would save the farthest door, probably the door to the master bedroom, for last.

***

Deirdre waited beside the tree. Its rough bark bit her skin as she pressed herself to it, trying to coax as much cover as possible from the slender trunk. She knew where they were; had narrowly missed blowing off John's head as he walked near the window.

She was ready now. There was another small window to the right – no doubt a bathroom – but it was too small to get out of. So she kept her rifle aimed at the center of the larger window, whose glass had already been blown out. She wanted to put down the rifle long enough to use her com-link to call Malachi and tell him where John and Fran were, but could not risk lowering her muzzle long enough to do so. She needed to be steady. Sooner or later one of the devil-spawn would rear a head, and she had to be ready to pull the trigger and blow them to hell in that instant.

A bead of sweat trickled down her cheek, tracking slowly across her chin, hanging for a long moment, and then dropping to the grass. The night was cool, but her concentration was of such a high level that it resulted in physical exertion.

Another drop of sweat began a similar journey down her face. Still she did not move. Nor would she. Not until she saw something in the window, and then it would be over.

She wouldn't miss.

***

Fran felt her body shaking as John pushed her into the small bathroom. It was atypically neat for a bachelor's private toilet area. Or perhaps not. Fran knew that most older, confirmed bachelors like her cousin were actually closer to being obsessively neat than they were to being the slobby stereotype so often depicted in the media. Indeed, she suspected that if Gabe had seen her place, he would have shuddered and left as soon as possible, extremely uncomfortable by what Nathan had jokingly called her "hands off" approach to housework.

The picture of Gabe shivering at her messy house reminded her that her cousin was dead. He would never come to see her house; would never visit her again. The thought filled her with sorrow, and she was hard-pressed to quell the feeling. She managed, however, pushing down the emotion so that she could attend to the job at hand: survival.

John didn't turn on the bathroom light, instead leaving the room darkened as he went and felt under the sink.

So dark.

It didn't matter that the bedroom let some light in, or that outside light entered through the small bathroom window, they were still in a dark place, and Fran felt her shudders grow stronger. She was cast back in time again, to the night that Nathan had died. The two men who gunned him down were like the ones chasing them now, though she sensed those two had not been nearly so dangerous as the mad pursuers that now sought them.

John grunted as he found what he was looking for, then slowly cracked the bathroom door open. He stayed to the side of the window, but no shots slammed through the window or nearby wall.

"They're waiting by the other window," she said, almost to herself. "They know this one's too small and the door out is probably covered, so they're waiting to kill us at the other window."

John looked surprised at her statement. But he nodded, and she thought she detected admiration in his eyes. That filled her with warmth, almost dispelling for a moment the cold gloom that had draped itself shroud-like over her heart. She felt her cheeks warm with a sudden glow, and knew that it was not the fear of danger and death that now had her heart beating so rapidly.

John pulled Fran back into the master bedroom, leaving her near the bathroom door, then went to the conductors' lamps, pulling all three from their brackets on the walls and quickly unscrewing their caps. He had to put the gun down to do it, and Fran decided that if she wanted to live, she'd better start helping.

She picked up the gun and aimed it at the door.

John started when she grabbed the gun, and his eyes found hers. Even in the darkness, she could see and sense the power in him. It was like a tightly bound spring, ready to explode with controlled energy at any moment.

She wasn't sure whether that made her feel safer or not. Surely, it was best to have him on her side. But at the same time she didn't know if having such a huge amount of energy near her was a good idea, no matter how controlled it appeared to be. She became aware in that instant of how deadly John really was, and briefly wondered if having him to protect her might not be like warding off a common burglar with a thermonuclear device. Then she remembered what she had seen, remembered the shots taking Gabe in the head and chest, and knew that John might not be enough to fight off such pure evil.

He smiled at her encouragingly when she took the gun. The smile warmed her even in her desperation, and the shakes that had gripped her subsided a bit, ebbing behind a wall of strength. She knew that such strength resided within her; that it had, in fact, kept her alive before. But always it took her by surprise when she felt that power rise within her. Her trembling subsided and she gripped the gun more tightly. Though not an expert as she sensed John was, she was familiar with its workings, and confident that she could kill anything that came in through the bedroom door while she was covering it.

Out of the corner of her eyes, Fran saw John dumping something into the kerosene lamps, a box of some kind of powder, then he screwed their tops back on. He took the lamps back to the door that led to the hall. It was a thick door, solid core construction. Like the rest of the house, it was also made in a quasi-old fashioned manner. That meant that in addition to being sturdily built and carefully crafted, it also had a large keyhole in it. Rather than the modern keyholes that ended only in tumblers and the inner workings of the door latch, Fran thought this keyhole would probably provide a clear view out of the room. Apparently she was right, for John knelt and looked into the hall.

***

Malachi stood in the hall. Two more rooms to go.

The second had been just as empty as the first, a pair of beds the only furnishings. They were conveniently unmade, as well, so Malachi could easily see below them by stooping for a moment. No draping bed skirts or blankets to hide what was beneath them. Nothing there.

Two more rooms to go.

He would be thorough, but Malachi knew where they would be. He could *feel* them, could hear the frightened pounding of their hearts as they cowered in fear before him. He knew where they would be, and where he would kill them.

The last bedroom.

***

John had only been a few steps away from her, but Fran nonetheless felt glad when he hurried back to her side. He was staying low, undoubtedly so the sniper outside couldn't draw a bead on him, either directly or by seeing some shadow and using it to extrapolate his position in the room. John snatched a lighter from Gabe's bedside stand and lit all three of the red conductors' lamps he held. He kept the wicks low, so they burned with only the barest flicker, and handed two of them to Fran, keeping one of them for himself and taking the rifle back from her as he whispered hurriedly.

"When I open the hall door, you throw one of these out the window at the same time. When I come back in the room, I'm going to run to the bathroom. As soon as I do, throw the other one outside as well, okay?"

"What at?" she asked.

"Doesn't matter. Just throw it hard, and stay back so that sniper can't hit you."

"But what am I trying to hit with the lantern?"

"Nothing," he answered. He must have seen the question in her eyes, because he continued, "You're just trying to spook them into moving when I want them to." It didn't really answer her question – what are you doing? – but Fran sensed it was as much talking as they could afford to do. They had to act now. She nodded. She was under control again. They had a plan, and even if she wasn't sure exactly what it was, she knew it felt better than the blind panic and running of the last few minutes.

John kissed her forehead. "Be safe," he said, and spent a precious moment lavishing a look of what she hoped was pure affection upon her before moving with his eerie stealth to the hall door.

***

John looked through the keyhole and saw Malachi come out of the bedroom about twenty feet from the door.

No time to hesitate. He threw open the door and came face to face with the man who wanted to kill both him and Fran.

John saw everything in slow motion. Malachi's gun was already up, and he knew there was no way he could beat the man in a shooting contest. Not under these conditions.

There would be one shot only, and the madman would be the one to fire.

***

Fran saw John throw open the door, and at the same moment she hurled her first lamp through the window. A split-second later she heard the crack of a shotgun behind her. It didn't sound like it came from where John was standing. Rather, it came from the hallway, and she knew that one of the lunatics had fired practically point blank at John.

***

Deirdre saw something fly out of the window. She almost shot it before she realized that it wasn't either of the targets she was worried about. Just a small thing. A bottle, it almost looked like, with a reddish tint. It hit about ten feet away from her, and shattered with a musical tinkle.

Deirdre never wavered the point of her rifle from the window, though. She kept her aim steady and true. She felt like she could have held that position until the end of time, like a heavenly strength was coursing through her muscles and strengthening her. The feeling grew more and more palpable, and her muscles felt warm.

She smiled, sure she was being sustained by her cause, until the warmth that swarmed over her muscles quickly became uncomfortable, then unbearable, and then painful.

She suddenly realized she was on fire.

She looked down at her clothes and saw bluish flame creeping along her pants. The leather started to crack and split almost instantly in the heat, and Deirdre threw herself into the dewy grass at her feet, rolling until the flames died.

Somehow, the people they were after had made some kind of bombs.

***

John sensed the madman's finger tightening on the trigger of his weapon even as he raised his arm and threw the lamp in the same instant.

He threw the lamp, then dropped and rolled as the Malachi discharged his weapon.

The round hit the lamp straight on, shattering it in midair. John had time to think what an amazing shot that was, how deadly an adversary this man must be.

Then thought was drowned out by sound as Malachi's shot passed through the lamp, igniting the kerosene and soap powder compound it had held. The mixture exploded as the gunfire passed through it, becoming a billion droplets of fire that flew through the air, setting the madman ablaze and showering him with burning shards of red glass.

John saw Malachi drop his gun and begin rolling on the carpet, trying to smother the flames that had ignited his clothing. John allowed himself a quick smile.

Burn, you monster, he thought. Hopefully the kerosene had soaked enough of Malachi's outfit that the lunatic would not be able to put out the flames before he was burned to death.

He slammed the door shut and ran to the bathroom as Fran heaved the next lamp through the window.

***

Deirdre saw the next container sail through the window, and this time she *did* move. The homemade bomb sailed directly at her, and Deirdre had no wish to be at ground zero of the explosion.

She hurried to the cover of another tree, hiding behind it as the one she had been at ignited.

Then she risked a peek from her hiding spot.

And saw Fran.

The woman was looking out through the window, trying to spot her.

Deirdre grinned and took one step forward, dropping to one knee, balancing perfectly and aiming rapidly in the night.

She wouldn't miss.

She gently pulled the trigger.

***

John rushed into the bathroom and looked out the small window.

As he had hoped, his mini-explosive forced the sniper out of hiding. But her attention was still on the main window, and she didn't notice John.

But before he could take aim at her, she had drawn back fully behind the tree. John had no angle and shooting her would be impossible. His plan had failed.

Then failure turned to sudden triumph as the woman came out from behind the tree and dropped to a crouch. John wondered what she was doing, until he realized she had a bead on someone.

Fran.

"No!" he screamed, and squeezed off a quick shot.

The impact of the bullet spun the black woman around, smashing her into the tree behind her. She lay still, but John had heard the simultaneous report of another bullet and knew she had gotten off a shot.

And in the same moment he heard a terrified scream.

Fran had been hit.

DOM#67A
LOSTON, COLORADO
AD 2013
8:56 PM MONDAY

John rushed back into the bedroom, gripping his rifle, and felt the look on his face change from terror to glee. "You're not hit," he said.

Fran shook her head. "The shot scared me. I figured out what you were doing and thought she'd be easier for you to hit if she was aiming at me." She motioned at the window frame, where a large chunk of wood was missing. "That was almost a bad idea."

John smiled widely, took her face in his hands, and kissed her warmly. The kiss was short, but sweet. She smiled when it was done, and she was beautiful.

"We have to go now," he said, and gestured at the window. "I think I got her, but I don't know how bad."

Fran nodded. Without a word she shoved some large glass shards out of the window pane, then rolled through the open gap, moving as fast and as well as anyone John had ever seen while in the service.

He heard her fall with a thump onto the roof, rolling to a stop only inches from the edge. A moment later, John came through the window, landing on his stomach beside her.

"Do we go?" Fran whispered.

He shook his head, scanning the landscape around the house. "Two down. There's one more. And we don't know where she is."

***

Jenna heard the shots from her position in front of the house. She waited, though, until they ceased, trying to breathe through her nose and not swallow too much of the blood that still streamed from her shattered gumline and the mangled remnants of her front teeth.

She waited.

Waited.

Waited.

Finally, she could stand it no longer. She entered through the front door, swinging her gun left and right, gripping it tightly in both hands with the elbows straightened. She was determined not to fail again, and knew that if she saw John or Fran again, they would not escape her.

Nothing. All was dark.

She moved to the stairwell, glancing up and seeing the body at the top of the stairs.

***

John continued scanning the environs.

"Anything?" Fran whispered.

He shrugged, still looking.

"Then let's go," she said.

"What? Why?"

This time it was her turn to grin at him, and he felt his spirits lift immediately.

"I guess I just feel lucky," she said, and rolled over the side of the eve, dropping to the ground and landing in a crouch.

He followed suit, landing near her.

"In a hurry?" he asked. He felt a laugh boiling inside him, trying to get out. Even in the middle of a nightmare, during one of the most horrifying and intense fights of his life, and this woman still could make him smile.

Now if only they could survive the night.

***

Malachi's eyes fluttered and then opened. Every inch of him hurt, but he knew he wouldn't die. He *couldn't* die. Not until his work was done and the Lord called him home.

So he would not die, but there was no denying that he *could* be hurt. He looked at himself, and saw that his clothing hung in tatters, pink flesh showing through in many places. Still, he didn't look or feel badly burned. More like a bad sunburn. Inconvenient and painful, but hardly crippling. He felt his temple, and his fingers came back sticky and red. Some piece of whatever John had thrown at him must have hit him in the head, knocking him out for a minute or two.

He noticed Jenna, then, staring down at him, on her hands and knees beside him and looking worried. Her mouth still bled copiously and she sucked at the blood, trying not to drool on him.

"You all right?" she asked.

He snapped completely awake then, adrenaline pumping through him as the implications of her presence coursed through his mind. "What are you doing in here?" he snapped.

"I heard the shots and I thought they might have –"

He cut her off with a hard right cross. She screamed and he felt the nubs of her teeth rasp across his knuckles, cutting them. His fist ached with the impact, but he knew her mouth felt far worse. That thought made him smile inwardly, though no trace of mirth or happiness could be seen in his expression, which was utterly devoid of humanity.

"Stupid whore!" he screamed. "I told you to wait outside!"

He rolled to his stomach, grabbed his rifle from the floor, then stood in spite of the myriad aches and pains that caused his bones to ache and his skin to crawl. He ran to the back bedroom, hoping that he would find John and Fran dead in the room, blown away by Deirdre.

In the bedroom he saw that the window was destroyed, but there were no bodies. No John. No Fran. He raced to the window and looked through the shattered remains of the frame. Outside he saw no trace of his quarry. No John. No Fran.

Just fire and Deirdre, laying in a crumpled heap at the base of a tree. He couldn't see if she was dead or not, but thought it likely she was. Though he knew John would have regrets about killing her, there would be nothing to stop him from carrying out the job if he was put in a position where her death became necessary to prevent his or Fran's demise. Malachi was protected: his holy nature would prevent John from taking fatal action against him. But Deirdre had no such heavenly protection. Malachi mentally adjusted his plans to accommodate the likelihood of her termination.

At the same time, anger welled within him, that same, incalculable rage that he felt more and more with every passing day. It boiled up like steam through a pipe, seeking egress before terminal pressure built up and caused an explosion. The requisite escape mechanism was triggered as Jenna entered the room, and Malachi felt himself bringing up the muzzle of his gun. "You let them get away! I should kill you and cut your body into pieces."

Jenna tried to smile through the bloody mess of her mouth, looking eerily like a clown, her blood-rimmed mouth standing out harshly from her pasty complexion. Her thoughts were clear: death was the ultimate release for those on a mission such as this. The dead were guaranteed a martyr's eternal bliss, cradled in the arms of God and forever knowing joy.

But Malachi cocked his weapon. "Don't go thinking that. You'd go straight to Hell, my dear. I'd make sure of it."

Jenna's smile disappeared. Malachi knew she was aware of his holiness, and so she must also be aware of his exalted standing before God. Even a martyr would not find heavenly peace should he testify before her at the gates of Heaven. For such as found his displeasure, their souls would be freely passed to Hell, for Satan to sift and grind them into dust.

A siren sounded in the distance. The sound presented an eerie, ululating melody to the threat that hung between them. It sang of death, and Malachi let Jenna think about that song for a moment.

Then he lowered his gun. "You're lucky I need you right now."

CONTROL HQ – RUSHM
AD 4013/AE 2013

Adam looked over sheet after sheet of readouts. Jason and Sheila stood at his side, reviewing the information as well.

"Two more bits down," he said.

"And John and Fran are apparently staying away from the streets, out of sight," said Sheila.

"So we can't see them until someone else does," added Jason, finishing his wife's sentence for her.

Adam's shoulders slumped. The situation was quickly spiraling into ever-worse scenarios. Things were getting out of hand. If they had ever been *in* hand to begin with.

"All right," he said. "Activate her tracker."

Sheila paled. "That'll put the whole place into second stage alert mode. They'll all go after John."

"I know!" said Adam. He paused and took a deep breath, then said the words they all knew were coming but none of them wanted to hear: "We need to get her back. And he's expendable."

With that, he pushed the button that would mean John's death. But perhaps it would also mean Fran's continued life, and so it was an action he had to take. The good of the future and the continued existence of the human race might depend on it.

DOM#67A
LOSTON, COLORADO
AD 2013
9:10 PM, MONDAY
*****ALERT MODE*****

John and Fran darted from bush to bush, trying to keep out of sight as much as possible. He knew he was moving fast, pressing her to keep up, but noted that she was doing well. In fact, she was doing better than a lot of the guys with whom he'd been through basic training. She was a survivor, a rare mixture of strength and beauty and intelligence.

"Why couldn't we take my car? Or Gabe's?" asked Fran during one of the short moments when they rested in the shelter of a larger bush behind yet another darkened house.

"Because they probably know what they look like," said John.

"Who's 'they'?"

"Damn good question," he replied, and took off again, trusting her to follow his movements. He had no answer for her, but somehow knew that he was right. It was not only important for them to stay away from the cars, it was imperative that they remain completely hidden. He had no plan beyond that, though. He was merely moving to keep putting distance between them and Gabe's house.

Gabe. Tears welled up behind his eyes as he thought about his friend. He was dead. One more person gone from his life. John blinked rapidly, pushing back the tears. Like love, grief was an emotion he could ill-afford to indulge in right now. There would be time for weeping later, if he managed to survive this night.

A few minutes later they stopped again, kneeling in the shadow of a tree some twenty or thirty feet from the back porch of yet another dark house. They had passed several dozen such homes, and with each one John grew more convinced that, whatever mysteries this night held, they were more all-encompassing than he had first supposed. It seemed as though the whole town was involved in some way. He could not understand how that could be, how it could be that the people he had known all his life were involved in a grand conspiracy without him so much as suspecting a threat existed. But each darkened house proved his ignorance anew; demonstrated that, though all the houses had extinguished their lights and the whole of Loston sat in shadows, only John and Fran were truly in the dark.

What's going on? he thought. What is happening to us? What mystery have we stumbled into, and why is it worth killing us?

Suddenly, the old scar on his shoulder twinged, and a strange thought flew through his mind with sparrow quickness.

Daddy, why you walkin'?

He grasped mentally at the thought, but it flew too quickly to be halted, and was gone as suddenly as it had come, leaving only new questions in its wake.

"Where are we going?" asked Fran, pulling John out of his thoughts.

"We've got to hole up for a while until I can figure out what's going on," he answered.

"Your house?"

He shook his head. "If they know our cars, they'll know where we live, too."

Fran opened her mouth to speak, but before she could utter a syllable, another voice pierced the night.

"John! Fran!"

John heard the voice and paled. He knew the voice, knew who it belonged to, and somehow knew instinctively what was about to happen.

If he had had the time, he would have started crying.

He spun around and saw Mertyl Breckman coming at him. Not to help him with filing or to find out why a student had been absent from his class, though. No, she ran at him to attack, sprinting off her nearby porch with a large kitchen knife clutched in her old fingers. Her spindly legs pumped back and forth under the folds of the nightgown she wore, and John had a split-second to notice how fast – impossibly fast – she ran before she was upon him.

"Mertyl," he managed before she lunged at him with the knife. She moved quickly. Too quickly for a woman her age. The old woman slashed at John like a blood-maddened cougar. He held her off with his rifle, using the barrel to blunt her attacks. He didn't want to kill her. And the way she was moving, he didn't know if he had the skill to do so, even if he had the desire. She moved so quickly that he almost did not have time to block her manic slashes with his rifle.

"Mertyl, please," he gasped as she cut at him again. He knew it would be no use; that she would be deaf to him as everyone else but Fran had been this night. Still, he had to try. He was getting tired, and a large part of that was the emotional toll that came with every act of violence he committed. He wasn't a hateful man or an angry one, not the kind of person who found destruction therapeutic. Violence saddened and weakened him, and he was feeling more and more strained as the night continued.

The combat took them around the small clearing that lay behind Mertyl's house, John losing track of time and his surroundings in that peculiar tunnel vision which takes hold of people locked in a fight to the death.

The world slowed to a crawl and centered itself around the gleaming edge of the wickedly sharp knife with which Mertyl lunged at him. Moonlight flashed off its surface in jeweled gleams, throwing spiderweb wisps of glinting light around them. John skittered aside, allowing the sparkling steel to pass beside him – too close, she would have him in a moment – before again blunting the follow-up attack with his rifle.

He was peripherally aware of Fran, trying to keep her behind him, to keep her safe. But Fran apparently would have none of that. When Mertyl lunged again at John, he parried it, jabbing Mertyl lightly on the arm, knocking her a bit off balance. Fran pounced then, jumping on the old woman's back.

Before she had sufficient purchase, though, John saw Mertyl spin in Fran's grasp. He gasped. The old woman hadn't just moved fast, she had moved *impossibly*, turning so quickly that she was a blur, grabbing Fran's arms and pulling them off her neck as easily as John might have separated a mosquito from his skin.

John felt his heart sink as Fran was instantly under the power of the crazed old woman. She was dead, he knew. Fran was dead. With the insane speed and power she was possessed of, it would be the work of a moment for the old woman to snap Fran in two. John was powerless to halt what would come next, and his heart sank in despair.

But Mertyl didn't do anything except put Fran down. And John noticed that, though the school secretary moved Fran with firmness, she took great care not to hurt the younger woman.

The same consideration did not apply to him, apparently, as Mertyl returned to the attack on him with vicious fury.

John felt himself tiring, but Mertyl wasn't even breathing hard.

What's happening? he thought. What's going on? His mind moved at a furious pace as he strove both to unravel the ever-more-tangled mysteries that presented themselves and to keep alive.

He knew he was tiring, and would have to end this quickly or fatigue would surely trip him up, so he attacked Mertyl in earnest, now driving *her* back, drawing on reserves he didn't know he had.

He saw an opening and clipped her hard with the muzzle of his rifle, striking her knife hand along the wrist. He heard bones crack with a withering, brittle finality. The knife fell from Mertyl's hands and he snatched it out of the air.

At the same time, her other hand extended toward him, fingers curled into old but deadly claws, like those of a harpy out of myth or nightmare. John swung the butt of his rifle around this time, swinging the weapon one-handed like a bat. The butt connected, snapping his assailant's other wrist.

He thought that would end it, but still she came, gnashing at him with yellowed teeth, kicking him with her old woman's legs that somehow had the power to break his skin and bruise his bone with every contact.

John held her off, and then something happened that frightened him badly. Worse than anything that had come before. Tal and Gabe rising from the dead had been one thing....

But Mertyl's *wrists* healing up in minutes was something else.

And they must have healed, for now she attacked him with her hands again, fingers snapping at him as he waved the knife in front of her eyes, crisscrossing deadly patterns of steel through the air before her. He saw that the wrists, limp and hanging at impossible angles only seconds before, were now strong and unbruised, as though he had never touched them. Thankfully, his horror at what was happening was pressed out of his mind by the pressing matter of how he would survive. He still continued to weaken, while Mertyl looked as fresh as ever.

She couldn't quite break through his defense, and he didn't want to kill her. They were at an impasse, but each passing second brought a greater likelihood of an unhappy ending to this encounter.

"Mertyl, please," he whispered, his voice hoarse.

The old woman stopped and backed off. For a moment John believed it was over; that he had found an island of refuge from the sea of terror that he floated in.

Until she opened her mouth.

"They're here!" she screamed. "Fran and John are here!" Her voice was louder than he had thought possible, almost shattering his eardrums with its volume and intensity.

Even as he reeled from the vocal blast, the neighborhood came alive as lights flashed on in all the houses. Doors began slamming, and John felt as though he was in the middle of the Red

Sea in the moments before it crashed down upon the soldiers of Pharaoh.

In seconds he and Fran would be engulfed.

Without pause, he swung his rifle, snapping Mertyl's chin back. She dropped, unconscious, and John grabbed Fran's hand and they ran.

***

Mertyl regained consciousness a moment later, dimly aware of dark shapes rushing past her, like specters in the black night of a haunted graveyard.

Her head throbbed, but not where John had hit her.

No, it throbbed throughout, an incessant, rhythmic beat that slammed through her skull with the force of a jackhammer.

Each pulse seemed to carry a feeling. Not one that she could articulate, but the closest she could come was one word:

Follow.

Follow.

Follow.

She clutched her head and squinted. Gradually she could make out the shapes that sped by her prone figure. They were her friends and neighbors. They were the people she had known all her life. They were the ones she loved.

They were strangers.

They ran with awkward, unsteady paces, and she knew they were all feeling the beat of that super-liminal cadence that Mertyl was hard-pressed not to dance to herself. They held guns, knives, bats, any kind of weapon at hand. Small children ran in the crowd, holding not play toys, not plastic guns painted bright orange, but knives and forks, small implements of death.

The pounding in Mertyl's head continued, and she rose, pushing herself up on hands and knees and then shakily standing.

But that was wrong, wasn't it?

What was wrong?

Something's wrong.

Her thoughts muddled about in her head, mixing up and becoming incomprehensible. She looked at her hands.

That was it. Her hands. She couldn't have pushed up on hands and knees. Her wrists were broken. John had broken her wrists.

And why didn't I scream when he did that? she thought. Why am I not screaming now?

She clenched a fist. Then the other. There was no pain. Her wrists were healed.

The confusion of her thoughts heightened to a dizzying altitude. Nonsense phrases from her youth mixed with memories of yesterday. The differences between what was and what should be grew more pronounced in her mind, the thoughts more jumbled, the confusion greater.

A great, heavy blanket of darkness seemed to coil around her consciousness, like a gruesome amoeboid preparing to envelope its prey and consume it at leisure. The darkness spread, and Mertyl felt herself going, losing control.

The darkness was madness.

And when it had completely captured her, Mertyl danced. She danced in a river of her loved ones as they ran past her, not seeing her, not caring about her as she no longer cared about them.

She danced, clawing herself, tearing at her eyes, raking cracked nails across her breast.

She danced to the maddening beat that was the only sense in the blackness.

Follow.

Follow.

Follow.

But she couldn't. The blackness held her firm, gripping her in an excruciating embrace that restrained her urge to follow.

Follow.

Follow.

She reached out and plucked a rifle from one of the passing mob. His fingers grabbed for it, but then he was past, swept away by the current.

Mertyl pressed the rifle barrel under her chin. Then something told her to move it lower. To the soft tissue where the jaw met the neck.

She pressed it there, feeling the cool roundness of the barrel penetrate the dark fog of her mind.

She pulled the trigger.

Most of Mertyl Breckman's head disintegrated in a splash of bone and blood, and her decapitated corpse fell to the ground. Her legs twitched spastically, her old heels kicking the soft grass beneath.

Even in death, Mertyl continued to dance.
***

Malachi heard the sounds grow, and it frightened him.

He knew *he* was in no danger, but if the town had been alerted, that meant that the Controllers were trying to actively track Fran through the bracelet on her wrist.

Standard practice, really. A bracelet, a gem, a ring. The Controllers planted them through a friend or loved one, who always gave the bauble with an admonition never to remove it.

In this case, Malachi knew, the bracelet had come from Fran's husband, Nathan. His lip curled as he thought of Fran, lying with her husband, never knowing her glorious destiny, never knowing the creature – no, the *thing* – that Nathan was.

So the sound of neighborhoods waking up frightened Malachi, because things were getting out of hand. Besides, though *he* was protected from the townsfolk, he knew Controllers would be coming soon. And he had no guarantee that all of *them* would respect his divine nature. Some of them might find themselves as powerless to harm him as were Loston's citizens. But others might discover that they were able to raise their hands against him. If that happened, Malachi might be killed.

He was outside the house where they had trapped John and Fran, and now he hurried to Deirdre's form, so still in the light of the fire that John had set with his lantern bombs. Deirdre moaned as Malachi approached, surprising him. He thought for sure she would be dead.

Not dead, though. Wounded, but Malachi could tell instantly that the bullet had merely scratched her, taking a layer of skin off the outside edge of her left shoulder and cauterizing as it passed.

She would live.

God *is* watching out for us, he thought. He always believed that, of course, but sometimes it was nice to have proof. It cemented his conviction more firmly: they would triumph this night. John would die, and with him Fran. And when they were gone, the future would die also. The Dream would become reality, and the world would burn.

Malachi helped Deirdre to her feet, and Jenna, who'd been standing nearby, reached out a hand to steady her.

"What's going on?" mumbled Deirdre, blinking unsteadily.

"They've put Loston on Alert," whispered Malachi.

Deirdre straightened as if shocked by a spear of white hot lightning. "What?" she whispered.

Malachi nodded and started leading her back to Gabriel's house. "Come on. We'll sit you down inside for a moment. You'll need all your strength to keep up.

"Things are about to get messy."

DOM#67A
LOSTON, COLORADO
AD 2013
9:10 PM, MONDAY
ALERT MODE

The stitch in Fran's side grew from a minor inconvenience to a major source of pain, a monster that was eagerly clawing out her insides. She clapped her free hand to it – the other John held in a tight grip, pulling her along with ever more speed – and tried not to pass out.

She considered herself to be in fairly good shape, running two miles every day and working out three times a week, a habit she had picked up in the health-conscious Los Angeles neighborhood she and Nathan had lived in. But no amount of weight training or aerobic exercise could have prepared her for the nightmare run they were now engaged in. Stealth was abandoned. Speed was all that mattered.

All around them sounds of a town, awakened as from a deep sleep of fairy lore, pummeled at them. They were strange, frightening sounds that Fran didn't want to hear but had to: the sounds of people moving, running, hundreds of them following, but not a one of them speaking a word.

They ran past a house and Fran saw a boy exit as they did. The boy held a hunting rifle that he aimed at them. Fran tried to warn John but the boy fired before she could, the noise deafening even a hundred feet away. The shot zinged past them and John, in one of those too-fast reactions that she knew had to come from some kind of special training, spun automatically and shot back.

The boy fell with a cry, a cry that was echoed in John's own ragged shriek of dismay.

"No!" he screamed. His voice was a study in anguish, and that anguish reflected itself on his face. "Dallas," he cried, and tears welled in his eyes. He stepped toward the porch that the still form lay on, and Fran knew John would go and kneel by the boy and wait to die.

That couldn't happen.

Now *she* grabbed *his* wrist and began pulling him. "No," she said. "Don't go!"

John was oblivious to her, pulling against her, dragging her with him.

Then she saw the boy's feet twitch and he slowly moved to his feet. Fran saw most of his head blown away. He was dead. He had to be dead.

But he moved.

"Oh my God!" she screamed. "What's going on?"

The sight of his former student's slowly animating corpse seemed to jolt John as well. He changed course, moving away from the boy with Fran.

They ran on.

They ran forever, it seemed, until their run dissolved into a long montage of Loston's townsfolk running after them, of hiding in ditches and beside buildings, moving ever onward, ever farther from the town.

Now the sun was peeking over the horizon, and Fran was sleeping on her feet.

She felt a tug as John jerked her awake.

"Come on, we're almost there," he said.

"Where?" she asked. He didn't answer, and Fran finally realized that the question had never made it past her fatigue-muted lips. She looked around her.

They were picking their way up a steep dirt incline, going up the side of a mountain. Fran shook off sleep, or tried to, in order to place her feet firmly on the loose silt of the trail.

"You sure know how to show a girl a night on the town."

"Nothing but the best," said John.

Fran's eyes closed again, and when she opened them they were halfway up the mountain, John quietly guiding Fran in the night.

"This is worse than before," she said, and closed her eyes again.

She didn't see John look at her, his brow wrinkled in confusion. And if she had, she would not have cared. She was too tired to care, too tired to even remain aware as she trudged in a daze on the trail that led up into darkness.

***

It was a meeting quite unlike Malachi had ever seen. Indeed, to his knowledge, *no one* had ever seen a meeting like this before. It was a standard procedure of an Alert, but Malachi knew that a full Alert had never before been necessary.

The high school gymnasium was crowded. People stood on bleachers, on the floor, every square inch of horizontal surface was occupied, with more people crowded outside. Of course, the place would have to be full. All of Loston was in attendance. Yet for all that, there were no sounds. No one shuffled back and forth from foot to foot. No one asked to be excused. No one said *anything* at all. They all focused intently on the man at the podium at the end of the hall.

He stepped to the microphone and began speaking. None of the usual tapping of the microphone; no "Testing, one-two-three"; not even a tiny joke.

Malachi had never seen the fat little man who now began to speak, but he knew from Controller protocol that it would be the mayor who gave instructions in this situation. It didn't really matter, of course, a two-year-old could have administered the directives and the townsfolk would have had no choice but to obey. Still, having the mayor do it lent a small semblance of normal life to the proceedings, and Malachi knew how important it was to the Controllers that everything seem real.

Jenna and Deirdre stood beside him, crushed against the people around them, all of whom took no heed of the visitors in their midst. Malachi knew that he could probably stand on someone's shoulders and urinate onto the crowd without any reaction. They were utterly focused on the mayor, and would not break that focus even if the entire world crumbled suddenly around them.

The mayor's voice, dry as a desert tumbleweed, sounded through the PA system. "We will first conduct a house to house search. All will return to their homes and look for the woman. As soon as you find her, detain her at all costs. The man will become violent. If possible, kill him before engaging the woman. If they are not in any of your homes, we will begin a search of Loston and its environs in the following manner...."

Someone flicked on an overhead projector and a map of the city flashed to life behind the mayor. Malachi marveled at how evenly planned out the town was. All the streets ran in perfect lines. All the blocks stood as perfect squares. Fields existed in perfect ratios to one another, in a mathematically-balanced composition.

Of course, there was no other way the place could have been designed, Malachi thought. Though later areas had been built with more flair and imagination, the designers that had first planned Loston were not noted for imagination. Not those soulless monstrosities.

The mayor used a laser pointer to highlight the areas he assigned as he continued. "All those residing on Cherry Tree Lane and South Avenue will search from the North River to the Foothills. All those residing...."

Malachi shut out the mayor's voice, looking at the map, seeking the most likely place. He knew that, like those that had built Loston, John would not be terribly imaginative in his flight. He would go to the most logical hiding place to make his plans with the woman.

Malachi's eyes danced as he studied the map of the Loston area.

And he smiled.

He knew where they were.

***

John helped Fran up the last part of the hill. She was dead on her feet, and John didn't feel much better than that himself. He had gone as long as four days without sleep, but he knew that after two days, people started losing control. In three days, most people hallucinated, and after four a kind of madness overwhelmed them.

It had only been twenty-four hours since his last rest, but adrenaline and fighting had taxed him physically and emotionally. He needed sleep as much as Fran did.

He walked to the Resurrection mineshaft, the destination he'd had in mind since they started running. It was locked, as he'd expected, a thick wood plank covering the door and secured with a heavy Master lock.

"We're going in there?" asked Fran, looking about her with eyes that barely remained open. Her voice was thick with fatigue.

John nodded. "There's about ten miles of tunnels down here: it's one of the largest mines in the country. It'll be hard to find us in here. Impossible to pin us down. And," he said, picking up a rock from nearby the entrance, "I know this place."

He pulled at the rock and it tore in half. Fran gasped, clearly astonished at his apparent ability to split solid granite with a mere tug. "It's not real," he said with a grin. He withdrew a key and used it to unlock the door, throwing it open. The tunnel that led into the bowels of the mountain gaped before them, like the open throat of a pitcher plant, waiting for its unwary insect victims to venture inside.

"How well do you know this place?" whispered Fran.

"Pretty well."

"We won't get lost?"

"No." He was silent a moment, then said, "My dad worked here."

He motioned her inside, then followed, swinging the door shut behind them. The external padlock meant he couldn't lock the access door from the inside, but to a casual observer it would appear the mine was closed as usual. Not that casual observers were likely. From what he could see, all of Loston was after them now, and anyone making their way up to the mine wouldn't have any casual business at all. Only the serious business of finding – and apparently killing – him and Fran.

Or perhaps only him. He remembered the incredible care with which Mertyl had placed Fran during the run-in they had. He had no clue why Fran merited better treatment, any more than he had a clue as to what was going on tonight. Further, he knew that he was not in possession of the facts necessary to clear up those mysteries, so he put away thoughts of what was going on for the moment. A few minutes more and he would feel safe enough to bend his mind to the task of figuring out what was happening. Until then, however, the questions must remain unanswered.

With the door shut, they stood in complete darkness. Fran let out a little cry as the mineshaft entrance swung shut behind her. John couldn't blame her. For all that everyone on earth lived half their lives in the night, very few had ever experienced the absolute darkness of a closed mineshaft. After a week of such darkness, your eyes could cease to function. You could go legally blind.

Miner lore was replete with stories of men coming out after being lost in the darkness only a week and never being able to see again. Other, more disquieting stories – stories told to every beginning miner, because they were true – told of those who remained for several weeks in the dark.

After as little as a week, you *could* go blind. But after thirty days, you *would* be insane.

John didn't plan on spending thirty days in Resurrection. But the stories rang in his head as he groped for Fran's hand. She held onto him tightly, and the warmth of her palm spread from his hand through the rest of his body, giving him strength that he did not possess alone.

"Come on," he said, and began feeling his way through the dark.

CONTROL HQ – RUSHM
AD 4013/AE 2013

Jason stood behind Adam and watched the monitors. He held Sheila close to him, clinging to her for support. He knew that many of the other Controllers viewed his decision to marry as nothing more than rank foolishness. Eventually he or his wife would begin the inevitable spiral into madness that all of them grappled with sooner or later, and that destructive plunge would be all the harder for the person left behind.

But in spite of that, he was glad that he had married her. She was dear to him, too dear to live without, and at times like this it felt good to have someone nearby to truly lean on. This was one of those times, when support was needed. The world seemed to be spinning out of control beneath them, loosed from its moorings by the actions of Malachi and his insane followers.

All the monitors showed the same thing: the citizens of Loston, literally tearing their homes apart in the search for John and Fran, but what they *didn't* show was any sign of the two.

Jason glanced at Adam. The older man scowled. A look at Sheila revealed her face set similarly. Both of them knew what Jason did; both of them knew that Fran was the most important person in the world.

She was the mother of the world, and only if she survived could the rest of humankind.

DOM#67A
LOSTON, COLORADO
AD 2013
5:50 AM TUESDAY
ALERT MODE

Fran squinted, trying to peer through the darkness as she slowly walked forward, led by John's sure hand. It was impossible, however. The blackness was not only complete, it was so thick that she felt it as a blanket of black velvet. It clung to her, covered her, enveloped her in an impermeable layer of night that could be neither pierced nor pushed away. This was darkness as she had never known it before, perhaps not even in her mother's womb.

A moment later a light snapped on. She blinked at the sudden glare.

"Sorry," said John. He stood near a switch held to the wall by brackets. It was by a small wooden rack that had been similarly hung. Thick jackets hung from the rack, and Fran suddenly realized how very cold it was in the mine. Less than ten meters from the entrance, and the temperature was at least twenty degrees cooler than it was outside.

John handed her a jacket and took one for himself. "It's a constant thirty degrees in here, even in winter," he said.

Above the jackets there rested a shelf on which lay miners' helmets: red and yellow painted hardhats with lights affixed to the fronts, batteries on the backs and sides. John plopped one on her head.

"Now you look like just like a fireman," he joked. Fran tried to laugh but was too tired. She just wanted to sleep. And maybe engage in a little therapeutic thumbsucking.

John flicked on her headlamp, then his own. The light that speared forth provided illumination but no warmth. Cold circles of luminescence surrounded them, but Fran felt no comfort, only some relief that the darkness had been cast back. The relief was mitigated, however, by the fact that beyond the small spheres of brightness provided by the headlamps, the darkness continued to lurk. It seemed to roil and pitch as a living sea of murky water, waiting only for the lights to wink out before claiming her for its own and burying them in its depths.

Beside her, John grabbed a thick flashlight from another shelf nearby, hefting its solid weight. Fran could tell it would be useful if it got really dark. Or if he needed to club someone.

Another shelf provided a thick coil of rope that John swung over his shoulder. The rifle he had taken from Gabe's house the night before – though it seemed to her a million years ago – lay in an at-rest position across his other shoulder. Fran wondered how many rounds were left.

John returned to her and flicked the wall switch off. The only light now came from their helmets, and Fran felt John's hand hold tightly to hers as he began to lead her deeper into the tunnel, straddling tracks which Fran guessed had been used for mine cars in years past.

They proceeded two or three hundred feet, then turned abruptly into a side passage. She almost stumbled over the tracks as they turned, but righted herself in time. Her breath fogged in front of her and she shivered again. She glanced to her left and saw her light refracted from a million shards of glass.

Not glass, she realized. Ice. A crystalline mat that unevenly coated the dirt walls.

"John," she said, "where are we –"

He cut her off with a finger to his lips.

"This is a bad part of the mine," he whispered. "Dangerous. Don't talk too loud."

Fran nodded, subdued. She looked up, and could imagine the thousands – no, millions, *billions* – of tons of dirt and rock that hung above them, held at bay by only a few pitiful wooden support columns placed here and there throughout the mines.

Because she was looking up, she didn't see the small ice patch. She stepped into the middle of it and slipped, stumbling again. She scrambled for balance, arms pinwheeling as she pitched headlong at the wall on her left, toward a set of wooden braces.

John rammed into her, body checking her painfully. They both flew back several feet, and Fran landed on a rail, bruising her hip. She literally bit back a cry of pain, digging her teeth into her lower lip so hard she knew she'd have a bloody mouth.

She needn't have bothered. Even before they hit the ground, John's hand went over her mouth to stop any noise that might have emerged. When he saw he didn't need to keep his hand there, he pulled it off, and she thought she saw admiration in his eyes. His look warmed her as the light from their headlamps had failed to do, though even it did not take away the pain that coursed through her body as she fell.

John leaned closer to her, and Fran became aware that he still lay across her. The pain in her hip finally disappeared from her consciousness as his face dipped closer to her, and she realized that she wanted him to make love to her. Not now, of course. Not here. But she wanted him. To hold him. To feel him.

"See that wall?" he whispered, his breath hot against her ear as he pointed to the area she had almost careened into. She nodded. "It's about sixty tons of rock that's been loosened up recently and it's just waiting to fall. I don't know if it would come down just from you touching it, but let's not take any chances, okay?"

John stood and helped her carefully to her feet.

"Are there any other places I should worry about?" she whispered.

"Just don't go near anything made of dirt."

Fran looked up and down the tunnel. "Don't touch the dirt. Right."

John turned away from her and began leading again.

"This whole damn place is made of dirt," she said to herself.
***

Malachi's brow furrowed in concentration as he looked at the map, searching for the exact spot. The people had all funneled out of the room ten minutes ago, not so much as sparing a glance in their direction, and now he, Jenna, and Deirdre stood in front of the empty school gymnasium, studying the overhead map that the townsfolk of Loston had left on when they left to begin their search.

"Well?" asked Jenna.

"They're in the mountains," said Malachi.

"Then let's go."

"I want to figure out *where* in the mountains they are," replied Malachi. "Now shut up and let me think."

Jenna quieted. Deirdre was already silent, standing wordlessly as a dark ghost, holding an Uzi she had also brought with her to Loston, though until now it had been stowed under her heavy coat. She hadn't used it before, preferring the shotgun, but since the town was on alert now, greater firepower might be required. She held the weapon at ready, able to fire it in an instant. More than likely the inhabitants of Loston wouldn't pay them much attention at all, but if they should become *aware* of the visitors in their midst...well, Malachi was glad that Deirdre was keeping her weapon ready.

Suddenly a voice, dry and hard and sharp as obsidian, slashed through the open space of the auditorium. "Who are you?"

Malachi turned to see a woman, face stripped of all emotion, entering the gym through a side door. She wore a pair of blue jeans and a striped blouse, a name pin with "Mary" scribbled across it her only adornment.

Deirdre answered her by pulling the trigger of her Uzi. The spray of bullets literally cut the woman's head off. The body fell to the floor, and before it had even hit Malachi had turned back to the map. Mary's death meant no more to him than would the death of a fly. Less, in fact, for the Lord had made flies, but only the Devil had been involved in Mary's birth.

"Got it," he said at last.

"Where?" asked Jenna, her voice still slushy from the beating John had given her.

"The mines," answered Malachi.

"Why there?" said Jenna.

"We know he'll be in the mountains. The mineral deposits will make long-distance tracking impossible. And if he goes to the mines, there's machinery that will further mask their locations."

"Would either of them think to go there?"

Malachi strode to the door of the gymnasium.

"The girl wouldn't. But him...I don't think he could think to go anywhere else."

***

John helped Fran onto the lift, steadying her. She looked down, and John saw her face pinch with fright. He didn't blame her; the same feeling had swept over him the first time he looked down while riding the mine elevator. The floor consisted of a steel reinforced mesh that allowed plenty of space to look down and see....

Nothing.

The mine shaft appeared to descend for thousands of feet. And the truth was it did. Bare rock walls could be seen for a few feet below them, but those walls rapidly disappeared in the awesome darkness that waited below, like the wide-stretched maw of some forgotten beast of stone.

Fran took off her jacket and he followed suit.

"Hot," she murmured.

John nodded. "It'll get hotter the deeper we get."

He hit the lift button, and the elevator began its descent, jerking into motion in and causing the cage to swing on its cables. Fran clutched him for a moment, her eyes darting in all directions like those of a trapped animal. The swaying steadied somewhat, but never truly ceased as they descended, and once again John was impressed by Fran's ability to deal with whatever came at her. She looked on the edge of panic, but she had not yet succumbed to it as so many would have done already in this situation. Indeed, John himself had done so earlier, when he shot Dallas, and would have surrendered utterly to madness and certain death had she not pulled him to her and in so doing yanked him back to comparatively rational thought.

Dallas. He still could not believe that he had shot the boy. He knew that the reaction had been one born of deeply inculcated habit; that rational thought had not been a party to the choice to fire. Nonetheless, the boy's injury rested heavily upon John's mind. He hoped the boy was not dead.

But then again, even if Dallas had been killed, the night had shown that death was no longer the one-way portal he had always understood it to be. Indeed, as they descended John fully expected to see Dallas waiting in one of the tunnels they passed on their trip downward.

Fran looked up, and John heard her gasp. "Wow."

John looked up, too. He had seen it before, but the sight always invigorated him with its beauty. Icicles glistened above them, hanging in impossibly long shafts, a small but steady drip of water coming off the tip of each one. They clung to the ceiling of the vertical shaft in silky, crystalline shards, ranging in size from inches to a hundred feet, from centimeters in diameter to many inches across. Again John felt as though he were in some gaping mouth, looking up now from the monster's gullet to see a glimmering network of pointed teeth above.

"That's a hundred years of miners breathing and steaming in the bottom of the mine where it's hot. The moisture comes up and hits the frozen ceiling of the shafts, and that's what you get."

As always, he tried using his helmet light to pierce the darkness that clouded the crystalline stalactites. The beam reflected back at him from a million reflective angles, creating a blossoming web of fiery luminescence that in turn gave birth to thousands of stars that hung above and around them. The resulting light created blurs in the gleaming icicles, so that he could not be sure whether he was seeing reality or merely a reflection when he looked at the glittering teeth. It was an awesome sight, and not a little frightening because of the sheer immensity of the hanging crystalline growths.

The icicles extended dozens – and John knew in some cases hundreds – of feet, ending finally at the top of the shaft, which had been dug far above them to accommodate such accumulations. The elevator cables were woven among the tops of the stalactites, then anchored in the rock at the ceiling of the shaft. Together, ice and steel blended in a strange hybrid of the natural and the synthetic, a metallic spiderweb encased in ice.

The crystals disappeared in the darkness above them as John and Fran continued to drop, passing level after level of mine shafts. But the surreal spell they wove stayed with them far after the teeth were swept from sight and eaten by the ever-present darkness.

"How far down are we going?" asked Fran.

John frowned. He had planned to drop only a few levels, but that didn't seem right. Something seemed to be pulling him ever lower, and suddenly John knew what his subconscious had been trying to tell him. It had been years since he had spent any time in the mine, but not enough time had passed to cleanse his subconscious memories of the important details of the mine's layout.

"We won't go all the way," he said, "but a bit farther. There's an old rest station with some cots. We can use them to get some shuteye."

"I don't think I'll be able to sleep," said Fran. She tried to chuckle, but to John's ears it sounded more like a sob.

He put his arm around her and squeezed, feeling her mold herself to him in response, holding him tightly. He well remembered his first trip into real battle. The fear, the tension, the exhilaration when he survived. He was amazed at how well Fran was holding up. But he knew that as soon as she laid down, she would fall asleep as her body's automatic systems took over. Emotionally charged and mentally wired or not, the human body could only stand so much exertion before it fell into dreamless sleep.

"You'll be surprised," he answered, and squeezed her again as they continued their descent into the belly of the mountain.

***

Malachi pulled the police cruiser off of the main street, scanning the street signs with Jenna in the back seat and Deirdre running point. He had memorized the directions to the Resurrection Mine – he thought the name strangely apropos – and now drove through the town in the early morning light of what the Controllers called a sun. Malachi knew it was nothing of the sort, but it shed light and he didn't care about it beyond that.

He supposed he could have gotten to the mine more quickly had he used the siren, but he didn't wish to draw attention from the wraithlike walkers that drifted across every street. As long as they appeared to be following a search pattern, Malachi and his team should drift beneath the awareness of those around them. But sirens might just jerk them into attention, and attention was something Malachi wished to avoid. He knew he could not die, but he could certainly be inconvenienced, and even inconvenience at this time could not be permitted. The end was too close, the work to which he had been ordained almost finished, and he would let nothing hinder him or even set him back a few minutes.

All around them, the people of Loston glided from house to house, from tree to tree. The very old stood without aid of walkers or crutches or chairs for the first time in years, while the very young pushed through underbrush with a determination and focus that belied their years.

Malachi knew what it was: Adam and the Controllers had put the people on full Alert. All through the town, people would be searching for John and Fran while the Controllers tried to home in on Fran's beacon in an attempt to rescue her.

Malachi smiled, moving the cruiser forward a bit faster. He knew that Adam was doubtless aware of his presence in the town; or if he was not, that he soon would be. But he also knew that Adam would be confined to the patterns and protocols that had been in place for centuries. Those would obstruct Adam's movements and restrict his ability to act. Malachi had the advantage in this situation, and could act more freely than could Adam, his old friend and mentor.

A young woman walked into the street ahead of him. She looked up as Malachi approached her in the cruiser, then looked straight ahead again and continued walking, perhaps confident that he would stop, or, more likely, in her present state of mind she was merely unaware of the threat that the car presented.

Malachi, feeling confidence rise within him like a fountain of living water, gunned the engine. The car hove forward with a slight screech of burning rubber. Jenna screamed in the backseat as the car hit the girl. Malachi hadn't had time to move the car to anything resembling its top speed, but still the impact was hard enough to grab the girl in an invisible but tight grip and then flip her over the top of the car.

Malachi hit the brakes and looked in the side mirror. He could see the girl behind the car, twitching, then sitting up. He looked out the side window. A woman, no doubt the girl's mother, watched him impassively. Malachi looked away from her, then put the car into reverse. He slammed the accelerator down, and the tires spun in the loose gravel below them before biting down and throwing the heavy cruiser backward with another lurch.

It knocked into the girl, pushing her down under the heavy-duty tires of the police car, crushing her below. Malachi jammed the brakes a second time, halting with the front right tire still resting on top of the girl. His smile grew wider: as a real person the girl would forever be a soulless failure. As a speed bump she was actually quite serviceable.

He looked out the window again. The girl's mother watched him for a moment more, then her visage changed. Malachi knew the look was not one of a parent angered by the sudden and unfair loss of a child, but rather the look of an intelligent weapon which has finally sensed a threat.

The woman ran to Malachi's car. He looked around as she approached. There was no one nearby. He waited until the woman got close, then rolled down the front window.

Her arm snaked in, grabbing him by the hair and yanking, trying to pull him out of the car. But seconds after it touched him her hand drew back as though the woman had been bitten by a cobra. She shook her head and her eyes cleared momentarily of the gauzy veil that had been draped across her mind.

Malachi gave her no time to come to an understanding of the situation, but quickly drew his gun and jabbed it at her face. He felt the barrel punch through her teeth, shattering them, and then came to a stop inside her mouth. He pulled the trigger, then laughed as the woman fell in a heap beside the car, laying only inches away from her daughter, who was mangled but still twitching below the front tire of the cruiser.

"Why did you do that?" asked Jenna from behind.

"Because it was fun," he replied.

He gunned the engine and continued on to the foothills.

CONT HQ – RUSHM
AD 4013/AE 2013

Adam saw another screen go blank from the corner of his eye. When he looked over, the word "OFFLINE" was playing across its surface.

"Replay that one," he told Jason. "And enlarge it."

The scene came on again, a first person point of view that showed a police cruiser with someone inside. Someone close, someone familiar.

"Malachi," Jason whispered.

Adam and Jason both watched as Malachi pulled his gun and jammed it at the camera. He pulled the trigger, then the screen went black.

"Damn," said Adam.

"Well, there's some good news," sighed Jason wearily. They'd been up forever, it seemed, watching the crisis worsen in Loston. Fatigue had filled Adam's mind, scratching at his eyes and causing them to blur, but now his gaze sharpened somewhat in surprise at his compatriot's statement.

"What's good about it?" he demanded.

Jason hit some keys, and another screen came on beside the first. It cued up to a view of Malachi and his followers in the prison: the scene from earlier, when Tal had gone offline.

Jason pointed at Todd in the screen. "He's not there anymore. Bet that John got him."

"That is good news, I suppose," said Adam.

"But?" said Jason, clearly hearing the unspoken conditional in the older man's hesitation.

Adam went to Jason's console, cueing up the first view again, the scene of Malachi in the cruiser. He stopped the action and pointed at the street sign visible over the top of the car. "See where they are?" he asked Jason.

"They're going to the mines," the younger man replied.

Adam nodded, simultaneously flicking an intercom. "Sheila?" he said into the machine.

"Yes?" came her voice after a moment.

"Is the recovery squad ready?"

"And waiting."

"Good. We're leaving in five minutes."

He turned off the intercom.

"You're going yourself?" asked Jason.

Adam nodded. "Loston is starting to disintegrate. We have to stop it. If we don't everyone there dies."

"And everyone here," said Jason.

Adam did not respond. What could he say? Jason was right. If Fran died, they all did. The future was contained in that woman's life, theirs as well as hers.

DOM#67A
LOSTON, COLORADO
AD 2013
6:30 AM TUESDAY
ALERT MODE

A thousand feet below the surface, John flicked on the lights.

A bare room – little more than a cave – greeted their view in the pale light of the low-wattage bulbs that were strung on the wall like miserly Christmas lights. Several dusty cots lined the dirty cave walls, dust-laden sheets covering some of them, while others stood bereft of bedding, their filthy mattresses perched almost carelessly atop spindly aluminum springs. Other than that, the room was featureless, all bare stone and dirt.

"This is it?" Fran asked, eyeing the cobwebs and the thick layer of dust that lay across everything like a heavy winter blanket.

"Yup," John answered, beginning to strip two of the less-filthy cots. "A veritable Shangri-La."

"What about rats?"

John thought that an odd question. Malachi and his band of anonymous killers were after them, the entire town of Loston seemed to be in some kind of Red Alert mode, and oh let's not forget about the fact that dead people are having this weird habit of walking around, he thought, but she's worried about rats.

John would have traded a billion rats for a return to reality, and almost said so before he saw the look in Fran's eyes. They were darting about wildly, as though terrified that at any moment one of the rodents might erupt from the solid walls around them and chew her throat out. Clearly now was not the time to joke, so John swiftly changed the response on his lips to something less flippant and more comforting. The fact that she was in distress concerned him. He suspected it wasn't really some irrational fear of rats, but rather the question was instead evidence of the fact that her mind had gone through too much for one night. He had seen it before:

men who had gone through a combat zone without breaking a sweat, and then broke down crying because when they finally got back to the relative safety of their base camp because someone had moved their toothbrush.

He touched her arm tenderly, reassuringly. It was not meant to evoke sexual response, but rather the touch of a concerned friend. Nonetheless, John was hard-pressed not to shudder at the sudden and all too pleasant warmth the contact stirred up within him. "It's okay," he said. "The only rats in here are mine rats. You'll like them. They have cute little fluffy tails."

"Still a rat."

"Don't worry." John turned back to the beds and finished stripping them down, shaking the bedding, trying to rid it of as much dust as possible. Fran grabbed a handful of sheets and began doing the same. Each shake of the sheets caused a miniature cloud of sediment to rise into the air, and John was glad he didn't work the mines often. He had no major aversion to dirt, but preferred to be clean when possible. "In all the years I've been here, I've never seen one. They're rare. Besides, the old miners say if you see one it's good luck."

"Lunatics and lucky rats. What a day."

They worked in silence a moment, replacing the now slightly cleaner bedding and then pulling the cots together, side by side. Neither asked if such a move was necessary; neither could stand to be farther from the other than possible. Not on this night.

Fran sat down on her cot, her eyes drooping in spite of her earlier voiced doubts that she wouldn't be able to sleep.

"Yeah, lucky rats," John said. "The story is that if you see one it's because they're leaving the mine, and you'll know to get out, too, because something bad is about to happen."

"Something bad?"

"Earthquake or subterranean slide. That's why they're lucky: they're God's early warning system."

"Does that happen?" she asked.

"What?"

"Earthquakes."

John chuckled at her apparent fear at the possibility. "Not in Colorado. No seismic activity to speak of for thousands of years."

"What about the subterranean slides?"

"Only if you bump into a loosely-shored wall or set off an explosion. So no breaking wind." He couldn't believe he had just said that. It was totally unlike him to be so comfortable with a comparative stranger that he could even hint at the sticky subject of human biological reactions, let alone joking about them. It had taken months of constant contact with Gabe before John had been able to make such comments, and even then he did so only rarely. But with Fran he was under constant threat of forgetting how new they were to one another. His heart clenched into a tight fist of sudden anxiety. Would she think him crude or disgusting now?

Apparently not, for she laughed slightly and lay down. "I'll do my best. Let's just hope the mine rats keep *their* gas to themselves, too."

Now it was John's turn to laugh as he followed her example, laying down on the cot beside hers. He closed his eyes and almost immediately began floating into that kind of sleep that is reserved for those who are utterly exhausted. Then his eyes snapped open as he remembered something

"Fran," he said, shaking her. She was already asleep, but her eyes fluttered. "Fran, wake up."

"Tired," she murmured.

"I know. I'm sorry. But when Mertyl came after –" he stopped, not wanting to remember the awful scene. "When we were running, you said, 'This is worse than the last time.'" He paused for a moment. "What did you mean by that?"

Fran's eyes jerked all the way open and she jumped to full alertness, sitting up on her cot. "I didn't say –"

"Yes, you did. Don't lie to me, Fran." His exhaustion affected him, making his voice sound gruffer than he intended. He continued quickly, softening his tone. "Sorry, I don't mean to snap, but if we're going to get through this we're going to have to trust each other. Now what were you talking about?"

"John, I can't –"

"You have to!" This time he let the steel show through in his voice. He felt that whatever she was keeping from him might be the key to unlocking this mystery: why all this was happening, and what had happened to his friends in Loston to drive them all mad.

Then he noticed she was two steps away from crying. His expression softened and he gathered her into his arms. "Shhh, shhh. I'm sorry. Don't worry about it." He rocked her back and forth, comforting her.

"No, you're right," she said, sniffling. A moment, then: "My husband died not long ago."

John's muscles clenched as the words triggered an image: Annie, shrunken and shriveled in a hospital bed that looked out of place around her tiny frame, crying and pleading for him to let her die.

Annie, taking a last breath, and smiling at him.

Gradually he became aware that Fran was still talking.

"...two men who showed up. They knocked and Nathan went to answer it and...." Fran's body shook as she wept in earnest now, shivers and sobs coursing through her. John held her tighter. "One said, 'Where's the woman?' Nate didn't answer quick enough, I guess, so they shot him. Over and over and over, and then in the head."

"Don't, Franny," said John, kissing her head. But she was beyond hearing him. She had retreated to a place that she probably hadn't been in years – hadn't allowed herself to go – and John knew the memory would have to run its course. In spite of his own self-imposed pessimism about life, he still believed that people were mostly good. He believed in their ability to find happiness in despair. But he knew also that sometimes to find that happiness, a person had to be allowed to wade through the sorrow, trudging through the grim muck of memory until they were clear of the swampy mires of past misfortune. Fran looked like she was having such an experience as she relived this horror in her mind.

"They blew his head off," she continued. "They killed my Nate." She shivered, and then continued in a smaller voice, "I was sitting right behind him. They didn't see me until he fell, then they came after me." She separated from John and gazed into his eyes. He looked back, seeking to pierce the veil of pain that lay over her soul, trying to find the warmth and goodness he had fallen in love with.

And it's true, he thought. I *am* in love with her.

A moment later, she pulled down the neckline of her shirt, revealing a wicked scar that curled around her shoulder. "They came in shooting. Screaming something about the last days and some prophecy. Insane. They hit me in the shoulder, but I made it to the kitchen and grabbed...."

She collapsed into John again. He waited.

"I grabbed a meat cleaver. Buried it in the forehead of the first guy. The other one just looked at his friend, and started crying."

"Because you killed one of them?" asked John

He felt her shake her head, simultaneously burying her face in the hollow of his neck. He could feel her breath as she spoke.

"He started hollering that it was his turn, and he was supposed to die, and it wasn't fair that the other guy got the honor."

"What did you do?"

"I ran as fast as I could. Into the bathroom. Jumped in the tub and prayed. The other guy ran after me and started firing through the door. Didn't hit me, though. And the cops were there a minute later. I was surprised because that was in L.A., and cops there are actually required by law to wait until at least forty-five minutes *after* you're dead before responding to your call, and I hadn't even had a chance to phone them yet. But they came in and caught the guy and dragged him away. He tried to escape later that night and they killed him."

She pulled away from John to look him in the eyes again. Her eyes were dry now. She was done with weeping. "I wish I could've killed him myself," she said.

John stared at her.

"Fran," he finally whispered.

She dropped her gaze, ashamed. "I know. I'm sorry," she said. "Cute little Fran is a bloodthirsty bitch at heart."

"No," he said quickly, putting his hand gently below her chin and raising her eyes to his. "Two guys kill your husband, then come after you, and you *apologize* for wanting them dead?" He shook his head. "Fran, I don't know what's going on out there, and I hope that sooner or later everyone goes back to normal. But I do know this: some people deserve to die. People like that bastard who's been chasing us all night long. People like that, people who have given up their humanity, renounce their right to live. As soon as they take it upon themselves to kill, they say that they themselves are ready to die. It sounds more and more like these people are some kind of cult that's targeted us – and you in particular – to die. I don't know why, but even if you were the mother of the Antichrist, I wouldn't hesitate to say that you deserve to live, no matter what."

"What if I *am*?" she asked in a small voice, and John could tell instantly that this was something that had bothered her: a fear that had plagued her since the night of the shooting. "What if they know something I don't, and they have to stop it by killing me? What if it we'd be better if I *were* dead?"

"No," John answered. "That isn't the way it is, and even if it were, I don't know that anyone has the right to decide that for you."

He paused, a bit surprised at his speech. Hadn't he killed in the war? And not only killed once, but numerous times, quickly and efficiently as anyone ever had. How could he condemn others for taking that same action?

He shook his head. It wasn't the same; couldn't be. He had fought for his country; for what he believed was a good cause.

But these people that were after them, they were different. They had to be. There was nothing of honor in the way they fought. John could see the dim smile that seemed to play around Malachi's lips as he threatened John in Devorough's house. There was no courage there, only madness and death. No prevention of some evil that could only be stopped by someone's death, either, for the eyes of Malachi and those of his followers were untouched by human concern.

Whatever their motive, it was a selfish one, and he believed – he *knew* – that what he had done in the past and what Fran had done to protect herself was as different from their motives as Gandhi's beliefs would be from Hitler's.

Fran sniffled, and John wasn't sure what else he could do to convince her that she was a good person; that she deserved to be alive. What he finally did was a product of instinct; an action he wouldn't have taken had he thought about it: he pulled down his shirt and showed her his scar. It was an eerie parallel to her own. She touched it. "How?"

"My father died when I was young. A man shot him. Just like the ones who shot your husband." He sighed. "I know about death. And I know that those who seek to steal lives need to be stopped."

"Were you there?"

John nodded, for a moment sinking into that long-past memory. He felt as always the wall at the far side of that memory, that implacable and blank buttress that kept him from seeing what had happened after his father was killed.

"What did you do?"

He did not know exactly how she meant him to take that question. Had he thought about it, he may have realized that she was likely asking how he dealt with the grief and the loss that followed; how he grappled with life without his father. But he did not think about it, for in that instant the wall that had held him back from understanding for so very long suddenly crumpled like cheap

263

aluminum siding. It folded before him, and in a single, dizzying instant he could see what lay beyond.

He hissed sharply, inhaling like a drowning man clawing desperately for breath. He was drowning, fallen into a deep pool of memory, engulfed by a torrent of remembrance that had been held back by the dam of his memory-wall for decades.

Dimly, he was aware of Fran shaking him. "John?" she asked. "John, what's wrong?"

He heard his own voice and it sounded strange and thin as an echo in his ears. It was as though he were hearing his own voice from across the Grand Canyon or some other gulf of titanic proportion. He had to strain to hear his own voice, to comprehend his own question as he asked, "Did the men who killed your husband – did either of them have a cross shaved in his head?"

Fran stared at him dumbly, and though she did not respond affirmatively, he knew her answer was yes. Terror and unbelief flared in her eyes. "How did you know?" she whispered.

"Because that's what the man who killed my father had," he answered quietly. And the thought ran flitted his mind, as it had earlier in the evening, while they were running from Gabe's house: *Daddy, why you walkin'?*

Only this time it was different. This time he knew what the thought meant, and the devastating fact of that knowledge slammed into him like a mountain, as though the mine had suddenly collapsed and buried him beneath it. His breath hitched again, then once more. He felt bile rise up in his throat and choked it back, only to have it replaced by equally traumatic hammer blows that seemed to rain down on him from everywhere at once and only gradually could be identified as the suddenly devastating pound of his own heart.

"John," said Fran, and now it was her turn to hold him, cradling him in her arms like a baby. She rocked slightly, trying to soothe him with those comforting motions that seemed to be hardwired into the human brain.

For John, however, the embrace and the rocking did not have the power to take his mind away from itself; to turn his thoughts away from memory and focus instead on the pleasant effect of her touch. Instead it thrust him deeper into the morass of memory that threatened to overwhelm him, each sway of her body taking him back a day, then a month, a year, whole decades, until he found himself reliving that day, that awful day.

He spoke as the details flooded through him, recounting the events of the day to Fran as each moment surfaced from subconscious to conscious understanding. She continued to rock him, but he was unaware of that fact. In fact, he was not even cognizant of the fact that he was speaking to her and recounting the events that unfolded themselves in his mind. He could not feel his lips moving, or hear his own voice. All he could feel and hear were the fear and blood and death of that day. The day the man with the cruciform pattern shaved in his scalp had shot his father.

His father lay beside him, one eyelid ripped off, the other eye gone, along with half of his head. Little Johnny, too, was wounded, shot still lodged in his shoulder, blood pooling below him and one arm useless, but he did not feel that. He just felt horror at the sight of his dead father.

The sight was all he could think of until his father's killer moved, bringing his weapon to bear on little Johnny as he said, "For my God and my Redeemer."

Johnny knew in that instant that he was going to die. There was no way to avoid it. Daddy was dead, and no one was close enough to save him from the shot that was coming to end his life.

But then Johnny's father moved. He was dead – *had* to be dead – but he moved. Too fast to see, but the killer shrieked and clutched an arm suddenly broken at the wrist.

The shotgun fell near Johnny and he scooped it up with his good hand, running to the back of the kitchen. He had no thoughts of using the weapon, only of getting it away from the gunman. Getting it away, and then getting *himself* away from the strange, impossible events that had invaded his house.

But he couldn't move far. His young mind froze as he watched his father. Daddy had been dead, Johnny was sure. Positive. But he was moving. Half his head gone, how could he be moving? But he was. Moving fast, with jerky motions that were nonetheless quick as those of a praying mantis.

His father reached the gunman, who had fallen and was scrabbling backwards like a crab, his hands finding little purchase on Johnny's mother's antiseptically clean white linoleum floor.

Johnny's father reached out his hand and caught the man's leg. Pulled it. Twisted. Wet-dry snaps shattered the air as the man's leg broke. He screamed.

Johnny's father grabbed the other leg. Pulled. Twisted. This time there were no snaps, but a sucking, ripping noise that was a thousand times worse than the shrieking splinters of shattering bones. The gunman's shriek grew high pitched. It climbed in volume until it was too loud to bear. Johnny dropped the gun at his feet and clapped his hands on his ears.

His father continued twisting, and the noise kept echoing painfully off the shining white floor as the gunman's leg slowly but inexorably separated from his body. It pulled out at the upper thigh, where the leg met the groin, and Johnny heard a high-pitched mewling that he gradually realized was coming out of his own mouth. Two great splashes of blood pumped out of the intruder's gaping leg socket. Then the gush slowed to a steady pumping, which in turn became only a trickle that beat rhythmically forth, keeping time with hollow cadence of the dying man's heartsong.

The man kept screaming. Kept screaming until Johnny's father stood and with a surgically precise movement reached out and crushed the man's trachea.

The scream cut off, instantly transforming to a whisper of painfully compressed air passages. The man grabbed Johnny's father's leg. Johnny's father stared at the would-be assailant out of his remaining eye. Then he kicked the man. The man's neck snapped backward with the force of the blow, blasting into a ninety degree angle. Another kick, and the head *popped off*, like an overripe watermelon kicked off its vine.

At last, the gunman was still.

Johnny's father stood there a moment, then turned to his son. Johnny was crying, weeping, wanting to know what was happening, but *not* wanting to know what was happening. He did not understand what could be going on, but knew that he did not like it; that he would be forever changed by it. Nothing was the same now, nothing would ever be the same again. Johnny felt a wrenching sensation in the pit of his stomach and knew that it was the feeling of his childhood withering and dying before its time

Daddy, why you walkin'? he thought

The question squeezed the last traces of life from his youthful innocence.

His father smiled, and two of his teeth fell out of the side of his mouth that was permanently open, because of the fact that he had no cheek and only half a lower palate.

"Shokay, shon. It'sh all right," said his father's corpse, his voice mushy and strained through flesh that hung off what remained of his lips.

He stopped. Johnny could see the one eye moving back and forth. Back and forth in what would have been confusion if the rest of his head had been there.

His father moved to the refrigerator. A mirror hung on the side of the appliance, where his mother had hung it. She said it was a joke, something that she put there because she was so busy cooking and cleaning that the only way she could find time to do her hair would be if she could do it in the kitchen while making breakfast.

Johnny's father looked in the mirror. His blood-covered hand went to his face. To the half that was left. Touched ruined mouth, disintegrated jaw. Then dipped inside the head, where the brain had been and where perhaps a bit of the brain still hid.

Johnny screamed when his father put his hand in his head and felt what was inside. Or what wasn't.

But as loud as he screamed, it was nothing to match his father. His father opened his mouth, and out spewed a sound of anguish and terror like nothing Johnny had ever heard.

His father screamed, and at first it was a wordless, mindless squeal, but it soon resolved into words. Into three words, over and over. The same words as his father advanced on Johnny.

Johnny shied away, pressing into the cupboard at his back. His father was dead. Had to be dead. And yet he still moved, so he must be a monster. Something that had killed one man and now would kill Johnny. And Johnny didn't believe the words the monster screamed. Not for one second.

But the monster wasn't about to touch Johnny. Wasn't about to pick him up and eat him. No, instead it took the shotgun Johnny clutched with white hands.

The thing slumped to the red-stained floor of the kitchen.

It looked down the shotgun barrel with one good eye.

Hooked a red-spattered toe through the trigger. Kicked once.

Johnny renewed his screams. Screamed until he was hoarse and there was no screaming left in him. Screamed until he couldn't even see anything but the scream. Screamed until he couldn't hear his father's last words.

"I'm not real."

DOM#67A
LOSTON, COLORADO
AD 2013
7:00 AM TUESDAY
ALERT MODE

Fran held John for long after his story ended, murmuring wordless nothings into his ears, pure sound modulated to provide comfort, caring, and love. She held him as he sobbed upon reaching the point where his father was shot, and kept holding him when he cried out in telling of the moment his father stood up and began walking again. She held him through the entirety of the strange tale that burst forth from him and must have purged him of a lifetime of self-doubt and mystery, while at the same time raising new and perhaps even more deadly questions for them both.

His sobs and cries gradually petered out, and he held her tightly to him, as though afraid she would disappear if he loosed his grip even slightly. But she would not disappear. She would stay for the duration of this nightmare, until they either both woke up or were claimed by death.

At last, he spoke again, in a voice that was calm and composed, quavering only the slightest bit at the edges. "Time travel," he said.

"What?" she asked, surprised at his sudden speech after long minutes of silence.

"Time travel," he repeated. He gently touched her arm, still wrapped protectively around his chest, and she felt warmth wherever he touched the skin, as though he were somehow branding her. If he was, she discovered that she didn't mind. She was his, if he wanted, and she suspected that he was hers, too. Nothing else could draw two people closer than passing through a nightmare together. Pain and fear were strong ropes, tying them tight to one another with unbreakable cords, and Fran was glad to be in this kind of bondage.

But that realization had to be set aside for a moment. Had to be left for another time, after their mysteries had been resolved and answers had been divined. Survival lay in understanding.

"What about time travel?" she asked.

***

"I saw the Skunk Man the day my dad was killed." John said. "Again in Iraq."

"That's when you said he – Skunk Guy – was killed."

"That's right. But in spite of that fact I saw him again just the other day. The only way that could be possible is through time travel."

"What are you talking about?"

John smiled at the question. He was a computer science teacher. That meant that at heart he was something of a nerd. Not in the stereotypical sense, of course. He had no particular penchant for white socks and floodpants, nor did his ensemble include pocket protectors or Scotch-taped glasses. But John felt a deep desire to know how things worked, to understand the ways things were put together and how they could be taken apart. He lived at least part of his life in the virtual world of computers, and that led him to be a dreamer of sorts, a man who could stare out a window one day and see the view, and then the next day he might see only imagination, entire vistas of questions and possibilities that bore little or no relation to what actually lay before him.

Also similar to most nerds – stereotypical or not – John had a tendency to become lost for days at a time in a good science fiction yarn. He had never actually planned on finding himself *in* one, of course, but the fact was that he had spent countless hours preparing himself for just such an occasion as this. He had studied devoutly at the feet of Professors Asimov and Heinlein, had feverishly pored through texts by Clarke and Card. He had even spent some time with adjunct faculty like Koontz and King, who though not exactly renowned as sci-fi authors, could rightly be counted as such for the alternate realities found in some of their books.

So John knew about time travel. Knew that if it were real, it would allow a man – the Skunk Man, for example – to skip across the ages without showing any sign of aging or wear. "Heck," he told Fran after explaining this to her, "it would also explain how he died and came back. Maybe he lived – or is it lives?" Fran shrugged, showing she, too, was at a loss. Proper grammar fell by the wayside when discussing time travel. John continued, talking as much to himself as to Fran, turning over his hypothesis as he spoke. "So he lives in the future. And on day one he goes back in time to my boyhood for some reason. Then returns to his time. Day two, he goes back in time again, this time showing up in what we think of as the last few days. Then returns again."

"And day three," finished Fran, comprehension dawning on her face, "he goes back in time a third time, to Iraq."

"Which for us happened in between thirty years ago and just last week," acknowledged John with a nod.

"And that's when he gets killed. So to us he died first, but to him it was the last thing."

"Right," said John. "And he could even show up again tomorrow. For all we know he made dozens of trips around time before finally getting killed."

"What if it isn't time travel, though?" asked Fran. "What if it's just triplets or something? Or father and son who look really similar?"

John considered the idea. Then shook his head. "No, it has to be time travel. In addition to the fact that Skunk Man changed zero – and even twins change over the years, to some extent – the guy who killed my dad was wearing some kind of glow suit. I don't know what fabric it was, but it wasn't polyester, and that was about as far as we had gotten when I was a kid. What he wore was weird. It had lights all over it, but not like a Christmas tree. It was more like one of those fiber-optic flashlights you can buy at party shops. Like the fabric was cut from a skein of photons instead of fabric." He shook his head again. "No, it's time travel. That's the only way to explain the Skunk Man."

"So you think that he came – comes, will come, or whatever – from the future?"

"Yeah."

She mulled over the idea. He could see she didn't like it; that it turned her idea of right and wrong in the world upside down and shook it like an Etch-A-Sketch, erasing reality and leaving the slate clean for some new creation. But he could also tell she was accepting it. "Okay, so that explains the Skunk Dude. What about Malachi? What about the crazies who came for Nathan and *especially* what about people getting killed and then standing up and going for a walk to a friend's house for tea and cakes?"

John pursed his lips. "I'm guessing that the men who killed Nathan and the man who killed my dad are connected with Malachi. He doesn't have the cross shaved in his head like they did, but their m.o. sure seems similar: bust in a door and start shooting with high-caliber weapons. I'm guessing that we represent a threat of some kind to them."

"Sure," she said. "We're caught in a rotten replay of *The Terminator*. Do you want to be Arnold or Linda Hamilton?"

"Fran –" he started, sensing the anger and fear that were welling up beneath the flippant words.

She cut him off. "No, seriously. For myself, I'm gonna be Robert Patrick. That way I can both have long metal arms *and* hang out with Scully in *X-Files*. Good times for all." Her tone was rising as she spoke, the tone growing higher and more strained as panic gripped her. He reached out a hand, intending to comfort and steady her, but she swatted it away, the shakiness of her hands revealing the depth of her terror. "Don't you understand what you're saying? If these people are from the future, then we can *never stop running*."

John could only respond with silence.

***

Fran could feel the fright bubbling up from a deep well bored through her soul. It was black and alive, curling through her bones and heart like oily black worms, eating her out from the inside. None of this night should be happening, but it was. None of it *could* be happening, but it was. She wanted to go home and curl up into a ball on her bed and go to sleep until she woke up from this nightmare she had somehow been sucked into. But she knew that she couldn't do that, because the likelihood was that someone would be waiting there: waiting to kill her like they had already tried to do once before, on the night Nathan died.

She wanted this to be over; wanted it to stop. But it wasn't over and it wouldn't stop. She knew that, and knew even more that what John was saying made sense. That it was likely that the goons after them were from the future. But that fact brought with it even more fear.

"If they're from the future," she said, "then they will know where we go, they can read the newspapers or watch a tricorder or whatever future thing they do to locate people and show up with guns at our door any time." Her voice was quavering in a way she did not like to hear. She was a person who preferred optimism. She *reveled* in it. So hearing this fountain of worst-case scenarios flowing from her lips was disturbing both because the scenarios seemed likely and for the fact that she was unable to think of a silver lining. For the first time in her life, she was scaling a cliff edge that hung out over a deep pit of true despair, and she found she did not like the view at all.

"If they can find us anywhere, anytime," she continued, fighting to keep her voice from breaking, "then we're never going to be able to go home, or get money from our bank, or even write to friends or families for fear that they might use that information to track us down and kill us."

John sighed, then nodded. "Maybe," he said quietly, and Fran felt some of her fear leave her as he spoke, felt that strange tightening in her bosom that she had only felt with Nathan: that sense of true trust and faith in another person. "But maybe not. You asked about the people who stand up and walk after being killed...."

Fran nodded, too worn out by all of the dire possibilities that snarled and howled at her door to be able to vocalize anything further. She hoped what John was about to say would supply her with a needed lifeline of hope, something long enough and strong enough to scale this cliff she found herself perched on and so get away from the despair-filled void below her.

"Well, near as I can tell they've only done that when the goons are doing the shooting."

"What?" she asked, relieved to feel a modicum of calm in her voice.

"The people we've seen get up again are my dad, Gabe, and the sheriff. And all of them were killed by the goons: by Malachi or people like him."

Fran nodded, seeing where he was going. "So you think that maybe that's some kind of response; something meant to help us?"

John nodded as well. "Sure. If Malachi and his people are from the future, maybe there are other people there, too. People trying to help us. Maybe they have some way of reanimating people so that they can protect us from the goons. So in comes Malachi, blows away the sheriff, and is about to kill me, too. But Tal resurrects somehow, and that gives me the time I need to get away. The same thing happened when my dad was killed. He *saved* me."

"How come Nathan didn't resurrect?" asked Fran, her voice small. The question was not one for which she wanted an answer, not really. She much preferred to leave her husband at peace, and discussing his death in this manner seemed akin to digging up his grave so she could jostle his remains around a bit.

"Maybe he did," answered John. "You were in the bathroom, remember? And besides, you said the police came within a minute. Maybe those weren't police. Maybe those were the good guys –"

"The anti-goons," Fran said, and was pleased that she could make such an attempt at levity, weak though it might be.

"Sure," said John with a smile. "Maybe the anti-goons were able to send their own people in as police, to help you out, so Nathan didn't even need to be reanimated."

Fran felt relief sweep through her. She didn't know if this particular bit of speculation was true or not, but it comforted her to think that her Nathan was at peace. That he was not stuck in a mahogany box, hideously resurrected from the grave like some ghoulish Lazarus, but unable to escape the coffin in which he had been lain to rest. He's asleep, she told herself. Asleep, and angels are watching his dreams and making sure he only has good ones.

The raw edge of her panic had been soothed by the hope John's theory offered. She felt her body unclench, and nodded. "Sure. So it's not just the bad guys. Not just the goons. There are anti-goons, too. Maybe helping us out."

"Right. And even if there aren't –"

Fran looked up at John sharply, suddenly afraid he was going to snip the line of hope he had been letting down to her, dropping her into that awful chasm of grief and fear. He must have understood the look she gave him, for he shook his head.

"Relax," he said. "I was going to tell you that even if we *did* have to go on the run forever, well..."

His voice petered off, and Fran got the strong impression that he wanted to tell her something, but was worried she might take it badly. Strangely curious at what might cause such boyish reticence, she put a hand on his. "What?" she gently asked.

The move seemed to have the opposite effect she was hoping for. John's face grew flushed and his mouth opened and closed like that of a fish trying to work a hook out of its lip. Fran couldn't help but laugh a bit. He was so sweet, so obviously concerned about her comfort, and so darn *cute* when he was embarrassed. She laughed again, and it felt good to laugh. Laughter was another rope to climb away from despair, so she laughed even harder, climbing that psychic cable to safety. Despair dwindled below her, growing ever smaller, and when John joined in her laughter, a full-throated belly laugh that shook his frame like a mirthful earthquake, the despair disappeared entirely.

She leaned forward and, still laughing, touched her lips to John's. He blushed again, she could feel his cheeks radiating warmth, but kissed her back. The contact was quick and light, not a kiss of lovers but one of friends, greeting one another after a long absence. It was fondness and friendship and hope. Fran smiled at him, and he smiled back.

Still blushing, he said, "If we *do* have to run, well...there are ways to hide and stay hidden forever. And I know them all."

Sobered, she said, "Well, that takes care of you, but I don't know any of them."

His face grew completely serious, all traces of laughter flown. "I would take care of you." He hesitated, and his mouth did the fish move again. Fran smiled, waiting for whatever was coming. "I..."

"Yes?"

His jaw stopped pumping. He took a deep breath as though to draw in strength from the dusty air around them, then simply said, "I love you."

She felt her smile deepen, and said in return, "Good. Because I love you, too."

This time he kissed her, and again it was sweet. But more lingering this time. Still friendship and hope, but also love and passion was in this kiss, as though both of them knew that the world was ending and this was all that remained and all that really mattered.

And perhaps it was.

DOM#67A
LOSTON, COLORADO
AD 2013
7:50 AM TUESDAY
*****ALERT MODE*****

Light speared into the shaft as Malachi threw open the wooden door that marked the entrance to the mine. Jenna and Deirdre looked on, fingering their weapons anxiously, clearly nervous at what they might discover within the mountain's belly. Already the night had proven more difficult than anticipated, and with the town now on full Alert, and Malachi knew they could only expect things to get worse.

He looked at them. They looked like hell. Burnt, bruised, or both. He knew that he must look a fright himself, but there was no time to remedy that. There would be time after they killed John and then Fran.

There would be time.

There would be an eternity.

Beyond their injuries, the two women also looked tired; worn down. Malachi knew that he should feel the same, but he didn't. He felt aware, alert. Alive. But it was a mad kind of life that glittered in his eyes, like a single photon trapped in glass ball of darkness, dancing back and forth in a manic hope for release.

Jenna stepped into the tunnel and Malachi covered her, though he didn't expect either John or Fran to be close. They would not wait in the tunnel's mouth, he knew. Ambush was not in John's nature. He would try to run, to hide. Above all, to protect Fran. But always running, because it would be ingrained in his nature to run. He would be deep within the mountain, trying to escape notice in the murky blackness of a million tons of dirt and stone.

"Nothing," said Jenna. Malachi's admiration grew for her just a bit. She hadn't complained at all about her shattered mouth, and during the last few hours had started acting a bit more like Deirdre: silent, self-contained, with the quiet confidence of a tiger with the scent of blood in her nostrils. Perhaps she would turn out to be useful, after all, and not the liability that she had thus far proven herself to be.

Malachi and Deirdre stepped into the tunnel, leaving the door open behind them.

Deirdre pointed wordlessly at a shelf with hats on it and a row of hooks with jackets hanging off them. It looked as though two of the jackets and two of the hats were missing. Malachi nodded.

"Which way?" asked Deirdre.

Malachi pulled a tracker from his pocket. The size of his hand, it glowed a deep green, like an emerald, only larger and brighter than any natural gem could ever be. This was one of the trinkets he had taken with him when he ceased being a Controller and ran away to join the group he now called his family. It would home in on the beacon implanted on Fran's bracelet, and would lead them to her. The beacon had only a short range, but he thought it likely that they were within that limited area.

He pointed the tracker down the tunnel, and it changed hue slightly, shifting to a light shade of pink.

"She's in here," he said, and moved down the tunnel.
***

The pale rose hues and blue casts of the morning sky over Loston broke suddenly in half.

Or at least, an observer would have thought so at first. Of course there were no observers; all those below were busy searching for John and Fran, under orders that they didn't know about but had no choice but to obey.

The sky, a peaceful blue with several clouds floating serenely through the air, seemed to crack open. A doorway appeared, allowing a view of a strange and disquieting sky beyond it: burnt red, the color of amber and flame. Then the sky beyond the sky was obscured as a ship dropped through the doorway between worlds.

Its engines hummed as it plummeted quickly through the opening in Loston's sky, which sealed behind the ship, leaving no trace of the craft's point of entrance.

Adam sat in the cockpit, next to the Controller who piloted the vessel. Both watched the nav-scopes intently. The ship had no windows whatsoever. Windows allowed too much of the deadly ultraviolet and gamma rays that pervaded the world of their time to enter the craft, damaging both equipment and personnel.

"Where to, sir?" asked the pilot.

"Resurrection," answered Adam. The name of the mine sent an icy insect scurrying over the nape of his neck, cold feet of dread tracking pinpricks of fear over his spine.

Resurrection follows death, he thought. Who will die tonight?

Unbidden, the answer also came to his mind:

All of us.

***

Malachi followed the deepening red of the tracker. The going was slow, for he had no way of knowing which of the offshoots were tunnels, which were rooms and which were dead ends. He had to follow the tracker, and in the catacomb of the mine system, their prey could be five feet away but impossible to find, standing on the other side of a thick rock wall that didn't connect to their tunnel for miles.

Malachi hoped such wasn't the case.

He wanted to find them. He would kill John immediately, of course. Fran was the prize. Deirdre and Jenna would want to kill her instantly as well, but Malachi hoped to keep her alive. He had plans for her, beyond mere death. He said a silent prayer:

Please, God, let her live. Give her to me.

A warm feeling spread through his soul as his body felt the answer. Peace overcame him and he knew what they would do: find the two, spray their hiding place with bullets. He had a deep conviction that they would kill John and somehow miss Fran, leaving her alive. He knew it was God speaking back to him, answering His most faithful servant.

God was giving him Fran.

And Malachi planned to keep the gift for a time.

She had to die, of course. That was the true endgame and the only thing standing between him and Heaven. But Heaven had waited for so long, he thought, that surely it would not begrudge him a few hours or days of time with her. She would scream beneath him, and he would spend himself on her.

When she died, so would they all, and Malachi intended to go out with a bang.

***

John and Fran slept on one cot. It was really too small for both of them, but neither had been willing to separate after the closeness they felt following their shared revelations. They lay so near to one another that each could feel the other's heartbeat, could feel the other's breath.

They were exhausted, and slept deeply. Even so, John sat up suddenly, yanked from the depths of fatigue back into sudden wakefulness. He recognized the sudden transition as a defensive response he had come to rely on in the army. It meant that his subconscious, ever active even while the rest of him was near-comatose, had picked up on something important. Perhaps dangerous.

Had he heard something? He didn't think so. The single light source in the room was still burning, and John found its low wattage glow distracting. He got up and turned off the switch in order to be able to concentrate more fully on his environment, on the telltale sounds of approaching enemies, if any were nearby. After a moment in the pure blackness of the underground world, he was forced to admit he could discern nothing out of the ordinary, and so lay back down again. He kept the light off, knowing that it would permit Fran to sleep deeper and be more rested. Nevertheless, a moment later the complete darkness became too much for him. He turned on the flashlight he had confiscated from the mine entrance and rolled it under the bed, so that only a dim glow emerged.

Fran pulled even closer against him. He smiled and kissed her hair.

Then slept again.

***

Malachi stopped as they approached a doorway and the jewel in his hand abruptly red-shifted, turning almost crimson. Light shined through the entrance to the nearby room. They had passed several such lit chambers, evidently on some timer or just permanently illuminated for some reason, but Malachi knew that this time the light must signal habitation. Their prizes were beyond the doorway.

He put the jewel back in his pocket, then signaled to Deirdre and Jenna. They nodded, and he held up three fingers, counting down.

Two.

One.

They jumped into the doorway, firing everything they had into the room. He heard Jenna screaming as they each emptied their weapons into the room. Deirdre was silent in the deafening thunder, hardly blinking as she expended the clip in her Uzi.

Nothing in the room could possibly survive the maelstrom, but Malachi *knew* that they would find Fran alive. God had promised it. She would be his, to serve him and pleasure him in the final agonizing hours of her existence. But John would be dead.

Sure enough, Fran and John stood before them, and just as he had foreseen, their shots took John apart while leaving Fran unscathed. Blood splashed everywhere as John took round after round to the arms, legs, chest, and head. Fran screamed in terror and fear, covering her eyes with her hands as John fell at her feet.

Jenna and Deirdre stopped firing beside him, but Malachi continued shooting, emptying his weapon into the room, into John's body where it curled on the floor behind him. Fran wept and cried and sank to her knees in supplication, holding out her hands for mercy. But mercy would not find her here, not in the darkness below the earth.

John was dead, and Fran would soon follow.

DOM#67A
LOSTON, COLORADO
AD 2013
10:10 AM TUESDAY
ALERT MODE

His last shot spent, Malachi had the delicious sensation of pure victory. Godly triumph welled through him, marred only by the fact that he felt Deirdre and Jenna gazing at him quizzically. He glanced at them, incensed that they were stealing precious moments of his victory.

"What are you doing?" asked Jenna.

He frowned and prepared to deliver a scathing reply, one that would bring this woman to her knees next to Fran, but before he could do so he realized that the room was empty. John and Fran were nowhere before them, in spite of the fact that he had clearly seen John die mere seconds ago, leaving only a whimpering, broken woman on her knees beside him.

Malachi blinked rapidly, surprise registering on his face as he comprehended that what he had seen was not real. It was a vision, and it would *become* real, as sure as there was a God. But it had not happened. Not yet. Fran and John would fall soon, but Malachi and his two remaining helpers had not yet killed them.

Rather than explain all this to the women, who continued to look at him strangely, Malachi looked again at the tracker. Still bright red. Fran had to be here.

He scanned the small room for side exits, trying to spot a way she and John could have escaped. There were none.

"Where are they?" asked Deirdre. She appeared shocked for the first time. Malachi knew how she felt. The tracker had signaled that they were within mere feet. Had signaled that this was where they were.

Unless....

"Oh, no," he said, and cursed.

"What?" asked Jenna.

He repocketed the jewel. "Fran's beacon transmits her location to a satellite, which then interprets the data and resends it to a receiver in the tracker. But the tracker doesn't have a proximity meter for Fran herself."

"What does that mean?" asked Deirdre. She was still looking at him with a bit of dismay, as though observing a bug. Malachi decided that, win or lose, Deirdre would not be coming home with them. She was too self-assured, and not enough afraid of him to be a truly strict adherent of the way of God.

Still, he answered, "It means that the tracker doesn't really track *Fran*. It tracks a latitude and longitude transmitted to it by the satellite. So we're probably right on top of Fran, but she must be on a different level. We picked them up laterally but can't find them vertically. We'll have to split up and search each level. They're somewhere right below us."

He left the room, heading back to the main shaft. There had to be an elevator somewhere nearby. They would find it and then find John and Fran. It was destiny, and it was his promise from God. They might have to tear the mountain apart looking for their prey, but Malachi would not be stopped. Not now.

***

The room remained as it had before the three entered it. The small addition of bullets meant nothing to the vast and ancient stone of the mountain. A few more bits of iron and lead and steel were nothing to it. They would be absorbed into its rocky self over the years, and would eventually become one with it, joined as truly and as firmly as if they had been born in the walls, rather than hurled there by the force of exploding gases pushing them through weapon muzzles.

Still, with the bullets had come noise. And with the noise the mountain sighed. A few small pebbles dislodged from where they had remained for eons, tumbling to the floor of the room.

A shower of dirt followed. It made hardly any sound, being merely a small shift, as ethereal as a whisper in the vastest desert.

But whispers could quickly become shouts.

The mountain trembled, on the verge of movement.
Then quieted.
For the moment.

DOM#67A
LOSTON, COLORADO
AD 2013
10:12 AM TUESDAY
ALERT MODE

"How long until we get there?" asked Adam.

"Not long," answered the pilot. He checked a screen.

"Let me know when we reach the mines," said Adam.

"Why the mines?" asked the pilot.

"The metal there blocks our homing device," answered Adam. "We'll have to be right on top of them, in the mine system itself, before we can find them." He motioned to a stone inset in one of the circuitry boards of the ship, a stone that was the mirror of one Malachi had taken when he defected. It was a dull green, signaling that Fran's beacon was not being picked up.

"Would John know that?" asked the pilot. "Would he know to get into the mine to avoid us?"

"Yes," answered Adam. "Not consciously, of course. But, like Fran, our John is so much more than he realizes, and his subconscious would send him there just as surely as a salmon would swim upstream to spawn."

***

Malachi, Jenna, and Deirdre descended through the shaft on the cage-like lift. Deirdre looked up and smiled. Malachi followed her gaze and saw the icy spears that hung over them, glistening like pointed crystal turrets, extending from a castle that was hopelessly inverted. He did not smile, however, unmoved by the crystalline structure above. Beauty to him was not found in ice. It was found in fire, and pain.

He brought the elevator to a halt at the next level down and motioned for Jenna to get off.

"Is your com-link charged?" he asked. She nodded. "Good. Signal me if you find anything. Kill them if you can, but get us if you need help."

Jenna nodded, and the Malachi thumbed the button again, dropping himself and Deirdre further down the shaft.

Another few levels, and he let Deirdre off. She took a few steps away, and Malachi continued his descent, dropping further until the darkness swallowed up Deirdre's light.

He was alone.

***

"Here we are," said the pilot.

Adam felt a soft thump as the ship set down.

In seconds he was outside, standing before Resurrection Mine with the Recovery team: ten men and women who were heavily armed and armored. Like the Cleanup Crew had been in the plane that took Fran from LAX to Denver, these men and women were Controllers. However, they were not here to turn back the clocks. No, these people were here to get Fran – and John, if possible – before Malachi did.

They all checked their instruments and weapons one last time. Adam did the same, checking to see if his pulse-gun was charged. He was grateful that Malachi did not have access to such advanced weaponry. Over the years, too many Controllers had defected to join Malachi and his ilk. When they left, it was often in possession of devices that would aid them in their quest for the eradication of humanity. But luckily they had not been able to steal many weapons.

What arms they did manage to smuggle out with them were generally small and soon lost their charges, becoming nothing more than conversation pieces. That meant that the Controllers would be better armed than Malachi and his adherents, who were forced to steal weapons while going from time to time looking for people to kill. Malachi's team would probably have rifles and shotguns, maybe even automatic weaponry, but they wouldn't have any pulse-shots or cathode arrays, thank goodness.

Adam led his team into the open mineshaft as the dropjet took off behind them. It would hide itself in the mountains nearby, the pilot waiting for Adam's pickup signal.

They entered the shaft and began splitting up, shearing off in ones and twos. Adam knew some of them might get lost, but they couldn't afford to go slowly. This race would go to the quick. Because there would only be one victor, and the rest would only earn death.

***

One of the Recovery team, a woman whose high cheekbones and dark skin bespoke a native American heritage, stumbled in the darkness. Esther had a light, as did they all, but it was woefully inadequate to illuminate her every footstep. Plus, she dimmed it periodically so as not to give away her position to any of Malachi's people that were down here.

Fanatics, or Fans, some of the Controllers called Malachi and his insane army. Esther knew the name was apt. Completely dedicated to their mission, single-minded in their pursuit of humanity's end, and zealous in their belief that God was with them, they were dangerous men and women. Esther knew they would fight to the death – and in some cases beyond death – to win their battles, so she turned off the light every few feet and walked in blackness in order to confuse any Fans who might be hiding down here.

That was why she walked in darkness. That was why she stumbled.

She fell forward, her hands reaching out automatically, grabbing the wall for support. She narrowly avoided a spill, but any relief at that small victory fled her mind instantly with the sound she heard.

It was a deep groan, like a million bass singers screaming an aria from the depths of the earth in angry protest of her hands touching the wall of the tunnel.

A tiny spray of silt fell on her head.

She brushed it off and looked around.

The Controllers lived inside a mountain, one of the only places that provided adequate shelter from the adverse conditions of the time and place they lived in. But it was nothing like this. It was steel and ferroconcrete all around them. This was bare rock, and dirt that would rain down on a person who merely fell into the wall.

She was afraid, and stood still for a moment, listening for more noise.

There was none, and in a moment she continued. She did not notice that in the darkness behind her, a fine mist of dust continued to spill downward from the ceiling, forming a small pile of sediment on the packed tunnel floor below.

DOM#67A
LOSTON, COLORADO
AD 2013
10:30 AM TUESDAY
ALERT MODE

John's eyes snapped open suddenly, and he had to stifle the urge to scream as a monster swam into focus before his eyes.

Sharp teeth that were a mile long, beady black eyes that seemed to swallow up the dim light that came from his flashlight, a mottled black and pink nose that wiggled cutely....

Wiggled?

John blinked, and realized he was nose to whiskers with a mine rat. It looked the same as other rats he had seen, though smaller and apparently more friendly. He pulled back slowly though, not wanting to startle the rodent that was illuminated dimly by the flashlight below the bed. He doubted rabies was a danger with subterranean creatures but didn't want to chance being bitten.

The little creature just stared at him, nose wiggling. It's tiny tail – a puff of fur that resembled a brown dandelion – twitched once, then it turned around and scampered off the bed, running through the door and disappearing in the blackness beyond.

John looked around, smiling at the cute little animal as it retreated. Only gradually did he become aware that there were several other rats in the room, appearing from cracks in the walls and running out into the corridor.

His smile disappeared, replaced by a frown.

He got out of bed, trying not to wake Fran up. She reached out to him in her sleep as he left, but he gently pushed her hand back to her side. Better that she keep resting, if she could. The more sleep she had, the better she would be able to function when they finally had to emerge from this underground oasis, to weather the fearful realities outside.

He grabbed the flashlight off the floor and walked into the tunnel, shining the light before him like a pale spear. His heart sank at the sight which greeted him there.

The tunnel was alive with rats. Millions, it seemed, stampeding down the shaft.

John raced back into the sleeping area and sat down hard on the bed. He shook Fran once, sharply, and began putting on his shoes.

"Fran, get up!" he shouted.

Her eyes blinked sluggishly. "What...."

"Get up, Fran. We have to go."

She caught the urgency in his voice and sat up immediately. John admired the way she threw off sleep so quickly, stepping into her shoes beside the cot and lacing them up before he had even gotten his on himself.

"What's going on?" she asked.

"I don't know," answered John. He watched another fluffy-tailed rat race by and disappear into the tunnel, joining its brothers and sisters in a brown stream of panic. As he watched, the stream slowed to a trickle, then disappeared entirely. But the fear he felt did not disappear. It grew only more intense as the flood of rodents dried up.

"I don't know," he repeated. "Something bad."

***

Deirdre glided down the tunnel. A small light illuminated a tiny sphere around her, but she turned it off and watched for other lights every couple of hundred feet, disappearing into the darkness as completely as a specter in a haunted house.

She hadn't found anything yet. In another couple of minutes she would go back to the elevator and try a different level.

Then she heard voices.

***

Malachi turned a corner, following the indications of the jewel he held. He was so intent on following his course that he cried out in surprise when he abruptly turned a corner and came face to face with two men.

In the instant that he dropped the tracker and raised his gun, it registered who they were.

Controllers. A Recovery crew, from the looks of their garb.

He fired at the same instant as they did, all three throwing themselves in different directions at the same time, trying to evade the spray of bullets that came from Malachi's gun and the weird blasts that came from those of the Controllers.

***

Jenna turned around. She couldn't find anything, and would have to give this level up as a lost cause. She wanted desperately to be the one who found them, though. She wanted to kill John, then Fran. She would bring back Fran's heart to Malachi, and redeem herself for her earlier mistakes.

She wanted to redeem herself. Redemption was what every single one of Malachi's followers dreamed about.

They were Fanatics, and all Fanatics wanted redemption, followed by death.

She reached the elevator shaft and punched the button that would call back the lift from the lower levels of the mine. After several minutes, she realized she had closed the wrong circuit, causing the elevator to descend instead of rise.

She cursed softly and hit the other switch. The cable in the open shaft before her began to spool up.

***

Malachi fled down the hall, turning back and forth, taking corridors at random in the hopes of losing his two pursuers. He glanced back and saw that the two Controllers he had bumped into had been joined by two more, a man and a woman. All four opened fire on Malachi. Their guns weren't the primitive ones he was using. They were pulse pistols, each holding an electromagnetic charge in the handle that shot out thumps of concentrated sonics. If one hit him, he would fall to the ground, twitching and immobilized, very possibly permanently paralyzed.

He knew they wouldn't kill him, but he wasn't sure exactly how important his bodily integrity would be to them. They might not have any problem with cutting his legs and arms off and taking him back to Controller Central like that.

After all, that was what he had trained them to do, back when he had been Adam's second in command.

So he ran as fast as he could, dodging the blasts, feeling the air heat around him, feeling dirt rain down on his head as the blasts pummeled the tunnel's ceiling and walls.

***

John handed Fran her jacket. They both wore their helmets again, but hadn't yet turned on the lights. The only illumination came from John's flashlight, which still shone brightly. Apparently they hadn't slept long enough to kill the heavy duty battery, for which both were now grateful.

John picked up his length of rope, slinging it over his shoulder, and they stood, ready to go.

He looked at Fran, shining the light under his chin and making a spooky face. She smiled at the antic, but was again struck by the premonition of doom that had ceased her before, outside Gabe's house, when John's face had looked like a skull to her. He winked, but fear gripped Fran in an unrelenting grasp.

John took her hand and turned with her to the door that led to the tunnel.

And in that moment the black woman, one of Malachi's supporting actors in this shadowy play of death, stepped in the room and opened fire with an automatic weapon.

DOM#67A
LOSTON, COLORADO
AD 2013
10:43 AM TUESDAY
ALERT MODE

Adam came up against yet another dead end.

He cursed under his breath. This was getting them nowhere.

Behind him the two Controllers – two women who were the Recovery team's most capable members – shuffled uneasily.

Adam stared at the blank wall before them for a moment before turning around once more. "Let's go back to the entrance," he said.

He had a feeling that waiting was the only thing he could do at this point.

***

Fran screamed as the woman opened fire. Luckily for them, the woman came in shooting blind, firing round after round into the room. Then Fran felt John stiffen beside her, and was sure he had been hit.

He hadn't, though. She had felt his muscles clench as he threw his heavy flashlight at the woman. The thick steel cylinder collided with the barrel of the Uzi, knocking the woman's weapon upward and sending her next shot into the ceiling.

The flashlight hit the ground with a heavy clatter, and the bulb shattered on impact, pitching them all into darkness.

Fran felt John grab her hand and pull her to the floor, then they both rolled under a bed. She felt him pushing her shoulders as above them the black woman continued to fire, the bursts deafening and the light blinding in the close quarters of the room.

Oh, well, thought Fran. With any luck the woman before them would be just as confused by her own fire as Fran found herself.

Fran felt John push her again, and finally realized he was trying to get her to crawl back to a stony outcropping she had earlier noticed in the back of the room. Perhaps that would provide some cover in this place that had abruptly become a whizzing arcade of death, a shooting gallery with real ammunition in which she and John served as the ducks lined up in a row. She moved with him, keeping her head low as gunfire sounded, immense in her ears, her hearing assaulted by the deafening thunder all around.

Bullets zinged around them, ricocheting off the walls, and Fran realized that even in the small area hidden behind the vertical shelf of stone, it would only be a matter of time before some bullet bounced into their hiding space and she or John – or both – were hit.

***

Malachi kept running from the four Controllers on his tail, the breaths surging in and out of his lungs in what felt like ragged chunks of wood that had been set ablaze. Cramps gripped his side, and he didn't know how much farther he could go at this sprinting pace.

He fell suddenly, rolling and shooting behind him as he did. The sight of the four Controllers scattering into offshoot tunnels gratified him, but he had no time to enjoy the tiny respite. He jumped to his feet and continued running.

He turned and ran again, hoping the elevator was still on his level. All other avenues of escape had been closed by the Controllers who now followed him.

He turned another corner and saw the open shaft before him. Saw the cable that trailed below the elevator. It was reeling upward, a sinuous snake clamped tight to some anchor high above, rippling slightly as it moved upward with the lift.

Malachi risked a look back and saw the Controllers still close behind. He had gained a bit of a lead, but had nowhere near the time he would need to recall the elevator. So he didn't bother to try. He kept running instead, and when he got to the shaft he pushed off from the lip of the tunnel, jumping desperately for the cable.

He caught it, and held tight. His grasp slipped on the cable and he thought for a moment that he was going to fall as he scrabbled for purchase on the thickly wrapped wires. Then his hands caught on frays and a few roughened edges on the black cord, and his short descent abruptly ceased. The elevator – so far above him that he couldn't see it – rose, and drew him up with it.

Malachi looked down and saw his pursuers appear at the shaft opening. He opened fire, gripping his rifle one-handed as he let forth a few short shots, and the Controllers disappeared back into the shaft like rats in their holes.

He looked up again, and saw the next level approaching.
***

In the lift, Jenna raised her gaze. The top was approaching. Beyond that hung the icicles, crystal teeth in the maw of a giant, a golem fashioned by some long-gone artisan out of stone and earth and clay. They glimmered as with saliva, bright and shimmering, water dripping steadily off their wickedly pointed ends.
***

John popped open the rifle, checking how many shots he had left.

One.

Shots still blasted all around them, ricocheting nearby, threatening their miniscule area of safety behind the rocky outcropping in the cave. He cursed inwardly. He had done pretty well during the evening, considering that he hadn't seen action in years. Even still, some of his habits were bound to be rusty.

Like remembering to keep on top of your ammo count.

Beyond the stony outcropping he and Fran hid behind, the black woman continued firing, sharp staccato bursts that were too close for comfort. One of the bullets ricocheted within inches of John's face, heating the air beside him.

John shot blindly in the direction of the doorway, hoping to get a lucky shot in. But Lady Luck was not interested in assisting his aim, it seemed, for the woman didn't even pause in her firing. John thought furiously, then pulled Fran close to him.

"Can you get to the tunnel from here?" he asked. He practically had to yell to be heard over the din of the shots, but he knew the sound would only carry as a distorted noise to the shooter; she would remain unaware what was being planned.

Fran nodded. The gunfire continued, but John noted that the woman wasn't coming any closer. She probably didn't know if they had any weapons or not. But soon enough she would realize that her fire wasn't being returned, and would begin a cautious advance. When that happened, they were as good as dead.

"I'm gonna rush her," said John. He felt Fran stiffen beside him, concerned, but there wasn't any other choice. "When I do, you get into the tunnel and run left. Do not touch the walls. As soon as you're out of firing range, turn on your headlamp and run as fast and as quiet as you can. Okay?"

Fran pulled John next to her. "What about you?" she asked.

"Don't you worry. When you get to the T-intersection in the tunnel, stop and wait for me. No matter what happens, just wait for me, okay?"

Fran nodded. John kissed her in the dark. Her lips sought his at the same moment, and he was struck by an odd feeling of destiny, as though all this was supposed to happen. He only hoped that their kiss wasn't the final touch of doomed lovers, a Romeo and Juliet whose lives were torn apart not by feuding Montagues and Capulets, but by something much more cruel and less easily-defined. Still, the feeling demanded that he add one more sentence to his instructions, one more line of dialogue that might have been plucked from any of a thousand melodramas, but that he meant nonetheless, from the bottom of his feet to the top of his head.

"I will come for you," he said.

He still didn't know what had happened in Loston, or why these people were out to kill him. But now wasn't the time to find out. Now was the time for action, for survival.

He separated from Fran, pulling away slightly in preparation for the coming movement.

"When I leave, you count to three and go, stay on the right, because I'm rushing her left, okay? But don't go until I leave, okay? No matter what I say, stay here until you feel me move away."

Fran nodded again, a movement he felt more than saw, almost preternaturally aware of her closeness and position next to him. Is this what love does? he thought. Takes someone we know and makes them so close they are a part of us?

Then he thought, And then they are taken away. He pushed that pessimistic line of thought away, shoving it out of his mind with all the force of his will. They would live. They had to live.

"All right," he said to Fran. Then in a loud voice, he screamed, "Now!"

He felt Fran stiffen beside him, reacting automatically, but she caught herself before leaping into the room. Good girl, he thought.

The woman in the door fired several rounds at his voice, then stopped shooting, listening for the sounds of a hit. In the silence, John removed the coil of rope from his shoulder, then took off his jacket before repositioning the rope so that it was still on his shoulder, but not blocking his movement in any way. He threw the jacket across the room and to the left, then ran out to the right.

The woman in the door heard the sound of the jacket and opened fire again, masking John's movements as he rushed her.

It was a risky move, one that he never would have tried if the situation didn't force it on him. Too many ways it could go wrong. She might sense the decoy and fire at him as he rushed. He might miss her in the blackness. Fran could rush out and get hit in continued fire, or trip on the coat that John had thrown in the middle of her intended escape route. Too many ills could come of his move, a crazy, desperate escape attempt that no sane man would engage in if he could avoid it any other way.

But he had no alternative.

***

Fran felt John leave as more than a physical departure. The sensation was a painful psychic rift that she felt at the center of her being, where she held her most delicate and painful and wonderful secrets. He scampered away, and Fran wanted to reach out, to hold onto him and wait for eternity together.

But then something inside her rose up, pushing aside the romantic notions and making room for her steelier side. This was the feeling she had when she buried the cleaver in the head of Nathan's killer, or rather the lack of feeling. Fear, love, *everything* shut down as her instinctive animal self rose from within and took calm control of her body. Life was all that mattered now, a life with John, a future with him. Which would not happen if she lost control, if she surrendered to the panic that gripped her in the moment of his departure.

She counted to three and then ran, staying low and trying to weave around the two cots she and John had moved next to each other to sleep on. She heard a grunt in front of her and the firing stopped, signaling that John had gotten to the woman; he had not been killed on his headlong flight into danger.

For a moment she thought about helping, then realized that her aid would be useless. She had seen John in action, and knew that if he couldn't handle the woman, neither could she. Her presence would only distract him, perhaps fatally. So she ran down the tunnel, turning on her headlamp as she did.

And being oh-so-careful not to touch the walls.

DOM#67A
LOSTON, COLORADO
AD 2013
10:46 AM TUESDAY
ALERT MODE

The cable pulled Malachi to the next level. He almost jumped off automatically, then realized that a free-hanging cable would provide no leverage with which to push off, and he would not jump but fall, a swift flight to the bottom of the shaft, to the center of the earth where he would be dashed to pieces, never to return. Unlike most of Loston's inhabitants, he could not come back to life if he was killed. The divinity that protected him from direct attack was also his weakness: he could die, so falling was not an acceptable option.

He swung the heavy cable back and forth like a child's swing, using his body to push jerkily back and forth. The cable whipped from side to side, and the entrance to the mine level he had just passed slowly sank before him. Malachi doubted if he would make it to the next level – one of the Controllers might shoot him long before he got there, sending him plummeting to his death in the deep bowels of the earth – so he let go.

He almost didn't make it, throwing his gun as he fell so it landed in the tunnel, and then grabbing onto the lip of the mineshaft floor with both hands. His shoulders felt as though scalding acid had been poured over them as the full weight of his wiry body pounded downward, wrested from gravity's grip by his own muscle and will.

He pulled himself up, gasping as he lay in the mouth of the tunnel, one arm hanging over the edge into nothingness.

What now? he asked himself.

What now?

***

One level below, the four Controllers watched the wire reel past. Then one of them – Elijah, the senior Recovery officer –

signaled for the group to move forward. All of them jumped as one, grabbing onto the wire and hanging on one-handed, rifles aimed steadily upward.

Elijah saw Malachi's arm and fired. The other three followed suit and fired as well, the sonic blasts dislodging bits of dirt from the sides of the shaft. The silt fell on them like black rain, and the arm disappeared.

Elijah hoped they had managed to hit Malachi, but doubted it. The bastard was slippery. Besides, Elijah could remember when Malachi had been a Controller and the head of the Recovery Operatives. He hadn't trained Elijah, but Elijah knew from Reco-Ops myth that Malachi was the best.

No, not just the best. The best ever. Someone capable of wiping them out. And they didn't know how many of them would be *allowed* to kill him, even if they were so lucky to get in a position where such became possible. Because his genetic makeup was something so rare that most of the Controllers would not be able to harm him, even if it meant dying themselves instead.

Stopping him would be hard.

Maybe impossible.

***

Jenna stumbled as the lift jerked around her. The cage rattled and the cable below it tautened suddenly, as though something below was suddenly pulling on it. The motor whined above, sending eerie echoes down the shaft. It sounded like the shriek of a baby being sliced with razors. Jenna had heard a baby dying that way once. Malachi had done it, had killed a child and brought back a video reproduction of it, played on the primitive media of that time and place. A videocassette, showing him killing the infant, draining it of blood, and kissing the dead child on the mouth after it was all done, after the cries had ended and all was celestial silence. She shuddered.

Then shuddered again as she reached the top level in the shaft, and thumbed the button. The elevator jerked to a halt, and she got out.

Time to wait.

***

Elijah almost lost his grip on the elevator cable when the elevator stopped. Two of the others *did* lose their grips, falling about a foot down the cord before regaining their hold and sliding to a stop.

They waited a moment, but the elevator didn't move again.

He looked at the troops. They still held their guns with one hand, each pulse blaster aimed upward, each person probably praying for Malachi to pop his head out, but Elijah knew that was a hollow hope. Malachi wouldn't do anything so foolish.

Elijah also knew they couldn't climb and cover themselves at the same time.

They were stuck.

***

Adam moved back and forth, trying to discern some distinguishing mark that would tell him where he was. He hated to admit it, but he was lost. He was positive the entrance to the mine shaft was nearby, but all the tunnels looked so similar that it was hard to find one that looked merely familiar, as opposed to the exactly the same as every other tunnel he had traversed.

Then he saw something in the tunnel ahead.

"The elevator," he whispered, and headed for the shaft, the three Controllers following behind.

***

Malachi lay on his back, weighing his options.

The Controllers had come en masse, that much was sure. He wanted to kill Fran and John. But he also needed to survive. That limited his range of choices.

He resisted the urge to look out and down the elevator shaft; it was a sure bet that the Controllers were waiting for him to do just that. Nor could he reach out and fire blindly downward, hoping to hit them. They were sure to be watching the lip of the floor where it merged with the elevator shaft, and if he put out his arm he had no doubt it would be hit and paralyzed by a pulse before he got off a single shot.

So he looked up instead.

The elevator was up there, though he couldn't see it. And as sure as anything, there were more Controllers above him, too. Adam was more than likely among them.

And don't forget the four Controllers below. Hanging below, waiting for a chance to come up and capture him.

The more he thought about what to do, the more his mind kept returning to the elevator. At first he thought his subconscious was telling him to call it down and ride it out. He rejected the idea. As soon as he got on, the Controllers below would fire up, puncturing the lift, paralyzing him. The elevator might fall as a result, but he knew they'd be more than willing to hurtle to their deaths if it meant stopping him. He didn't think that they'd be able to do willingly cause his death, but an accidental murder might be within their action parameters, and he'd be just as dead as if they'd done it on purpose. So he would stay off the elevator.

The elevator.____

He smiled then as he realized what his subconscious had been trying to tell him, then wiggled out as far as he could onto the lip of the tunnel. It projected a bit into the shaft, providing him an unobstructed view straight up while still shielding him from any shots ascending from below.

He aimed his gun up the shaft and pulled the trigger. Not once, but many times. The pinging of bullets tearing into the lift above sounded in response to his actions, and Malachi imagined the bullets punching holes, tearing through machinery.

Shearing cables.

The cable that trailed below the lift began to swing wildly, and he heard screams from below.

Let them cry, he thought. Let the Controllers weep in their last moments and feel the emptiness that comes to those who have no souls.

They wouldn't die, he knew. They couldn't.

Because most of the Controllers, like the berserk inhabitants of Loston, were machines.

DOM#67A
LOSTON, COLORADO
AD 2013
10:47 AM TUESDAY
ALERT MODE

Adam reached the elevator a moment before the shooting. It was empty, and one of the Controllers – a woman named Del – reached out her hand to open the gate. Sudden shots pounded up from somewhere down below, causing the lift to twitch back and forth like an enraged animal on an electrified floor.

The edge of the lift caught Del's shin, knocking her over into the center of the cage. She lay in a fetal position, arms shielding her head, as bullets shot through the floor all around her. Miraculously, none hit her, though the floor of the lift looked like a cheese grater when the firing stopped.

Adam thought for a moment that God might actually be doing a miracle of some kind, impossibly saving the woman's life, before a snap ripped through the turbulent air and the elevator plunged out of sight.

A few seconds later, something else fell past them.

Adam couldn't really make it out. But it had glistened like a diamond.

A long diamond, in the shape of a spear.
***

Elijah was still trying to figure out the best way to proceed, how to get himself up the cable and onto solid ground again before he either fell or Malachi killed him and the three other Controllers hanging out in empty space below the elevator. He needed time, he needed peace and quiet for thinking and some time to decide how to proceed. But peace and quiet were not to be found in this place, it seemed, and time was the one thing he couldn't have, for in that instant he felt the cable slacken in his hands and knew that he was falling.

It was over.

The thoughts in his head tumbled over themselves in an almost childishly silly patter of twists and convolutions, making no sense and all sense at once, marking his end not with the peaceful understanding that he had hoped for as he entered the eternities, but rather with confusion, with disorientation, with despair. His thoughts were jumbled even as he was, plummeting in fast loops and barrel rolls as he fell through the silence of the mine shaft. He could not see where he was going, or where the other three Controllers who had been on the cable with him were. But he could feel the wind rip through his clothing and pierce his skin as he fell, picking up speed as he dropped like a stone down a deep and empty well.

He fell forever, it seemed, and at one point felt himself collide with the wall of the shaft, which sheared off his right hand cleanly. He was already screaming by then, and the pain registered hardly at all.

Hundreds of feet. Forever. Eternity wasn't Heaven or Hell, it was a fall through a dark tunnel to the pit of the world, clutching a sonic pistol in one hand and nothing at all in the hand that fell disembodied beside you.

Then he hit the ground, finally, and all sounds, including his own, were silent.

But not gone. He wasn't gone. He was alive, with all that meant, and he felt himself – now a prisoner in his body and not the owner at all – push up on hands that were shattered that were attached to arms that were broken that in turn hung off a torso whose innards were mush.

Elijah could feel it, though. He could feel the bones re-knit themselves within him, and he knew what it meant.

I'm a machine, he thought, and darkness rose within him.

He looked over and saw one of the other Controllers – he couldn't even tell who it was, so mangled was the body – also twitching. Slower that Elijah, though. More internal damage. The other two Controllers were nowhere to be seen, and the analytical part of Elijah – that part of him that was quickly disappearing beneath a soft, dark blanket of madness that he could feel settling down in his mind like black snow – reasoned that they must have been utterly pulverized in the fall, colliding with the wall of the elevator shaft so many times and with such force that they had simply disintegrated under the pummeling.

Then he noticed the cable. It was still dropping from above, wrapping around the floor of the shaft like an obscenely long snake that would twist in on itself and then begin to eat the whole earth from the inside out.

Elijah knew the elevator itself must be falling, and he began to shuffle to the side of the shaft, hands and knees working slowly as they mended themselves and tried to carry him out of the danger zone at the same time.

He made it.

He turned as the elevator hit, seeing it slam into the other living – or unliving, as it were – Controller, smashing he/she/it into the earth, allowing no more life, crushing the last bits of animation out of the machine. Blood splashed and dust rose in a great cloud as the earth shivered with the force of the impact.

Elijah lay there in the dark, feeling his body mend.

I'm a machine, he thought again. His whole life, the memories he had, the loves he felt, the friends he knew, all turned away from him as he realized that his existence was a lie. His memories were constructed, and his birth had been from in a bio-lab, not a womb.

He began screaming again, his lungs now able once more to process oxygen (Not *breathe*! screamed the rapidly diminishing portion of his mind that still remembered being a man. *Process oxygen.*) and then stopped as he heard a new sound.

It was a terrible, silent sound. The sound of the earth in stasis before an earthquake, that awful stillness before cataclysm.

Elijah – the thing that had once been Elijah – looked up. Darkness greeted him, but then something sparkled above.

He saw the icicle that had cracked off its base hundreds of feet above him a mere fraction of a second before crashed down.

The needle sharp shaft pierced him, slamming through him like a pin through an entomologist's favorite specimen. It exploded through his face in a bright flash of white, and Elijah felt it enter the tiny part of his thalamus that was all that was keeping him alive in spite of his body's anxious desire to embrace death.

Elijah, the man and the machine, died.

And was not unhappy.

DOM#67A
LOSTON, COLORADO
AD 2013
10:48 AM TUESDAY
*****ALERT MODE*****

John slammed into Deirdre, feeling her in the complete blackness of the room. The move caught her by surprise, and him too: he had expected to be gunned down in the darkness. He knocked into the barrel of her weapon, and grappled for it, gasping as the gun barrel – hot from the Uzi's high bullet expenditure – burnt his hand. The woman tightened her hold almost immediately, no doubt aware as John was that letting go would be tantamount to signing her own death sentence.

The struggle was a silent one as John and the woman slammed against the cave wall, each trying to gain the upper hand in the darkness. He felt a breath of cool air whisk by him in the void, and knew it was Fran, once again following his directives perfectly. He managed a grim smile even in the thick of the struggle.

He saw a light flick on down the tunnel and again knew it must be Fran, clicking on her headlamp. At the same moment, he felt his enemy's body tense. The woman redoubled her efforts, trying now not so much to win as to get away.

To follow Fran, John thought. And again he wondered what they wanted of her.

The thought distracted him enough that the woman was able to get in a hit. She loosened her grip on the gun and slammed her palm into John's cheek. It wasn't a hard blow – her leverage was bad – but the contact dazed him, and she was able to push him away. He heard her running and made out her dim outline, sprinting toward the light that marked Fran's location.

He knew he'd never catch up in time, and his reaction was more instinct than thought.

In one swift move, he pulled the coil of rope off his shoulder. It was thick gauge, meant for hauling miners up and down new shafts, for lashing temporary support braces and other strength work. So it was heavy, almost a cable, with a good heft to it.

John threw the rope and dimly saw it fly through the air in tight curls like an airborne tarantula. It hit the woman's legs, tangling them, and she tripped. Her arms reached out to break her fall, and in the time she was going down, John leapt to his feet and ran toward her. She careened into a wall brace, then fell to her knees in the dusky gloom of the tunnel.

If he could get to her before she stood, he felt sure he could kill her. But he was still twenty feet away when she jumped up, gun aimed at him. Point blank, and no way to miss.

***

Deirdre's knee hurt where she had hit the ground. Her knuckles were skinned from the impact with the wall, and her whole body was bruised from the short but intense fight in the dark. She knew her mission was to get the girl, but now she had the chance to make sure John didn't get in their way anymore. He was in her sights, hard to see in the dim light, but still impossible to miss at this close range. She could see that his hands were raised in a ridiculous stance of defeat, as though he thought she would let him go.

"Die," she snarled. He leaped to the side, but she didn't pull the trigger. She didn't want to waste any ammo, so she would wait a fraction of a second longer, then kill him when he stopped his sideways move.

In the fraction of a second she waited, a thin trickle of dirt fell on her head.

Then, with a deep rumble, a hundred tons of rock rolled out of the wall, slamming into her with a life-ending torrent that masked any slight noise she might have made in the millisecond between realizing what was happening and becoming a permanent fixture of the mountain's structure.

***

Fran heard the collapse behind her and launched herself forward, shielding her head with her arms and landing in a fetal position on the ground. She felt a cloud of dust roil over her like an angry and biting wind, and then there was only stillness, a silence that was as deep and profound as the darkness she had experienced in this place beneath the world. Silent and dark, quiet and deep. The mountain seemed to her as though it was holding its breath, deciding whether to let loose another torrent of rock and dirt. There was another deep rumble, and then silence again.

She looked behind her. A solid wall of rock and rubble greeted her.

"John!" she screamed.

No answer.

She looked the other way down the hall. There was nothing, just twenty feet of straight shaft, then an intersection. John had told her to wait at the intersection. No matter what.

So she stood and walked to it, knowing she would wait there as if he were alive, because her heart would not allow her to believe he was dead. Besides, she knew that she would never be able to find her way out of this place on her own. If John didn't appear to help her, she could wander this subterranean labyrinth for a year without ever coming close to finding the way back to the surface.

She waited, gripped by a loneliness she had never felt before, one that few people *had* experienced, but which one of the miners could have told her went with being in the ground. It was the peculiar sensation that all above is gone, a dream, and only she and the earth still existed. But the existence was dark and solitary, with rock columns for companions, and the ever-present ink that painted everything the same bleak shade of black hovering beyond the reach of her small headlamp. Loneliness was the way of the earth, and now for all Fran knew she would die in this profound solitude.

Still, she clung to the thought of John. She prayed he was alive.

***

Adam stood before the shaft. The elevator was gone. So was Del, one more Controller gone from the ever-dwindling population of would-be saviors of humanity. He didn't know how to get down without the elevator, so all he could do was guard the entrance and hope against hope that John – and more importantly, Fran – surfaced.

The remaining Controllers knew the same thing. They shuffled nervously as they waited for Adam to move. None of them was really sure how to get back to the entrance. For all the technological advances they may have enjoyed in their own place and time, here under the mountain they found themselves bereft of advantage. The ground had stolen their skill, and left them alone to fend for themselves with only primal instinct as their guides. And instinct was found wanting in people who had not had to use such a thing in millennia.

A distant rumble sounded, and all of them stiffened. They didn't know what the sound meant, but it sounded ominous.

"Subterranean slide," whispered one of the Controllers. Adam didn't know. It certainly could have been a subterranean slide.

Then again, it could have been a giant kangaroo hopping on the mountaintop in steel-toed ballet shoes for all Adam knew. He was no expert in geology, and knew his spelunking experience was even more limited than his knowledge of the different rock strata in which he now found himself encased.

A moment later, he started walking. They were at the elevator, he reasoned, so the tunnel opening couldn't be far.

At least, he hoped not.

***

Fran struggled against tears in the darkness. The light from her headlamp was on, but it only illuminated a dim cone in the thick dust that still hadn't settled completely after the cave in.

Alone.

Never had that word ushered such dread into her heart as it did now. Even in the dark days and months directly after Nathan had died, her sense of loneliness had been tempered by the outpouring of love and sympathy she received as a daily allowance from friends and relatives. She had never truly felt alone in the way she did now.

This is how the dead must feel, she thought, locked in a silent tomb with nothing but the earth and their own steady decay for company.

She sniffled, then coughed as the dust entered her nostrils and lungs. It was thick and sharper than any dust she was used to, composed of tiny slivers of silicon and volcanic rock that could cause what the miners called black lung or the bleeding. She didn't worry particularly about contracting silicosis, not in the short time that she had been here, but the air irritated her mucus membranes, making her nose run and her eyes water.

She covered her mouth and coughed, and then heard something coming down one of the side corridors. She swung her light around to see what it was, worried that new horrors awaited her, demons that had lingered until now, until she was completely alone, before coming with their obsidian eyes and razor claws to claim her life.

A dark shape hurtled out of the darkness, and Fran screamed.

"Fran, it's me!" shouted John, and her scream instantly dissolved into a whimper as she clung to him. She was trying to be brave, but everything she had been through in the past twenty-four hours had drained her.

"I'm so tired," she said.

John nodded. "Me, too," he said. "Come on, let's get out of this hole."

DOM#67A
LOSTON, COLORADO
AD 2013
11:02 AM TUESDAY
*****ALERT MODE*****

Malachi heard the sound of the falling elevator cut through the air and caught a glimpse of one of the Controllers – he thought he recognized Del laying in the cage, but couldn't be sure – as it hurtled by.

He smiled. One less Controller was good news.

He also smiled at the cries of pain that disappeared almost as soon as they began as the four Controllers on the cable below the lift fell to the bottom of the shaft. He knew they were gone for good: even if they survived the fall, they would quickly go insane as they realized their inhumanity. It always happened that way. Fed by a lifetime of programming, their biomechanical minds hadn't the defense mechanisms necessary to cope with the sudden discovery of their own lifelessness.

Cogito, ergo sum, he thought. I think, therefore I am. It was a saying from Before, from the old days before all this had become necessary. It was what the philosophers had reasoned out to explain their own existence. And there seemed to be some truth in it, for unlike a real man or woman, the machines masquerading as people always went insane when confronted with the fact of their true nature.

Enlightenment bred understanding, understanding bred insanity, and insanity brought death.

He stood and walked carefully down the tunnel, searching in the dimness for a way to get out of the mine. After a short time he found a ladder. It went up. And up was where Malachi wanted to go.

***

John climbed, leading Fran up the small ladder that extended up a long shaft. He had never taken this ladder before, but knew it was one of the ways into and out of the mine, though it was long-abandoned in favor of other, easier methods of egress like the lift. They had been climbing for what seemed like hours, and his arms were tired. He knew that Fran's arms must be on fire, feeling like her shoulders were pulling out of their sockets, but she made no sound, whispered no complaints.

The ladder felt no similar need to refrain from grumbling. It crackled and splintered during their entire ascent, noises that disquieted John. He tried to remember how long ago the ladder had been built. It had been decades at least, he knew. That was part of why the lift was put in: the ladder was not only inefficient, it was dangerous. Several times during the climb he stopped and signaled Fran to do the same, worried that their combined weight in a trouble spot would pull the ladder away from the wall or just splinter it under their hands, casting them back into the depths of the earth. He would navigate the dangerous area himself, carefully testing each rung for strength, before allowing Fran to follow behind him.

In spite of his misgivings, however, the ladder held, and when John looked up for what felt like the millionth time, he saw a glorious sight: the top of the slim shaft. He couldn't remember for sure, but it seemed to him that the top was within feet of the tunnel entrance. He redoubled his efforts, climbing faster.

"Why the rush?" panted Fran from below him.

"We're almost out," he said.

He heard her move faster behind him as well, gaining strength with the news of their impending exit from the depths of the mountain. Splinters from the old wooden ladder bit into his hands, but he didn't care. He wanted to leave.

He pulled himself up over the lip of the shaft, then reached down to help Fran up the last few feet.

She reached out a hand.

And the ladder, old and weary from years of neglect, at last did exactly what John had most feared. It fell away. It crackled and snapped like a log in the fire, then shattered into several large pieces. Short segments of the ladder remained anchored to the wall of the shaft, tethered by tenacious bolts that had rusted solid and so dirty they were nearly invisible. The rest of the ladder plummeted into the darkness, its skeletal outlines disappearing into the black below long before sounds of the splintering and cracking that marked its final dissolution had ceased.

Fran screamed, and John heard an echoing noise escape his own lips as Fran desperately lurched upward, catching onto his hand. The ladder section she had been resting on fell from beneath her, leaving her suspended over a dark and bottomless well.

"Oh, God, John, help me!" she cried.

"I've got you, Fran!"

"Help me, John!"

"I've got you! I won't let go!"

He felt himself slipping toward the rim, her body weight pulling against him and the bad angle of his body on the tunnel floor giving him no leverage. He reached out his free hand, trying to gain purchase on something. He found only loose sand and dirt, and tried to stop himself by jabbing his palm hard onto the dirt floor, as though he could pummel the mountain into submission and force it to provide him with a handhold.

It didn't work. He was still slipping, scrabbling desperately for a grip on the hardpack dirt floor of the mine. Pebbles and gravel came away in silty handfuls, and he knew he was going to lose Fran.

"Help!" he cried out, though no one was there to save them. Only Malachi and his goons might be around, and they had hardly shown themselves to be the saving type.

Fran was going to fall, he realized. He also knew that he wouldn't let go of her, so her fall would be quickly followed by his own.

Then something stopped him. Pain lanced through his hand and his forward movement stopped. He looked over and saw a cleated bootsole, grinding onto the back of his hand, trapping it against the floor of the tunnel.

"Jenna," said the person who wore the boot, one of the women who had been trying to kill him and Fran. Her mouth was caked with blood from where he had hit her while they struggled at Gabe's house twelve hours and a lifetime before. He could make out the damp shards of broken teeth jutting out through her mangled lips. "My name is Jenna," she hissed. Blood drooled from her mouth in ropey strands, but she smiled like a little girl who she had just been given a pony for her birthday.

Her gun pressed against John's cheek. He didn't move as she looked over the edge of the shaft, looking at Fran who still hung helplessly from John's rapidly tiring grip. Jenna's macabre grin grew even wider, the gnarled remnants of her teeth seeming to swell and twist in among themselves in the dim light of the mine entrance.

"I just wanted you to know who sent you to hell," she rasped, and John saw her finger tighten on the trigger.

DOM#67A
LOSTON, COLORADO
AD 2013
1:15 PM TUESDAY
ALERT MODE

The shot rang out, and John felt his fingers slip away, heard Fran shriek once and then go silent, and waited for the end. He expected a sudden burst of pain, a white light, and then the deep black of oblivion, a darkness so pervasive and all-encompassing that the deepest tunnels of Resurrection would seem light by comparison.

But none of that came.

Instead, he felt the boot come off his hand, granting him sudden relief from the pressure and accompanied by an equally sudden jab of pain as the nerve endings in the abraded skin were exposed to the damp air of the cave.

He looked at Jenna, still not sure what had just happened. Blood poured from her mouth, but this time it was more than the blood leaking from the wounds John had inflicted upon her. She was hemorrhaging, and dark arterial blood welled over her lips and fell in a stream onto her chest. Jenna stumbled once, looking surprised at the blossoming stain on her bosom where blood flowed thick and fast. Then she fell past him, tripping into the open shaft and disappearing without a sound.

A man stood behind her, lowering his gun. It was a strange gun, but clearly a gun nonetheless. He was an older man, his hair white and his face deeply creased with age and worry. Even in the dim light, John could see that the man's eyes were the most startlingly blue he had ever seen.

Several others stood behind the man, all dressed in strange clothing and body armor, all holding the same strange weaponry as the man who had shot Jenna.

He saw all of them watching him, but he didn't care to know who they were, or how they came to be here, or why they had saved him. He turned to look back down the shaft. Fran was gone, he knew, and his vision swam as tears blurred his sight. But still he had to look.

He swept his head back and forth, looking down in spite of the impossibility of finding her alive. All that mattered was Fran.

Please, God, he prayed. Please let her be there.

The thought that he had not prayed since Annie's death came to him, and he wondered if God would even listen to him at all, much less answer such a prayer. When we turn our backs on Him, thought John, does He turn His back on us as well?

A moment later he had his answer. Or at least, he had as close to an answer as he was ever likely to get: Apparently He doesn't.

John sobbed as he saw Fran, upside down and unconscious, her legs tangled in one of the sections of ladder that remained bolted to the wall. She was far out of reach, he knew, but he tried to lower himself farther anyway, unwilling to give her up.

The piece of a ladder that she hung from started to creak, beginning to give.

"No!" shouted John, and redoubled his efforts, straining as though by mere thought or physical effort he might be able to add another inch to his reach.

He felt a hand on his shoulder, pulling him back from the edge. It was the man who had saved him. The blue-eyed old man.

John fought against him. "I can't let her die!" he said, almost in tears.

The man shook him. "You won't. But you're exhausted and you're likely to miscalculate. Let one of my people take care of her."

John struggled a moment longer, before the man's words penetrated his fatigued and pain-fogged brain. He nodded. Immediately the man gestured at one of his crew, a thick, burly man who stepped forward instantly. His clothing, mostly some kind of body armor that John was unfamiliar with, almost glistened in the darkness of the shaft. It wasn't any material John had ever seen. But it *was* similar to the fabric worn by the man who killed John's father.

Answers might be within his reach, he realized. He might at last know who had killed his father, and how his father had risen from the dead to save him. Perhaps he would even learn what had happened to transform the town and the people he knew and loved into undying killers. But not now. Now, Fran needed to be saved, and if that didn't happen, the rest could fall into the shaft and be lost with her for all he cared.

The burly man withdrew a tiny device from an inner pocket. He pressed a small button on its face, then dropped it to the ground near the rim of the shaft, where it affixed itself with a solid thunk. Then the man slid out over the lip himself, easing himself downward farther and farther and then finally letting go. John saw him float downward toward Fran, and wondered if, on top of all that had happened in the last few days, he was now about to find out that people could fly, too. In a moment, however, he realized that the man wasn't actually floating, but was hanging from some kind of micro-fiber. The filament was affixed to the man's belt, and a continuous feed of the thread came forth from the device the man had affixed to the shaft rim above him. He descended like a spider, suspended from a single silken line that was clearly too thin and weak to hold him.

Yet hold him it did. John watched as the man drifted down to Fran, then carefully unhooked her legs and pulled her into his arms. John heard the men and women who stood nearby him sigh, and realized that they had been just as afraid as he. Fran's safety meant something to them. The thought comforted him as nothing else in this long nightmare had been able to do. Perhaps he was safe. Perhaps he and Fran would no longer have to run.

John heard the white-haired man speak to another one of the men and women who stood nearby: "Call the jet."

The man holding Fran started up again, the machine attached to the shaft's edge reeling in the slim fiber that held them aloft against gravity's insistent tug. Soon they were both at the level of the tunnel floor, and John pulled Fran over to him. A wound on her scalp bled profusely, but John could see instantly that it wasn't deep. Head wounds bled copiously, but were often of superficial importance. More frightening was the possibility of internal injuries. He began inspecting her expertly, checking her for obvious signs of trauma, then probing gently to see if he could find any edema or other signs of internal damage.

"Please," said the man who had helped them, the white haired man with the sorrowful eyes, "why don't we do that after we arrive?"

"Arrive?" said John, continuing his examination. He was beyond fear or any other strong sensations, the night having burned out his capacity for normal feeling, cauterizing the ragged edges of his emotion and leaving only unfeeling scar tissue behind. All he felt now was concern for Fran, and he wasn't going to stop trying to help her to make small talk with this man, whoever or whatever he was. "Arrive where? Who the hell are you, Mister, and why is everyone I know so intent on killing me?"

"All will be explained."

"Explain it now. Who are you?"

"*Deus ex machina*," answered the man, speaking with the tone of one who was making a private joke, though his eyes did not glint with any kind of merriment. Rather, they seemed to look even more sorrowful, if such were possible.

If the response *was* a joke, John didn't get it. Fear and amazement fraying his patience to mere threads, he repeated his question more emphatically, making it clear that he wasn't going to tolerate any more nonsense.

"Answer me, dammit."

The other man's eyes grew cold and flinty, and now John discovered that they were capable of filling with more than just sadness and wisdom. They contained strength beyond anything John had ever before seen. Clearly this was a man who was accustomed to being obeyed. But John also sensed something more than the existence of a man of power. This man was not one of those pale dictators and petty tyrants whom John had dedicated much of his life to putting down. Instead, the man before him seemed to wear the mantle and bearing of a true king, evoking a sense that he must be obeyed not merely because he was the monarch, but because he was *right*.

"Really, John," said the man. "We've devoted quite a large of amount of effort to you. The least you can do is come with us."

The men and women standing near the man leveled their weapons at John. It wasn't a request.

"Who are you?" asked John again, his tone pleading this time. It was a defeatist gesture, he knew, begging at least a morsel of information in return for his acquiescence to their wishes.

The man nodded and looked as though he felt pity for John, his face clearly conveying a sense that he hated all this, but that for some reason it was necessary. "My name is Adam," he said, and nodded at his crew. Two of them holstered their weapons and moved as though to pick up Fran. John gathered her into his arms and stood before they could do so, standing before Adam, daring the man to try and take her from him.

Adam nodded, conceding John's right to hold the unconscious woman, and gestured for him to move.

John looked down the tunnel the way the man had pointed. "We going back into the mine?" he asked.

"What? No, we're leaving," said Adam.

"Then we go this way," said John, walking in the direction opposite to the way Adam had indicated. He walked a few feet, turned the corner, and headed to the entrance, feeling a bit better knowing that, for all their mystery and apparent technology, these newcomers couldn't get out of a hole in the ground without his help.

A few feet from the mine entrance, scant meters from being able to finally leave Resurrection, he stopped in his tracks.

There was something in front of the mine entrance. It looked like a small private jet, only it had absolutely no windows or visible doors. It hovered in midair before the mine, soundlessly hanging in the still air of midday, so still that it seemed to be less a construct of steel and metal than an inanimate rendition done by some itinerant artist who specialized in painting mechanical miracles on canvas of air.

Adam came and stood at his side. "After you, John," he said. At that moment, the side of the jet split open and a ramp dropped out.

John looked around him. He still didn't know what was going on, but again the presence of the guns leveled at him convinced him that the graciousness and politeness that had so far abounded could quickly change to hostility.

He stepped the rest of the way out of the mine, approaching the opening. Two more people dressed in the same strange garb as Adam came down the ramp out of the jet and held out their hands to help him in.

John glanced down the mountainside as he shuffled into the strange craft. He saw a thin line of people, some of them his friends, all of them known to him, following several hounds up the mountain trail. The queue undulated in perfect synchronization, every person marching to the hypnotic cadence of an unknown drummer.

It was the entire town, making its way up the mountain. John's stomach lurched with renewed dread. They were coming for him, he knew. This nightmare was not yet over.

Adam saw them too, but did not react with terror as had John. He calmly pulled what looked like a button from his pocket.

"Control," he said into the tiny device.

"Yes," answered a woman's voice, emerging from the button. It must be some sort of radio or communications device, but the voice that came from the small machine Adam held was unaccompanied by the tinny sound that John expected from field communicators. It was crystal clear, as though the speaker was standing by them, unseen but present.

"Sheila, this is Adam. We have them."

"Thank God."

"Thank Him later. Right now initiate shut-down on Loston. And roll everyone back two days."

"Understood."

Adam repocketed the button and looked down the hill again. John followed his gaze and saw the men and women and children making their way up the hill suddenly stop. They swayed as in a breeze for a long moment, then slowly crumpled and slumped to the ground.

Adam pushed John gently into the craft before them. The rest of the Controllers followed, and the ramp retracted into the ship, sealing it behind them.

***

Malachi poked his head into the tunnel, watching John carry Fran out, followed closely by Adam and his group of Controller drones.

Malachi couldn't take them on. Deirdre and Jenna were undoubtedly dead, and for him to attack all the Controllers on his own would be tantamount to suicide. But, if he was lucky, if he was *blessed*, the situation could still turn to his advantage.

He watched carefully, ready to dart back into the side room where he had secreted himself upon emerging from the depths of the mountain only minutes before John and Fran had arrived. He could be gone in an instant should Adam or anyone in his group turn this way. But no one did, and he followed them cautiously down the tunnel. He saw them get into the dropjet, and it started to rise. Malachi ran out of the mine, pulling a tracer pin from his belt. He threw it at the rising craft, heard it click to the metal and knew that it would instantly solder itself to the metal of the jet.

The jet was taking Adam home.

And home was where the heart was. The Controllers had moved their headquarters since his defection from their ranks, and every one of the Fans who had tried to pinpoint its new location had met with failure. But there was nowhere else this jet could possibly be going than back to its own time and place, to care for Fran. The risk of her dying was one that frightened them enough that they would take her there to care for, in a place where she could receive the best possible medical attention. They would probably also wipe her memory.

Of course, Malachi hoped to stop all that. Fran had escaped, for the moment. But now he could follow her. Could follow them all, and that meant he could at last find the Control HQ and do what he wanted to.

He would see the world in flames.

THREE – INTO THE OUTSIDE

SUBJECT ACQUISITION/
TRANSIT LOG

John stared at Adam, who returned his gaze steadily. Fran lay across John's lap, still unconscious, and that worried him. She was in a coma, he feared, and he didn't know what to do about that. He was in some sort of a ship with people – if they were people; John hadn't ruled out the alternate possibility that they were some strange alien race – who had saved his life and then forced him at gunpoint to accompany them. He just wasn't sure what to think or what was going to happen to him.

He looked again at Adam, studying the man who sat across from him. The man's eyes were so blue that John thought he could see the sky in them. He could also see worry and anguish in those orbs, as though the weight of the world rested on this man's shoulders. Or more than that. They were eyes that spoke of trust, and care, and love. But John would not be fooled. He would not be at ease until he and Fran were home again, and safe.

Safety. Was that even a possibility anymore?

"Where are we going?" John asked.

Adam smiled. "Just wait," he said. "All will be explained."

"Why not now?"

Again, that enigmatic smile. "Because you wouldn't believe it if I told you."

"Try me."

Adam shrugged, as if to say, you asked for it. "We're going to Virginia."

John had prepared himself for nearly any answer, but had certainly expected something more along the lines of "The third star in the Alpha Centauri system" or "We will be disintegrated and our particles beamed to a starship, where we will go where no man has gone before" or even "Booga booga, haven't you figured out that you're insane?" But "Virginia" was the last thing he thought he would hear. The men and women around him must have seen his discomfiture, for they laughed heartily. The sound made him relax a bit.

Laughter. Very human laughter. Surely people who laughed so openly couldn't be evil, could they? John knew he was doing more than just grasping at straws with that line of thought. He was inventing reasons to hope. But as that was all he had left to him, that was what he would do.

Adam leaned forward and put a hand on John's knee. The worry still clouded the other man's sky blue eyes, but a twinkle also shone in them. "It's not outer space, but don't worry. I think you'll be surprised anyway."

The crew around John laughed again.

How about that? he thought. I'm on a space ship going to Virginia with a bunch of commandos out of a Buck Rogers show. And it's all so terribly funny.

It wasn't, but somehow the events of the past week had awakened something in him. He realized that he felt *good* all of a sudden, in a way that he had not felt since Annie's death. He felt as though he had purpose, a reason to be alive. It felt right. As though he was speeding, not to some unimaginable future, but toward a home.

FAN HQ
AD 2013/AE 4013

Malachi walked into the place that was his home, and within seconds his people surrounded him, asking a thousand questions: "Are you all right?" "Was it successful?" "Did you kill her?" "Where are the others?"

A thousand questions, a thousand hands touching him, caressing him. He closed his eyes for a moment and felt of the warmth that sprang from their souls like a spring of cleanest water, something unknown to his world for two thousand years.

He lived in Newark, New Jersey.

At least, he *thought* it was New Jersey. That was what he guessed based on the small bits of the past that were unearthed in the subterranean caverns where the Fans took refuge from the cruel world outside. He could not be sure, of course, for Newark had not existed as a living place for some two thousand years. But that was his guess, and he supposed that Newark was as good a place as any. Jerusalem or one of the hallowed lands of the Bible would have been more fitting to his mission, but since Fran and the Controllers were located somewhere on this continent, the Fans had to make their homes here as well.

He looked upon his people, a small army of men and women who gazed up at him with something akin to worship. Each was dressed differently, each wearing clothing stolen from a different time, each holding weapons that had been invented during distinct historical epochs. Some of his people looked quite normal. Others were ravaged by the cosmic rays that constantly swept over this doomed earth's face. They lived underground, below a thick barrier of sand and stone, in order to avoid those deadly emissions, but the nature of their work took them out often enough that most Fans were destined to die of cancer or other, more virulent forms of radiation poisoning.

Malachi felt no revulsion at the sight of half-eaten faces, no chill at the touch of hands that left bloody marks on his clothing.

These were his people, his brothers and sisters, his sons and daughters in the kingdom they were building.

When everyone had gathered around, cramming into the room which served as their assembly hall and as their chapel, he spoke.

"She is still alive," he said. A ripple went through the assemblage. Sadness, despair. He held up a hand to quell the burgeoning sense of helplessness that was the constant companion of every one of them. "The others," he said at last, speaking of Todd, Deirdre, and Jenna, "have gone on to their reward. The three of you who went out have not come back. One was a machine, but two were lost to us without divulging their true natures." He bowed his head as though praying, then raised it and said, "Let it be known that they were human. They were real, and they shall rest in eternity for their great work."

A great sigh swept through the group. A few began crying, not with sadness but with envy. The rest waited for the remainder of Malachi's report. Return and report: it was the way they had done it for almost two thousand years now, and though Malachi was the newest in a long line of priest-kings and had changed many things, this aspect would never change. He would return and report, so that the work could go on, no matter what.

"The girl is still alive. So is her protector," he said, a sneer curling his lips at the last word. "A Recovery team came into Loston and saved them."

Again the sigh rippled through his people. More sadness. He held up his hands, and even the tiny whispers and murmurs melted instantly away, like snowflakes on the scorched ground above them.

"There is blessing, though," he said. He held up his tracker. "They still have Fran, but I'm tracking them – *all* of them – back to Control."

The silence that followed that statement was deafening, like the absolute silence that must have been heard in the second before

God first said "Let there be light." It was the stillness of promise, of knowledge that what was to come would be glory.

Malachi allowed himself a smile. "Arm yourselves," he said. "All of you. We attack them as soon as you are prepared. We end it all"

A great cheer went up and the group divided into a hundred smaller units, putting on gear, dividing up weapons. Preparing.

Malachi watched it all. He took a deep breath, and his body cried out with the strain of the last two days. But at the same time he felt light and ready for what came.

He closed his eyes, and again felt the hot breath of fire, fire that burned across the world and completed what had begun two thousand years before.

Today was the day.

Armageddon, begun two millennia ago, would at last be complete.

CONTROL HQ – RUSHM
AD 4013/AE 2013

A thump signaled their arrival at wherever it was they were headed. Adam had said their destination was Virginia, but John didn't really expect to see the place he knew from travel books and TV shows as Virginia, with the rolling hills and mountains and signs pointing out the historic sights.

He wasn't disappointed. The view that greeted him upon arrival was nothing he was prepared for. It was utterly alien, and that sense of displacement was only heightened by Adam calling it Virginia.

The door cracked open and once again Adam gestured for John to go first. He didn't resist this time, stepping out with Fran still in his arms. He entered what appeared to be some kind of hangar, but it was like no other hangar he'd ever seen or heard of. It was bathed in a strange red light that poured like blood through the hangar opening. Several other craft like the ones he'd flown in on hung in the air nearby, and several carlike contraptions squatted at their sides. The vehicles were short and boxy, and looked like dune-buggies with tank treads instead of wheels.

He had barely had a moment to take it all in when five men scrambled toward him. They were large, muscles straining against the strange fabric of their shirts, and John realized that they meant to take Fran from him.

A sudden rage gripped him. Adam had betrayed them, the good feelings nothing but a front and a lie. John resisted the groping hands of the men, but there were too many of them, and he was encumbered by Fran's still unmoving form. He managed to take two of them out with swift kicks to the knees and inner thighs that left them curled on the steel floor of the hangar in various stages of hurt.

Then he realized – vaguely, as all his thoughts floated in a cottony haze of confusion, fear, fatigue, and anger – that not only were the three remaining men still coming at him, but the people who had come with Adam were doing their best to peel Fran away from him.

"No!" he screamed, and redoubled his efforts to escape. But he couldn't. It was impossible.

He kicked another person, one of the women who had come with Adam, and then turned to see one of the burly men club at him with a rifle. The butt of the weapon smashed John in the face, point blank, and all went dark.

He faded into blackness, and the last thing he remembered was Adam's voice.

"Dammit, you killed him."

FAN HQ
AD 4013/AE 2013

Malachi knelt on the central floor, his followers around him. There were only about three hundred of them, far fewer than the number of Controllers, but he did not fear. He knew that their faith would make them strong, and he would fear no evil.

They all prayed, holding weapons in front of their chests like exotic prayer beads, mumbling words to God and all asking for the same thing:

Let today be the day.

Malachi finished his prayer, wiped his eyes, and stood.

"It's time."

CONTROL HQ – RUSHM
AD 2013/AE 4013

Adam watched John carefully. Blood flowed copiously from the wound on his temple, enough that a casual observer would have bet John soon would be dead, if he wasn't already.

Yet Adam knew the man was in no danger. Not from the head wound, at least.

In moments, John's eyes flickered, then opened fully.

"Do you think God loves machines, John?" asked Adam.

John did not respond. His gaze moved around as he tried to take in his surroundings. Adam knew what John was seeing: a dark room, a large desk, and the man who had taken Fran sitting behind it. He saw John tense, saw him steel himself to attack Adam, and held up his hand.

"Try it and Fran will die before you even touch me."

Adam deplored the lie, but knew John was too frightened to be compliant, unless perhaps he believed his good behavior might somehow benefit or protect Fran. It worked. The fight went out of John all at once, as though he were a giant hot air balloon whose air had been crushed from it by the grasp of a giant, leaving it deflated and useless.

"What's going on?" asked John. His voice was weary and strained. Adam regretted the course he had put John through, but knew it had been necessary. So many hard choices, and so few of them right, it seemed. Did the ends justify the means? he asked himself, but as always there came no answer, just more questions to haunt his conscience.

"I do regret all this," he said to the confused man who sat before him, "but some precautions are necessary. An entire species depends on what you and I do here."

"What are you talking about? Where's Fran?"

Adam leaned back in his chair, steepling his fingers in front of him. "She's nearby. Being treated for her wounds. She'll be fine, I assure you."

Adam watched as John looked around, apparently trying to gain some kind of understanding from the empty room they sat in. Adam knew that he would find no enlightenment in this Spartan space, so he spoke. "You want to know what's happening," he said, making it a statement and not a question. "You want to know why everyone you've known and loved your whole life is suddenly a stranger. Why they all want to kill you. Why they don't stay dead when *they* are killed. Who killed your father. Why everyone is after you and Fran."

John nodded. His face was stony, not giving anything to Adam. That was to be expected, under the circumstances, and Adam smiled at John, a genuinely friendly smile. "What year is it, John?"

"Two thousand thirteen."

"Wrong. It's two thousand thirteen, all right, but not A.D. It's two thousand thirteen *A.E.* That's After Endwar, which doesn't mean anything to you right now," said Adam, responding to John's confused look. "So let me translate for you. In your reckoning of time, it's A.D. *four thousand* thirteen."

***

Adam did something as he delivered this pronouncement – John couldn't see exactly what – and one wall of the room slid away, revealing a gargantuan control room filled with people checking monitors, keying in information on computers, and all looking as busy as the cliché bee. One entire wall of the mammoth room held stacks of glowing cubes John thought were TV screens, until he realized that their images were three-dimensional, and they appeared to be hanging in the air without the benefit of any surrounding chassis.

Adam rose from behind his desk and motioned for John to step into the room. "Go on, John. See where we run the world."

John stood, feeling a bit wobbly. The technology that surrounded him was obviously so far beyond what he knew that he felt like a Neanderthal man holding a Nintendo game. He stepped in and looked at the people, the computers, the monitors. He noticed one of the screens held a view of the inside of his house and pointed at it.

"What's that?"

Adam looked at where John was pointing. "That's Mayor Barnes. He was probably waiting at your home on the off chance you would return there, and that's where he remained when we shut down Loston. You're seeing through the mini-cams in his eyes."

John snapped his gaze back to Adam. "What?"

Adam shrugged and then delivered the kicker: "All the robots have them."

He turned and went back through the opening, into the office again. John followed and the wall shut behind them, again isolating once more in a featureless space of shadow and gloom. Adam sat back down at his desk and tapped a control, motioning with his other hand for John to be seated again.

"I'm going to paint you a picture, John, and I hope you listen carefully, because this will be unpleasant, and I have no desire to repeat any of it."

A picture appeared in the air between them, a 3-D cube like the ones John had seen in the other room. Pictures of reporters, like any he would see on CNN or Fox News or MSNBC, flashed across the holograph. Each one of them was obviously speaking into the camera, though John heard no sound, and all of them held looks of despair. They pictures skittered and lurched oddly, and without sound it took him a few moments to realize he was watching a futuristic equivalent of fast-forwarding.

"Around the year two thousand," said Adam, speaking from behind the cube, "several of the smaller countries acquired enough nuclear capacity to give the old U.S.A. a run for her money."

John watched as the video cube changed, showing shots of what he recognized as nuclear warheads, though the designs were slightly different from the ones he'd been trained to recognize. Men stood around the weapons, wearing what were clearly military or paramilitary uniforms, though John did not recognize their insignia at all. The men worked on the nukes, tinkering and adjusting them in preparation for whatever was coming next. John felt a sinking dread in the base of his stomach that seemed like pure acid, scalding him and creating a bitter taste in his mouth.

Adam continued. "Within a few months tensions were high enough that someone did the worst thing possible: they fired a warning shot. A sixty-megaton warning shot." The cube disappeared abruptly, leaving John in complete darkness, Adam's voice wafting through it like a ghost from some nightmare version of a Dickens tale.

"Within one month, most of the earth had been burned over."

The cube reappeared then, and John gasped. It was a picture of a news anchor again. It could have been any of the faces John saw on the nightly newscasts he watched, but there was no way to tell for sure, because the person's face was ravaged by radiation poisoning. One eye had burned away, skin hung in stringy peels from the bone of his skull, and great tufts of hair fell out even as the living corpse spoke. He read from a pair of pages held in his wasted hands, and John heard sound with the video this time, the terrible voice of this world's past.

"I'm bringing you the latest," said the man. His voice was rough, gravelly, the voice of a corpse who hasn't the sense to die. He coughed wetly, then put down the papers. "Is there anyone listening? Is there anyone even alive? I'm here in this studio, it's automated. Just me and the machines. Me and the machines. Don't bother trying to call in, the phone lines are gone. Everything is. I doubt this signal is even going out."

Blood began to drip from his nose, spattering across his desk. The drip turned into a steady stream as he continued speaking, pooling in a crimson puddle beneath him, running in rivulets over the side of the desk. "It's just me and the machines, but I have to try. Have...to....."

His head slumped and hit the desk with a wet splat. His eyes were still open, but he was clearly dead. John couldn't pull his eyes away from the vision, as though he were seeing the death of Pestilence, one of the Four Horsemen, himself. Adam spoke, the dead newsman providing eerie proof of his words.

"Ninety-nine point nine percent of the earth's population was dead, and the last one tenth of one percent looked like it would soon follow. Radiation was everywhere, and no one had any way of escape. The human race was destined for certain extinction."

"But – " John said.

Adam continued over him. "People survive, John. They always do. That's God's plan. I truly believe that, and you should too."

The view on the video cube flickered and then disappeared, mercifully taking the apparition of the newscaster with it. The lights came on in the room and John let out the breath he hadn't realized he'd been holding and looked at Adam.

"So in a hundred years," continued the older man, "there were more people. Still not many, though, and they were still in constant danger of dying off. The earth had been changed by the war – we call it Endwar – the ice caps melted, most of the vegetation gone forever. So the remaining few constructed domed cities, safe havens from the elements."

"Like zoos," said John.

"Very much so." Adam leaned forward, his blue eyes searing into John's like icy lasers. "But people don't do well in captivity, even the self-imposed kind. Most of them either went crazy or killed themselves. Radiation levels were up beyond what humans are made for, and one of the results was a new genetic predisposition to insanity. A few of those who went mad – the Fanatics, they call themselves – believed that Endwar was the harbinger of Armageddon, the battle of Gog and Magog. They believed that God was trying to destroy His wicked children, so they took it upon themselves to finish the job for Him."

John started. "One of the people who tried to kill Fran and me said something about his salvation or something."

"That was Malachi. He's their leader. Their priest. Dedicated to killing off all humankind. They draw their numbers from the domes, and even a few of us," he waved, gesturing so that John would understand that by "us" he meant the people who worked with him, "join them. It's a controlled madness and a rather strange religion, with only one important new scripture. I have it memorized. Want to hear it?"

John wanted to say – to *scream* – "No!" To shake his head and close his eyes like he had when he was three and his mother tried to feed him peas. But he didn't. He nodded soundlessly, more afraid of not knowing than he was of discovering the truth. He was realizing now that not knowing was the state in which he had spent his entire life. Not knowing had led him to death, and to this dead place in the future that was also, somehow, the present.

Adam sat back again, closing his eyes. "'After thou hast killed all others, thy final act will be to come unto Me.'"

"Jesus."

"I hope not." Adam smiled grimly at the joke. "Malachi's a real danger. Used to be second in command here. Then it all got to him."

"Why didn't you stop him, then?"

Adam pursed his lips as though this were a sore point. "We live a strange life here, John. One of the strange aspects of it is that we try to live in perfect emotional control. Not only does that free us to make hard decisions, but it also provides an early warning sign of impending insanity. Almost every one of the Controllers will go mad if not killed by a Fan or by radiation poisoning. So we teach ourselves to live in control of our feelings. When we can no longer contain our emotions, when we start to show too much passion, that gives those around us a sign that our mental processes are starting to deteriorate. But it didn't happen that way with Malachi. He maintained perfect presence of mind, it seemed, up until the very day he ran from Control HQ, and joined the Fans."

"And became their leader," said John.

"Correct. The Fans came after us, or at least they tried to. We used to be located under Old Salt Lake City, but we closed down as soon as he left and came here instead. It's standard procedure to move from place to place after a defection."

"You must move a lot,"

"Rarely," answered Malachi.

"But you said everyone goes nuts. So don't they all join his crew?"

"Of course not," answered Adam. "We kill most of them before that happens."

CONTROL HQ – RUSHM
AD 2013/AE 4013

John was silent for a moment, of necessity taking some time to digest the awesome amount of information that threatened to overload his mental processes.

"You kill them?" he repeated at last.

Adam nodded, wearily it seemed, and shut his eyes. "Yes. Try not to judge us too harshly for that. We are all that stands between the Fans and the end of humanity. So we can afford to take no chances with those who show signs of dementia or madness. Because when we miss one, like we missed Malachi, that person becomes just one more soldier in the crusade against our survival. Malachi went over to the Fans, and he's been killing people in the domes and looking for our headquarters ever since."

"If he's been doing so much killing, then why isn't everyone dead?"

Adam's eyes opened again, answering John's question incorrectly, perhaps intentionally so. "Technology moved fast in the last year before Endwar. They could take a single atom and inscribe the words from an entire library on its face. They could take a man apart and put him together again." Adam paused, taking a deep breath. "And they could create life...or a reasonable facsimile thereof."

Again, John's mind reeled with the implications of what had been said and what he sensed Adam was about to say. The older man stood and gestured for John to follow him. They went to another part of the wall that looked no different from the other surfaces around them, but when they approached it split open, creating a narrow door that allowed them to exit. Adam stepped through and led John down a series of corridors before going through yet another door. The new room they entered was a lab. Completely mechanized, lined by huge tubes with clear faces. Adam gestured, inviting John to look in the clearest tube.

"Recognize anything?" asked Adam.

"Gabriel," whispered John. "Oh, my God, it's Gabe."

Gabriel reclined in the tube, eyes closed as though asleep. But he couldn't be asleep, because from the waist down he was nothing but bone. Literally. The bones of his pelvis and hips emerged below the line of his waist, continuing down to attach to leg bones, patellae, and the small bones of his feet and ankles. Then as John watched, a slick substance built up around the bones. Soon it sheathed the entire structure, and began to darken.

"Tissue formation," said Adam. Then he said, "It's not Gabe, it's a robot. Another robot, like the first Gabe was."

John turned to Adam, aghast and horrified. "What do you mean?" he asked.

"Your best friend was a biomechanical construct. This one is to replace him."

"No, he wasn't, he couldn't," said John. He didn't like the voice he heard coming from his mouth, whining and frightened. "All the memories he had," he continued. "Everything he had done...."

"Were real. Within certain parameters. We permit them to live their lives out as they will, mostly, but there are certain requirements we have programmed into them," answered Adam. "He was real, and he led a real life, but he was just a machine. Like everyone else in Loston."

John looked at the other tubes. Mertyl lay in one, slowly being reformed, no doubt complete with her old memories and soon to be reigning supreme in the school office once more. Adam pointed at the tubes, all of which were full. "We have to remake the ones we've lost and reinsert them into Loston, because we hope that soon it will be safe enough for you and Fran to go back there."

John felt weak and fought to remain standing. His world spun around him as the implications of Adam's words burrowed into his brain. He looked around the room and saw other tubes, other bodies. Some of them were incredibly tiny, like....

"Babies," said Adam, noting where John's gaze had fallen. "That's the one thing we could never create: a viable living form,

343

one that could not only survive but reproduce. So we make them here and a few other places, then ship them to their domes. They grow normally but all their implanted programming parameters are already there, waiting to be activated at the appropriate times. And they can't breed. That's why you and Fran are so very important."

John stared at one of the babies. He reached out and touched the glass that separated him from the small form, and suddenly the body animated, the little chest expanding as breath was drawn into its lungs. John's hand jerked away, and the thought that he had caused the baby's movement gripped him. Then he realized that the baby was still unconscious, its body merely reacting to unseen directives given to it by the machines.

"They can't breed," said Adam again, as if this was the most important thing about them, and then continued, "but if you can't tell the difference, and they can't tell the difference, then who's to say there even *is* a difference?"

John's gaze returned to Gabriel's still form. The tissue around his legs was more formed now, growing incredibly rapidly. Above the tube a readout suddenly clicked on, reading 00:00:48:00:00.

"That's the Calibrator," said Adam. "We're bringing everyone – all Loston robots – online with the memories they had 48 hours ago, so that in Loston none of this will have ever happened."

John sank to the floor. He felt as though a vision of hell had opened up before him, and the worst thing about it was that he was already there.

"Everyone?" he said. His voice was small and weak. Training had given him the skills to overcome physical threats, but this was more. This information threatened not just his body, but his mind and soul.

"Everyone," replied Adam. He was looking at the tubes with the clinical expression of a doctor or a computer engineer: disassociated, dispassionate. "The 'bots are completely undetectable, completely *human,* unless we put them on alert or their sensors indicate a threat to their primary functions. Then they change. They can withstand all but the most violent deaths, have extreme strength, and even resurrect themselves."

John jerked slightly, Adam's words bringing to vivid recollection the events of the past hours, the strange night of reanimating corpses and living dead.

"There's a supercomputer – a biological networking computer – at the base of each 'bot's thalamus. It regulates the organism, makes sure everything's going smoothly. The physics and biology that are involved wouldn't make any sense to you, but in times of need the computer triggers a series of electro-chemical changes that keep the organism alive."

"That's why they went for the heads," whispered John.

Adam nodded. "Malachi knows that to destroy the computer you have to destroy its networking center. Kill the thalamus."

Both men looked at Gabriel. The man looked so peaceful from the waist up, and so frightening and alien from the waist down. His tissue continued to generate, and John could see the individual strands of ropy muscle begin to form. Soon skin and hair covered them, and Gabriel was complete. A pair of cables, glistening with some kind of lubricant, snaked into the tube and inserted themselves into Gabe's ears. His eyes jerked open and his mouth rounded in a silent scream.

John almost screamed himself before Gabe's eyes closed and he resumed his peaceful position. Adam gripped John's arm. "It's just downloading," he said. "We have to give him the memories he needs to be Gabe again."

"He won't be Gabe," said John.

"Oh, but he will. He'll be everything Gabe ever was up to two days ago. We build them well. In fact, the only thing we could never beat was the fact that they go insane if they find out the truth about themselves."

"How can a robot go insane?"

"How would you feel, John, if one day something triggered you – triggered something inside you that you didn't even know was there? And all of a sudden you're doing things you know are impossible and your body has become something different than you've known. You realize that all your most cherished memories are lies. Not only are you not *you*, you're not even a real person." Adam nodded at Gabriel's body. "As long as they live the lie, they're fine. But when they realize it for what it is...rather than face that bleakness, they go mad. We make them too well, perhaps. Undetectable. Human."

Both men were silent for a moment, staring at Gabriel's body, which slept in its strange and macabre way, an analog to the life that John now knew was forever beyond the coach's grasp.

"Do you think," said Adam, "that God loves them as His own, or do you think they are anathema to Him?"

The tubes in Gabe's ears crackled, and Gabe drew a deep breath, beginning to breathe regularly as the tubes withdrew.

John turned his head and vomited.

***

Fran's eyes fluttered, but all was a mist of gray and confusion, as though someone had padded her brain in cotton batting like the kind her grandmother had used once long ago to make quilts that reminded one of a gentler time, a time when people were good to each other and didn't die and then stand up again, but had the good sense and courtesy to stay dead.

What does that mean? she wondered to herself.

A light appeared in the mist, and she realized that her eyes were open. She was trying to see, but for some reason resolution and clarity were evading her. The light grew bright, then was blocked by a pair of forms, like two dense clouds traveling through a lighter fog that hung over a fairy land.

Her thoughts were muddled. Where's Nathan? she thought. And why isn't John here, either?

One of the clouds spoke.

"She's coming out of it."

The other cloud moved, and Fran thought she felt something touch her arm. Immediately the mist that surrounded her thickened into a more impenetrable darkness.

"Keep her down," said another voice. "Adam wants her under for as long as she's here."

CONTROL HQ – RUSHM
AD 2013/AE 4013

"You people are monsters," said John, and Adam's eyes filled with tears as the statement stabbed him to the core.

"Please," whispered Adam. John's words caused a pain in his heart that was reflective of the self-doubt he felt, of the belief that John might be right. "Please don't think that. We're not monsters, just people doing what we have to to keep humankind alive."

"What about *you*?" asked John. "Are you human?"

Adam picked up a small box that lay near Gabe's tube. He held it next to John's head, and a panel on it glowed green. "Human," he said, then handed the box to John. "You can scan me if you want. I've never done it. I believe I'm human, but that could be the programming. You hold my soul – or if I don't have one, then my sanity – in your hands."

John looked at the box, obviously tempted to use it. "You'd go crazy if you knew?"

Adam nodded.

"What about the guy I saw in Iraq? Hell, what about *Iraq*?" asked John.

Adam felt relief at the question, one he was actually prepared to answer. "The man – Devorough – was what we call a bit."

"A bit?" repeated John.

"Short for bit player," explained Adam. "It's a robot model we use over and over again. It saves us a lot of time and difficulty, because each new face is made from scratch, basically. So there are thousands of recycled templates we use, and most people won't notice the face in the mall that they also happened to see thirty years ago in the movie theater. Or if they *do* notice, they chalk it up to *déjà vu* or indigestion or a strange dream or any of a thousand other things. You, on the other hand, *did* notice, so we tried to transfer him out."

"But he was in his house when I went looking."

Adam's brow furrowed, though he tried to hide his expression from John. This was one of the things that most concerned him: not only had Devorough shown up at Loston with a daughter, which his programming wasn't designed to support, but to all appearances the bit either hadn't responded to its directive to leave Loston, or it hadn't received the order. The former alternative meant that the bit had somehow resisted its programming.

And the latter meant that, somewhere, there was a traitor among the Controllers.

***

Jason watched the monitors. Sheila stood beside him, also watching through Loston's eyes as the Cleanup Crew replaced everyone, putting them into the positions they had occupied forty-eight hours before.

It all had to be perfect.

But Jason watched with only half his attention. The rest of him was turned inward, thinking through the plans he'd made over the long years, beginning when he finally realized that the Fans were winning, and the Controllers destined to utterly fail in their self-appointed task. Today would be the day. The final day.

Today the Fanatics would come. He had to be ready to welcome them appropriately.

He felt at his side for Sheila's hand, and felt it curl around his. It was warm, soft, everything that real flesh should be. He wondered if he could kill her to fulfill his mission, and realized that he had come to love her.

But he also realized that, yes, he *could* kill her if it became necessary to do what he had to. Just as Adam would kill *him*, if he discovered Jason's plans, if he were to find out that Jason had betrayed them all.

The Fans were coming.

The end was at hand.

***

"But he attacked me," said John. Something in what Adam had told him wasn't making sense, but he couldn't quite put his finger on it.

"Yes," answered Adam. They were back in the older man's office now, back in the place where John had awakened. He hadn't been able to handle looking at the "new" bodies of his friends any longer, so Adam had brought them back here. "When you mentioned seeing him before, it triggered a mode we call shut down. He tried to keep you from spreading the idea around."

"By killing me. Tal attacked me, too, when I told him I saw Devorough before."

"Those were automatic reactions. They had to keep Loston intact, especially with Fran coming in."

"Fran," John breathed. He had almost forgotten about her in the all but overwhelming crush of ideas that had pounded into him in the last hours.

"Fran," said Adam, "Is quite possibly the most important person in the world."

"How so?"

"To explain that, I have to tell you a bit more about us, about the Controllers. We are all recruited from dome life. All of us were born in one zoo or another, and the then-Controllers observed us and noted that we had characteristics that would allow us to be good Controllers in turn. So after a formative period, we are taken from the domes and brought to headquarters for training. But doing that exposes us to radiation, and sterilizes us within a short time. No babies from our ranks."

"None?" asked John. Once more, he didn't know where this strange conversation was headed, but once more he felt fear's clutching hands tightening around his heart.

"None," said Adam. "We continue our existence by harvesting our members from the inhabitants of the domed zoos, like Loston. But none of us can reproduce. Not one of us is a viable, fertile organism."

"Wouldn't that mean that you are all machines? If all of your lives are bent toward making sure the human race continues, would it make sense for you to come out of the domes if you're human?"

Adam winced as a spasm seemed to run through him, a shudder that could have been pain or fear. "We certainly hope we are human, and merely chosen to sacrifice our reproductive future for the greater good of humanity."

"But you don't know?"

Adam shook his head. "No. No one really does. Only a few computers that have been around since all this began have a complete database of who is real and who is not. So though the odds are completely against it, although it is more likely than not that each and every one of the Controllers is a robot, a machine called into existence by other machines, each of us hopes that we are, in fact, human. We know that Malachi is, for instance. And it could be that others among us are also human. After all, as I said, only the computers know for sure who is who. We ourselves are kept in the dark about each person's nature. Only when a threat emerges are we informed as to the nature of the threat and the nature of the life that is threatened. That's how we became aware of you. It's also how we became aware that Fran was so important: a computer monitoring Denver took note of the threat when she was attacked by Fans, the night her husband was killed."

"But if you don't know who is real until they're threatened, how do the Fans know?" asked John.

"The reason we don't know is that we don't want to know, because knowing would threaten our sanity and our existence. And by extension, the existence of humanity. But the knowledge *is* there, if someone knows how to look."

"Someone like Malachi," guessed John.

"Exactly," agreed Adam. "He knows. He knows where the real people are, or at least he managed to find out their names and dome locations before he left us. The real people are the ones who can carry us forth, who can hopefully bring humanity back from the brink."

"And Fran is one of them," whispered John, guessing how this would turn out. He guessed half of the truth.

"Fran is," agreed Adam, nodding. "She's also the fertile last fertile female alive in the world. If she dies before reproducing, then so does humanity. And all that's left is a world of machines."

OUTSIDE CONTROL HQ – RUSHM
AD 4013/AE 2013

Malachi looked behind him. His legions followed closely, riding their stolen hoverjets and cycles over the rocky, barren soil that covered the whole earth. Death had already won on this planet, and only a few didn't accept that reality.

Well today they would be instructed of that fact. Malachi knew that God was with them, and the thing that made God into God was the fact that He never lost.

Never.

Today Malachi would be God's instrument. He closed his eyes for a moment, savoring the idea of heavenly wrath descending once again to finish the job that nuclear weaponry had begun two millennia before. The Controllers dead, Fran destroyed, the world would follow irrevocably. But this time the world would not be consumed by nuclear fire, it would be destroyed by fiery insanity and a flood of madness more complete than the Noachian tide that covered the earth once upon a time.

The old Bible had said that God gave the rainbow as a sign that He would never again cover the earth with a flood. But after Endwar, the sky had not permitted rainbows. They were a thing of the past. The promise was no more, and the flood was coming.

Malachi focused on the tracker that was leading him and his people to the hidden Controller hideout.

Rainbows were gone. And in a few hours, hope would follow those bright arcs of years past, disappearing in the darkness of death and eternal night.

CONTROL HQ – RUSHM
AD 4013/AE 2013

John blinked rapidly, feeling as though he were emerging from a dream so real that it doesn't surrender its grip upon waking. "Fran's the last?" he asked.

"The last," answered Adam. "After the wars of the early twenty-first century, there was a significantly higher radiation count. And one thing it affected more than anything else was the reproductive process. There were fewer females born than males. We've been harvesting sperm from the real men scattered through the world, but that doesn't change the fact that females have been an ever-shrinking number. Fran's the last."

When Adam mentioned the wars of the late twentieth century, it spawned another question. It seemed that for everything Adam explained, fifty new mysteries arose. "What about what I did in the army? The wars I fought in?" he asked. Adam hesitated. "Tell me," John insisted.

"This is going to be hard to understand, but the things you did were nothing but a fabrication. Vietnam, Korea, both World Wars, the others. In the twentieth and twenty-first centuries – the real ones, not the times we built for people like you and Fran to live in – they never really happened. There *were* wars, but they were terrible things."

John shivered, remembering the eyes of the little girl who'd looked at him while he hid in a hole in the sand, remembering the possibility that he might have had to kill her. "The things I saw *were* terrible."

"Not compared to the reality of two thousand years ago."

"Then why invent something like what I went through?"

"To prepare you. We needed to have a good reason to draft people into the armies, so that they could train and be ready."

"Ready?"

"The 'bots in your city are programmed to protect you. Their thalamic operations sense the proximity of a real person –

you, for instance – and they orient to keep it safe. But what if there's a glitch? Like what's happened to you. How long would you have lasted if you hadn't been in Special Forces?"

John didn't have to think very long to arrive at an answer: "About four seconds."

"Exactly. The war you fought was for your benefit. You and a few other humans were the only real participants. And you were always protected, despite what may have appeared to you as direst peril, in what you remember as a tragedy that took thousands of lives. But it prepared you for the eventuality of something like what's happened in the last few days. It kept you and Fran alive. And hopefully you two will have children and the human race will be one step closer to living on its own again."

Both men paused a moment. Then Adam continued, in a softer voice, "I know what you're thinking. There would be other ways of preparing you. Why invent a horrible war? Why cause suffering?" John was silent, but knew that his eyes told Adam he was thinking exactly that. "Think about it, John. There has to be difficulty. Opposition is what makes us strong, what makes us appreciate the easy times, too. So we created worlds that held opposition in them, hoping that living in those environments would teach you – and all humans – how to be strong and good. So that someday, when and if there were enough real people, they could be strong and good enough to heal the world and make it a home again."

Adam hit a button on his desk and a ladder slipped quietly from the ceiling. He handed John a pair of goggles, motioning him to put them on, and slipped a matching pair over his head. John put on the eyewear, wondering what would happen when he did.

Nothing. The lenses were clear, and he looked at Adam quizzically.

"Protection," said the older man, and hit another button on his desk.

A trapdoor at the top of the ladder slid open, and John winced at the strange, red light that streamed in through the opening.

Adam climbed the ladder, motioning John to follow. He did, climbing up and out and finding himself on bare rock under a red, hazy sky. John stood, looking right and left. He could not discern where he was. He only knew that he stood on a high spot, looking down at a landscape that was burned and scarred beyond recognition.

"Wouldn't the radiation have dissipated by now?" he asked. "Two thousand years is longer than the half life of a lot of nuclear byproducts."

"Of course," answered Adam. "But the nuclear strikes utterly destroyed much of the atmospheric filters that are meant to keep the world safe from microwaves, gamma rays, and a host of other nasty cosmic attackers."

"Oh," said John. "Then – " He stopped speaking suddenly as his stomach, still clenched in fear's cold grip, now threatened to be crushed by the jagged grasp of sheerest terror. He stopped speaking as his world tumbled again, dropping around him in shards of reality that were forever broken and changed. He stopped speaking as he recognized where he was.

He stood on Mount Rushmore.

Below him were Lincoln, Roosevelt, Jefferson, and Washington. Now two thousand years older than he knew, the tops of their heads clearly visible to him and pitted and scarred from millennia of harsh climate.

John looked down and saw the valleys below. No trees, no nothing. Only bleak barrenness under a red sky and a sun that glowed a strange purple. Domes dotted the horizon, though, dozens of them standing across the sweep of the pitted land, huge constructs of metal and plastic that seemed to gleam in the weird light.

Adam pointed at the largest. "That's Los Angeles dome, where Fran came from. It's the biggest. She flew out in a plane we picked up, then we sedated her and transported her overland to that one," he pointed at another, much smaller. "That one is Denver airport, where people 'land' before we re-drug them and ship them to their final destinations. They just think they've had a nice nap all the way from home." He pointed out another place. "Chicago dome. Twenty two humans in there that we are aware of. All male of course. There was a female, but Malachi killed her a short time ago." His arm moved slightly, pointing to yet another. "Loston," he said.

John looked at it, automatically memorizing its placement among the others.

"They're all in different times, too," said Adam

"What?"

Adam smiled. "The Los Angeles dome is set in twenty-thirteen, like Loston. The Chicago dome is in the nineteen-twenties. Others are in other times. We've been experimenting for the last two hundred years or so to find out which time period works the best for our purposes, which one creates the proper mix of protection and stimulation. So far the early twenty-first century is ahead." Adam looked up at the strange sky. "We'd better go back inside. You're probably already sunburned."

He dropped back down into the office, John following quickly after.

OUTSIDE CONTROL HQ – RUSHM
AD 4013/AE 2013

Malachi stared at the mountain that lay before them, still small in the distance but easily recognizable. "Rushmore," he said, and began laughing.

It was so perfect. He should have guessed.

He raised his hand, and his people moved again. They were the army of Israel, come again to liberate Cana. And as it had been to the Israelites, so it would be with Malachi's followers: they would destroy the interlopers, and the promised land would be theirs.

CONTROL HQ – RUSHM
AD 4013/AE 2013

John sat back down, not only physically drained but now also emotionally exhausted. The weight of his newfound knowledge and understanding was almost more than he could bear. It pressed upon him like his nightmares had so often done before. Only unlike his nightmares, this burden would not dissipate with the light of the day. Indeed, the daylight would only add to its cumbersome weight, for if John ever returned to Loston, he would look up and know that the sky was not real. It was an illusion crafted by technology beyond his grasp or understanding. It was a dream, and caught in that dream forever, John would have no safe place in which to hide from his nightmare existence.

"My father wasn't real," he said.

"I'm sorry," said Adam, looking genuinely sorrowful. "We take viable children from their parents, and tell them they died in birth or soon after delivery. And we give them to other parents, who will be able to provide a higher level of care in the event of an emergency." He paused, and then added, "In your case, it saved your life."

"So what now?" asked John.

"We send you and Fran back to Loston. She's been asleep since the mines, and she'll stay that way. At least then we won't have to explain all this. We've given her something, too, that will incline her towards thinking that the last few days were just a very vivid dream. You get married, live happily ever after. Most of all, you try to have children."

John was silent for a moment as the enormity of what Adam was saying sunk in.

Adam, he thought, *shouldn't that be* my *name? With Fran as my Eve?*

What he said was, "How do you know what she and I will make it? That we'll...love each other?"

359

Again, Adam was silent a moment before answering. "Because we programmed your ex-wife to be just like her. And we programmed her ex-husband to be just like you."

John felt his hands clench at his sides as he began to truly understand just how choreographed his life had been. Nothing left to chance. Not even love. Not even his own heart. "You bastard," he said.

Adam winced. "Please understand, I had nothing to do with those decisions. As I told you, the Controllers are rarely even aware of who is human and who is not. The computers that have been running events for over a thousand years decided your fate, not me." Adam dropped his eyes for a moment, as though penitent. Perhaps he was. But then he raised them and said, "Though I would have done the same thing they did. We needed you two to fall in love. Just sleeping together would have been enough, I suppose, but we have found that humans do better in a family environment, married, and we wanted you two to have as many children as possible."

John flinched. "I'm sorry to say it that way, but it's true. The crudity and the importance of it is that we need you two to have sex all the time, and the computers figured you'd be more likely to do that with someone you truly loved. So they created perfect matches for both of you, then gradually changed them to match the real mate you would eventually both meet. Then we planned to retire the 'bots. Give Fran a great job in Loston, where her cousin, who just happened to be your best friend, would be trying to set her up. And *voila*."

It registered in the back of John's mind that Adam hadn't said any of this proudly. It wasn't as though he was showing off the brilliant system they'd set up here. He said it like he was tired. Tired of having to play the one role that a man could never be capacitated to play: that of God.

But John only felt that realization peripherally, as he hadn't heard much past what he felt keenly as the most painful and important word in Adam's explanation of the cold mechanics of a computerized fate.

"So you 'retired' my wife?"

Adam closed his eyes.

John heard a savage growl escape his throat. The growl turned to a scream, and he leapt across the desk, sliding over the surface that separated him from Adam. He grabbed the older man by the throat, weeping madly, then hurled Adam to the ground and stood over him, tears streaming from his eyes.

"And if Fran's husband hadn't been conveniently killed by the Fans at the proper time, would you have 'retired' him, too? Would you have intentionally put her through the same hell I've been living in for the past two years?"

There was no hesitation in Adam's voice. Weariness, yes. Sorrow, certainly. But no hesitation. "Yes," he answered.

John screamed again. He raised a fist to *kill* this sonofabitch and Adam stared up at him, not cowering, not angry, not sad, not anything but tired. John fell to the floor beside the other man, crying and clutching his stomach.

He felt Adam's hand on his shoulder. "I'm sorry. I really am. And I'm tired. I'm exhausted from the effort of keeping humanity alive, even for one more day. But more than any of that – more than anything at all – I want you to live." His grip tightened, pulling John closer, almost to an embrace as the two men lay side by side on the cold ground of Adam's room. "And I think you really, truly have a woman who will love you. And you will love her. More than you ever loved your wife. I know it. Does it matter whether that happiness has come because of fate or machines, or because of the machinations of a tired and lonely old man? Won't that light make the darkness worth passing through?"

But John couldn't hear him. He rocked back and forth, saying, "Annie, Annie...," over and over, as though by repeating her name he could call her forth from her grave and make the whole bad dream that was his life disappear. Oblivion would be welcome, for he had always believed that his wife had gone to

Heaven, but now he knew that if she had then that meant God was a machine.

No, there would be no Annie in Heaven, for there had never been an Annie at all.

He felt Adam's arms encircle him, the older man taking John in his arms and rocking him back and forth like a baby. In a remote part of his mind, he was struck by the strangeness of it all: of seeing a man from the future comforting a man who had just lost his past. But it was, at the same time, right. John realized that this man was the closest thing he would ever again have to a father, to someone who would watch out for him, and pick him up when he fell.

John's weeping slowed, and his tears dried.

There was silence.

And then the alarm sounded.

***

Sheila tried to make sense of it all, to stay in control, but she felt like she was struggling to remain afloat while at the apex of a tidal wave, aware not of the height but of the depth of the force that threatened to overwhelm her. Jason was nowhere to be seen, and though she always missed her husband's presence whenever he was absent, at times like this, times of crisis, she felt his lack more keenly.

She breathed a sigh of relief when Adam entered from his office. John stood behind him, eyes red and troubled.

"What's happening?" asked Adam.

Sheila pointed at a bank of monitors. These weren't hooked up to any 'bots, rather they showed the installation inside Rushmore. Fights could be seen on all the screens.

"Attack," she said.

"Fans?"

Sheila nodded. She pointed to one of the monitors. Onscreen, Malachi blew the head off a Controller, a man she'd worked with and known all her life. She jerked as though the shot had hit her, then jerked again as Malachi aimed the gun at the vid-unit and pulled the trigger.

The screen went black.

"How did they find us?" whispered Adam. Sheila shrugged. Then shrugged again as Adam said, "Where's Jason?"

"I don't know," she answered. "He said he was going to check on some things, and a minute later this happened."

"How many are there?" asked Adam.

"A few hundred is what it looks like."

She caught another glimpse of Malachi on one of the monitors, running down one of the halls. Adam saw it too, and blanched, his already pale skin draining completely of color as he ran out the door.

"Where are you going?" she screamed after him, desperately afraid of what was going to happen.

"He's heading to the infirmary. He's going after Fran!" hollered Adam over his shoulder. John ran out after him, and Sheila was alone again. In charge of the Doomsday situation that they'd all hoped and prayed would never happen.

***

John followed Adam through a nightmare twisting and turning of tunnel paths. He realized after a moment that it was familiar, and wondered why.

Then he realized that it was similar to the layout of the Resurrection mine. Not exactly, but similar. Clearly the machines that had designed each little world in the make-believe reality of the dome zoos had taken bits and pieces of already-existing structures and strung them together to create facsimiles of cities and towns, and even mines.

He followed Adam around a corner and suddenly found himself in a fight with two of what Adam had called Fanatics. They held old-fashioned six-guns, straight out of a spaghetti western. Both Fans reacted as Adam and John dove away from them, shooting their guns and shrieking at the tops of their lungs.

John saw Adam spin around as one of the shots took him in the shoulder. Then he felt himself hit the ground. Immediately he rebounded, springing back at one of the Fans in a quick move that took the man by surprise. John grabbed the man and spun him around in front of him as the other Fan fired, shooting his compatriot in the chest. John grabbed his captive's gun from hands that were suddenly limp, and shot the other Fan. The bullet took the man in the eye and the Fanatic pitched backward.

John ran to Adam, who held a hand against his shoulder. "Shoot them again," he gasped. "In the head, toward where the neck joins. Have to kill the master computer."

John nodded and returned to the men, both of whom were twitching again. He shot each, placing the muzzle carefully at the base of their skulls and pulling the trigger. The killing sickened him; it felt like murder, though it was done in self-defense and though they were machines.

His grisly task done, he returned to Adam and helped him to his feet.

***

Malachi found the door he was looking for. He put away his shotgun and drew a new weapon, a hideous, fat-barreled thing that looked like a deadly slug.

He pressed the door release and stepped in.

Not into the infirmary, though. He entered Central Control, the nerve center that kept all the domes alive.

Controllers sat at their stations, the good little machines they were, and were surprised when he stepped through the door and pulled the trigger.

Liquid fire coursed from the barrel of his weapon, a flamethrower he had brought with him for this purpose. The incendiary stream sluiced through the air and hit the nearest Controller with a flowing beauty that Malachi loved, because he recognized it as the beginnings of the Dream made real.

All of the world would burn.

All of the earth would perish.

The Controller shrieked as the weapon – one that dated back to the real twentieth century and which Malachi had saved for an occasion such as this – discharged and set him ablaze, his skin charring and his blood beginning to boil and steam within his veins almost instantly.

Malachi turned to the next Controller.

Sheila.

Her weapon was in her hands, already aimed at his heart. Malachi smiled at her, waiting for her – *daring* her – to pull the trigger.

She didn't, as he knew she wouldn't. "Primary function, deary," he said to her, "Protect the real people." He pulled the trigger again, and the fire coursed over her, as well, cooking her and melting the eyes out of her head. He held the trigger down, and turned the spray on everything that surrounded him, Controllers, monitors, computers.

All around him, machines were dying.

Malachi smiled and laughed as he burned them. He burned them all, and felt his dream coming true. Perhaps he had Dreamed too great a dreaming, he thought. Perhaps the *entire* earth would not be covered in flame. But though the whole earth might not be burned, this was the earth's heart, and it would die by fire.

CONTROL HQ – RUSHM
AD 4013/AE 2013
((((INTEGRITY BREACH))))

John stood before the door, fear for Fran threatening to overwhelm him. Had Malachi found her yet? The possibility was too awful to think about. Forget about her importance in the grand scheme of ongoing human existence. He loved her, and refused to contemplate life without her.

"This is the place," said Adam, wincing. John glanced at Adam's wound, which still flowed freely. Adam hoisted the other gun they had taken from the Fans, the mirror of John's own, and said, "I'm all right. I'll cover you."

John nodded. Adam pressed a button on the doorframe and the portal whispered open. John launched himself through it, gun at the ready, and almost pulled the trigger before he realized that the man and woman standing over Fran's inert form weren't harming her.

"They're doctors," said Adam, bringing his own gun down as he entered a split-second after John.

"What's happening?" asked the man who stood protectively over Fran, the woman at his side mirroring the question with her eyes.

"Fans," said Adam.

"How did they find us?" the woman asked.

"It was bound to happen sooner or later," answered Adam, apparently unable to answer that himself.

The lights flickered, then went out, pitching the room into blackness for a moment before emergency lights switched on at the room's corners, bathing the place in a soft amber glow. John kept his gun aimed at the entryway, covering it against any unwelcome entrants.

Adam swore under his breath. "Malachi must be in the control room," he said. The man and woman grabbed weapons from a nearby cabinet and ran out without being told. Adam swung around to look at John, who stepped back a half-step under the intensity of the man's gaze.

"Take Fran," said Adam. "Go down this corridor to the end. Turn left. You'll end up in the hangar. There are crawlers there – they look like what you know as dune buggies."

John nodded. "I remember."

"Take one and go back to Loston."

"Everyone in Loston's trying to kill us, too."

"They've been reprogrammed. To them it's Sunday afternoon. If you reenter the dome through one of the side hatches, they'll never know anything different ever happened. Tell Fran you took her hiking and she fell."

John's visage hardened. How could he trust this man, after he had admitted that he had planned an intricate lie and called it a life? How could he trust anything that happened now? Nothing was the same, and never again would he be able to just do something with the simple belief that his actions were what they seemed to be. All had purpose, even though he didn't understand it.

Adam shook his head as though he were reading John's mind. "I know you think I'm a bastard. But I'm the bastard who's devoted his whole existence to keeping you alive."

John nodded at that. Maybe Adam was no more the game master than he, but was just another playing piece, a larger one perhaps, one with greater range of movement, like the knight on a chess board, but still one whose actions were not under his own control.

John picked up Fran, throwing her over his shoulder. He hoped he wasn't aggravating any injuries she had, but knew that speed and ease of movement were of the essence. "What are you going to do?" he asked Adam.

"I have to take care of someone," answered the older man. He fingered his gun, and John knew that he was talking about Malachi, about going head to head with the great demon that had come and stolen Eden from him. Fighting Malachi would be like trying to kill Satan himself, John thought, and did not envy the Adam his task.

John gripped Adam's arm, silently wishing the man luck, then left the infirmary, running down the hall in the direction Adam had indicated. Within a hundred feet he came upon the first of several groups of corpses. The bodies were locked together in death, like the last combatants of a long-fallen race.

One of them gripped an M16. John discarded his six-shooter in favor of the larger weapon, stopping only to make sure it had enough ammo before continuing on his way. He hoped he didn't have to use it. But he planned to be ready for the eventuality.

***

Adam burst into Central Control and looked around. The place was rubble, piles of melted metal and glass laying everywhere. Other charred heaps lay among the rubble, and Adam realized they were the remains of the Controllers who had manned the room.

His coworkers.

His friends.

His loved ones.

Adam's face twisted as he surveyed the wreckage, his expression matching each horror with another twist and wrinkle. Soon he wore a visage of pure wrath as he saw that all were dead, Central Control in ruins.

Most of them couldn't be rebuilt, either. Almost all had been robots, but he had no way of finding out which were which without going into the files, and he feared if he did that he might see his own name among the names of the machines, among the list of the dead...it would be tantamount to putting a gun in his own mouth and pulling the trigger. The end result would be slower in coming, but death for all would be no less certain.

So his friends were gone, and no bringing them back. Even godlike powers had their limits. All he could do now was stop the madness before it continued any farther and make sure that the perpetrator of this deed was punished.

He left the room, searching for Malachi in the smoke of Rushmore.

***

John entered the hangar, his footsteps heavy. Fran was a slim woman, and couldn't have weighed more than one hundred and twenty pounds, but she felt like ten thousand to John's overstressed muscles.

He went to one of the groundcars and lay Fran across the seat, wrestling her limp body into the straps. A Fan jumped out of the smoky haze of the hangar, screaming and firing a Glock at John. He let go of Fran, bringing the muzzle of his M16 to bear on the attacker. He pulled the trigger, the gun's recoil driving the stock deep into his shoulder, and the Fan danced a mad jig of death before falling to the ground. His feet twitched and John hurried to his body, shooting a quick burst from close range that obliterated the man's head and neck.

The feet stopped twitching.

John returned to the groundcar, hoping that the controls would be simple enough for him to figure out. They were, just a steering wheel and a lever marked "Forward" and "Reverse." But he also saw that several suits were attached to the back of the groundcar, with clear plastic helmets affixed to them, and realized that they had to be worn outside, or prolonged exposure to this newly discovered earth could be fatal.

It was a hard process, getting Fran inside the first suit, and it felt like it took a million years. Gunfire sounded throughout the installation, and John had to stop and check his surroundings every time he heard a noise. The hangar remained empty, though, until finally Fran was safely ensconced in a plastic cocoon that he hoped would protect her against the adverse elements of the world. The world he had always thought he knew but was in fact about to see and really experience for the first time. He lay Fran gently across the seat, then turned to grab a suit for himself...and felt the warm muzzle of a gun against his cheek.

"Hello, bit," said Malachi.

John said nothing, his synapses firing like light-speed pistons as he searched for a way to kill this man, this devil made flesh. But nothing presented itself, and John knew he and Fran were about to die.

Despair threatened to overwhelm him as Malachi smiled. "Typical. They program you so well," said the Fan. "But you're mad. You know that, don't you? You're insanity just waiting to happen."

"That might hurt my feelings if it wasn't coming from a psychotic killer."

For a moment, Malachi's cloudy eyes grew sharp as he dug the gun further into John's cheek. "Shut up!" Then he almost instantly calmed again. "My God tells me what to do. And I do it. I do it well." Malachi's eyes flickered over to Fran, who still lay upright in the seat. "The sleeping princess. There's a fairy tale about the sleeping princess in the world they wrote for you, isn't there, bit? A woman who slept until she was wakened by a kiss?" Malachi's eyes grew dreamy again, and he gazed lustfully at Fran.

John's eyes moved wildly back and forth, seeking some way he could gain the upper hand. Malachi smiled at him. Smoke and dust from the fighting swirled around them, giving Malachi a Faustian appearance. He was the Devil, come to claim the souls he had stolen. John tensed, preparing to make a move that he knew would end in defeat. But he had to try. Doing nothing was surrender, and John refused to give up and allow victory to this demon cloaked in human form. He would throw himself at Malachi, and the lunatic would pull the trigger of his gun and blow John's brains out. John knew he was no machine; he would not come back. But perhaps he would survive long enough to hurt Malachi, maybe even to kill him. He would never see Fran again, but perhaps he could purchase her life with her own.

He never got the chance.

CONTROL HQ – RUSHM
AD 4013/AE 2013
((((INTEGRITY BREACH))))

Adam emerged from the smoke that surrounded them all, jabbing his gun into Malachi's back. His clothes were stained and spattered with blood, and he had no doubts as to what he wanted to do. He wanted to kill Malachi. The question was, would he be able to?

"Drop the weapon, Malachi."

Malachi smiled in spite of the gun digging into his back. "Remember the old days, Adam?" he said, his tone light as that of an old woman gossiping on the porch swing. "Remember when we worked together? Good times. Time for me to think and realize that I was fighting for a bunch of machines who didn't even grasp their own nature and for a pitiful shard of humanity that should have died two thousand years ago."

Adam's finger tightened a little bit more. "Now, Malachi. Drop it. You're human, and if I kill you you won't get back up."

"So arrogant," answered Malachi. "Always so arrogant, even in your pretended humility and your questions about the nature of God and what He thinks of the things you've done. Well, I've *answered* those questions. I've *found* God and it turns out He's on my side."

Malachi still wasn't moving. Adam wanted to blow him away, but he recognized the gun Malachi was holding and knew that if he shot the man, Malachi might reflexively pull the trigger. If that happened, both John and Fran would be hit. Both would die, and all that had been suffered would be for naught. He decided to try a different tack. Force could not be exerted, so though he knew it was all but futile, he decided to try persuasion.

"I do remember working with you, Malachi. I remember asking you if God loved the machines. You never answered."

Malachi stiffened, then relaxed. His finger released from the trigger of his gun, and Adam thought it might have worked. He thought for a moment that he had found whatever fragment of sanity and humanity still hid within Malachi's soul.

The hopes were dashed when Malachi handed him the gun and said, "Shoot me."

***

Malachi smiled as Adam's face contorted. The old man – and Malachi noticed how very old Adam now looked; the years had not been kind to him – tensed as he bent his will to pulling the trigger. He cried out with the strain of it, and Malachi laughed. Still laughing, he took his gun from Adam's hand, then removed Adam's gun as well.

"Does God love machines?" he asked, repeating Adam's question. Malachi cast a look over his shoulder at John, who stood silent and apparently dumbfounded behind him. "Why don't you tell me yourself, if you see Him?" he said. Then he shot Adam. He used Adam's own gun, a six-shooter he must have taken from one of the members of Malachi's army, emptying it into him.

But careful, oh so careful, not to hit him in the head.

Adam crumpled to the iron deck of the hangar. He cried out in agony as each iron slug bit into his body.

But after the six-shooter had been emptied, Adam wasn't dead. No, Malachi left him alive. As alive as a robot could be. But death would come soon. And Malachi smiled because after death would come madness, and that would serve as a just punishment for the man who played at understanding God; for the false prophet who had claimed to know God's will.

He leaned down, whispering into Adam's ear, "How could He love you? He didn't even give you a will of your own."

Malachi turned to John.

And to Fran.

The End was coming.

CONTROL HQ – RUSHM
AD 4013/AE 2013
((((INTEGRITY BREACH)))

John watched Malachi gun Adam down, watched the old man's body twist with the bullets' impact, fall, and lie still. Through it all he couldn't move, couldn't bring himself to react to what had happened.

What *had* happened?

John's mind still struggled with it as Malachi threw away Adam's gun and turned back to John, pointing the weapon he had brought at him and Fran. "Adam told you you were human," he said. "Probably even rigged a scanner to 'prove' it to you." Malachi approached John, closing the few feet between them, his gun pointed at John's face. "But did he explain why you've been so adamant about protecting Fran? Did he explain how it is you haven't been able to kill me? You had a rifle in Gabriel's house. Why didn't you use it on me? Why did you just throw the lamp at me?" Malachi leaned in close to him, and John could smell the monster's stale breath as he whispered tightly, "Because you knew I was human, you felt it, and that was my life insurance. You can't kill a human."

John stared at Malachi, sweat from the heat and fear in the room dripping off his face. "I'm human," he said, meaning the words to come out defiantly. Instead, they came out in a high voice that sounded less like defiance than begging.

Malachi laughed, and did with him what he had done with Adam. He handed John the gun. "Shoot me, then."

John held the gun; cradled it in his hands like a fragile porcelain doll that might crack with the slightest careless movement. Malachi's barking laugh jolted his gaze to the man's insane eyes.

"Come on, John," Malachi taunted. "Any real human would be able to do it."

John looked at the gun, fearing what an attempt to kill Malachi would mean.

What the hell? he thought. You'll die anyway if you don't try.

He closed his eyes for a moment, then, slowly...he brought the gun up, savoring Malachi's expression as the man realized he was about to die. The moment attenuated into a short eternity as his finger tightened on the trigger of the gun, pulling it to the firing point.

And then letting go.

"No," he said. "I choose not to."

"What?" Malachi's expression twisted in a way that would have seemed almost comical had John been watching it on a TV show at home.

"If you're human," answered John, "then human is something I don't want to be." He nodded at Adam's form, which lay still on the floor. "And if that's a robot, then I'd rather be a robot. At least they have the sense to put some value on life." He saw Malachi's eyes boil over with rage and added the kicker: "They're closer to God than men like you ever will be."

Malachi flew at John, beating at his face, arms, chest. John didn't do anything to withstand the attack, consciously keeping his hands loose and his arms limp. Malachi's fists smashed at him, and John felt the pain, but it was as though it came from a million miles away, distant and unreal as the stars that had always hung in the lying sky of Loston.

Malachi paused, winded, and John spoke again. "Keep going. Prove me right. Everything you've ever done was twisted and hateful. You could have killed me several times, but you didn't. Because death is too quick. You wanted me to suffer. Just like you suffer." He took a deep breath. "I feel sorry for you," he said.

Tears of frustration welled from Malachi's eyes. "Don't you dare pity me!" he wailed. "You're not even human! You couldn't kill me if you wanted to, and all the rest is rationalization."

"Maybe you're right," answered John. "But whether you are or not, I have nothing more to say to you."

The words flowed from John's mouth without his thinking, and it felt as though he were drinking a cool draught of the purest water. All the time, he realized, since Annie had died, he had been cursing fate. He had bemoaned his plight, and shaken his fist at the heavens. Now he knew that that was the problem. He had been viewing life as a thing he was owed; as a thing he was born to have. Now he knew that life was fleeting, and often perhaps even illusory. No one could control it, and so all that he could do – all that anyone could do – was control how he reacted toward it. It was time to stop fighting a battle he could not win. Tomorrow would be tomorrow, and hard or easy, if he was alive to see it he would view it as a blessing.

This was what he had been missing all his life. This was what he had never seen when Annie had been alive. She was such a blessing to him, without struggle or pain, and when so when the pain of her passage came upon him, he was ill-prepared to cope. But now he had seen death, and life, and death again, and knew that whatever came he would honor it for the great gift it all was. No one had a right to live, life was a present, and he to spend it in bitterness or mourning was to grind it to dust underfoot.

So he would not bow to the likes of this screaming monster who wept bitter tears before him. He would not let anger or its emissaries cloud his ability to feel love. He had loved Annie, he now loved Fran. He would enjoy that as long as it lasted, and be content. Whether there was a Heaven, he could not say. Whether there was a Hell, he did not have the power to know. But he did have the power to turn his back on hate and fear and try to discover if maybe – just perhaps – Heaven was simply the name people gave to being happy right here and right now. So he would not spend one more minute talking to this angry madman who stood between him and home, between him and an existence with Fran.

Life was just too damn short for that.

He turned his back on Malachi and began unbuckling the second suit, getting ready to put it on.

A sound behind him, the ruffle of cloth on cloth, alerted him to some kind of movement. He turned and saw Malachi pull another gun out of the wraps of his clothing, saw his finger whiten as he pulled the trigger, and heard the deafening bellow of a shot resound through the hangar.

CONTROL HQ – RUSHM
AD 4013/AE 2013
(((INTEGRITY BREACH)))

Malachi fell to his knees before John. Blood poured from a spurting hole in his chest. More dripped from his lips.

"But, God was on my side," he said.

And then he died.

John looked at the man who stood behind Malachi. A Controller. He reholstered his gun, nodding at John to continue getting into the suit. Then the man turned to Adam's body.

He saw Adam, half-delirious and fading fast, grab hold of the man who had rescued them all, and whisper, "Jason."

The man looked at John. "Get going," he said, and John did not have to be told twice.

***

Jason knelt next to Adam's shattered body, holding the old man's hand in his own. "Jason," Adam whispered again, seeming to pour the last of his strength into the word. "Kill me. Stop me from coming back."

Jason hesitated, but the anguish in his friend's eyes was too much for him to bear. He removed his gun from the holster and placed it at the base of Adam's chin, where he would destroy the thalamus on the first shot.

Adam closed his eyes, and peace seemed to sweep over him. He took a final breath, and let it out again. Then he was still. Gone.

Jason dropped his gun. He gathered up Adam's body in his arms, and ran from the hangar, down the hall to the birthing lab. Adam began twitching before they were halfway there, and Jason knew the old man's bones were reknitting and his veins and arteries mending inside him.

Soon, he would awake to a black future of despair.

Jason had to prevent that.

He ran to the lab, which stood still and silent and mercifully unharmed by the Fan attack. The attack itself was fading away, as though they had sensed their leader's death and with him had gone their spirit. The fight was done, and victory for the Controllers – for life and humanity – was at hand.

Jason hurried to an empty tube and put Adam inside. The old man began to struggle a bit against him, and Jason fought to put him all the way in before slamming the door shut. He punched a button and the upload/download links coiled their way through Adam's ears, the microscopic fibers connecting with his brain and beginning the reconstruction process. Immediately Adam's body jerked as tissue regeneration began.

It had all led to this. Jason had overridden Devorough's return command, leaving him in Loston for John to find. It had been a desperate gamble, one calculated to Activate Loston and bring the Fans out, to bring Malachi to Control, for Jason had realized when Malachi killed Lucas in the Ohio dome that the fight had to end. The Fans killed a few every year, and Fran was the only woman left. They had to be stopped, the fight had to be taken to *them*, or the Fans would win.

He knew they would find her eventually anyway, so he used Fran as bait. He hated himself, for he had drawn her out and put her with John, knowing that she would appear an easier target while in Loston, hoping that John would be able to fight off the Fans. He had put her at risk, and had killed many of his friends and loved ones by giving Malachi all the opportunities he needed to find Central Control, hoping that the man would be crazy enough to bring all the Fans with him in a last, final, desperate attack.

Jason loathed the decisions he had made. But it had all worked. The Fans were broken. Malachi was dead. So was Sheila, whom he had loved.

He didn't want to lose Adam, too.

Jason set the calibrator that sat atop the tube: 00:00:00:20:00.

Twenty minutes. He hoped it would be enough.

FOUR – LOSTON REFOUND

DOM#67A
LOSTON, COLORADO
AD 2013
2:00 PM SUNDAY
(RECALIBRATED)

It seemed a day like any other. Except the clouds hung motionless in the sky, defying geothermal physics to remain absolutely still. No birds sang, no cougars roared their terrible roar. Not a blade of grass moved.

And then, a sound. The side of a rock broke in two as John stepped through the suddenly-appearing doorway, pulling Fran with him. He cracked the pitted helmet off his suit, then stripped himself of the bulky outfit. Ten minutes later he had taken Fran's suit off her as well, and threw them both back outside, squinting against the harsh alien sunlight that shone outside the dome.

He pulled a handle on the outer surface of the cage he called home, then darted back inside as the dome sealed behind him. The rock, split in half only moments before, mended itself and in seconds appeared solid and sure. John resisted the urge to reach out and touch what appeared to be empty air next to the rock. It was not empty, he knew now. It was a wall that, through technology he could not understand, looked exactly like a rock, and air, and dirt, and life. It was the bars on the cage where he would live out his life.

He rested a moment, then picked up Fran and began the last walk home.

***

Fran woke up feeling...well, fuzzy was the best word for it. Dark blurs gradually resolved into lighter ones and one of those slowly morphed into the shape of her cousin.

"Hey, cuz," whispered Gabriel. His voice sounded far away, strange. "Sorry you gotta see me first thing. Helluva way to wake up."

"Wha...," she managed. The tiny effort made her head feel as though it was being slammed in a car door. And not a small one, like a Toyota or a Nissan. Something huge. The door of a monster truck sponsored by Excedrin's evil, migraine-causing twin. She raised one hand to her burning eyes and realized that bandages swathed about her forehead like a turban.

"Seems you took a slip in the mines. I told John not to take you, but –"

Fran bolted upright. "The mines!" she shouted. "They're after us! We've got to –"

A hand pushed her gently back down. She looked at the arm that the hand belonged to. Then the body. The face.

"John," she breathed, and his presence was enough to make everything seem all right.

"It's okay," he said.

Then a strange look came over his face, as though he wanted to tell her something.

CONTROL HQ – RUSHM
AD 4013/AE 2013

Adam watched Fran's face on the monitor. Controllers picked through the refuse around them, finding the bits and pieces of machinery that Malachi hadn't destroyed and getting them up and running again.

Jason stood at his right hand, quiet. He had been quiet since the attack, and no wonder. His wife was gone. Adam didn't know what had happened – he'd been knocked unconscious early on in the fight and remembered little beyond telling John to get out with Fran – but Jason had told him that Sheila was dead, and so, apparently, was Malachi.

Adam had knelt over Malachi's body, and shed a tear. So much potential. But the man had chosen another path.

Now, Adam felt himself hold his breath. What would John say? Would he go along with the plan Adam had suggested to him? Would he tell Fran that it was all a dream? Or would he destroy all their work by telling her the truth?

Then the voice came through the monitor: "It was a dream," said John. "You're home...you're in Loston."

Fran's face, larger than life on the three-dimensional screen, twisted as she fought to remember what had happened.

"I was so afraid," she managed.

Again, John's disembodied voice came through the screen. "I know, honey. I know. But it's all right now."

The view changed as the camera shifted, bringing Gabriel's face into frame. "You shouldn't have taken her into the mine, pal," said the coach.

"I know," said John, his voice floating through the cave like that of a ghost, a disembodied soul. "I feel awful about it."

Jason thumbed a button. The sound muted and he looked at Adam.

"Do you think he knows?" Jason asked.

Adam thought a moment, then shook his head. "No. John still thinks he's human. Amazing how he asked me all those questions and never thought to ask the obvious ones: why Malachi never tried to kill *him* as a primary target; why all the attacks were against Fran. Why every person in Loston was free to attack him, even though they weren't able to harm those they knew to be human. Why he couldn't kill Malachi."

"I heard him talking to Malachi before I killed him," answered Jason. "He said...he said he didn't want to."

Adam nodded. "That's the magic of the Series Sevens. They can rationalize the choices they make so they fit into the existence they have no choice but to accept. The Sevens have a greater illusion of free will, and that is what saves them."

"Have we found a likely mate for Fran yet?" asked Jason.

Adam shook his head. "No. We'll let them stay together a while. He'll do an even better job protecting her than her last husband did."

"But the Fans are gone," said Jason, obviously startled at the implication that Fran would *need* more protecting.

Adam shrugged. "For now," was all he said. "We'll leave them together for a while."

"I'm glad," said Jason. "I don't really want to have to retire him."

"Neither do I," answered Adam. "He's a good Seven. A good man. But we'll do it when the time comes, to make sure the race goes on. We'll kill John off and bring her a viable husband. And they'll have babies and we will go on as ever, watching and protecting them."

Adam looked at the screen again, looked out through John's eyes, through the eyes of a machine, and almost laughed.

"What?" asked Jason.

"A good man," said Adam. "That's what I said, and now I wonder: what if he *is*? We know so little, here in this room where we play at being blind gods who are told what to do by still greater gods who are quite possibly as blind as we. But those greater gods, those computers who tell us what to do each day, who to kill, who to save, who matters and who does not..."

"Yes?" prodded Jason, and Adam thought for a moment he saw something in Jason's eyes, some fleeting sense of secrecy, of shadows.

Then the look was gone, and Adam shrugged. "Maybe they lie," he finished. "Maybe John *is* a real man, and the computers just told us otherwise for some reason beyond our understanding." He was silent a moment, then smiled, wider than he had smiled since he became a Controller, since he gave up his life to serve. "I will choose to believe he is. That's all I'm allowed to do, is choose what I believe, but I think...I think that will be enough. To do what I must, whatever that will be."

Adam glanced at the monitor again. "Sometimes I can't believe how easy it is," he whispered.

"How easy what is?" asked Jason

"To make them believe the lie. Or to make us believe it." He turned to look at Jason. He smiled, then gripped his friend's arm. He thought for a moment he saw something behind his right hand man's eyes. Thought again that Jason knew something.

Then it was gone. Gone, as if it never was.

He turned back to the monitor, Jason at his right hand, and together they continued to do their jobs.

Afterword

People ask me where I get my ideas from. The answer is easy and hard: I have no froikin' clue. Everywhere. Nowhere.

Sometimes I hear stuff on the news and think: booyah! Story!

Sometimes I am "researching" (playing on the internet) and I find something so fascinating that it becomes a kernel of an idea.

Once I woke up with an entire story in my head, done and ready to be written – I kid you not.

Usually, though, it involves a combination of all of that. Dreams, interests, random junk floating through my extremely messy mental filing system. Then I sit down and rework it until the rough idea is something I think will sustain an interesting story. A mixture of alchemy and drudgery.

With *RUN*, though, the answer is easy: the idea came from a vacation.

I was in college. While there I worked several jobs to pay extra expenses. Before college I was a missionary for my church – a job that averaged upwards of eighty hours a week. Before *that* I worked to earn money so I could be a missionary and then go to college.

So it had been years since I had worked less than fifty hours a week. My mother was going to visit family in Colorado and more or less kidnapped me. She's cool like that.

Off we went. It was a great trip. And the highlight for me was, of course, the part that scared me to death.

We went and visited a working silver mine. And by "working" I mean "holy crap there are still dudes down there digging stuff out of the ground!"

It was cool. It was crazy. It was *terrifying*. Particularly because we were guided along by an old miner who clearly delighted in telling us the lore of the mines – not the fun stuff about gold and silver and maybe the occasional Morlock/C.H.U.D. sighting, but blindness and subterranean avalanches and *madness*.

At one point they turned out the lights, to demonstrate what "true darkness" was.

Sold.

I was already writing then. Nothing saleable (I was still in the middle of that first million words you have to plow through before you start to figure out how to put a sentence together), but the *ideas* were there.

And this dark, low-ceilinged, frightening place provided, if not a full *idea*, then a great *impetus*. Namely: I wanted to write a thriller that ended up with a chase in a silver mine. Because that would be a giant double helping of sweetness with a side portion of bitchin'.

But, being me, I couldn't just have something start and finish in the silver mine. No, our heroes had to be *in extremis* when they got there.

Why?

Uhhh...

"Because they're being chased!"

Why?

"Because everyone wants to kill them!"

Why?

[Yes, conversations with myself tend to resemble conversations with an addled toddler.]

"Because everyone is...a *robot!*"

Why?

And so *RUN* was born.

I worked on it for years. Honed it. Crafted it to the best of my ability.

Sent it to publishers.

Rejection.

Rejection.

Mean, nasty rejection.

Rejection.

No one wanted it.

It sat around for a few more years.

Then I bumped into this thing on the internet called a "Kindle." And discovered that I could sell the book myself.

Woohoo!

I put the book up on Amazon, and a few other places.

Grand total sales the first month: something like six. And I think my parents bought all of them.

But still, I had done it. I had written something and put it out there.

And a few months later, something weird happened: *RUN* started selling. A lot. Enough to be the number one bestselling title on Amazon's Horror and Sci-Fi lists, and number two on its thriller lists.

Now I was hooked! I was a published author! I was making money!

That happened about three years ago. Since then I've written about two dozen books, a dozen screenplays, and countless other shorter works. I've discovered that writing is one of the hardest, weirdest, most frustrating, and ultimately wonderful jobs in the world.

I've also discovered that my wife is a saint, and my children are going to have to deal with someone they are likely to perceive as a crazy man for much of their lives.

So, was that trip to the silver mine worth it? Certainly it was a mixed bag. I love what I do. I love meeting fans at conventions, and hearing from them via Facebook and Twitter and emails. I enjoy telling stories.

I do *not* love the stress that comes every time I tackle a new project and realize that *this* is the one I am going to completely screw up. Or the fact that "professional writer" is code for "newly unemployed when you wake up every morning." Or the reality that everyone has theories about how to succeed in this business, but [SPOILER ALERT] no one *really* knows (if anyone did, Creative Writing would be offered as a Bachelor of Science degree, it would be much more boring, and the average pay would be better).

Was that trip to the silver mine a good thing?

Ask me on a good day: yes!

Ask me on a bad day: *&$^#!

Ask my wife any day – actually, don't do that. She's got enough on her plate just dealing with me all the time.

So I don't know.

I guess what will tip it is you. The readers. Professional writing is *always* a collaborative exercise. The writer should have the audience in mind. If the writer does his job, he communicates ideas with clarity and insight and (hopefully) a level of fun. I wrote *RUN* thinking not just of what I thought would be cool, but what I hoped *you* would like, too.

So here's hoping we succeeded together.

Here's hoping it was fun.

And (if you'll pardon the pun) that the *RUN* continues.

- Michaelbrent Collings

2013

*

FOLLOW MICHAELBRENT

Twitter: twitter.com/mbcollings

Facebook: facebook.com/MichaelbrentCollings

NOVELS BY MICHAELBRENT COLLINGS

DARKLING SMILES: Tales of Brightness Darkled

TERMINAL

PREDATORS

THE DARKLIGHTS

THE LONGEST CON

THE HOUSE THAT DEATH BUILT

THE DEEP

TWISTED

THIS DARKNESS LIGHT

CRIME SEEN

STRANGERS

DARKBOUND

BLOOD RELATIONS:
   A GOOD MORMON GIRL MYSTERY

THE HAUNTED

APPARITION

THE LOON

MR. GRAY (aka THE MERIDIANS)

RUN

RISING FEARS

THE COLONY SAGA:

THE COLONY: GENESIS (THE COLONY, Vol. 1)

THE COLONY: RENEGADES (THE COLONY, Vol. 2)

THE COLONY: DESCENT (THE COLONY, VOL. 3)

THE COLONY: VELOCITY (THE COLONY, VOL. 4)

THE COLONY: SHIFT (THE COLONY, VOL. 5)
THE COLONY: BURIED (THE COLONY, VOL. 6)
THE COLONY: RECKONING (THE COLONY, VOL. 7)
THE COLONY OMNIBUS
THE COLONY OMNIBUS II
THE COMPLETE COLONY SAGA BOX SET

YOUNG ADULT AND MIDDLE GRADE FICTION:

THE SWORD CHRONICLES
THE SWORD CHRONICLES: CHILD OF THE EMPIRE
THE SWORD CHRONICLES: CHILD OF SORROWS
THE SWORD CHRONICLES: CHILD OF ASH

THE RIDEALONG
PETER & WENDY: A TALE OF THE LOST
    (aka HOOKED: A TRUE FAERIE TALE)
KILLING TIME

THE BILLY SAGA:
BILLY: MESSENGER OF POWERS (BOOK 1)
BILLY: SEEKER OF POWERS (BOOK 2)
BILLY: DESTROYER OF POWERS (BOOK 3)
THE COMPLETE BILLY SAGA (BOOKS 1-3)

PRAISE FOR THE WORK OF
MICHAELBRENT COLLINGS

"Epic fantasy meets superheroes, with lots of action and great characters.... Collings is a great storyteller." - Larry Correia, New York Times bestselling author of *Monster Hunter International* and *Son of the Black Sword*

"... intense... one slice of action after another... a great book and what looks to be an interesting start of a series that could be amazing." - Game Industry News

"Collings is so proficient at what he does, he crooks his finger to get you inside his world and before you know it, you are along for the ride. You don't even see it coming; he is that good." – *Only Five Star Book Reviews*

"What a ride.... This is one you will not be able to put down and one you will remember for a long time to come. Very highly recommended." – *Midwest Book Review*

"I would be remiss if I didn't say he's done it again. Twists and turns, and an out-come that will leave one saying, 'I so did not see that coming.'" – *Audiobook Reviewer*

"His prose is brilliant, his writing is visceral and violent, dark and enthralling." – *InD'Tale Magazine*

"I literally found my heart racing as I zoomed through each chapter to get to the next page." – *Media Mikes*

Cover image element by La Bella Studio and ventdusud

under license from Shutterstock

cover design by Michaelbrent Collings

website: http://writteninsomnia.com

email: info@writteninsomnia.com

For more information on Michaelbrent's books, including specials and sales; and for info about

signings, appearances, and media,

check out his webpage,

Like his Facebook fanpage

or

Follow him on Twitter.

Made in United States
North Haven, CT
24 March 2023